THE
KNOWING
WITCH

OMNIS BOOK ONE

M.M. PARKS

Book Cover by Samantha Sanderson-Marshall

Edited by Jessica McKelden

CONTENTS

AUTHOR'S NOTE

This book is intended for adults only, and contains subject matter that may be difficult or disturbing for some readers. Sensitive material includes, but is not limited to: profanity, violence, animal death and dismemberment, animal sacrifice, death of a parent (off page), grief/loss, and explicit sexual content.

Reader discretion is advised.

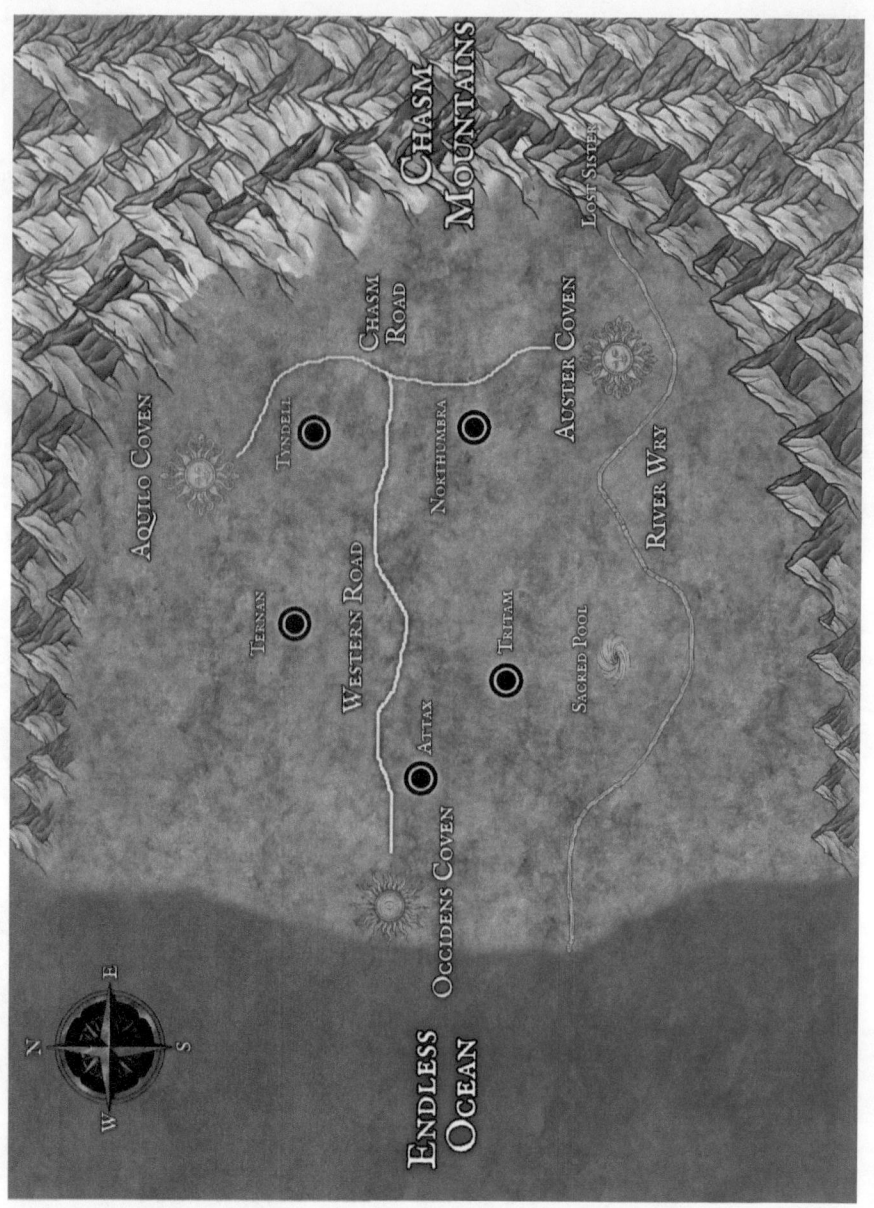

To all those who feel lost.
Do not be afraid to choose the unknown path.

CHAPTER ONE

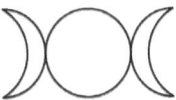

ENA WALKED THROUGH THE woods, listening for signs. She stepped lightly, letting her Knowing guide her. Sunlight filtered through the dense oak and pine forest, and life teemed at every crunch of her boot along the leaf-covered ground. She'd been walking for hours and butterflies filled her stomach with every minute that passed. Dusk was approaching and she needed to return soon, but she hadn't gotten what she'd come for yet.

Her worn brown-leather boots nearly blended in amongst the multicolored downed leaves. It was fall in the Turning, and the air was fresh from the recent rain. But Ena's eyes were trained on the ground, waiting and scouring for what she needed.

There.

A small gray mouse scurried, gathering pieces of acorns. But the forest detritus also signaled another presence—the one she was looking for.

The psilosnake lay coiled tightly in wait beneath a half-rotted log, its goal evident in the still patience of its long, black body. She Knew its intent like she knew her own. The mouse's whiskers twitched as it approached, mortally unaware of the signs.

The snake was fast as it struck, reaching to snatch the mouse in its powerful grasp—but Ena was faster.

Using her booted foot, she crunched through its hiding place and pinned the snake's venomous head firmly to the forest floor. Then, unsheathing the knife from her hip, she bent down and quickly sliced its head from its body, watching reverently as blood oozed from the cut.

Leaving the snake's lower half for the owl she Knew was dozing in the oak tree nearby, she picked up the bloody, severed head and wrapped it in a cloth before placing it in the wicker basket she carried.

Relief flooded her now that her task was finally complete, but it was short-lived, because as she turned to head back to her village, the nerves that had fluttered through her all day returned.

She knew it was normal to be nervous. Who wouldn't be, knowing they would soon face the unknown? She had never been fully exposed to Gaia before, and didn't know what it would be like. Would it hurt? Would she feel fear? All witches faced the Summoning ceremony on their twenty-seventh birthday and emerged with their newfound Gift from Gaia. She shouldn't fear what so many others had successfully completed. And she shouldn't fear her Goddess, whose magic surrounded her and whose will guided her. But she felt unsettled, and she couldn't help the pit of dread that filled her stomach.

As she reached the edge of the forest and the trees began to thin, her village came into view. Homely stone houses with roughshod wooden shingles covered in a thick layer of green and brown moss dotted the woods. They were so humble that they almost blended into the landscape of cedar, oak, and maple trees. The single-story houses were all similar in appearance, with small, square windows and chimneys puffing out smoke from the hearth fires within. Well-worn dirt pathways were carved through the ferns and grasses on the ground, and they led between the houses, weaving in and out of the fenced-in gardens and chicken coops that flanked each house. A particularly large log barn, housing the horses and goats, stood at the far end of the gathering of houses. Past that, one particularly well-beaten path veered south away from the village and towards the River Wry, where it dead-ended at the Sacred Grove.

Tonight at dusk, she would stand there amongst her Coven, nestled in the clearing that was surrounded by the oldest grove of trees this side of the Chasm Mountains, and give herself to Gaia. Lately, the thought filled her with apprehension. She'd once looked forward to the day she would become a full-fledged member of the Coven, and her true path to serving Gaia would be revealed. Ena had worked hard her whole life studying the magic of Gaia, learning how and when to interpret her will. She was endlessly improving her use of spellwords and memorizing potion ingredients. She was ready. But somehow, now that the event was upon her, the idea of having her path finally decided for her, having no more unknowns in her life, left her with an overwhelming feeling of suffocation and panic.

She continued walking past the square to the far edge of the village, where the Coven matriarch lived. Heran's house was large, almost stately, in comparison to those of the other witches who lived clustered around her. It was two stories tall, and was surrounded by a garden so large, it seemed to swallow the structure whole, as if the garden was growing a house and not the other way around. Squash and pumpkin vines covered the ground, nestled around half-rotted corn and sunflower stalks. Though they should have been long gone, the summer vegetable plants—tomatoes, peppers, and ground cherries—were still sporting some harvestable fruit, thanks to her sister Greya's magic.

Ena walked up the front path which wove through the section of the garden growing every herb imaginable, and entered the arched front door. Fergus, the small black cat, ran along her leg in greeting. She read his signs and Knew he was happy to see her. She walked through the cozy sitting room filled with overstuffed chairs and a saggy couch to the expansive kitchen that took up the entire back side of the house.

There, her sister Greya stood at the large wooden island grinding herbs with a mortar and pestle. The walls of the kitchen were filled with hanging pots, bunches of herbs, and shelves crammed with jars and sacks containing every ingredient and foodstuff known to this side of the Chasm Mountains.

Greya turned to look at her as she entered. "Did you get it?" she asked, looking hopefully at Ena.

"Of course. Did you think I wouldn't?" Ena smirked, belying her inner turmoil.

"Thank Gaia. If anyone could do it, it'd be you, but you and I both know it's difficult to find psilosnakes this close to Samhain."

"Well, Gaia granted me, I guess."

Greya tossed her pale-blonde braid over her shoulder before she reached for a pot bubbling over the fire in the enormous hearth. Several other pots were also simmering within the fireplace, which was large enough for several people to stand in, and held multiple small blazes, but Greya was focused on scraping the contents of the mortar into the dark-red mixture that bubbled in the ceremonial iron cauldron.

"Are you nervous about the Summoning?" she asked. Her tone was almost too casual, as her brown eyes, so distinct from Ena's bright-blue ones, remained focused on her work.

"A little," Ena replied cautiously. She didn't know why, but she couldn't bring herself to tell Greya about the depths of her fears. She didn't want to worry her.

"That's normal, you know. I was as well. But don't worry, Haren won't let you descend."

"I know," she said. And she did. She trusted Heran, who had practically raised her and Greya after their parents died of a swift and all-consuming fever when Ena was just two years old. The matriarch had conducted the Summoning of every witch in their Coven for the last twenty years and never once had a witch descended and been rejected by Gaia. Heran was a force of nature, and Ena trusted her implicitly.

"I just worry I won't like the Gift I'm given. It will determine my whole future...my path with the Coven."

"Gaia would not give you the Gift if it wasn't meant for you. And as for your path, I have no doubt you're meant for something great. You're one of the most talented witches in the Coven. You know almost as many spellwords and potions as Heran. I know Gaia has a special purpose for you." Greya spoke with the utmost confidence, as if she'd spoken with Gaia herself on the matter.

"You think?" Ena replied, unsurely.

"I *know*."

Ena was comforted by her sister's wisdom. Only three years her senior, Greya had always seemed in control and assured of her place. She was on track to become matriarch herself one day, thanks to her Gift and the ease with which others looked to her for guidance. Three years ago during her own Summoning, she had been Gifted *vita*, a magic that allowed her to force a living thing through the phases of life. She could take a flower bud, force it to bloom, then make it wither and die in the span of seconds. It was a rare, special Gift, which, along with the respect she garnered from the rest of the Coven, made her path with the Coven one of leadership.

But beyond Ena's concerns about her own path, she was also nervous about the ceremony itself. Although she had attended several Summonings for other witches, including her sister's, she did not know what would happen when she met Gaia, and that unknown weighed on her. Even the witches who went through it only came out with fuzzy memories of the event. What if it was horribly painful *and* she was given a Gift that required her to milk goats all day, like her friend Thyla? Thyla didn't seem to mind using her *glacio* to chill the milk, but Ena would go crazy if that was her path. She didn't know why, but she needed something...different. She just didn't know how to get it.

For the last several years, it was as if she'd been frozen in place. She didn't even remember the last time she'd felt truly challenged and...alive.

A warm summer sunset illuminating a pair of striking green eyes flashed unbidden through her mind.

Okay, that was a lie. She *did* remember, even though she often tried to forget. And now that the Summoning approached, she dreaded the inertia of her path. What if she never felt that way again? What if she remained this stuck forever, and her Gift was the last thread sewing her firmly in place?

"You should go upstairs and get ready. I already filled the tub for you," Greya said, breaking Ena out of her spiraling thoughts. "We've only got an hour before dusk. I'll come get you when it's time and we'll walk to the Grove together, okay?"

"Okay. Thanks, sis," Ena replied, giving her a small smile.

Leaving her basket with the psilosnake head on the table, Ena left her sister to the rest of the preparations for the Summoning as she went to climb the creaky stairs to her bedroom. The sun was falling fast and she needed to prepare her body to meet her Goddess.

As she entered her small room containing only a bed, a side table, and an armoire with an old, tarnished mirror on the front, she untied her dark-green cloak and tossed it on her unkempt bed. Quickly disrobing down to only her shift, she walked down the hall to the bathing room to find a steaming-hot bath awaiting her in a large copper tub. Silently thanking her sister yet again, Ena took off her shift and sank into the water.

As was customary before a Summoning, the bath was filled with marjoram, cedar berries, and lemongrass—a potent combination meant to cleanse and purify her body in preparation for the sacred rite. As she methodically scrubbed her body using a pumice stone, she tried to focus on each action as a way to quiet her mind. *These are my feet. This is my stomach. Now I'm rinsing my hair.*

But she couldn't stop the depressing, unbidden thought that soon, even though she would be different, everything would still remain the same.

CHAPTER TWO

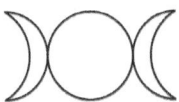

ENA STOOD IN THE center of the Sacred Grove. Towering evergreen trees guarded the edges of the large clearing, their steadfast presence a balm to her nerves. The skirt of her white silk gown, made especially for this occasion by her own hand, fluttered in the gentle breeze. It was long-sleeved with a modest neckline, but it fit her like a glove. The waist was tapered to accentuate her curves, and the edges of the sleeves were detailed lace, as was the neckline and hem. A long row of buttons went all the way up the back, and for once, she wore a decorative, lace-detailed corset underneath rather than a bodice over top.

She looked up at the sky through the gap in the trees to see that the sun was setting, casting the sky in a dusky purple, but around her, it was already dark in the woods. She Knew animals were beginning to stir beyond where she could see, emerging and prowling as night began its descent.

A giant bonfire sparked and crackled behind her, lighting up the sea of faces encircling her, watching her—waiting. She had spent the last half hour intricately braiding her long, dark-brown hair into a tight bun, knowing it would likely slip loose anyway before the Summoning was complete. Regardless, she felt beautiful, strong, and strangely calm as she looked out on the faces of her Coven, men and women she'd known her whole life, who stood around her in a circle with their hands joined. They each wore a black, hooded robe that hid their faces and bodies from Gaia. Ena was to be the sole focus tonight. Looking to her left to where Greya stood, she gave a slight smile of reassurance, letting her sister know she was okay. She couldn't make out her face, but she Knew Greya smiled back.

As the last sliver of the sun dipped below the horizon, she turned to face Heran, who stood beside her in the center of the circle. The matriarch of the Coven smiled kindly at her. Her wrinkled face was softened by the firelight, but her gray eyes were sharp and cunning as ever. Her gray- and brown-streaked hair was tied back in a low knot at the nape of her neck, but her strong voice rang out across the clearing, at odds with her aged appearance.

"Kneel before Gaia, child," she said, as she took Ena's hands and helped lower her to her knees.

Ena lowered herself to her knees, facing Heran, who reached behind her to accept two silver ceremonial chalices in her hands from another witch, who promptly returned to the circle. One chalice, decorated with an upside down crescent moon above three teardrops, a symbol of the blessing to come, contained the blood-red mixture concocted by Greya. Ena had been there herself when Greya had slaughtered the goat, harvested its blood, and set it to boil with cloves and dandelion root over a fire made from ash wood.

Ena closed her eyes and tilted her face up as Heran slowly poured the contents of the chalice over her forehead. She felt the thick blood drip down her face, smelling of iron and herbs. She resisted the urge to lick it away from her lips and instead pursed them tighter so none could get inside.

"Mother Gaia, Giver of life and Bringer of death, she who maintains the Turning of the seasons and celestial bodies, and balances the Light with the Dark, accept this witch to your service, so she may use her true Gift as you intend."

Ena slowly opened her eyes, blinking away drops of blood that rested on her lashes.

She knew what came next.

Heran handed her the second chalice. This one, decorated with the three phases of the moon representing the Goddess Gaia, was filled with a dark-red wine laced with the venom of the psilosnake she'd killed just hours before.

Ena took the chalice and lifted it to her lips. The first sip was sweet, mixed with a hint of blood from her lips. The second sip was bitter, the venom burning as it coursed down her throat. Bile rose in her throat and she actively fought the urge to vomit. Afraid she'd lose her nerve, she breathed through her nose and tilted her head back as she downed the rest in one large fiery swallow.

She felt the chalice slide from her hand as her eyes rolled back and everything went black.

***

She was nowhere. She was everywhere. She felt her heart beating acutely in her chest but she had no body. She felt the wind on her skin as she, too, blew through the leaves that remained on the trees. She Knew life was around her—she felt it throbbing in the dirt—but death and decay drained her also.

She felt the bugs crawling on her skin, which was crumbly, black, and moist. She felt a bird fly through the tendrils of her white mist hair as they condensed in a sky of deep blue. She felt claws rip at her throat, and the blood leaking out, draining, draining, until her lungs were still. Then she felt them expand again, her first breath filling her like an ocean wave.

She burned through the land, leaving ash in her wake as she split the ground in two, her chasm swallowing everything whole. She felt joy and laughter as she bubbled with the streams. She felt agony and despair as she cried with the rain. Her veins were the tree branches and the river's winding path, just as her sweat dripped down, turning to ice as she froze and thawed, then boiled and steamed.

There was so much to do, so much to Know, so much to be.

She had no idea how long she remained this way. Being and Knowing and feeling a million things at once. It was interesting, it was new, and she forgot why she was here.

And then came a blinding light. Or was it a void? It was so bright, like staring at the sun, and yet it was the darkest black she'd ever known. The warmth of it enveloped her, making her shiver. For a second, she was terrified. She felt utterly exposed and at the mercy of the unknown. Her life could be forfeit before she could even gasp and she would be nothing but humus underground.

But then she felt it enter her—and all at once, she felt unutterably safe and peaceful. She heard a voice that made no sound speak to her, and she couldn't quite make out what it was saying, but she Knew it in her bones.

Here was her purpose. Here was her path.

***

She woke up lying on the ground, the chalice she'd dropped rolling gently away from her outstretched hand. She slowly sat up, gradually getting her bearings, and there was Heran, smiling warmly down at her.

"Rise, daughter of Gaia, and join your Coven."

She took Heran's outstretched hand and stood, feeling off-kilter from the venom and, honestly, the wine too.

How long had she been out? It had felt like a while, but the sky was still the same tinged dark blue as when she had drunk from the chalice. The wind whipped the flames in the bonfire next to her, and though she should feel relieved to have awoken feeling relatively normal, she was still trying to grasp what had happened, the memories of what she'd seen and done slipping away like a dream.

Heran looked behind her to where Greya approached them, holding a wide wooden bowl filled with water from the Sacred Pool between them. The bowl was worn smooth with age, but clearly had been oiled and well maintained.

"Place your hands in the bowl, Ena, and we will see what Gaia has Gifted you," Heran instructed.

Cautiously, Ena placed her fingertips into the cool water. It felt refreshing on her warm skin. Heran did the same, placing her fingers in the bowl on the other side, and closed her eyes.

"Reach down into your Knowing, Ena, and we will see what arises," Heran said.

Ena did as she was told, closing her eyes and reaching down into her innate sense of Knowing, that sense which was Gifted to all witches upon their birth. It was her Knowing which allowed her to read the signs of the life around her and gave her a witch's intuition. Only now, quieting her mind and reaching down into it, she felt something new. Something that hadn't been there before. She reached for it like she would her Knowing, and it began to grow like a vine, spreading through her like wildfire, filling her from her fingertips to the soles of her feet. And she Knew.

It was her Gift.

It multiplied inside her, making her feel strong, powerful, and it pushed her to do...something. She wasn't quite sure. But the pull of the power was alarming. She quickly felt lost to it and struggled to reign it back. She didn't know what letting it grow would do.

Just as she felt a bolt of terror at her own lack of control, Heran gasped and withdrew her fingers from the water. The sudden change broke Ena's concentration, and her Gift melted back down to where it had come from.

"*Visanis*," Heran whispered.

Small gasps echoed around the circle, breaking the eerie silence that had governed her Coven up until now.

"W-what?" Ena asked, her eyes flying open to find Heran staring at her, her brow wrinkled with concern. "What's that?"

"That's your Gift. It is not...common among witches." Heran was staring at her intently now, a cautious look on her face. "How did it feel, child?"

"It felt...overwhelming." Ena struggled to put into words what she had felt when she touched her Gift. "It took over, like I was being swept away by the river's current."

"I'm not surprised to hear that. *Visanis* is a powerful Gift, and it can be dangerous. You will need to control it."

"But what is it? What can it do?"

"It is a Power of the mind. It can...enforce your will, your desires upon another."

"A Power of the mind? But I thought witches did not have those. Powers of the mind are given by...Iblis," Ena said the last word quietly, almost a whisper. She was now acutely aware of the other members of the Coven fidgeting and looking around at one another cautiously.

"They are. Clearly, this is an exception. I will need to look into the Coven histories and commune with Gaia to understand this more," Heran said, her brow wrinkling in thought. "But for now, I encourage you to not draw on your Gift until we figure out why Gaia has given this to you. Do you understand?"

"Yes, Heran," Ena said obediently. If her Gift had Heran this concerned, maybe that was for the best.

"Good. Then the Summoning is complete. Blessed be, Ena."

"Blessed be, Ena, daughter of Gaia," the witches around her chanted.

The circle slowly dissolved around her as the witches pulled back their hoods and came forward to congratulate her. The faces of those she'd known since her birth, lived with her whole life, for the first time were filled with a trepidation she had never seen before as they cautiously patted her arm or hugged her. Some offered tentative smiles and encouragement, while others avoided her completely. Summonings did not usually end on such a confusing note.

Eventually, she found herself face to face with Greya who, having discarded the bowl, brought her in for a tight hug.

"You did so well," she said, smiling reassuringly.

"Thanks, I think," Ena said warily.

"Don't worry about all that at the end. It will sort itself out. It's an honor to be given a rare Gift. I should know," Greya added jokingly, clearly trying to lighten the mood. "It just means your path to serving Gaia is unique. The important part is that Gaia found you worthy, and now you can fully join the Coven and follow your path. I'm so proud of you," her sister said warmly, pulling her in for another hug. And despite her own confusion, Ena did feel a little reassured.

"That psilovenom stings like a bitch, doesn't it?"

Ena turned around to see Perse as he approached them. He smiled widely and gave her a friendly clap on the shoulder.

Ena laughed, feeling some of the tension drain out of her. "Absolutely."

"I'm proud of you too," he said, bringing her in for a hug of his own. Perse, as Greya's betrothed, had always been like a big brother to her. His kind hazel eyes and joyful presence helped calm her nerves, too, but she was still unsettled.

Slowly, the witches began to filter out of the Grove and back towards their homes. Following Greya and Perse, Ena started down the path back towards the village.

She knew she should feel elated at having successfully completed the Summoning, but that same dread that had haunted her earlier in the day returned, only now it was worse. She had a Gift, a rare one. But she couldn't use it. Her path was no clearer than it had been before. Did that make her upset or...relieved? She wasn't sure.

She turned around to look back at the empty clearing; the embers of the bonfire and a stain of blood on the ground were the only signs of activity that remained. Then she turned to look into the forest. She could see only darkness, but her Knowing told her there was more there, so much more, just beyond her view.

It was as if that unknown called to her, urging her to come seek it out, the same way her Gift had urged her to use it. As if it was telling her that this path, the one she walked back to her Coven, was not all there was. But she didn't know how to take that first step, or which direction to go. So instead, she turned back and continued on the well-worn path to her village, following her sister.

CHAPTER THREE

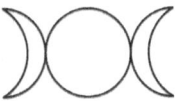

ENA AWOKE THE NEXT morning with the mother of all headaches. Head pounding, she sat up and reached for the cup of water on her bedside table, but it was empty. She was much too tired and in way too much pain to walk downstairs and get water from the cistern, so instead, she held the ceramic cup in two hands and reached down into her Knowing. She could feel the particles of water that surrounded her in the air, like tiny, invisible drops just waiting to be brought together, and she spoke.

{Aqus}

Slowly, the water condensated from the air, filling the cup. Once it was full, she brought it to her lips and downed the water in seconds. Feeling more hydrated, but slightly more tired from the use of her magic, she slowly got out of bed and trudged downstairs to the kitchen, grabbing a large shawl to wrap herself in along the way.

"Good morning, sunshine," Greya greeted. She was sitting at the large oak table that filled half of the room, a needle and thread in one hand and a black eye mask in the other. She placed her sewing project on the sturdy, knick- and dent-covered table as she looked up at Ena. Six simple oak chairs surrounded the table, all of them tucked in except for the one right next to Greya, as if she had been expecting Ena any second and had prepared it expressly for her. The smell of freshly baked biscuits filled the warm air, but Ena's stomach was currently immune to their charms.

"Mmhmm," Ena grumbled in reply.

"The lingering effects of the psilovenom are no fun, huh? Remember after my Summoning? I threw up for hours the next day."

"Don't talk about throwing up," Ena pleaded as her stomach turned at the thought.

Greya laughed. "Sorry. Here, I thought you might feel this way, so I made you some peppermint tea."

Greya stood and walked to where a large black kettle sat on a small shelf built into the hearth. Grabbing a simple mug, she poured Ena a cup of the fragrant peppermint tea and handed it to her.

"Thanks."

Grabbing the cup and breathing in the warm steam, Ena took a cautious sip and felt her stomach begin to settle. She moved to sit down at the table in the chair Greya had set out for her. Grabbing a biscuit for herself, Greya joined her. Ena watched silently as Greya grabbed the crock of butter and slathered it onto her biscuit, followed by a heaping dose of blackberry jam. The thought of eating anything right now was abhorrent, so Ena eyed her sister skeptically as she ate.

"That mask is beautiful," Ena said, when she finally finished and went back to her sewing. The center of the mask had a sturdy piece of tan leather folded over the center to form the likeness of a beak, and Greya had intricately stitched white feathers around the eyeholes using silver thread to make it look like the face of an atra owl. Greya had always loved the rare birds and certainly embodied their wise elegance. It was the perfect choice for her Samhain mask.

"Thank you," Greya replied proudly. "Have you finished yours yet?"

"Not yet, but almost. I can't believe Samhain is less than a fortnight away. I was so focused on surviving the Summoning, I almost forgot."

"Is Cris coming this year?" Greya asked innocently, feigning intense focus on her mask.

"I'm not sure," Ena replied cautiously, knowing exactly where this conversation was heading.

"You know, now that you've completed the Summoning, you're free to handfast and start a family," Greya said.

It was true—witches were generally forbidden from handfasting with another prior to receiving their Gift from Gaia. Not only did this ensure that they were old enough for such a commitment, but knowing one's Gift meant your path to serving Gaia had been revealed, whether that was to assist in healing ailments, contributing to the flourishing of life in gardens or agricultural fields, helping foster alliances with mortal villages, or assisting in the rituals required to commune with Gaia, among other paths. Witches often made strategic decisions to handfast and procreate with witches on a path that was complementary to their own.

Ena eyed her sister. "Wow. Subtle, Greya."

"What? Oh, come on, you know he's been head over heels for you for years. I'm just wondering where you stand."

"We've had... fun together, that's true. He's a great guy. But he's not for me. He's not...he's just not for me."

Greya paused. Looking up from her sewing, she studied Ena. "Wow. Still?"

"Still what?"

"It's been nine years, Ena. You need to move on and trust someone else. You need to commit to someone. Not all men will abandon you."

Ena stared at her sister in shock. "Well damn...say what you really think, Greya," Ena replied sarcastically, her ire rising. "That's not what this is about. Not at all. I'm so over that."

Greya eyed her suspiciously.

"Really, Greya, that's not what this is about. Cris is just not a good fit for me long term. I gave it a chance between us, but I don't see it lasting. It *hasn't* lasted. It's over. I'm content to be on my own right now."

"Okay," Greya replied skeptically. "I just wanted to make sure. And I don't mean to be harsh. I know how bad all that messed you up and I just worry sometimes. I haven't seen you care about anyone, really, deeply, since then. I just want to make sure you're not holding out for someone who's never coming back."

Greya's words gutted her, and she didn't know why. She knew he wasn't coming back. She'd known that for years.

Gaia, she was pathetic. A few days with a boy nine years ago and she couldn't move on.

No, that wasn't true. She *had* moved on—definitely, truly, had moved on. She rarely thought about him anymore. Yesterday before the Summoning was an anomaly.

"I'm not," she said with a conviction she desperately wanted to feel. "And why are you bringing all this back up now? It's been nine years, as you accurately pointed out. That was a lifetime ago."

"I know, and I won't bring it up anymore, I promise. Like I said, I just worry about you sometimes. I know it must be hard to never get closure from your first love."

"He wasn't my first love. It was just a summer fling. And I have moved on. I'll find someone else—eventually. Or I won't, and I'll just live with you and Perse forever," Ena said, smiling sweetly at her sister.

"Oh no, there's not a chance in the Underworld I'm letting you live with us after the handfasting," Greya replied, shaking her head and smiling in return. But Ena knew she was only teasing. She really would let her live with them forever if she needed it. Greya was just that good of a sister. Greya would never abandon her. They'd pretty much only had each other after their parents died. Ena didn't even remember them, since she'd been so young when they succumbed to the fever, but she knew Greya had some memories of them. Especially of the trauma of their unexpected passing. Secretly, Ena was glad that she didn't remember that. In her memories, it had always been just the two of them. And Heran, of course. Heran had taken them in and raised them like a grandmother would. They still lived in the matriarch's house, too, although Greya would be moving out once she was handfasted with Perse.

"Speaking of, have you and Perse given any more thought as to when your handfasting will be?" Ena was extremely grateful to change the subject from her failed love life, and instead took joy in her sister's thriving one.

"We're thinking about doing it around Yule. Winter is Perse's favorite season and he wants to take our vows after the first snowfall."

"That sounds wonderful," Ena replied with a smile. Perse and Greya had danced around each other for years before they finally committed. She was endlessly happy that she'd soon be able to count Perse as part of her family. Not only that, but she knew how happy he made Greya. The two were sickeningly in love.

The thought made her suddenly sad, though. She wasn't jealous of them, but she was confused—confused about what her true path was, even with her Gift having been granted. How could she possibly commit to Cris or anyone else when everything still felt...off?

Ena took another large sip of her tea and pushed herself up to standing. "Okay, I'm going to wash up and get dressed. Heran told me last night to come speak with her this morning about my Gift."

"Okay, I'll see you later. But Ena..."

Ena turned to look at her sister before she walked away.

"Don't worry. Your path will be revealed in due time too."

***

Ena made her way back upstairs, trying to pull her mind from the long buried past that Greya had so lovingly dredged up. Instead, she chose to dwell on more recent troubling events—specifically everything that had occurred during the Summoning last night. She'd woken up today with everything much the same as it was before, but she did feel different—she couldn't deny that. She Knew her Gift lay somewhere inside, and although she was curious about it, she didn't dare reach for it again. Not after Heran's and the rest of the Coven's reactions. She hoped Heran could find some answers for her. What did it mean that Gaia had given her such a rare, powerful Gift? Powers of the mind were usually reserved for those who followed Iblis—daemons who existed only to disrupt the balance of life and death that witches, followers of Gaia, sought to maintain.

She had never seen a daemon before, but she knew of their works. Two months ago, a pestilence had spread through a neighboring mortal village, wiping out their entire wheat crop for the summer. And six months before that, an explosion of the wolf population in the north had led to a decimation of game in the region, leading to outbreaks of starvation among the villagers who lived there. Such extreme, unnatural occurrences were always the work of daemons doing Iblis's bidding.

After washing up with the pitcher of water and basin in the bathing room, Ena dressed in her everyday wear consisting of a long linen shift, knee-high woolen stockings, and a gray woolen dress topped with a black bodice. After brushing her hair and braiding it simply over one shoulder, she went back downstairs and past the kitchen to seek Heran in the altar room.

The room was dark as she entered, and it took a second for her eyes to adjust. Sparse candles lit the space, which had no windows. The walls of the room were covered by towering bookshelves laden with spellbooks detailing every kind of magic imaginable, histories of the three Covens, and the journals of past matriarchs of their own Auster Coven. Ceremonial bowls, pendants, chalices, animal skulls, and various gemstones littered the shelves, as well, and nearly every inch of the floor was covered with trunks storing jars and vials of various spell and potion ingredients.

In the center of the room, she found Heran kneeling at a small rounded table covered in a lace tablecloth with a single candle upon it. She had various gemstones and animal bones scattered on the table before her. It was Heran's job as the matriarch to commune with Gaia and interpret her will. This allowed her to determine how to direct their Coven to serve the balance. As one of only three Covens this side of the Chasm Mountains, they were frequently visited by mortals seeking help with their crops, their illnesses, and their livelihoods. Communing with Gaia through divination allowed Heran to determine which requests to allow, and what we required in return.

Looking up as Ena entered the room, Heran greeted her warmly. "Good, child, you're here. How are you feeling today?"

"Well," Ena replied simply.

"And your Gift? Have you attempted to access it again?"

"No, as you instructed. But I can feel it. It's there."

"Good. I spent much of last night reviewing the Coven histories back centuries, but could not find another recorded instance of *visanis* among any of the Covens."

"Oh," Ena replied, feeling disappointed. She really hoped Heran would be able to find answers for her. To find *something* about her Gift and what it meant for her path.

"However," Heran continued, "Gaia graced me with her presence in my dreams last night, and she encouraged me to reveal something to you—something that I think is highly relevant to this Gift and which may help us to determine her intentions for your path."

Heran stood slowly and went to one of the smaller trunks in the corner of the room. She opened it and took out a large old-looking book with a worn, dark-green leather cover and handed it to Ena. The book was heavy as she balanced it on her two hands. The binding had clearly become loose from repeated use, so Ena was gentle as she rested it on her left forearm and flipped back the cover to reveal the title page. In a handwritten decorative script that was faded with age, was the title: *The Evolution of Magic*.

While Ena had spent hours in this room growing up, flipping through the journals and grimoires of previous matriarchs, and studying intensely the various methods of healing and herbal magics, she had never seen this book before.

"What is it?" she asked.

"A book," Heran replied matter-of-factly.

"Yes, of course, matriarch," Ena said, smiling gently. People often underestimated Heran's dry sense of humor, but having lived with her almost her entire life, Ena was used to it. "I meant, what does it say?"

"Many things—things which may help explain why Gaia granted you such a rare Gift."

Ena began to look through the book silently, waiting for Heran to go on.

"Did you know that all magic comes from the same source?" she began. "Long ago, only mortals walked the earth, but one day, Gaia and Iblis came together and granted magic to a chosen few. For a while, all those with magic, and those without, coexisted peacefully. But conflicts arose, events transpired, and eventually, those with magic came to a divide. Daemons, whose Powers are naturally inclined to sow chaos, confusion, discontent, and discord, chose to serve Iblis, and he became their Master. And witches, as you know, chose to use their Gifts to maintain the balance and to perpetuate the Turning, and they went to serve Gaia. Their magic still comes from the same source, however, so sometimes Gifts and Powers can be shared among them."

"So *visanis*...my Gift. It's one that a daemon can have as well?"

"Yes. That is my theory, at least, but I can't say for sure. We have no contact with daemons, as you well know, not since the divide. This is why you must be careful. *Visanis* is a powerful Gift that must only be used to serve Gaia and maintain the balance, lest you accidentally fulfill an intention of Iblis's."

Ena's hands gripped the book tighter at Heran's warning. She knew that witches could unintentionally tap into Iblis's will and do his bidding, but she had never heard of it truly happening. She'd thought it was just a story, something told to witch children to scare them into behaving and keeping them on the proper path to serving Gaia.

"As such," Heran continued, "you may only use it in special circumstances, and only once I commune with Gaia to confirm that it serves her, otherwise it is strictly forbidden. Do you understand?"

"Yes, Heran," Ena replied.

"Good. I'm sure this is not what you wish to hear, but trust that this is what Gaia requires of you."

"Yes, Heran," she repeated. She had so many questions, but she'd learned long ago not to pester Heran with them. Her declarations brooked no argument or discussion.

"Oh, and Ena," Heran called as Ena turned to leave. "I hope it goes without saying that this information I've shared with you is not common knowledge, and it should remain that way. If too many were to learn this history, it could be dangerous."

"How so?" Ena asked, brows creasing. Hopefully Heran would allow her this one.

"Well, there are some who might come to see daemons as our equals and wish to welcome them back into mortal and witch society. This, of course, would only lead to further chaos. I'm trusting you with this knowledge so that you may better understand your Gift and why you must be cautious with it. I know you'll treat this knowledge responsibly."

"Of course, Heran." Ena smiled in reassurance.

Feeling that she was dismissed, Ena left the altar room, a feeling of unease following her. She was all at once disappointed, disturbed, and confused by everything Heran had told her. She was disappointed that she wouldn't be able to use her Gift like everyone else. She was certainly wary of it, given what it could do, but to learn that her Gift could also be daemonic? Well, that disturbed her. Ena had had no idea that Gifts and Powers could be shared between witches and daemons, or that their magic once came from the same source. And if she were being honest, she was confused as to why Heran had insisted she keep this history a secret. This knowledge seemed important for others to know, to understand. If anything, to know that daemons once had so much in common with witches and had chosen a separate path, one of discord and destruction, was *more* damning of daemons and their choices than thinking they were always separate. It did not make her inclined to welcome daemons back into society.

And then there was the fact that, despite knowing all this about her Gift and where it came from, it still called to her. She would be lying if she said she wasn't curious about it—what it felt like, what it could do...

But she wouldn't use it. She would do what Heran asked of her, like she always did.

Ena went about her chores for the remainder of the day, plastering on a big, fake smile when she joined Greya in the gardens to harvest herbs. She explained what Heran had told her about not using her Gift unless she expressly communicated with Gaia, but left out the historical details. She hoped that Greya would learn this one day anyway, when she became matriarch and was entrusted with all the knowledge that entailed.

She spent the rest of the day trying fervently to keep her mind from these recent events and focus on her path, and like everything she put her mind to, she was largely successful.

But later that night, as Ena drifted off to sleep, she could not stop her mind from turning once again to old memories, and that restless feeling from the night before returned. And while she knew she should be grateful for everything Gaia had given her and that she should be steadfast in finding her path with the Coven, in her dreams, she saw a different, dark path, and she yearned to walk down it.

CHAPTER FOUR

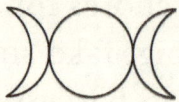

Nine years and four months ago...

THE LITHA CELEBRATIONS WERE *well underway by the time Ena finished her chores and made it to the Sacred Grove. Witches from the Aquilo Coven, their closest allies, were there, as were visitors from several nearby mortal villages, and other travelers from farther away who were passing through to attend the gathering. They had all been filtering in slowly over the last week and their makeshift camps now extended deep into the forest surrounding the village, filling the air with campfire smoke and the sounds of voices laughing and chatting. All these visitors were putting a strain on her Coven's hosting capacity, and Ena's chores had increased tenfold. For the last several hours, she'd been busy hauling extra water from the river, since the witches' magic could only produce so much, and harvesting and preparing foods and potions for trade. But there was an undeniable energy in the air that Ena loved, and she was intoxicated on all the new faces and signs.*

It was late afternoon when Ena finally arrived to wander among the revelers milling about in the clearing in the middle of the Grove. The lively music was loud and drowned out the constant rush of the nearby River Wry. The birds and animals that dwelled in the forest had long ago removed themselves to quieter trees and hovels, their everyday noises replaced by fiddles, drums, flutes, and a cacophony of voices. The rumble of so many people laughing and talking created an underlying hum that seemed to resonate in the earth, and the feel of it vibrated through her.

Ena made her way over to the edge of the clearing which housed giant barrels of mead, ale, and wine sitting side by side on stands next to a large wooden table groaning with the abundant foods of early summer. Ena perused the fresh berries, cheeses, pea and leek fritters, roasted asparagus, and various baked savory breads and sweetcakes with interest, noting several items to try later. One of the visitors from Tyndell had brought a large sow all the way just for the occasion, and the smell of it roasting on a spit over the simmering fire filled the air. Ena watched as the juices dripped down into the coals, wafting up to create a delectable steam.

After filling a wooden mug with ale, Ena turned to casually observe the madness. Over near the musicians and dancers, she saw Greya and her friend Thyla, already deep in their cups, laughing and talking to some mortal boys. Perse stood in the group, too, and she noticed the way his eyes never seemed to stray from Greya.

Perse was tall and thin, with long, chestnut-brown hair tied back in a low ponytail and large hazel eyes. It was painfully obvious to Ena how in love with Greya he was, especially given how close he was standing to her, as if he could shield her from other male attention. But while Perse was tall, his demeanor was kind and unintimidating, so it was definitely not detracting the other boys from flirting openly. Ena rolled her eyes, wondering when he would get up the courage to make his feelings known.

Smiling to herself, Ena let her eyes roam over the rest of the gathering. Despite the heat and mugginess of the late afternoon, witches and mortals of all ages were talking, dancing, and laughing—celebrating the triumph of the light on the longest day of the year. It would be hours before the sun would set, and the air was alive with the signs of life.

Distracted by all the goings on, Ena didn't hear the young man's approach.

"Hey."

Ena turned her head and was met with the face of the most gorgeous boy she'd ever laid eyes on.

He was tall, enough that she had to tilt her head upward to meet his gaze. And what a gaze it was. His eyes were mostly light green, the same color as the new growth on the pine trees, with a dark-green ring around them. They were framed by dark lashes and heavy brows that were just a shade darker than his light-brown hair. Dragging her gaze up, she saw his hair was slightly mussed, and had grown to a shaggy length that made him appear unkempt in a delicious way. His face was clean-shaven and the sharp line of his jaw could cut glass. On top of all that, he was smiling at her with impossibly straight teeth.

"H-hi," she replied, caught off guard.

"Will you dance with me?" he asked, with the calm confidence of someone who was clearly used to hearing yes.

Something about that sense of unwarranted assuredness made her bristle. She was not one to fall at a boy's feet, no matter how cute.

"You don't even know my name and you want me to dance with you? What if I'm a horrible dancer?"

"Are you?" he asked, those dark brows rising in challenge.

"No, I'm an excellent dancer."

"Great, so dance with me."

Ena scoffed. In all honesty, she was so flustered by his attractiveness that her heart was beating out of her chest, and she didn't quite know what to do.

"I can't. I already promised I'd dance with someone else."

It wasn't a lie. Cris, a witch from the Aquilo Coven visiting for Litha, had found her early this morning gathering water from the river and had asked her to save him a dance at the celebration. But he was currently occupied playing a rowdy game of Three Covens with several other boys their age, and given the way they were all shouting and throwing their cards down on the table, he likely wouldn't even notice if she did dance with someone else.

"Alright, then," he replied, but he made no move to walk away. The way he was looking at her was so intense, staring right into her eyes and hardly blinking, as if he was a predator locked on his prey.

"Okay, so...bye." She gave him a tight-lipped smile and walked away.

What in the Underworld was that? Her cheeks flamed in embarrassment. Gaia, she was an idiot. Why didn't she say yes? It would have been so easy to just say, "Yes, actually, I'd love to dance with you. Please dance with me all night long and keep smiling at me while I stare at your face." Okay, well, maybe not that last part, but the first part would've been the wise choice.

She was all at once mortified for being so awkward and mad at herself for missing such a wonderful opportunity. Not looking back, she went to refill her cup—with wine this time—and made her way over to Greya.

Her sister's face lit up as she approached. "Hey there. Having fun?"

"Yeah, yeah, it's so busy. Lots of visitors for the gathering this year!" she said hurriedly, and even she noticed the slight hint of mania in her voice. Sweat was dripping down her back all of a sudden, which was to be expected given the heat of the day, but she was keenly aware of it, and quickly took a drink of her wine.

"I saw you talking to that boy over there. Who is he?" Greya asked, gesturing to the young man who had approached her, who was now over by the table of food talking to a few older men whom she also didn't recognize.

"Oh, him? Yeah, I don't know. A traveler, I guess. Probably a mortal from Northumbra or Tyndell. He asked me to dance."

"Did you say yes?" Greya asked, giving her a look and smiling ear to ear.

"No, obviously not, because I'm standing here with you."

"Oh, okay. And why didn't you say yes?"

"I don't know, he's a stranger. And he just came up to me out of nowhere. I bet he's asking every girl at the gathering."

Dragging her gaze away from Greya, it landed on the boy once again. Well, "boy" was maybe not the right term. He looked to be close to Ena's own age of seventeen, maybe a year or two older. She watched as his group was approached by two witches in their early twenties who were a part of the same Coven as Cris. The boy was smiling and talking to one of them. His eyes flicked up briefly to make eye contact with Ena, who was openly staring at him. She quickly looked away and refocused on Greya.

"See?" she said. "He's already chatting up that witch from the Aquilo Coven. And besides, I told Cris I would dance with him."

"Speaking of..." Greya's eyes peered over Ena's shoulder. Turning around, she saw Cris approaching her.

"Hey, Ena, ready for that dance?" he asked, smiling widely at her and extending his hand. Cris was cute. He had a friendly face, with fair blond hair cut short to his head and kind blue eyes. He was easy to talk to, and she'd always felt safe with him. Their Covens, Aquilo and Auster, were allies. They were both located along the Chasm Road, the main trade route that ran parallel to the Chasm Mountains, with Aquilo to the north, and her own Coven, Auster, to the south. Members from each Coven often visited the other, so she'd known him since she was a child.

"Sure, Cris." Ena smiled back. Taking his hand, they moved to the space in front of the musicians that was packed with dancers. Without preamble, he grabbed her hands and spun her around. Cris was a good dancer, and Ena soon found herself laughing and stomping her feet to the music with him. Still, she couldn't help but notice when the boy from before entered the dance floor, too, accompanied by a blonde witch from the Aquilo Coven named Lylith. Purposefully avoiding his gaze, she focused on Cris.

One song turned into the next, and the next, and soon she was drenched in sweat and in desperate need of a drink. Explaining as much to Cris, she walked away to fill her cup.

Taking a deep drink of ale and a few pieces of pork to nibble on, she surveyed the gathering again. Dusk was beginning to settle in, but the celebration would last well into the night. She tried not to look for him, but despite herself, she noticed *that the boy from before was nowhere to be found. Not ready to dive back into the dance floor, and feeling a tad dizzy from the heat and ale, she wandered away from the gathering to get some quiet, cooler air by the river.*

The path from the Grove to the river was well-worn, and she heard shadowed figures giggling in the woods as she walked along it. Breaking through the trees, she meandered down the bank of the wide, crystal-clear river until she reached her favored spot: a small beach of pebbles and sand that jutted out into a large bend in the river. Hidden by poplar and ash trees, the beach was quiet, so she took off her shoes and stepped into the cool water.

The river moved slower here around the bend, and she watched as it swirled around her feet. She got so lost in the feeling of her toes squishing in the sand, and the overwhelming sense of life and possibility that always hung in the air this time of year, that again she missed the signs of someone approaching until she heard the splash of a rock skipping into the water.

"Gaia!" Ena gasped, whirling to find the boy from before standing a few feet behind her. "You scared me."

"My apologies," he replied, grinning in a way that said he wasn't really sorry, but amused.

That irked Ena. As a witch, she wasn't used to being snuck up on. Her Knowing usually prevented it.

"How do you move so quietly? It's annoying."

He laughed. An infectious sort of sound that tugged at the corners of her mouth.

"Just a natural talent, I guess."

"What are you doing here? Did you follow me?" she asked incredulously.

"Oh, come on, I'm not that pathetic. I was walking along the river myself and saw this spot. It's beautiful," he said, staring out at the water.

"Yeah, it is, but I was here first, so it's mine," she replied, smiling tightly at him.

Gaia, why was she acting so childish? She felt so flustered by his presence again. She really needed to stop acting like such a fool. Gathering herself, she forced her brain to think of something somewhat nice to say.

"But... I guess I can't fault you for having a similar sense of beauty," she said begrudgingly.

"How gracious of you," he drawled, picking up another flat rock and skipping it in the water. It jumped almost six times before falling in. He did it so nonchalantly, Ena thought it had to be an act.

"Is that supposed to impress me?" Ena asked, raising a brow at him.

"I don't know, does it?" He smiled again.

"Not particularly, though you clearly have many talents."

"I do?" he asked, brows rising, clearly amused. "What are they?"

"Well, sneaking up on people for one. And convincing girls to dance with you," Ena listed as she walked through the water a little closer to him.

"Oh, I don't know about that. It clearly didn't work on you," he said, taking a step towards her himself.

"True, but it worked on several others," Ena teased, referring to the string of girls she'd seen him dancing with after Lylith.

"Jealous?" He grinned, giving her a knowing look.

Ena scoffed. "Hardly. Just good to know where I stand. One of many, it seems."

"Hey, you turned me down. What was I supposed to do? Just stand around by myself?"

"No, no, of course not. I'm glad you found some other company," she replied, trying to sound sincere but coming off bitter, even to her own ears.

Silence fell between them again as the boy continued to watch her like a hawk.

"What's your name?" he finally asked.

"Ena."

"Eh-na," he said slowly, as if feeling out the name on his tongue. His voice was deep and a little raspy. She wasn't sure why, but hearing him speak her name made her heart beat faster, like she'd allowed this predator into some quiet, safe part of herself.

"I'm Ty," he said. "And if you don't want me to, I won't dance with anyone else. You're the only one I really wanted to dance with, anyway."

Ena blinked, taken back at the offer. She'd never admit it, but her heart warmed at his words. Ena met his intense gaze yet again, suddenly skeptical of his intentions, especially since she'd reacted so strongly. He was so good-looking and charming, she was acutely aware that he could be playing with her.

"Where are you from, Ty?" she asked, trying to change the subject.

"Yalta. It's a small village on the other side of the Chasm Mountains."

"So you're a mortal, then?"

"Yes," he replied, bending down to pick up and discard several more rocks.

That was fascinating to Ena. If she were being honest, she'd never felt herself this...intrigued by a mortal before. Although she'd interacted with plenty of them before, even befriended some, intimate relationships between mortals and witches were rare. Not out of any sort of prejudice, just because their ways of life were so different that handfasting usually occurred within one's own group. But then again, she'd also never met anyone from the other side of the Chasm Mountains before. Not much was known about what lay on the other side since no one that she knew had ever made the treacherous crossing over the snowy peaks. She knew from reading some old Auster matriarch journals that groups of non-magical people lived on the other side and sometimes traveled over to trade, but it was not common. He'd clearly traveled a long way to be here.

"What brought you all the way over here?" she asked, her curiosity piquing.

"My uncles and I are just passing through, cultivating new trade relationships for our metal goods. My village is near to a large iron ore deposit and specializes in blacksmithing."

"Oh," Ena replied lamely. She honestly had a million questions about what it was like on the other side of the Chasm Mountains and the journey over it, but she also felt increasingly nervous around him and it was making her mouth feel as though it had been stuffed full of cotton. Tucking her hair behind her ear to cover her awkwardness, she walked deeper into the water. "What's it like Yal—" Her words cut off as she heard a rustle of clothing and turned around to find Ty taking off his shirt.

"What in the Underworld are you doing?" she asked incredulously.

"*Going for a swim. It's hot,*" *he replied casually as he tossed his linen shirt on the beach behind him.*

Ena swallowed. As if his face wasn't beautiful enough, his body was more so. His long limbs still held the thinness of youth, but were not gangly by any means. Hard, wiry muscles shaped his arms and shoulders, and the ridges of his abdomen were clear even in the dimming light.

Kicking off his boots, Ty walked into the river until the water reached his thighs and then dove in, swimming to the eddy on the other side of the river bend. Popping up and smoothing his hair back from his face, he turned back to Ena. "You should come in," he called. "The water feels amazing."

"No thanks," Ena said awkwardly. She paused for a second, then felt the need to explain. "I can't swim actually."

"Really?" he asked, sounding surprised. "Not even a little bit?"

"No. I never learned. I tried, but the water..." Her words drifted off as she stared at the river, trying to think of how to explain this to a mortal.

"What about the water?" he asked, as if truly fascinated by what she had to say.

"Well, I don't know how much you know about our kind, but I can feel it, with my Knowing. Water is always wanting to get to the ocean. It's always rushing, rushing, rushing, and it's... overwhelming. I always worried I would be swept away."

Ty paused for a second as if to ponder that. "Here. Come in, and I'll hold on to you," he said as he gracefully swam back towards her.

"No way," Ena said quickly, shaking her head.

"Come on. You don't strike me as the type of person who is okay with not being able to do everything she puts her

mind to. Am I wrong?" He grinned at her wolfishly. How he knew that about her after only having known her for five minutes, she had no idea. Did something about her just scream "perfectionist"?

"Come on," he repeated as she eyed him skeptically. "I won't let you get swept away."

Ena was afraid, but for some Gaia-forsaken reason, she wanted to impress this boy. And she saw this for what it was—a challenge. He was testing her. Was she brave enough to do this? Maybe it was misguided, but she refused to appear meek in front of this predator. Besides, he did look sturdy enough to withstand the current.

"Fine," she conceded, rolling her eyes as if her heart wasn't beating out of her chest at the idea. Cautiously, she untied the strings on her brown bodice. Sliding it over her head, she tossed it on the beach behind her. Next, she slipped off her lightweight leather shoes. Since it was summer and hot, she now stood in just her thin white linen dress. Her nipples peaked underneath, and she felt his gaze on them before he looked up to meet her eyes once more.

Gaia, she'd never been this exposed with a boy before. Fooled around with a couple, yes, but she knew once she got in the water, most of her body would be visible through the thin dress, and she'd just met him not even an hour ago.

Remembering her regret at missing the opportunity to dance with him, she mustered her courage and walked slowly into the water. He walked towards her and held out his hand. Slowly, he led her into the water, deeper, deeper, until it was to her waist. Gaia, it felt wonderful—cold, but not too cold, and the air was still warm from the heat of the sun, which had slowly set behind the trees, bathing them in purple darkness.

Looking down at her, Ty moved closer and reached around her waist, tugging her into him. Above the fresh smell of the water, she could smell his skin. A heady combination of cedar and stone. Woodsmoke and honey.

"How's that?" he asked, swallowing visibly as their bodies touched. This was the first time she'd seen him even slightly out of sorts. She could tell he was just as affected by this as she was.

"That's good," she said.

He held her as he slowly walked them deeper into the water, until her toes no longer touched the bottom. She felt the moment his feet left the river bottom too, and he started to tread water. She reached her arms up around his neck and held tight, fear gripping her suddenly.

"Don't worry, I've got you." He grinned down at her. "Just hold on to me and I'll take you for a swim."

He released her waist as she clutched her arms around his neck tighter, bringing her face next to his. Using his arms, he pushed them around the water in smooth, relaxing glides. Ena smiled despite herself. It felt otherworldly. She could feel the current rushing around them, and Knew the water wanted them to join it, but Ty was strong enough to keep them from flowing into it. She found herself enjoying the sensation as he swam them across to the eddy on the other side.

"Okay, now for the dip."

"What?" Ena barely got the word out before he grabbed her waist and pulled her under with him. She felt the water cover her for one second, then two, before they came bursting to the surface. She gasped for air, using one hand to wipe her hair out of her face and the water from her eyes, while the other clutched tightly to Ty's hard shoulder.

"What the fuck?!" she sputtered.

Ty, water dripping from his long lashes, looked at her and laughed.

Taking her knee, Ena rammed it as hard as she could into his thigh, but the resistance from the water softened the blow so it was actually more of a nudge. Feeling that her point had not come across, she took her free hand and went to slap him on the shoulder, but he caught her wrist.

"Oh, come on. You loved it," he said, grinning at her mischievously.

Despite herself, she couldn't help the small echoing smile that tugged at her mouth as her heart raced. Now that the initial adrenaline rush was wearing off, it was finally hitting her. She had gone under the water—she was swimming! A swell of pride and contentment filled her chest.

She laughed back at him lightly, shaking her head. "You're reckless," she said.

"That's probably true," he replied, as he started gliding them around in the water again.

They continued on that way for several minutes, enjoying the quiet of the evening, and the cooling air. The current bubbled serenely around them, the sound and motion soothing, and Ena soon found herself relaxing in Ty's arms as he swam them back and forth across the river.

When the stars began to come out, he slowly made his way back to the shore, and they both emerged from the water dripping wet. As they trudged up onto the beach side by side, Ena couldn't help but notice the way the water made his pants hang low on his hips, highlighting the v-shaped muscles that disappeared below them.

Quickly glancing away, she hurried to retrieve her bodice, feeling his eyes on her as she did so. Looking down at herself, she could see that her dress was plastered to her body, displaying her shape and the rosy color of her areolas. Facing away from him, she picked up her bodice and pulled it back over her head before she re-tightened the laces on the front. Turning around, now semi-decent, she found him looking at her with that intense gaze again.

She cleared her throat. "Thanks for the swim," she said, trying to break the tension.

"Anytime," he replied, one corner of his mouth tipping up into a smile. The tension refused to break as he continued looking at her.

"Well, I guess we should get back to the gathering," she offered.

"Actually, I've got to go back to my camp for the night. My uncles are probably waiting for me," he replied, sounding regretful.

"Oh." Ena nodded at his explanation, trying to hide her disappointment.

"Can I see you tomorrow?" he asked.

"Tomorrow?" she repeated, her hope renewed.

"Yeah, we'll still be here for a few more days trading and gathering supplies for the journey home."

"Oh, okay. Sure. I'll have chores to attend to in the morning, but I could meet you in the afternoon," Ena replied, still trying to catch up to her whiplashed emotions.

"Good," he said, giving her that charming smile again. "I'll meet you here at midday."

"Alright," she replied, giving him a smile in return.

He paused, looking down at her. His eyes seemed to glow in the moonlight, and Ena felt a shiver run through her at the sight.

"Good night, Ena," *he said quietly, then he turned to walk back into the darkening woods.*

CHAPTER FIVE

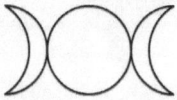

ENA AWOKE WITH A start, her heart pounding and her mind confused. Her dream...that face. It was no wonder she'd dreamt of *him* after the way Greya had very unceremoniously brought him up the other day. She used to dream about him all the time, her memories of the past always mixing with her day-to-day life in some sort of tortuous wish-fulfillment fantasy. But it'd been years since she'd had a dream about him, let alone *that* dream—the recurring one where he came back and took her over the Chasm Mountains. But it always ended the same, where she turned her back for one second and he was gone. She searched and searched, shivering and trudging through the deep snow, but she couldn't find him, until eventually, she'd wake up, feeling empty and alone.

Rolling over to go back to sleep, she tried to rebury those memories, both real and oneiric. Of course, this just made her think about him even more, so she got up, even though the sun was still hours from rising, and lit a candle to work on her mask for Samhain.

The black lace mask was some of her best work. It was decorated with emerald-green thread in the shape of two serpents on either side of the eye holes, the tails of the serpents looping around each eye to intertwine in the center. The look was completed by an extremely valuable piece of decorative emerald ribbon that she used to secure the mask around her head. She'd had to trade several batches of healing potions for various illnesses and a growth elixir for agricultural fields that had taken an entire year to cure in order to buy it, but it was her absolute favorite color, so it was well worth it.

Not to mention, Samhain was her favorite celebration of the year. While she loved the thrum of life during Litha, and the cozy warmth of Yule, the crisp darkness of Samhain made her feel...powerful. Samhain was halfway between Mabon, the autumnal equinox, and Yule, the longest night of the year, and it was a time of great liminality and change in the Turning. As the abundant life of summer began to dwindle, death became closer than ever. The closeness of death led to an intense intoxication with life among the witches, who sought to be closer than ever to it in order to maintain the balance. Every year, the Coven and its guests gathered in the Sacred Grove for a masked bacchanal to celebrate life and worship death. There was dancing, drunkenness, sometimes nudity, and, in general, a carefree wildness that was exhilarating to witness. It was the last gasp of summer and fall before the harshness and solitude of winter set in.

The next several days were filled with preparations for Samhain. Over the course of the week, travelers and visitors from nearby villages began to arrive, once again populating the forest surrounding their village with tents and small campfires. Ena and the other witches were busy doing their daily tasks—tending to the animals, harvesting the last of the season's abundance in their gardens, and curing and preserving foods for the winter. On top of that, they were charged with creating potions and spells to trade with visitors for the goods they did not produce themselves, and preparing the Grove for the festivities.

On the eve of Samhain, Ena and Greya found themselves in the matriarch's garden. Some villagers from Northumbra had requested healing potions for a plague of boils that was rampant among the elderly in their village. Heran had deemed that, in exchange for the grain they provided to the Coven, this was an acceptable trade in the service of Gaia, so she'd sent the two sisters to harvest yarrow.

The garden was an unruly, overgrown mess of black, yellow, and brown this time of year, filled with plants that were already dead and those in the process of losing their leaves and going dormant for the winter. Despite the natural season for the yarrow being long ended, Greya was able to use her Gift to grow the plant from seed on command.

Ena watched, always endlessly fascinated, as Greya carefully placed the tiny seeds they'd stored from this year's natural harvest into the dark black soil and covered them over. She brought her hand to hover above where the tiny seeds were tucked away and, as she called on her Gift, her hand began to glow with the light of the sun itself. Ena watched as the seed split open and erupted from the dirt in a tiny white-green sprout. In seconds, it grew into a young sprig, its leaves unfurling as if it were several weeks old. After about a minute, it sprouted into a full-grown plant with feather-like leaves and clusters of small, white flowers that bloomed as if in their full summer splendor. Continuing to draw on her Gift, Greya made the yarrow wither and dry, mimicking the late summer sun that normally dried the plant naturally. Once the stalks were brittle enough to snap easily, Greya removed her hand and allowed Ena to gather the plants into bunches, ready to be carried inside and crushed into a powder for the potion.

Watching Greya use her magic, Ena couldn't help but feel a hint of jealousy. She envied how naturally Greya was able to use her Gift, with minimal supervision or oversight. She was doing as Heran had asked and ignoring her own Gift, but it called to her still, and she couldn't help the curious part of her mind that wondered how it worked, what it was like, and when she might get to use it. Greya's Gift seemed to organically serve Gaia's purpose, and Ena had wracked her brain trying to think of ways hers could be used to help maintain the balance, but no matter what scenarios she conjured, she couldn't deny that her Gift was dangerous and could so easily lead to chaos and discord. How could taking away someone's free will ever be Gaia's intent?

Ena was contemplating these somewhat depressing thoughts when Perse approached them, escorting a newly arrived group of travelers through the village and gesturing to where they might camp across the far side. There were three of them on horseback, two men and a woman, with one of them trailing a large cart filled with sacks and crated goods. Ena couldn't help the ingrained reaction that passed through her to quickly scan the faces of the visitors, searching for one in particular. That was ridiculous, of course, and something she thought she'd stopped doing years ago, so she mentally kicked herself for being so pathetic and turned her attention to Perse, who waved goodbye to the visitors and entered the garden gate with a concerned look on his face.

"Hello, love," he greeted as he leaned down to kiss Greya on the cheek.

She smiled up at him with a contented expression on her face, which promptly fell as she noticed the tightness to his features. "What's wrong?" she asked, standing up to face him.

"One of the Northumbra men was just telling me about a group of bandits that's formed in the north. There was a village that was wiped out by wildfires this summer, and those who weren't able to find other homes have turned to thieving and killing. They've been hitting the region west of the Aquilo Coven pretty hard." Perse shook his head, as if at a loss of what to do. "Those travelers were just telling me they're looking to trade for weapons to protect themselves, so I directed them to the Tyndell visitors' camp on the other side of the village that brought a few extra knives and such."

"Oh no," Greya whispered, her brow pinching in concern. "That's horrible. I'll let Heran know and see if Gaia intends for us to intervene."

The sisters exchanged a look and Ena nodded in silent affirmation. Thievery and banditry were usually directly or indirectly the result of daemonic activity, and so it was often Gaia's will that they intervene as best they could to reinstate the balance. They would see to it that supplies were sent to the affected villages to mitigate the damage, and, while they would not provide magical assistance in apprehending the bandits—killing mortals was not usually Gaia's will—they would allow the mortal villagers in the region to do as they saw fit with the bandits. Ena's mind immediately started to wander, thinking through which potions she would ask Heran's permission to send. There was one in particular she'd been practicing which increased egg production in chickens, which could help those impacted to maintain a food supply through the winter...or there was another she was already adept at that enhanced the blood's ability to clot, which could help those who were wounded.

"If you two are all done here, do you want to grab some lunch?" Perse asked, startling her from her whirling thoughts.

"Yes, please. I'm starving after using all that magic," Greya replied, smiling up at him.

"You coming, Ena?" Perse asked her, trying and failing to fully drag his gaze from her sister.

"No, you two go on ahead. I'll bring these bunches of yarrow inside." Ena smiled reassuringly at them. She was definitely hungry, too, but she knew they needed their couple alone time, and she really didn't feel like being a third wheel right now.

"Okay. We'll miss you, kid. See you later," he said, patting her on the shoulder and turning to put his arm around Greya as he led her inside the house. He would likely be treated to a delicious lunch prepared by Greya of cured meats, pickles, and the goat cheese that was her specialty on a slice of the freshly baked bread Ena had seen her make that morning. The man was skinny as a twig, but he sure could eat, and Greya loved to cook.

Ena stared at them, a small smile on her face. She loved seeing her sister so happy, so settled, but she would admit it was hard to see how perfectly they fit, with each other and the Coven, when she felt so far from that herself.

Slowly, she gathered up the bunches of yarrow in her basket and went to bring them into the drying shed around the back of the house, all the while trying desperately not to feel so lost.

CHAPTER SIX

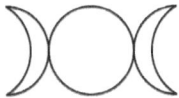

ON THE NIGHT OF Samhain, Ena stood in her bed-room, staring at herself in the full-length mirror. She'd donned her mask, along with a floor-length, long-sleeved black dress. It was low-cut and made from soft wool to keep her warm in the cool, fall night air. The built-in bodice, complete with laces made from the same dark-green ribbon that was on her mask, hugged her curves exquisitely. It was by far the most she'd dressed up in a while, although she wasn't quite sure who would be at the bacchanal to impress. But still, sometimes, it was just nice to look nice, especially on her favorite night of the year.

She fussed with her long, wavy hair before ultimately deciding to leave it down, then she leaned closer to the mirror to inspect her face. The black and dark green of her mask made her bright-blue eyes stand out even more than usual, but caused the delicate pink-rose color of her lips to look a bit washed out against the paleness of her skin. There was nothing she could do about that—she'd always been exceptionally pale, so much so that the blue veins in her arms and on her chest looked close enough to touch. But at least the mask hid the dark circles that had recently appeared under her eyes thanks to the recurring dream she'd been having.

Deeming her look acceptable, she turned away from herself to head downstairs. She wasn't even outside before she could sense the energy in the air, the growing anticipation and buzz of her Knowing alerting her to the presence of many new people at the gathering. She followed the sound of voices outside to find Greya and Thyla waiting for her by the garden gate. The sun had just set, and the night air was crisp and refreshing. Ena could see other groups of witches and mortals walking down the village's main path towards the Sacred Grove. Her heart felt lighter at the sight of it. Despite her recent feelings of alienation, she loved celebrating Samhain with her Coven, and she was hopeful that losing herself in the revelry would give her a reprieve from her discontentment, at least for a night.

She approached her sister and friend with a genuine smile on her face.

"You look fantastic!" Thyla greeted with a big smile of her own. The witch, who was Greya's age, was wearing a bright-orange mask decorated with tan and black cloth to resemble a fox's face. It was exquisite and must have taken her forever to make. Aside from her skill with the animals and in preservation techniques, thanks to her Gift, Thyla was also particularly adept at sewing and dressmaking, so Ena wasn't surprised. The mask suited her dark-red hair extremely well, as did her cream-colored dress with flowing sleeves.

"Thanks. You too," Ena replied, leaning in to hug her friend.

Greya stood next to her, looking regal in a gray silk dress with white beads embroidered on the bodice and her atra owl mask. Knowing that her path was to one day become Coven matriarch, Heran had spared no expense in trading for the finest fabric for Greya's outfit. It was important for her to appear powerful, especially when witches from other Covens were present. Even though they were allies, the Aquilo and Auster Covens were constantly vying for greater influence over the surrounding mortal villages. The more they were revered and respected by the mortals, the more people sought their Coven's potions and spells, and in exchange, the greater access that Coven had to resources received in trade. Appearances were not only important for establishing that Greya had a favored path with Gaia, as the intended future matriarch of the Coven, but also for the Coven itself, which she would represent when Heran passed.

Turning to look at her sister, she noticed that her tall shadow was missing. "Where's Perse?" she asked.

"He's already in the clearing starting the music with Adim," Greya replied. Perse's Gift of *sonia* was highly sought after on celebration days like Samhain. Not only did it allow him to amplify sounds, including music, but he was able to manipulate them as well, creating some of the most beautiful music with his fiddle that you'd ever heard. Music that sang to your blood and reverberated in your bones. Ena loved dancing to Perse's creations.

Exiting the gate, Ena, Greya, and Thyla chatted excitedly amongst themselves as they joined the others on the path to the Grove. The clearing was already nearly full with revelers by the time they got there, the wild fiddle music and beating drums filling the quiet of the night. A large bonfire burned in the center of the clearing, with several smaller fires scattered throughout.

Unlike the light and joyful exuberance of Litha, Samhain was a dark gathering focused on the outlandish and obscene. There were no food tables or barrels of ale, only large open bowls of a strong, red wine. No cups were provided, however, only large ladles, as it was tradition to have the wine ladled into one's mouth by another. This inevitably caused wine to spill all down one's front, and last year, Ena's lavender dress had been ruined beyond repair when Greya had giggled a little too hard pouring the wine into her mouth. Hence the black dress this year.

Clusters of people filled the surrounding forest, hidden by the darkness of the woods as they laughed and canoodled. Ena knew some of those couplings would turn into outright public fornication before the night was through—last year, she'd been close to being one of them when she'd gotten a bit carried away with Cris. She mostly blamed the wine and the intoxication of Samhain for that misjudgment. She really did like Cris, but she'd realized long ago that they were better suited to being friends. She just hoped he realized that, too, because despite the...encounters they'd had in the past, Ena was not looking for anything more from him.

Surrounding the bonfires was the main event—dancers both fully and partially dressed moving wantonly to the music Perse and Adim created, letting their bodies writhe freely as a tribute to Gaia and the dwindling energies of summer as they Turned to fall. As Greya made her excuses and went off to dance for Perse, Ena hung back with Thyla and scanned the crowd, noting several familiar faces. Unintentionally, her eyes locked on one face in particular as he stared at her. Cris was in a bear-shaped mask over by one of the smaller fires and gave a small wave when they made eye contact.

"Is that Cris?" Thyla asked, her big brown eyes lighting up at the sight of him.

"Yeah, you should go say hi," Ena encouraged. She knew Thyla had always had an unacknowledged crush on Cris, and she hoped that by pushing them together, Cris might take the hint.

Smiling politely in his direction, then turning away so as to discourage him from coming over, Ena looked up at the clear night sky. It was filled brilliantly with stars that twinkled and beckoned. Watching them, she took a deep breath. The crisp night air filled her lungs and that feeling, that call to the unknown, again ran through her.

She needed to go somewhere, needed to do *something*, but she wasn't sure what. All at once, she was practically itching out of her skin, so she fidgeted by reaching behind her head to tighten the ribbon holding her mask in place, but she pulled too tightly and felt it break, separating from the side of her mask.

"Damn it!"

"Oh, no, did your mask just break?" Thyla asked, her brows bunching in concern as she drew her attention away from where she'd been eying Cris.

"Yeah. It's okay, though. You go ahead. I'll run back to the house and fix it really quickly."

Pushing her way through the crowds in the clearing, Ena swam upstream through the flows of people coming down the path and walked quickly back to the village. It was quiet when she made it to Heran's house, everyone having made their way to the bacchanal already.

She walked up the path through the garden and spotted Fergus the cat slinking around by the front door. Instantly, her Knowing told her something was wrong. His tail twitched and he seemed perturbed. "Fergus?" Ena asked. "What is it?" Reaching down to scratch his soft, black ears, she heard a loud thud come from inside the house.

"Heran?" she called, walking in the front door. "Everything okay? I heard something drop."

Silence was the only reply. She walked cautiously to the altar room, where she'd heard the noise come from. Then a deep voice came from behind the closed door.

"It's not here. I've looked everywhere."

Ena froze. Someone was in the altar room. Someone whose voice she didn't recognize.

"Well, look again. It has to be here," a different male voice replied in a hushed tone.

Thieves, maybe? Mortals didn't usually dare steal from witches, not given how much they relied on their services, and because everyone knew they were no match for witches' magic. These men were clearly sorely mistaken about whose house this was, or they were simply stupid.

Mustering her best powerful, pissed-off witch face, Ena approached the door and threw it open. "What in Gaia's name do you think you're doing in here?"

The altar room was in complete disarray with books strewn everywhere and chests opened, their contents emptied onto the floor. It was obvious they'd been searching for something. Standing in the mess were two large men wearing Samhain masks, one in the shape of a gray wolf, and the other a black-eyed raccoon. They both whipped their heads to look at her, clearly startled by her sudden appearance. Then malice filled their eyes as they moved towards her.

Realizing her intimidation hadn't worked, Ena reached down into her Knowing, planning to call on a spellword to knock them down with a blast of wind while she ran to get help, when she felt her *visanis* surge upward, begging to be used. It filled her body with the same warm, growing sensation she'd felt during the Summoning. The feeling of it startled her, and in that extra second of hesitation, she saw the eyes of the two men flick over her shoulder, looking at something behind her in the doorway. She went to turn when a strong arm looped around her waist, pinning her arms to her sides, followed by a large hand that covered her mouth, preventing her from speaking her spellword.

"I wouldn't do that, little viper."

Ena froze. That voice...it was familiar. She inhaled sharply through her nose, and then the scent hit her. Stone and cedar. Woodsmoke and honey. No way.

"It's not here," the man with the raccoon mask said, speaking to her captor. "What do we do?"

"We need to move now, before more of them find us," the other with the wolf mask added.

"How will we find it now? We need something to go on," the raccoon man said frantically.

"It's fine. If it's not here, I know how we'll find it. Grab those ropes," the man holding her said, nodding his head in the direction of the ceremonial bindings used for handfasting that were sitting in a bowl on one of the bookshelves.

The wolf man grabbed them and walked over towards Ena. "What's your plan?" he asked the man holding her.

"Tie her up, rip up that tablecloth over there, and gag her with one of the strips. She's coming with us."

The man in the wolf mask didn't hesitate to follow her captor's orders as he approached her with the rope while the raccoon man ripped the tablecloth off the altar table and tore it in shreds. Ena started thrashing frantically, and yelling as much as the man's hand over her mouth would allow, but when the raccoon man joined in to hold her still, the three of them easily overpowered her.

Pushing her hands together, they wrapped the handfasting bindings around her wrists. Then, as the man holding her removed his hand from her mouth, they violently stuffed a large ripped-off piece of the tablecloth into her mouth and secured it with another long strip tied tightly around her head. The feeling of suffocation was intense, and the cloth dried out her mouth, making her want to gag. Fighting the urge to vomit, which would inevitably cause her to choke given that her mouth was blocked, she inhaled deeply through her nose.

The man who'd been holding her turned her around and, tilting her head up, she finally saw him. His face was partially covered by a reddish-brown and tan mask decorated with feathers to look like a hawk, but she'd recognize those light-green eyes anywhere.

Too shocked to move, she just stared at him. He glanced down at her with zero recognition, then grabbed her and heaved her over his shoulder. Finally snapping out of her stupor, she started wriggling wildly again, but his arm clamped around her legs, stilling her movements. Without the use of her hands, she was wholly incapacitated. Fear set in at the intense feeling of powerlessness.

"Quick, let's get her to the horses," he said to the others.

"What if they follow us?" the man with the wolf mask asked him.

He paused for a second, then spoke decisively. "Burn it down."

"Wha—??" Ena tried to speak around her gag. Twisting her head, she saw the man with the raccoon mask raise his hand. It was glowing a deep red, like hot coals in a fire, and she could feel the heat emanating from it even though she was several feet away from him. He placed his hand on a pile of books on the ground, and they caught fire instantly.

In that moment, Ena knew she was not dealing with mortals.

These were daemons.

As the fire from the books began to spread, they fled through the kitchen and out the back door of the house, her captor gripping Ena tightly over his shoulder. They moved quickly past the herb-drying shed and laundry tub, then into the dark forest that surrounded their village.

Ena couldn't raise her head enough to see, but she could hear the flames of the fire spreading, spitting, crackling in the house behind them. Could no one at the bacchanal see it yet? They would soon, and they'd come running to put it out.

But while they were putting it out, these men would have ample time to escape in the dark...with her.

She started to scream, trying desperately to call for help, but her sounds were muffled by the gag in her mouth, and her tongue couldn't move properly to form any words.

The men continued to jog quickly, moving deeper into the woods. After a while, her voice started to get raw with the effort, and she had to stop. She couldn't hear or see the light from the fire anymore; they were surrounded by only trees and darkness.

Sorrow and hopelessness wrenched at her as it truly sunk in that Heran's house—the only home she'd ever truly known—was burning. What if it spread to the other homes? What would the Coven do? All that knowledge in the books in Heran's altar room would be lost. Ena squeezed her eyes shut tight to fight off the tears and she struggled to keep her breathing steady as she began to panic. She bounced along on her captor's shoulder, trying to calm her frantic mind and think logically of how to escape. They couldn't be too far from her village—they were just moving on foot—but the man was holding too tight to her body and her voice was too muffled to scream, so she couldn't do much of anything except lie there uselessly, his hard shoulder digging into her abdomen.

Eventually, once the blood had all rushed to her head and her stomach was screaming in pain, Ena heard the snuffling of horses and the men came to a sudden stop.

The man carrying her—she still refused to think his name, as it couldn't possibly be him—unceremoniously flung her down on top of one of the horses so she was sitting side saddle. Her head spun with the sudden movement, and it took a second to get her bearings. Realizing that he now just had a hold of her waist, she tried desperately to kick him, thrashing and squirming to get down off the horse so she could run, but he was eerily strong and grabbed her legs in a death grip, pinning them together and to the horse's side. Ena grunted and fought with all her might, but her captor barely seemed to be out of breath.

"Steig," he called to the man in the wolf mask, "come grab her other leg while I get up."

Steig walked around to the opposite side of the horse she was sitting on and wrenched the leg closest to him over the horse's neck so she sat properly in the saddle. Still holding her other thigh so hard it would bruise, her captor in the hawk mask used the stirrup to gracefully swing himself up into the saddle behind her. He promptly wrapped his arm around her waist again, grabbed the reins in his other hand, and spurred the horse into motion. Before she could even think, they were moving at a quick pace through the trees, enough that Ena realized it was no longer safe to try to fling herself from the horse.

Turning around in the saddle as much as she could with the man holding her waist, she saw that the other two men had mounted their horses and were following closely behind them.

It was dark, the moon just a waxing crescent. The clouds had rolled in and were blocking most of the stars so she couldn't tell which direction they were moving and could just barely make out the shadowy trees surrounding them.

Ena shivered as the horses moved as swiftly as they could in the dark environment. She was glad they didn't move any faster because surely someone had noticed she was gone and would be following soon. On top of that, it was getting colder as the night wore on, and if the horse moved any faster, the wind would make her blood chill even further.

Gritting her teeth against the cold, Ena's mind spun. What did these men want with her? What were they looking for in the altar room? Which way were they heading? They had to stop at some point, and when they did, she'd try to get her bearings so she could figure out how to escape and get back to her village.

But one question dominated her spiraling thoughts: Was it really him? Had she just been confused in the rush of the attack and was imagining things? It had been so long since she'd seen him last. Over nine years. She was probably mistaken. He had been mortal, and these men were clearly daemons. Unless only some of them were daemons, and they were working *with* mortals?

Ena didn't have any answers, but as they rode on into the night, she vowed to get some.

CHAPTER SEVEN

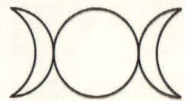

Nine years and four months ago...

THE MORNING AFTER LITHA, Ena flitted around in a state of intense excitement. She tended to her chores, helping Greya make breakfast for the two of them and Heran, collecting eggs from the chicken coop, and milking the goats in the barn, but her mind was fervently replaying the events of last night.

Had that all really happened? It seemed like a dream. She clearly couldn't stop smiling like a fool because pretty soon, Greya noticed.

"Why do you look like that?" she asked.

Ena was busy washing laundry in a giant barrel behind the house while Greya hung the clean clothes up to dry on a line. The smell of the harsh lye and wood-ash soap filled Ena's nose as she used a giant paddle to dreamily stir the soiled clothes around in the hot water.

"Huh?" Ena looked up, shaken from her reverie.

"You look all...dopey. And you've let the water get cold. What's up?" Greya asked, gazing at her suspiciously.

Ena just shrugged, trying to seem nonchalant, and refocused on the washing. Reaching down into her Knowing, she sensed the heat of the sun that lingered in the air. It was a warm day, so she didn't have to work very hard as she touched the side of the barrel and spoke.

{Fervis}

She felt the water reheat instantly to the perfect temperature, just shy of scalding. Keeping her eyes firmly on the washing, she kept stirring, hoping Greya would drop it.

"Oh, Gaia, it's that boy, isn't it?" Greya said, her eyes going wide. "I knew when you wandered off from the celebration yesterday that something must've happened!"

Damn her. Greya was way too perceptive for her own good, even without using her Knowing.

"Fine, okay, yes," Ena admitted sheepishly. "He found me down by the river last night and we ended up...talking."

"And...?" Greya prompted, grinning from ear to ear.

"Swimming."

"You went swimming?" Greya asked incredulously.

"Yes...sort of."

"Wow, you must really like this boy if he was able to convince you to get in the water," Greya teased. "Are you gonna see him again?"

"He wants me to meet him again this afternoon."

"That's so cute! Little Ena, falling in love," she said dreamily.

Using the paddle, Ena flung droplets of hot water towards Greya in retaliation.

"Hey!" Greya yelled, dodging the hot water, and laughing.

"Leave me alone," Ena ordered, but couldn't help the laugh that bubbled out of her too. "Besides, you're one to talk. You've got Perse following you around like a lost puppy. Want to talk about that?"

"What? No, Perse and I are just friends," Greya replied, shaking her head and refocusing on the clothes Ena had finished scrubbing.

"Mmhmm, sure," Ena said skeptically.

"What are you talking about? He's never shown any interest in me whatsoever. He didn't even ask me to dance last night."

"Greya, come on. He's clearly obsessed with you and is just too shy to do anything. You should make a move."

Greya rolled her eyes, but Ena could see the blush that crossed her face. "Gaia, fine, just go ahead and go already if you're gonna give me a hard time. I'll finish this washing on my own."

"Seriously?" Ena asked. She'd love to stay and continue to convince Greya to work her shit out with Perse, but she was also really eager to go see Ty. When her sister nodded in the affirmative, she didn't argue.

"Thanks, Greya! You're the best!"

Dropping the paddle like it was hot, Ena rushed back inside to change and fix her hair. Ty had said to meet him at midday, and the sun was already past its highest point, so even if he wasn't there yet, she figured she'd go hang out down by the river until he showed up.

She stripped off her water- and soap-soaked dress and pulled on a clean, light-brown linen dress with a dark-blue bodice on top. She brushed out her hair as best she could and braided it down one shoulder before securing it with a piece of dark-blue ribbon. She still looked sweaty and her hands smelled like lye, but it was the best she could do.

After slipping on her light leather shoes, she practically ran out of the house and then tried to look casual as she walked down the main path through the village and towards the *river. When she got to the beach, he was there already, sitting casually with his back leaning against a tree and using a whetstone to sharpen his surprisingly high-quality knife.*

"Hey," Ena said, hoping she'd be the one to startle him this time.

Looking up at her, definitely not startled, he smiled, and she felt a million butterflies gather in her stomach. "Hi," he said.

Gaia, he was just as gorgeous as she remembered from last night. Averting her eyes lest she start staring like a fool, she took a quick scan around the beach. There were clearly remnants of a small campfire, along with an apple core, and what looked to be Ty's discarded shoes by the riverside. He clearly had been here for a while already.

"So, been waiting here for me all day, have you?" she asked, teasing.

"Well, it's a beautiful spot and you're...a really beautiful girl," he said seriously.

Ena blushed. Damn, this boy was charming as fuck.

"So," she started, changing the subject. "Did you have something in mind for this afternoon?"

Ty stood up and put his knife back in the sheath at his side. "I was hoping you could show me around a bit. The landscape here is...different from what I'm used to back home."

"Sure, I could do that," Ena replied, nodding at him. For a brief moment, they locked eyes, and she remembered what it felt like being pressed up against him in the water last night. Her face flushed all over again and she had to look away. "Let's go this way," she said, gesturing upriver. "The river becomes a gorge as you get closer to the foothills of the mountains, and there's a path that leads through the forest and around to the top of a cliff. The view from up there is gorgeous."

"Okay, that sounds great. Lead the way," he said, gesturing for her to go first.

Following the bank of the river, they walked side by side, both of them stealing quick glances at the other. Ena was not particularly short, being about average height compared to the other girls her age, but walking beside Ty, she was struck yet again by their height difference, and she all of a sudden felt very small. They'd spent most of their time the night before face to face in the water together, so this was her first time really appreciating his height, and it was...attractive, to say the least.

The land began to slope up the farther they got from the village, and the river lowered gradually below them as the deep gorge formed. They moved in companionable silence for a while, but soon, Ena's curiosity got the better of her.

"So, you're here with your uncles, you said?"

"Yeah," he replied, as if they hadn't just been walking in silence for fifteen minutes. He was clearly a man of few words and Gaia, he was making her work for them.

"Where are they?" she asked.

"They're negotiating a trade deal with the matriarch. My village is in need of medicinal potions for healing burns, broken bones, and the like."

"Oh, great. Heran will give them a fair deal. She's very generous," Ena replied.

"Are you close with her?" he asked.

"Yes, very. She raised me and my sister Greya after our parents died. I've lived with her practically my whole life."

Ty was quiet for a beat, as though he was debating what to say. "How did they die? Your parents."

"It was a fever, or so I'm told. I was only two, so I don't really remember it."

"Don't you witches have potions for fevers? The way you're talked about in Yalta, you're practically immortal."

Ena laughed lightly at that. "No, unfortunately not. We do have many potions for many illnesses, but sometimes they are not ready in time to heal those who need healing, or sometimes the sickness is just too strong."

"I'm sorry to hear that," Ty said in all seriousness. "Were they both witches too?"

"Yes, my mom was from Auster and my dad was from Aquilo, but they lived here." She could have left it there, but there was something about Ty's stillness, the way he listened intently, giving her the opportunity to say more, that made her keep speaking. "I don't know much else about them, really, only what Heran and the other members of my Coven have told me over the years. I know my mom looked like Greya, and I take after my father. She had the Gift of arbores and maintained the fruit grove, and he had a form of animalium that allowed him to communicate with birds, but just facts like that. There's a lot I don't know. A lot I'll never know."

Ty nodded silently in understanding. "I know what that's like. Losing your parents, I mean," he offered, speaking hesitantly, as if sharing this was new for him. "I lost mine as well. Well, I lost my dad a few years ago. I never knew my mother."

"I'm sorry to hear that," Ena replied. As tough as it was for her to not have known her parents, she couldn't imagine having grown up with them for years, forging that bond, only to lose them. Ty's loss seemed all the more cruel. "How did your father die?" she asked gently, posing the same question he had to her.

"*A stomach ailment,*" Ty responded stoically.

"*And your mother...?*" Ena asked cautiously.

Ty looked away, as if hiding a shameful secret. "*She left when I was a baby,*" he said.

Ena had more questions, but she knew how to take a hint. The pain that tightened Ty's voice, the way he looked away—he clearly didn't want to go into more details, so she didn't push, and soon the conversation stalled as the land became steeper and they both breathed heavily.

Eventually, they left the riverbank and moved into the forest where there was a path that cut back and forth up the ridge to the top of the cliff. As they rounded a switchback, Ena's Knowing alerted her to a presence.

Grabbing Ty's arm, she stopped him. He looked down at her in question as she silently put a finger to her lips, telling him to be quiet. She didn't miss the way his eyes stared at her lips a beat longer than necessary.

She used her Knowing to read the signs of the forest, and then she spotted it and had to hold in her gasp.

A gigantic Canus Elk stood about ten horse lengths away from them, nibbling at plants in the dirt. Ena stared at it in wonder, not daring to move a muscle. Its hide was covered in fluffy, stark-white fur, with not a drop of mud or crust of dirt anywhere to be seen. Its huge, branching antlers, which began as a light-brown color at the base and gradually turned silver at the tips, seemed to shine and sparkle in the light that filtered through the forest canopy. Not only that, but the Canus Elk was enormous. It was larger than most horses, and the breadth of its monstrous antlers spanned her entire body length.

She turned to Ty to find him staring at it in complete awe. He looked down at her and smiled so widely, with such boyish charm and excitement, that it caused her own smile to break across her face, taking joy in his joy. They stood silently and watched it for a while, until it wandered away on silent hooves.

Once it was out of sight, Ty signaled to her that they should keep walking, and they continued along the path.

"That was incredible," he said. "I've never seen anything like it. What was it?"

"A Canus Elk. I've never seen one before either, but I've heard tales of them. They're incredibly rare. Have you never heard of them in Yalta?" Ena asked.

"No," he said, shaking his head. "The land is less forested there, so we don't get creatures like that. What else do you know about them?"

"Well, Canus Elks in general are said to be immortal—they're impossible to hunt and kill, so they just never die. Seeing one is supposed to bring good fortune—it's a blessing from Gaia. They've often been seen before major events, like the alliance between the Aquilo and Auster Covens, and before certain handfastings between powerful witches. And I know this one in particular was hungry and looking for chickweed."

Ty laughed at that. "How do you know what it was looking for?"

"It's...my Knowing. That innate sense that witches have. It allows us to...understand animals, plants, even water and rock to an extent. We can sense where they are, sometimes their intentions, by reading their signs."

"What signs?"

"The signs that are all around—noises, movements, colors, that kind of thing. Mortals can sense them, too, but they are *just heightened for witches, allowing us to read and under-stand their meanings more easily."*

"Huh," Ty replied, as if he was processing this information. "Is there anything your Knowing doesn't work on?"

"Daemons."

"Really?" he said, glancing cautiously at her. "That seems...inconvenient."

"It is, that's why they're so dangerous. It's said that their magic is such a foil opposite to ours that the two systems can-cel each other out, rendering our magic completely unusable against one another. The Covens want to help mortals, heal them, obviously, but when daemons get involved and use their Powers to disrupt Gaia's balance, witches are often unable to help or prevent it because we just don't Know they're there."

"Hmm," Ty said, going quiet for a minute. "Have you ever met a daemon?"

"No, thank Gaia. I don't think there's very many of them left anymore," Ena replied, huffing a laugh.

Soon, they approached a narrowing of the path that forced them to walk single file, and their conversation halted again as they trudged up the steep slopes.

"How much farther?" Ty asked from behind her.

"A little bit. Why, getting tired? This can't possibly be hard-er than the trek over the Chasm Mountains," Ena teased, glancing back at him with a wry grin.

"No," he replied, smiling back, "not at all. That took weeks. Although, we did have horses," he added as an aside. "But wouldn't it be faster if we just climbed this way?" He gestured to a face of bare rock that stretched to the top of the cliff, bypassing the steep switchbacks.

"Well, yes, but we'd have to climb."

"So let's climb."

Ena's heart beat faster at the idea. She wasn't much of a climber. The path was the safer route.

"I don't know," she said hesitantly, eying the rock face.

"Oh, come on. You can do it." Ty looked at her as if this was the most obvious thing in the world. As if he had absolutely no doubt that she could. "You go first. I'll coach you as you climb up. And I'll catch you if you fall," he added, grinning at her.

Ena looked up at the rock wall, then back at Ty. Again, he was giving her that challenging look. Are you gonna back down from this? his eyes seemed to say. Ena got the sense that he thoroughly enjoyed pushing people—or at least, pushing her. And she'd be damned if she didn't push back.

"Okay," she said, her competitiveness kicking in. "But if I fall and die, I'll be very upset with you."

Ty laughed and came to stand behind her as she faced the rock wall. She quickly knotted her dress above her knees so she had better freedom of movement. There was a very good chance he would soon be able to see straight up her dress from his vantage point as she climbed, and she wondered how he would respond to that challenge.

Grabbing a good handhold on the stone, she slowly started to work her hands and feet up.

"Good," Ty said.

His praise filled her with warmth and determination as she continued to climb. She felt steady for the first few handholds, looking up to chart her climb as she went, her confidence growing with every foot she climbed.

Once she passed the halfway mark, she felt her fingers begin to cramp. She continued on for a few more feet, pushing through the pain, and then she made the mistake of glancing

*down. She was high—very high. Looking around, she sudden-
ly didn't know where to put her hand next. She was already
almost fifteen feet up the rock face—far enough that if she fell,
Ty might be able to catch her, but she also very well might just
crush him with her body weight and hurt them both.*

"Uh... Ty?" she asked, her fear starting to creep into her voice.

*"You've got this," Ty said calmly. "Put your foot on that little
step up to your right."*

*Ena looked down and saw the step he was talking about. She
did as he said and cautiously put her foot there.*

*"Good. Now you should be able to push up and reach that
small rock jutting out to your left."*

*Ena cautiously let go with her left hand, put her weight on
her right foot, and pushed up until she could reach the tiny
bump in the cliff face that he had indicated. Her toes gripped
the rock through her thin leather shoes, and she was eternally
grateful for all the finger strength she gained from kneading
dough.*

"Perfect. Now you're almost there."

*Looking up, Ena saw that she was just a couple feet from the
top.*

*She was able to locate her last couple of hand and foot
placements herself, and soon, she was pulling herself over the
ledge and slumping down onto the cliff top. Her heart was
pounding and her body was throbbing with adrenaline.*

*She couldn't believe she'd just done that. She couldn't believe
she'd agreed to do that. She panted on her hands and knees
for a minute until her heart calmed down, and then, silently
thanking Gaia for not letting her fall, she brought herself to
her feet and turned around to look down to where Ty still
waited.*

He was grinning up at her so widely it warmed her heart all over again.

"I did it!" she called down to him, starting to feel incredibly proud of herself now that the adrenaline was wearing off. She'd never done anything like that before, and even though her arms were weak and her fingers would certainly be sore tomorrow, she felt infinitely stronger. Gaia help her, but earning the admiration of this boy and meeting his challenges was becoming addictive.

"See? I was right," Ty said cockily as he approached the rock wall and started to climb.

Ena rolled her eyes in response, but quickly couldn't look away as Ty scaled the cliffside like he was made for it. His large hands gripped the rocks as his forearm muscles tightened, ascending the rock wall like it was as easy as walking. In an embarrassingly short amount of time compared to how long it took Ena, he pulled himself over the top just as she had.

"Wow, you must climb a lot," Ena said, not bothering to hide the admiration in her voice.

"Yeah, there are a lot of...caves and stuff back home. I grew up climbing," he said nonchalantly as he caught his breath.

Ena was once again filled with curiosity about Yalta and what it was like, but the questions died in her throat as she watched Ty take in the view from the top.

Trees as far as the eye could see blanketed the valley floor. Far below them, the river gorge cut a dark, meandering ravine through the sea of green until it ended in the blue, flat haze of the Endless Ocean in the distance. Looming tall behind them were the Chasm Mountains, their snowy peaks cutting through the horizon, dwarfing the cliffside they stood on.

"This is gorgeous," he said, looking out across the landscape with a contented look on his face.

"I know," Ena said, matching his reverential tone. "I come up here sometimes just to look at the mountains and the ocean. They make me feel..." Ena trailed off, not knowing how to put the feeling into words.

"Make you feel what?" he asked, turning to look at her.

She looked back, meeting his gaze as he waited for her to continue. As if he were hanging on every word. "Small. Insignificant in the Turning. Just one tiny being in a much, much larger world. But..." she added, staring towards the ocean again, "safe somehow. Like I have a place here. Like I fit."

"Hmm," Ty said, sounding skeptical.

"What? Does that sound dumb?" Ena replied, smirking.

"No, not at all," he said, shaking his head. "It's just, I don't think you're small at all. You seem like a force of nature to me... Maybe that's why you fit."

His gaze turned serious now, the intensity of it reminding her of the way he'd looked at her last night. The sun was already starting to get lower, turning the sky a deep blue with a layer of orange and yellow along the horizon. This high up, away from the forest, blue was all Ena could see behind him, and his green eyes seemed to glow in the light.

Feeling self-conscious under his gaze, Ena turned away. "Do you see the ocean?" she asked, changing the subject and pointing to the hazy blue line in the distance. "Sometimes on a really clear day, you can see the white caps on the waves."

"Hmm. No, I can't see." Ty bunched his brows together, squinting like he couldn't quite make it out.

"Seriously? Look," Ena said, grabbing his arm and tugging him next to her. Standing up on her tippy toes, she put her face right next to his and turned to stare at the horizon with him, pointing in the direction of the ocean. "See?" she said. "Right there."

Ty turned his face away from where she was pointing to look at her instead. He was so close she could feel his breath on her cheek. "Now I see," he said.

She turned towards him, their faces just inches apart. Ena couldn't help but look down at his mouth. His full lips were quirked upwards on one side in a devastatingly handsome smile. This close to him, she was surrounded by his scent, as she had been last night. Cedar, stone, woodsmoke, and honey. Unintentionally, she inhaled deeply, letting her eyes flutter closed as she appreciated the heady combination. Realizing what she'd just done, embarrassment jolted through her. Her eyes snapped open as she went to turn away, but Ty reached out with his hand to cradle the side of her face, holding her there.

His eyes locked with hers as he gently stroked his thumb across her cheek. "Can I kiss you?" he asked.

Ena wanted nothing more in that moment, but butterflies filled her stomach. Was this real? She wasn't sure. This felt like a dream. Not her real life. Everything since she'd seen him last night at the Litha gathering had been a blur.

But, even if it were a dream, she realized she didn't really care. She'd already achieved an overwhelming high by climbing a cliff. How could she resist throwing herself off this one?

"Yes," she replied, heart hammering.

Ty pulled her face close to his and lowered his head. Already on her tippy toes, she placed her arms on his shoulders and closed her eyes as their lips touched.

His mouth was warm and soft and felt like home and the greatest unknown at the same time. The kiss was light and gentle, as if he were holding back, but it didn't matter; the feel of his lips moving against hers overwhelmed her senses and teased her in a way that sent shivers down her spine. She instantly felt an ache settle between her thighs and was acutely aware of how close their bodies were.

Then Ty pulled back. He looked into her eyes and didn't move a muscle, as if he were waiting to see what she would do next. They stared at each other, a million unspoken things passing between them. They could stop right here, not go any further. She could step back and walk away, change the subject. But Ena didn't want to do any of those things.

"Kiss me again," she said.

"Absolutely," he said, sounding relieved as he pulled her towards him again.

This kiss was firmer, needier. Ena followed Ty's lead as he naturally guided her mouth open with his own. She gasped slightly, breathing in his air.

Ena had kissed boys before, but it was nothing like this. Kissing Ty felt so natural, so right. He tasted like mint and honey, and when his tongue slowly slipped into her mouth and swirled against hers, she couldn't help but meet it greedily with her own.

She took a step closer to him without thinking, pressing her body flush with his. His chest was hard and warm, and her breasts pressed against him, tingling at the contact, as he wrapped his arm around her waist and pulled her into him.

The feel of him heated her blood to boiling, every nerve in her body coming alive. She let out a small whimper as his hand left the side of her face to twine into her hair, making her breathless as the kiss continued to escalate. His tongue expertly delved into her mouth, coaxing her, tantalizing her, and then she broke. Losing awareness of the world around her, Ena wrapped her arms tightly around his neck, letting one hand roam into his hair. She wanted more, wanted everything, and couldn't get close enough.

Their mouths and tongues began to move together like they were starving, like they'd been waiting their whole lives to taste one another. Ty seemed to sense her desperation as his hand left her hair and roamed slowly down her back to grab her ass through her thin dress, pushing her aching center against him. She felt his cock grow hard between them, pressed against her belly, and arched her hips into him. His touch was electric, his taste was addictive. She lost herself to the feeling, to him, and she wanted more.

The overwhelming feeling of it was so strong it shocked her, and all of a sudden, Ena hesitated. This was all happening so fast, and everything she was feeling was so intense it scared her a little. She pulled back, both of them breathing heavily.

Ena stared up at Ty, his eyes heavy lidded with lust. Clearing her throat, she suddenly felt awkward and didn't know what to say, how to explain her hesitation. What could she say? "I'm worried that I want you too much? That kiss was too fucking good and I was scared I wouldn't stop and we'd end up having sex on this cliff but I just met you yesterday and you're leaving soon?" *Lowering herself back onto flat feet and pulling back to put some distance between them, she felt his grip around her loosen as a brief look of confusion fell over his face.*

"It's... uh...starting to get dark," she said. "We should probably head back."

It wasn't totally an excuse. Looking around as if he, too, had completely forgotten where they were, Ty seemed to realize that it was, in fact, getting dark, and that they were on top of a cliff with a long hike back to the village.

Ty cleared his throat before he spoke, his voice coming out rough. "Yeah, yes. You're right. We should head back."

Ty released her fully from his grip, and she took another step back from him. She saw him release a deep breath, as if to calm himself, and she'd be lying if she said she didn't need the same herself.

Seeking to break the tension a little, she looked cautiously down at the rock wall they'd climbed up to get here. "Please tell me you're okay to walk back on the path this time."

Ty chuckled, watching her every move like she was impossible to look away from. "Whatever you want, Ena," he said.

She smiled at that, and turned to walk down the path, making him follow her.

CHAPTER EIGHT

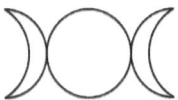

ENA'S BODY HURT ALL over. Her wrists were chafed raw from the handfast bindings, her thighs were shaking from holding herself upright on the horse for hours, and her head pounded. The sun was just starting to crest the horizon, bathing the forest in a delicate blue light. Birds were starting to shuffle around in the trees, and in the distance, Ena heard a creek bubbling cheerfully. She wasn't sure which direction they had been riding all night, but she figured the creek must be one of the smaller tributaries that ran into the River Wry.

Her theory was confirmed once the creek came into sight. It was a decent size, about ten feet across, and filled with large boulders and downed logs which formed small eddies and rapids. But just glancing downriver, she could tell it meandered widely, which meant that if she were to escape, she could try to follow its flow to the River Wry, but it would likely take her far longer than the route they'd just taken from her village.

She'd had a million thoughts like this all night—thinking through every possible escape route, every possible way she might be able to slip away from them and find her way back before they got too far. But they'd ridden fast all night without stopping, and not a single opportunity had presented itself. Besides, her hands and mouth were still gagged, which put her at a significant disadvantage.

As they approached the bank of the creek, the man in the hawk mask, who she'd refused to even glance back at while riding all night, called to the others. "We'll stop here to water the horses and take a short break, then we'll ride on. We need to put more distance between us and her Coven in case they come looking."

The man pulled their horse to a stop, then dismounted. He turned to face Ena and gripped her waist with large hands. Lifting her off the horse after him, he put her down directly in front of him. Ena was too tired to fight him, and her legs wobbled as she tried to stand. The man held her by the shoulders, his grip somewhat gentle, as he said, "I'd like to remove your gag so I can give you some water. I know you must be thirsty. If you try to scream and draw attention, I'll just have to put it right back in. You should know, we're far enough away that I don't think anyone will hear you anyway, so it would be useless to try, but I won't take any chances. Do you understand?"

Ena stared daggers at the man, but nodded obediently nonetheless. At this point, she had no choice but to acquiesce. She wanted water and this gag out of her mouth so badly.

The man reached behind her head to untie the gag and pulled the cloth out of her mouth. Ena sighed in relief, using her tongue to remoisten her impossibly dry mouth.

"Here," he said, offering her a leather waterskin that he pulled from one of the saddlebags. "You're also welcome to relieve yourself behind that tree over there if you have to, but if you go too far, or try to run, I will just have to catch you. And I will, so don't even try it. Understand me?"

"Yes, *Master*," Ena replied sarcastically, venom dripping with every word. She meant it as an insult. Only daemons called Iblis "Master," and among witches, to call someone that was like calling someone a sadist. But it clearly didn't have her desired effect, because the man just looked satisfied as a small devilish smile graced his lips.

Turning away from him, she lifted the waterskin to her lips and chugged the cool water. It felt like heaven in her mouth and down her dry, scratchy throat. Taking a peek over her shoulder, she saw the three men leading the horses to the creek and talking quietly amongst themselves. She felt relieved at their momentary distraction and wandered over to the tree the man had pointed to. As she crouched down to relieve her bladder, she took the private moment to frantically think of a plan.

She had to get her bearings and figure out where she was. Now that the sun was up, she would hopefully be able to see landmarks more clearly, or if they came to a high point in the land, she could try to orient herself to the Chasm Mountains and the sun's angle. As it were, being this deep in the heavily canopied forest, it was hard to tell from which direction the sun was even rising.

Coming back around from behind the tree, Ena saw the men washing up and filling up their waterskins in the creek, and it was the first time she'd gotten a good look at them in the daylight. They were all dressed similarly, in the same type of clothing anyone would wear this time of year: gray or brown woolen trousers and leather boots, linen shirts, and thigh-length black woolen coats with polished bone buttons. They carried more weapons than usual travelers, which made sense now that she knew their purposes. Each of them had a dagger strapped to their sides, and the tall one she'd been riding with had an axe strapped to his back. Weapons for killing other people were usually hard to come by on this side of the Chasm Mountains. The villages and the Covens usually existed in peace, and any skirmishes between mortals were usually brief and stayed confined to those villages involved. People more often than not used the farming and kitchen tools they had to defend themselves if anything went wrong, but there usually wasn't much theft or violence. The fact that these men had weapons at all was certainly suspicious.

As they turned away from the creek to huddle together in conversation once more, she realized that they'd also removed their masks and she could see their faces clearly for the first time. When the one she thought she recognized turned to face her, her heart leapt to her throat.

Seeing his face, maskless, in the early-morning light, there was no doubt. It was Ty.

He was clearly older, in his late twenties now, and he was bulkier than she remembered. His limbs had lost the thinness of youth and his arms and shoulders were more densely packed with muscle. His hair was different too. Instead of the slightly too-long, shaggy cut she remembered, he now had shorter hair that was shaved on either side of his head, revealing a series of tattoos along his scalp. And he had a beard. It was full and dark, perfectly complementing the darkness of his brows, which framed his unmistakable light-green eyes. Those hadn't changed at all.

He caught her looking at him and she quickly looked away, busying herself with the mouth of the waterskin she'd been given.

She'd gotten a good glimpse of the other two men, who had revealed their faces as well. The one called Steig looked to be about thirty years old, with short, curly black hair and dark eyes, but the other one who had been wearing the raccoon mask—and who'd burned down Heran's house—looked younger, though by how much she wasn't sure. His short hair was dirty blond and his eyes a striking blue, but overall, his face had a surprising innocence about it. They were both strong-looking, as well, and from what she could see of their arms and hands where their shirts were rolled up as they had washed in the creek, they were covered in tattoos too.

Ena's hands were still bound and clasped around her waterskin like it was her only lifeline as she walked back towards her captors, who were readying the horses again.

"Ready?" Ty asked her. There was still no hint of recognition in his eyes, no sign that he remembered her. Was she really that forgettable?

"Do I have a choice?" she asked bitterly.

"Good point," he said, as he reached for her waist and lifted her up onto his horse. Again, Ena didn't fight him. She knew her best course of action was to figure out her whereabouts before she made her escape, rather than blindly running and yelling through the woods. These men could certainly outrun her in her current state anyway.

They rode all day, stopping only briefly to relieve themselves a couple times. Ty graciously offered Ena some dried meat of some kind and an apple at one point to eat in the saddle. She ate them both begrudgingly, only to keep her strength up. She spent the rest of the time letting her Knowing soak up all the information around her. What animals and birds were there? What types of trees were around? Where was the water flowing? What direction was the sunlight coming from? All of these clues led her to believe that they were likely west of her village, a direction the witches in her Coven did not usually travel—and for good reason. But she couldn't say for sure. She needed to confirm her theory before she escaped. She didn't want to end up wandering aimlessly through the woods, as that was a surefire way to die.

She also spent time contemplating what the hell these men wanted with her. They clearly didn't want to hurt her, which they easily could have done by this point. This led her to believe that they probably wanted to use her for something. They had obviously been looking for something at Heran's house. But what could that be? She knew at least one of them was a daemon, the one whose name she did not yet know but who she'd seen burn down Heran's house with his bare, heat-wielding hand. However, she wasn't sure about Steig. And Ty...well she thought he had been mortal. She needed a way to confirm what they were so she knew what she was dealing with. Luckily, she had a method at her disposal.

She reached out with her Knowing.

Usually, using one's Knowing on other people, and especially other witches, was frowned upon. To use one's magic to interpret someone's intentions or uncover things about themselves they may not want you to know was considered a severe violation of privacy, so Ena rarely did it. Of course, sometimes she Knew things without intending to, and when that happened, she tried her best to ignore it or keep it to herself.

But this time, she absolutely intended to Know more about her kidnappers, so she read their signs. She turned her head surreptitiously to watch Steig where he rode his large, dapple gray horse to her left. She concentrated on his movements, the way he swayed in the saddle, the way his hands gripped the reins. She watched the way he breathed and the direction of his gaze. She took in all the signs she could and she felt...nothing. There was no sense of his intentions, no sense of his presence at all, really. There was just nothing. A void where her sense of reality should be. It was eerie now that she focused on it. She'd never felt that from anything or anyone before. He must be a daemon too.

And Ty... She slowly turned in the saddle and glanced back at him out of the corner of her eye. She saw his eyebrow quirk up as she looked back at him intently.

"Your Knowing won't work on me, witch," he said gruffly.

"And why's that?" she replied, facing forward again, feeling slightly perturbed at having been called out on what she was trying to do.

"I think you know."

"No, I don't actually. My Knowing doesn't work on you, remember? You just said it." Wow, what a childish comeback. But Ena didn't care. He was annoying her with his cocky bullshit.

"I know you don't *Know*," he replied, leaning closer to her to whisper in her ear, "but you're smart enough to figure it out."

As his breath coasted over her face, his woodsmoke and honey scent hit her again. The feelings and memories it stirred in her were instantaneous, and they were followed quickly by a sharp pang of longing in her chest. It was *him*, after all this time.

But as quickly as that feeling came, it was replaced by a wave of intense anger. How many years had she spent pining for that scent? Longing to see him again, to hear from him? Too long. And now all of a sudden, he was here—only he wasn't. This wasn't the boy she remembered. This man was someone else entirely. He'd obviously lied to her all those years ago about who he was. And, on top of all that, she clearly meant nothing to him. Less than nothing. He didn't even remember her. She had always assumed that something had prevented Ty from returning. She'd worried for years that maybe he'd been hurt or killed on the journey over the Chasm Mountains. But now it was painfully obvious that wasn't the case. Clearly, their time together had just meant much more to her than it did to him, since he had given no indication that he knew her name or recognized who she was at all.

Ena's heart ached with betrayal, but she knew that feeling would not serve her now, so she shoved that hurt to a deep, dark place inside her, and instead she latched onto hate.

"You're a daemon," she said with conviction, spitting the word out as her lip curled.

"Iblis take me, I think she's finally got it," Ty replied mockingly, huffing a laugh.

The four of them fell back into silence for a while until the sun started to set. Ena wasn't sure if they were keeping quiet for her sake, afraid of revealing any further information to her, or because they were still concerned about being followed. But either way, Ena was grateful for it. She couldn't take hearing his voice any more than necessary. She briefly considered calling him out, telling him she knew who he was, forcing him to remember her, but no matter how angry she got as she stewed in her feelings, she couldn't do it. She just couldn't expose that small, vulnerable part of herself. She could never let him know how much this hurt. So, if he'd forgotten her, then she would forget him too. Or at least, she'd appear that way.

Her feelings of bitterness and hatred were all that fueled her as the sky turned dark once more, her body long since exhausted from minimal food, water, and sleep. When Ty made them all stop to make camp, Ena whispered a silent prayer of thanks to Gaia.

"We're far enough away from her village now. I think we'll be safe to stop here for the night," he explained to the others.

Once again, he lifted her off the horse and placed her on the ground. Then, gripping her elbow, he led her over to a large tree and pointed to the ground at the base of it.

"Sit here where I can see you while we make camp," he said gruffly.

Eternally grateful to be off that fucking horse, Ena sat down as she was told and leaned back against the tree. She watched while they loosely tied up the horses so they could graze on the ground plants in the area, and gathered sticks and downed branches to make a fire. Of course, the younger-looking man's Power made the starting of it extremely easy.

She wondered briefly how his Power worked. It was so similar to the way witches used their spellwords to create fire, but his magic clearly didn't require a spellword and instead came directly from his body. The advantage of that was clear, given how limited Ena had been with the gag in her mouth. She briefly considered using a spellword now to make the fire blow up in their faces; even though her magic wouldn't work directly *on* them, maybe she could use it near them as a distraction to escape. But she decided that a momentary distraction wouldn't help her cause, not when there were three of them and they had much longer strides than her. And besides, she still hadn't gotten her bearings enough to know which way to go.

The sun set quickly this time of year, and soon it was pitch black and cold where Ena leaned against the tree. She watched enviously as the three men sat huddled around the fire, their voices low as they discussed something intently. Were they going to leave her over here all night? She would freeze. She was only wearing her woolen Samhain dress since none of the men clearly had had the decency or forethought to grab her a goddamn cloak before they kidnapped her.

After a few minutes of staring murderously at them, they seemed to come to an understanding in their conversation, and Ty stood up to approach her. Reaching towards her, he held out his hand as if to pull her up.

"Come by the fire. It's warmer there, and we need to talk."

Ena eyed his outstretched hand suspiciously, like it was likely to bite her.

"Don't be stubborn," he said. "If you cooperate, you'll be free of us all the more quickly."

Ena really didn't want to do anything he asked of her, even though she was freezing. She was exhausted and sore and so sick of being dragged around by these daemons. Daemons! She still could not believe, after all these years of hearing stories about them, that they were here in front of her and they held her captive. Her anger rose again, and she strongly considered remaining where she was, making them drag her to the fire if need be. But she also really, really wanted to go home. And if cooperating with them got her out of here, she'd do it. Grudgingly.

She lifted her tied hands up to his as he grabbed one and pulled up. She winced as the ropes chafed her wrists again. They were nearly raw in two spots where they'd rubbed all day, anytime she'd shifted positions on the horse. The handfasting ropes were of a high quality, but were decorative, and only meant to be used in ceremony. They were certainly not meant to be worn continuously or used to restrain someone.

Noticing her reaction, Ty paused. "Here," he said, reaching for her joined hands and gently untying the rope from her wrists.

She clasped her raw wrists to her chest, relieved to finally have her freedom of movement back. She looked up suspiciously at him. "I'd say thank you, but you're the ones who put them on in the first place, so I think *fuck you* is more appropriate," she said bitterly.

She expected her words to be cutting and maybe provoke his ire, but Ty just stared at her as a reluctant smile lit up his face and he huffed a small laugh. For a split second, she was transported back to those warm summer days nine years ago. Her eyes widened slightly in shock as Ty's face lit up with the motion, softening the harshness of his features.

"You got me there," he said wryly. But just as quickly, that vision of the old Ty was gone. His smile died as quickly as it had come and his eyes turned dark and aloof again as he turned back toward the fire, gesturing for Ena to follow.

She joined Ty and the other daemons around the roaring fire. Sitting next to its crackling warmth and light centered her. She stared at it and Knew its intensity, its desire to burn and consume until nothing was left. It soothed her somehow. Fire was always a necessary part of Gaia's plan, clearing dead trees to make space for new life, the ashes of the old feeding the soil. Only when fires were amplified by daemons to become more destructive than they should did they upset the balance. Right now, this fire felt like a kindred spirit; its destructive desire mirrored her own as she sat with these daemons, waiting for them to tell her what the fuck they wanted with her.

She realized she'd become lost in her thoughts when the younger-looking daemon—Turner, she'd heard the other two call him when they'd stopped to make camp—handed her some dried meat, a hunk of old cheese, and the same waterskin she'd had before. She took it, again grudgingly, and started eating in silence. When she'd finished, she found the three men looking at her expectantly.

"We want to make you a deal," Ty said with authority.

"What kind of deal?" Ena replied, brushing the cheese crumbs nonchalantly off her dress, as if her life and well-being were not in the balance here. Not for the first time, she wished she could read their signs better and understand their intentions, but she had no choice but to keep her own cards close to her chest. And right now, letting them know how scared she was, how much she wanted to go home, would not be in her best interest.

"The kind where you help us, and we let you go," he said.

"Help you with what?" she replied, her tone cool and even.

Ty looked briefly at both his companions, then explained. "We're looking for something. A magical object. We'd like you to help us find it."

"You'd 'like' me to?" Ena scoffed, some of her anger slipping out despite her efforts. "You dragged me away from my home and burned the matriarch's house to the ground. Why would I ever help you?"

"If you help us find it, we'll let you go. Unharmed," Ty replied, unfazed by her anger.

"And if I don't?" she asked in challenge.

"Well, then we'll have no choice but to keep you. In the Underworld."

Ena's spine went stiff. He couldn't be serious. The Underworld was an almost mythical place of dark depravity where daemons dwelled, or so she'd heard. She only knew what she'd been told about it, mostly through stories meant to scare young witches. But it was said that all manner of atrocities occurred there, that it was a place where daemons delighted in violence and inhumane behavior against one another and the mortals and witches that were unfortunate enough to be captured and taken there, never to return. The entrance to the Underworld was a heavily guarded secret among the daemons—no witch or mortal alive knew where it was. If Ty was serious... Fear gripped her at the thought.

She forced herself to think practically. She had to assume, for now, that his threat was serious. But even so, Ena assumed it would take them a while to travel there, so she considered her options. She could refuse to help them and keep looking for opportunities to escape while they traveled to the Underworld. Ena had no doubt that once she figured out her whereabouts, that she'd be able to make a plan and get away from them. They clearly underestimated her and what her magic could do if they'd taken off the ropes and gag.

On the other hand, if she did help them, she had the opportunity to find out more about what they wanted. She was not a fool. She knew that they could easily be lying to her and would not let her go after she helped them. They'd likely kill her, or bring her to the Underworld anyway, just out of spite. What nefarious purposes they'd have for a witch in the Underworld she did not want to know. If she could find out what they were looking for and why, she could escape with useful information, and then maybe her and her Coven could foil their undoubtedly sinister machinations. Going along with them was a risk, but at this point, Ena was filled with such hatred and loathing for these men and what they had done to her, that she wanted revenge. She knew what she had to do.

"Fine. I'll help you," she said, meeting Ty's gaze unerringly. "I can do a locator spell to help you find the object." There was no point in hiding this ability—they clearly suspected she could do something of the sort, or they wouldn't have asked for her help. She'd have to appear to be helping them in good faith while she gathered information. "But," she continued, "I need to know more about it to complete the spell. And I'll need some supplies."

Ty exchanged looks with his companions again. "What supplies?"

"Potion ingredients—specific herbs, an apple. Some blood...and fresh bones. Leg bones, specifically."

"What kind of blood?" Ty asked cautiously.

"Any kind."

"Okay. And what kind of leg bones?"

"Are you volunteering?" Ena smirked at him.

"No," he said, unamused. "I mean, will the leg bones of an animal suffice?"

"Yes."

"Okay, fine. Done. We can get you those things," he said dismissively.

"And the herbs?"

"If you tell me what you need, I have a plan for that too."

"Bay leaves, belladonna, sage, and wormwood."

"Okay."

"And the details about the object?" Ena asked innocently.

This was dangerous ground. They clearly did not want to share more about it, but she wasn't lying when she said she'd need more details to complete the spell. She'd only completed a locator spell a few other times before, but they could be very finicky. The more they could share with her, the better chance she'd have of getting it right.

Ty took a deep breath then sighed, rubbing his hand through his beard in uncertainty. She had him right where she wanted him.

"It's an amulet," he said, clearly having come to a decision. "A powerful one."

Ena was surprised. An amulet? She'd heard of them, but they were extremely rare. Used by witches to amplify powers or spells, they were kept as closely guarded secrets among the three Covens. Ena didn't even know if her own Coven had one, but clearly the daemons thought they had if they were searching Heran's house for one.

"What does it look like?" Ena asked, her curiosity piquing.

Ty paused again, as if sharing this information was physically painful for him. "Our sources say it is a large, uncut, deep-purple amethyst in a circular silver setting, decorated with Wiccan symbols. It is hung on a chain of intricately braided silver strands."

Ena paused, waiting for him to continue. When he didn't provide any more details, she prompted him. "Anything else? Anything about the Wiccan symbols on it?"

He shook his head. "That's all we know."

"Why did you think *my* Coven had it?"

"You don't need to know that."

Ena had expected that answer, but it still exasperated her. "Okay, then why do you want it?" she asked, trying to seem casual.

Ty grinned at her menacingly. "Careful there, little viper."

Ena grit her teeth at the nickname. She'd known he wouldn't tell her why they wanted it, but it didn't hurt to try.

"Fine," she replied. "That should be enough information to complete the spell, I guess."

"Good. We'll get your supplies in the morning, after we've rested," Ty said with an air of finality. Then he stood up and left the fire, seemingly to tend to his horse.

Having been essentially dismissed, and having absolutely no desire to make small talk with Steig and Turner, who remained by the fire debating amicably about the proper way to sharpen their knives, Ena lay down and curled up on her side in the dirt. Her back was to the fire, keeping her nice and warm for now, but she reached out at the plants around her to create a crude nest of leaves and ferns to insulate her even more.

She began to get sleepy, staring deep into the darkness of the forest, her body exhausted beyond anything she could ever remember feeling before. As her eyes drifted closed, she saw Ty emerge from the woods just at the periphery of her vision. He was leaning against a tree, staring into the fire. His face was lit up by the glow as it highlighted the harsh, masculine planes of his face. His eyes were contemplative and...troubled. A line had formed between his brows and he looked deep in thought. Ena allowed herself this one unabashed moment to take him in as he now was. To note how he'd changed, and how he was the same. Her eyes traced the lines of his beautiful face, his arms, his legs. This person who'd meant so much to her, who she'd dreamt about for *years*.

And in the cold night, as she drifted off to sleep, she was glad that she'd already lost that small, hopelessly romantic part of herself that she'd once held on to for so long. It wasn't real; what she'd had with him wasn't real. It was the daydream of a naïve, young girl. She'd suspected that already, but now, seeing him again, she knew it to be true.

But it was okay, because she wasn't that girl anymore. She'd said goodbye to her long ago. She'd said goodbye in the long, lonely nights, and every summer day that had passed since they'd met. And so, reminding herself of who she was now, she vowed to emerge from this betrayal stronger and wiser. She would make this man regret ever knowing and forgetting her.

CHAPTER NINE

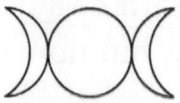

Nine years and four months ago...

THE NEXT DAY, ENA *was sent to search for mushrooms in the forest. Their stores were low on some critical species that they used both for potions and cooking, so she grabbed her harvesting basket and took off into the woods surrounding their village. She walked along a stretch of the River Wry past the clearing in the Sacred Grove, searching for pineroot mushrooms, but all she could think about was Ty.*

That kiss had been...well, it was intense. Just like everything with Ty. She knew she shouldn't dwell on it too much. He was leaving tomorrow. He'd probably be spending the rest of the day readying to leave and breaking camp, so they likely wouldn't see each other again. But still, the thought of him sent butterflies through her stomach. He was gorgeous, yes—too gorgeous. And he had an air of danger and mystery about him that was unique, for a mortal. Gaia, that combination alone drew her in like a moth to a flame.

But beyond that, he challenged her. She had already been way more adventurous with him in the last two days than she had her whole life. And it was because he made her feel capable—powerful in a way she'd never felt before, and yet also...safe. She found herself telling him things she wasn't sure she'd told anyone else. If she were being honest, it was those things that made a smile drift unbidden across her face as she thought of him, and that left her wanting more of him, even if she knew it was a fool's hope.

She was so lost in thoughts of something that couldn't last, but indulging herself anyway, she didn't realize she'd wandered over by some of the travelers' camps. Small campfires dotted the landscape, along with canvas tents and bedrolls as visitors milled about, packing up their camps and readying to journey home now that Litha had passed.

Then she saw him. Ty was shirtless, loading crates into a horse-drawn cart. His tanned skin was fully on display, his arm and back muscles rippling with every lift. Not of her own volition, she stopped and couldn't help but watch him. He moved so gracefully for such a tall person. There was another man helping him. He was older, maybe in his late forties, with dark hair and a powerful build that was covered in tattoos. Tattoos were not uncommon among some mortals, but these ones looked very distinct. He must be one of the uncles Ty had mentioned.

As if sensing her presence, Ty looked her way and caught her staring. A wide grin broke out on his face. He quickly said something to the other man, who threw a suspicious look Ena's way, then hopped down from the cart and walked towards her.

"Ena," he called, his long strides bringing him quickly to her. "How are you?"

Ena just stared for a second. He was slightly sweaty and out of breath from the lifting. The sound of his voice, deep and strong, sent tiny shivers up her spine. She tried very hard not to stare down at his exquisitely chiseled abs.

Clearing her throat, she said, "I'm good. Just mushroom hunting." She held up her basket for effect.

Silence fell between them. All the comfort they'd developed with one another last night had seemingly evaporated in the daylight.

"I was wondering," Ty said, rubbing the back of his neck. Was he nervous? "I have a lot of packing to do since we're leaving tomorrow morning, but I was hoping you'd have dinner with me later tonight."

"Dinner?" Ena repeated.

"Nothing fancy. I'd just like to see you again, before I go."

Before he goes... Ena's heart lurched at the idea of having to say goodbye to him, but it tripped over itself at his invitation.

"Yeah, dinner sounds good." Ena smiled widely at him, and he smiled back.

"Great, okay. Meet me at the beach an hour before sunset?"

"Okay," she said, her heart leaping at the idea.

"Good."

They were grinning at each other like fools, but Ena didn't care.

She gave him a delicate wave and kept walking past him. She felt him watch her for a few seconds after her back was turned, then heard him walk back towards his camp to resume loading their horse cart.

The rest of the day passed by in an anticipation-induced blur. By the time her chores were finished and evening had settled, Ena rushed to her room to bathe and get ready. She fretted for an embarrassingly long time over what to wear, but settled on a dark-blue linen dress with a built-in bodice that laced up the front with a length of black ribbon. The neckline formed a low scoop, accentuating her breasts in a seductive yet tasteful way, if she did say so herself. And she knew without a doubt that the color brought out her eyes, which were the same ocean blue as her dress. Not knowing what else to do, she simply left her hair down, the gentle, dark-brown curls tumbling down her back.

Not for the first time, she chastised herself for putting in too much effort, for caring too much. Ty was leaving tomorrow, likely never to return. Nothing could come of their relationship. She knew that. This should just remain a casual fling. She was having fun, she told herself. That's all this was, and all it would ever be.

Making her excuses to Greya and Heran, she walked along the well-worn path through the clearing which dead-ended at the river. Then she followed it upstream to her beach, the route second nature by this point.

What she saw when she arrived made her stomach flip and brought a wide smile to her face. Ty was there, sitting on a large blanket that was spread across the pebbles and sand of the beach. He'd started a small fire nearby, which cast a warm glow over his beautiful face as he watched the water. Arranged atop the blanket was a large green bottle of something and two chipped ceramic mugs, as well as an assortment of foods in wooden bowls that she couldn't quite make out in the low light of dusk.

"What's all this?" she asked as she approached him.

Ty turned to her, seeming startled by her appearance. Ena smiled lightly to herself at finally having snuck up on him for a change.

"Ena," he said, standing up. He stared at her for a second, as if not quite believing she was really there. His eyes slowly roamed her up and down, and she saw his throat bob as he swallowed. "You look..." he started, trailing off.

"Beautiful? Stunning? Exquisite?" Ena offered flippantly at his hesitation.

"Yes," he said, his tone deadly serious. "All of that...and more." Then grinning, he added, "My apologies. Words seem to have escaped me for a moment."

He reached out a hand to guide her to the blanket. Gaia, he was charming. The casual grace and confidence with which he moved was incredibly sexy. And his stare, always so intense, sent shivers down her spine.

Feeling like she needed to break the tension, she gestured towards the blanket and asked, "What food did you bring?"

"Ah, some delicacies," he described, gesturing grandly to the spread of food. "Strawberries that I traded one of the other Auster witches for, some cheese from the Northumbra travelers, and some corn cakes that I made over our campfire. And of course, some cherry wine," he said proudly, holding up the mystery bottle.

"Wow, you cooked for me? I'm impressed," Ena said.

"Finally," Ty replied jokingly, rolling his eyes. "I've never met someone so hard to impress, you know."

"Hmm. Well, I guess I'm just not easy prey. Not like all those other girls you impressed with your dancing prowess."

Ty chuckled, deep and dark. "You're still on about that? I told you, those girls are long forgotten. I don't remember their names, what they looked like. I wouldn't even recognize them if they were standing right in front of me."

"Oh, I see. And will I be so easily forgotten too?" Ena said, teasing.

"You?" he asked, all hints of playfulness vanishing. A contemplative expression passed across his face as he watched Ena, as if she were some unknown entity he couldn't quite figure out. "No," he said quietly. "No, I could never forget you."

Looking away, he picked up the bottle of wine and filled up both mugs, handing one to Ena.

The conversation turned once again to lighter subject matter as they picked at the food. The corn cakes were absolutely delicious, and Ty was entirely too cocky after hearing Ena's praise. They drank the cherry wine cheerfully as Ena regaled Ty with stories of her and her sister growing up under the strict guidance of matriarch Heran, like the time Ena had accidentally started a very small forest fire when she was learning how to use her spellwords. Luckily, Greya had put it out before anyone noticed, but to this day, Greya didn't allow her to start campfires.

Then Ty described what it was like growing up with his surly uncles and extensive relations back home, including how one beloved younger cousin had followed him around so much as a child that they referred to him as Ty's shadow. Ena also peppered him endlessly with questions about Yalta and what it was like on the other side of the Chasm Mountains, but Ty remained fairly tight-lipped about his home, insisting that it was nothing special, given how isolated and hard to get to it was.

As the stars began to emerge in the sky, Ty regaled her with a particularly hilarious story wherein he and his best friend went spelunking in a relatively dangerous and unused section of the caves near their village and got lost for three days before they found their way out. They had to survive by eating bugs and salamanders from the underground cave pools, so now Ty refused to travel anywhere without several extra days' worth of food, just in case.

Wiping tears of laughter from her eyes as he finished the story, Ena said, "So I was right then. You are reckless."

"I prefer...adventurous," Ty replied, grinning mischievously in return.

"Ah, I see. Well, that's where you and I differ." Ena sighed, her laughter finally calming as she shook her head.

"You're not adventurous?" Ty asked. "As someone who watched you climb that cliff yesterday with very little convincing, I might disagree with you."

Ena laughed at that, but quickly turned serious as the conversation seemed to hit a sore spot for her. "I've never done anything like that before. Sometimes...I want to be adventurous. But like with learning to swim, I just get scared the worst will happen or I'll lose control and it's just...easier to stay on the safe path, the known one. So that's what I choose."

Ty seemed to ponder that for a moment. "Yeah, that's true. It is safer. And I'm sure I could use some of that temperance, at least according to my dad." Ty smiled sadly at the mention of his father. "But I can't seem to help myself. There's too much to gain from the unknown paths. There's so much to discover, and that adrenaline rush that hits when you find something amazing...there's nothing like it." Ty's face lit up with that mischievous grin again, and Ena could help but smile back at him.

"You make me feel like I could do that, you know," she said quietly.

"Do what?"

"Face the unknown."

They looked at each other for a moment, their gazes full of anticipation. Ena knew what was coming, what was inevitable, but she wasn't sure she was ready for it quite yet.

Together, they turned to look at the sky. The night was clear, only a few wispy clouds covering the moon. A river of stars that mirrored the one flowing next to them filled the sky, and all together, the sea of tiny lights was so bright it nearly outshone the moon. It was beautiful.

"What do witches know of the stars?" Ty asked her casually, breaking the tension.

"Hmm. Well, Gaia created them to guide us, so we might always find our way and know how to orient ourselves to her path. But they can also tell us stories."

"Stories?" he asked, seeming rapt by this knowledge.

"Yes," Ena replied, smiling lightly at his enthusiasm. "The shapes they form tell us the way things once were, and how they may be again. Their movements are one of the ways we interpret Gaia's will."

"I see," Ty said, seeming to contemplate this. "What's that mean then?" he asked, pointing to a cluster of stars that formed a vague serpent shape.

"I believe that's Draco. He is a terrifying snake-like creature with wings."

"Wow, and he used to exist?"

"Used to, or will one day. We're not sure yet." Ena smiled lightly again as she watched Ty stare in awe at the stars. "You don't know all this? About the stars?"

"No," he said, shaking his head as he stared. "We don't see them much where I live. It's...cloudy a lot."

Ena nodded in understanding as they fell into a companionable silence, watching the stars and the light wisps of clouds drifting across the sky. Looking over at Ty, she took in his features and found herself loving his wonder at the things she took for granted. She didn't know why it hit her then, but all of a sudden, the words came spilling out.

"I think I'll miss you," she said quietly. "When you leave."

Ty was silent for a second, then said, "I'll miss you too."

Ena was suddenly filled with an overwhelming sadness, her chest aching and tears beginning to pool in her eyes. Everything she'd told herself, all the lies about this just being a fling, something just for fun, came crashing down around her as she realized that what she had here, with him, was special. It was something she'd never experienced before. But Gaia, it made her feel alive, and she didn't want to let it go.

"Do you think we'll ever see each other again?" she asked.

"I'm not sure," Ty replied quietly. She could hear the strain in his voice, as if it pained him greatly to say so.

Ena looked away, wiping at her eyes and feeling foolish for falling so hard, so fast for this boy. Part of her wanted to pull away, leave right now before she became even more attached. But a louder, braver part of her urged her to be bold, and seize this moment while she had it. Because it might never come again.

"You know, I realized what word it was I couldn't think of when you arrived earlier," Ty said, bringing her out of her thoughts.

"What's that?" she asked.

"Perfect," he said, looking at her as if she were as beautiful as the night sky. "You look perfect."

Before she knew what she was doing, Ena leaned into him. She put her mouth on his, breathing in his masculine scent. His lips were as soft as she remembered and they opened instantly *for her. He quickly took control of the kiss, like he'd been waiting for it all night. He grabbed the back of her head, twining his fingers into her hair, and pulled her closer. Their tongues twisted together, tasting of cherry wine and summer heat.*

Reaching forward, Ena grabbed his shirt and pulled him closer, but it still wasn't close enough. The sadness she had felt was quickly replaced by pure, mind-numbing lust as his tongue moved deftly against her own, licking into her mouth and making every nerve in her body come alive. She let her desire guide her as she brought her leg around to straddle him until she was sitting on his lap.

He responded with a groan, deep in his throat, almost like a growl. He released her hair and brought both hands down to cup her bottom, squeezing lightly and pulling her closer to him. Beneath his trousers, she could feel his hardness growing. Instinctively, she ground up against it, seeking the friction on her sensitive flesh. That spot between her legs began to throb, aching for more. She felt herself spiraling, spiraling out of control as she yearned for Ty to touch her there, touch her everywhere. Their kiss grew fevered and frantic as he sucked on her tongue and she wrapped her arms around his neck, riding him through his pants.

Sensing her urgency, Ty pulled back. "Ena," he gasped. "Tell me now if you want to stop. I don't want to go further than you want to."

"Don't stop," she said, shaking her head and meeting his gaze. "I want you. All of you."

"Are you sure?" Ty asked, breathing just as heavily as she was.

"Yes," she said, but through her lust-fogged brain, a hint of insecurity crept in. "But I...I've never done it before. Had sex, I mean. Have you?" she asked.

She knew it was probably dumb to ask. The way he'd had girls fawning over him at the Litha gathering clearly demonstrated that he'd had the opportunity before.

"Yes," Ty said, and she wasn't sure if it made her feel better or worse.

He studied her for a second, but his face wasn't filled with shock or disappointment. It was filled with understanding, like he saw her now. Truly. Fully.

Gently, he said, "I take a monthly contraceptive, so we could, if you want to. Or we could just kiss, or talk. Whatever you want, Ena."

Ena considered this for a moment. She knew this was fast—they'd only known each other a few days. She'd come close to having sex a few other times with different boys, but she'd never gone through with it because she'd never felt...like this. Like she would die if he didn't keep touching her. Like she wanted to breathe him into her lungs and make him a part of her. She knew it was probably naïve, because she'd only known him for such a short time, but she felt safe with him. She trusted him.

"I want to," she said, the realization dawning on her. "Even if we never see each other again, I don't want to forget this. Forget you. You're...you're everything I've ever wanted."

"Oh, Ena," he said, holding her face in his hands tenderly. "You're more than I've ever dreamed."

Then he kissed her again. Harder this time, fiercer, like he, too, couldn't fathom the idea of letting her go. Ena let her boldness guide her yet again and grasped at his shirt, tugging *it up. Following her lead, Ty broke the kiss briefly to bring it over his head. As soon as he tossed it aside, his lips were on hers again, as if drawn to her like a magnet.*

She ran her hands down his smooth, hard torso, feeling the ripples of his muscles down his stomach. Reaching between them, he began to slowly unlace the front of her dress. The anticipation she felt in that moment made her almost light-headed. She felt her skin heat and her nipples tighten where his hands brushed against them over her dress. Once the bodice was loose, Ty gently pushed the dress off her shoulders and down her arms, leaving it to pool at her waist.

Her breasts were fully exposed, her rosy nipples peaked in the cool night air. Ty looked down and stared at her in awe. She'd never had a boy stare at her so reverently before. As if he was seconds away from getting on his knees and worshiping at her feet.

Ty's large, warm hands came up to cup her breasts, his thumbs sweeping lightly over her nipples. "You are so beautiful, Ena," he whispered, resting his forehead against hers. "It almost hurts to look at you."

Ena huffed a small laugh. "Close your eyes then," she said.

"I wouldn't dare," he replied. Tilting his head, he kissed her again, deeply, thoroughly, as he kneaded her breasts in his hands. Releasing one, he lightly stroked his hand up her bare back, and brought it once again into her hair.

Reaching down, Ena began to undo his trousers. She felt his eagerness grow as she undid each button, and the way he sucked on her tongue left her whimpering into his mouth. Once they were undone, Ena rose up briefly on her knees so Ty could push his pants down his legs. Then Ena moved the layers of her dress out of the way so nothing remained between them.

She could feel his cock throbbing with warmth under her sex. It was hard and silky smooth. She slowly reached down with her hand to touch it and found it already slightly slick with her wetness, just from her sitting on it. She swirled her thumb gently around the tip, and Ty hissed, tilting his head back in pleasure.

"Fuck, Ena, are you sure you've never done this before?"

Ena laughed seductively, loving the effect her touch had on him. "Well, I didn't say I hadn't done anything.*"*

Looking back at her, he also slid his hand between them. His warm thumb brushed over her clit, sending sparks of pleasure through her.

"Gaia," Ena gasped. "That feels—" She couldn't even finish her sentence as he gently rubbed her in tight circles. She could feel herself getting wetter and wetter as he watched her writhe on top of him. Her eyes drifted closed as she chased his movements.

"Are you ready for me, Ena?" he asked, his voice tight with desire.

"Gaia, yes," she said breathlessly.

Opening her eyes, she looked down to see him grab the base of his cock. Lifting herself up on her knees and grabbing on to his shoulders, he lined himself at her entrance. They locked eyes, and Ena paused to take a deep breath before she slowly sank down onto his length.

Despite being more wet than she'd ever been in her life, the first inch was tight, and it stung. She squeezed her eyes shut and buried her face in his shoulder for a second.

"Are you okay?" he asked, as he cupped the back of her head. "Do you want me to stop?"

"No. I mean yes, I'm okay. Just stay still for a second."

Taking a deep breath, Ena felt her body gradually adjust to the stretch. Slowly, slowly, she lowered herself the rest of the way onto him.

The feeling of fullness was new and intense. Despite the slight pain, it felt natural. It felt right. *After giving herself another second to adjust, she looked back at Ty, and found his face enraptured.*

"Fuck, Ena. I won't move an inch if you don't want me to, but you feel so amazing."

Feeling braver at his praise, she slowly began to rock back and forth, testing the movement. The stinging started to dissipate, and she moved faster. Ty began to meet her movements slowly with his own thrusts, and when he did, his lower stomach began to rub against her clit in the most perfect way.

Moving faster, Ena felt her muscles tighten as her orgasm built. Ty reached under her dress to grab her bare ass, pulling her flush with him for more friction. Grabbing his shoulders tightly, she chased her pleasure, grinding on him as she got closer, closer. Her eyes began to flutter closed as her head tilted back.

Grabbing her chin lightly, Ty forced her gaze back on him. His pupils were blown so wide, almost nothing of the green of his irises remained. He looked feral, and his voice was rough and desperate when he said, "Please, Ena, let me see you."

Meeting his gaze, she let go and her orgasm broke, sending waves of pleasure through her body.

She let out a cry of ecstasy. "Fuck, Ty," she almost sobbed, collapsing onto his shoulder as her muscles went lax.

The orgasm had loosened her even further and their bodies began to move faster together. Ty gripped her ass tighter and began to thrust harder, frantically, his controlled movements finally breaking into wild abandon.

"Iblis, Ena, I'm about to—" Ena felt Ty spill inside her with a groan, leaning his head against her neck.

They stayed like that for several minutes, limbs entangled, breathing heavily. There was a peace to it, a still contentment that was just as new as everything else had been.

Eventually, Ty lifted his head, pushing a strand of hair from Ena's face, and he kissed her, gently, thoroughly. When he finally broke it, he asked, "Was that— I mean, are you—"

"I'm wonderful," Ena replied, smiling at him.

He smiled back, looking even more gorgeous with his hair slightly disheveled and his skin damp with sweat. "Good," he said.

Ena slowly slid off of him and stood up to fix her dress, while Ty fixed his own clothes. As the high of what they'd just done drifted away, she didn't know what to say. She was simultaneously happier than she'd ever been, and had never been more scared in her life. Everything they'd just shared had been...well, she was still processing how life-changing it felt. It was better than she could have ever imagined. But she knew what was coming next, and quiet dread filled her. The sun was starting to lighten the sky, and she knew they should head back to the village.

Silently, she helped him pack up the blanket and food he'd brought. Ty seemed lost in his thoughts, and Ena was unsure of what was going through his head. But once everything was gathered into the blanket and they turned to walk back towards the village, Ty took her hand. The firmness of his grip as his large hand enveloped hers steadied her. Ena held on tightly, trying hard to not dwell on how in the world she could possibly say goodbye after everything that had just happened.

They walked quietly downriver, and along the path that led through the clearing. The village was silent as a grave as they walked down the main path towards her house, everyone still sleeping as the sun began to crest the sky. It wasn't until they reached the garden gate outside Heran's house that Ty pulled her to a stop.

"Ena, wait," he said. Turning to face her, he reached out to hold both her hands. "I've been thinking, and I know we said we'd probably never see each other again, but what if I come back, next year?"

"Next year for Litha? You think you can?" Ena tried hard to hide her excitement, her desperation at the prospect of seeing him again, of not having to truly say goodbye to the only person who'd ever made her feel this way. But inside, her heart soared.

"I'll make it so. This can't be the end."

Ty leaned down to kiss her, slowly, sweetly. She breathed in his stone and cedar scent, hoping it would fill her and never leave.

"I have to go. The sun is coming up and my uncles will be wondering where I am." Ty cupped her cheek and pinned her with that intense gaze that seemed to see everything about her.

"Next year? You promise?" Ena asked.

"I promise," Ty replied.

He let her go, and as she turned to walk into her house, she believed him.

Chapter Ten

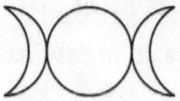

ENA SLOWLY OPENED HER eyes. Her entire body was stiff from sleeping on the ground and her eyes felt dry and irritated from the campfire smoke. She had rolled over at some point during the night so she was facing the fire, probably seeking its warmth, but she was paying the price this morning.

Pushing herself up into a sitting position with an audible groan, she caught Ty watching her from across a newly stoked fire, an enigmatic expression on his face. She would have said it was hatred, given its intensity, but underneath was something...softer—something almost like longing—but that couldn't be right.

Not for the first time, she wished she could read his signs better. How was it possible that she hadn't noticed that her Knowing didn't work on him all those years ago? She guessed that was just another indicator of how willfully blind she'd been. Blinded by his good looks. Blinded by her naïveté. It was just another reminder of how wrong she'd been about him and everything that had happened between them.

Looking away from her, he stood up. "It's time to go," he said. "We're heading out to a nearby village to get your supplies."

Slowly lifting herself to stand, she looked down at her dirt-covered dress. Leaves and twigs stuck to the wool, and she was pretty sure the horse smell would never come out. It was a party dress, not suited for everyday wearing, and certainly not backwoods camping, but she guessed she should count her blessings that her breasts hadn't spilled out of it overnight. She groaned, wondering what the chances were of finding a spare pair of clothes for her at the village too.

After dusting herself off as best as she could, she picked up the waterskin she'd been given last night and took a long, cold drink. From behind her, she heard footsteps crunching through the downed leaves. She turned to find Steig and Turner returning to the campsite from deeper in the woods.

"Trap's all set," Turner said, looking at Ty and then at her with a cautious smile. "Should have a rabbit or two ensnared by the time we get back tonight."

Ena cocked her brow at finally being addressed by one of them other than Ty. Clearly, the moratorium on speaking to her had been lifted after their agreement last night.

"Are you finally planning to feed me something other than these dried bricks of meat?" Ena asked sullenly, ripping off a piece of one of said bricks that she'd saved from last night with her teeth.

"Well, that depends," Steig said, crossing his arms and keeping his distance as if she were poisonous.

"On?" Ena asked.

"On how many we catch and how many we need to sacrifice for your little spell."

"Oh," Ena replied, pleased that they'd already been considering how to get the ingredients she'd need, but annoyed that they hadn't included her. "You should have brought me with you. I can sense rabbit burrows with my eyes closed."

Well, not *literally* with her eyes closed, but pretty damn close, given how often she'd used her Knowing to find them in the past.

"I think we managed just fine on our own. And besides, we don't need you using your witchy senses any more than you already are," Steig replied gruffly.

She bristled at his tone. Witches had always been revered by everyone she knew, especially mortals. Their magic was seen as a blessing and an asset. But these men, Steig especially, treated her like a trickster and a pariah.

"Come on," Ty said, untethering his horse from the tree. "We've got to get a move on if we want to make it back before dark."

Since Ena was cooperating—for now—she walked over to the horse and used the stirrup to lift herself up on its back. In the daylight, she could appreciate what a beautiful brown mare it was. It looked well-cared for and was sufficiently large to carry both her and Ty without much trouble. She read its signs and Knew it was a gentle and well-tempered horse, and she had to stop herself from leaning forward and scratching behind its ears in thanks.

Ty climbed up behind her and reached around to grab the reins. She would never admit it, but she was relieved to be tucked so close to his body heat. It was a chilly fall morning, and, once again, she bemoaned the fact that she had no cloak to keep out the chill. But still, she resisted the urge to lean further back against him. She had far too much pride for that.

They rode silently for about an hour until her curiosity got the better of her. Since she had agreed to their demands, she figured she was owed at least some inkling of where they were going and what to expect.

"How far away is the village we're heading to?" she asked, trying for a casual and innocent tone.

"About half a day's ride," Ty replied shortly.

"What are you planning to trade for the belladonna? It can be quite costly in my experience."

"Don't you worry your pretty little head about that," Ty replied condescendingly.

Ena bristled, turning slightly in the saddle to look at him. "Why can't you just tell me? I'll find out soon enough anyway."

"We'll tell you what you need to know, when you need to know it," he said with finality.

Ena huffed but fell silent. They clearly still didn't trust her any further than they could throw her, despite her having agreed to do the locator spell. But that was just fine for now. She could be patient. They'd let something slip eventually about their plans, she was sure of it.

They continued to ride in silence for much of the morning, weaving through the dense oak and pine forest. Despite being without her sister or her Coven, Ena felt at home in the forest. The birds shuffled in the leaves on the ground, looking for bugs, and squirrels scurried up and down the trees, collecting and storing acorns for winter. The trees swayed in the occasional breeze, more of their leaves dropping gracefully with every gust. The everyday signs of life and death were a comfort to her, and she knew that she was never alone. Gaia's presence was everywhere, guiding her.

Losing herself in the signs all around her, she *almost* forgot about her human company. The three men didn't speak much, only occasionally exchanging a few words. It made her wonder what their relationships were to each other. They didn't look much alike, so they were likely not closely related. But Ty was obviously the leader. The other two deferred to him and followed his decisions, but whether that was just because of his personality or any sort of formal leadership position he held among the daemons, she wasn't sure. Come to think of it, she didn't know much at all about the organization of daemonic society.

Beyond that, though, they also felt like...friends. The way they spoke to one another, and the way they seemed to operate with a certain level of unspoken understanding between them, it was clear they'd known each other for a while. She definitely felt like an intruder into their tight-knit dynamic, but that was their own doing, not hers.

Around mid-morning, Turner reached into one of his saddlebags and pulled out two apples. Wordlessly, he directed his horse a bit closer to Ty's and handed one to him before offering one to her.

"Thanks," she said, slightly surprised at the gesture, since Ty had been the only one to offer her food so far.

Turner simply nodded in reply and kept riding. Steig, on the other hand, clearly had a stick up his ass about something. He'd barely looked her way all morning, and when he did, it was just to scowl in her general direction.

She ignored him and ate the apple gladly, wiping the juices off her chin when she finished.

Towards the afternoon, they arrived at a road. They'd likely been keeping to the backwoods since they fled her village so they'd be harder to track and follow, but arriving at the road meant they were getting closer to civilization. There were only so many established roads this side of the Chasm Mountains, the main ones being the Chasm Road, which ran parallel to the mountain range and connected the Auster and Aquilo Covens, and the Western Road, which led to the Occidens Coven and the Endless Ocean. There were other smaller roads which branched off from those as well, connecting various villages to one another. But this road, if it could even be called that, was clearly not a main road. It was barely large enough to pull a single horse-drawn cart down and could only tightly fit two of them abreast on horseback. It was the least significant road Ena had ever been on.

Not for the first time, Ena wondered where exactly they were. While she had regularly traveled north along the Chasm Road to visit the Aquilo Coven and assist the villages that ran along it, she'd only been west exactly once in her life. When she was fourteen, Heran had taken her and Greya to visit a Sacred Pool that was about halfway between her Coven's village and the coast of the Endless Ocean. Even though members of her Coven were forbidden from traveling west, Heran had made an exception because the sacred waters of the pool were necessary for certain potions, so they'd made the trip expressly for the purpose of collecting the water, and they had not lingered. They hadn't stopped at any villages along the way, and they had kept to the backwoods. So her current unfamiliarity with her surroundings made her, again, think that they had traveled west.

It was quiet as Ena and the daemons walked along the barely there road, the only sounds the clomping of their horses' hooves on the packed earth. The road was clearly not frequented by travelers; they didn't see a single person or horse track the entire time. After about an hour, Steig signaled something to the others and they came to a stop. At first, Ena questioned why they were stopping. She almost missed seeing the path; it was so hidden by the trees and undergrowth that it wasn't until Ty's horse turned off onto it that she realized it *was* a path.

They walked single file down the path through the woods for a few more miles until the small clearing of a village became just visible through the trees. Ty signaled to the others to stop as they dismounted one by one, readying to walk their horses the rest of the way into the village. Ty offered her his hand to help dismount, but Ena ignored it and swung her leg over the tall horse herself, nearly losing her balance as her

short legs reached for the ground. As soon as she righted herself, Ty grabbed her shoulders and spun her to
face him. The men and their horses surrounded her.

"Okay, witch, here's what's gonna happen," Ty said.
"We're metalworks traders here on a scouting visit.
We'll go together to the village's guesthouse, where
you'll sit at a table with Turner while I talk to the villagers." He gestured to the younger daemon. "You won't
speak unless spoken to, and you won't leave Turner's
side. When I create the distraction, Steig will slip into
their kitchen and get what we need. On my cue, we'll
leave quickly and quietly and meet Steig back here in
the woods."

"Wait a second," Ena said, putting two and two together and feeling pissed at the result. "You're gonna *steal*
the ingredients? Why don't you just trade for them?"
she asked incredulously.

It made sense that they were posing as metalworks
traders, just as Ty had all those years ago. She'd
glimpsed one of their saddlebags filled to the brim with
various metal goods, including knives, daggers, hatch-
ets, ornate goblets, *and* silverware. She knew they could
easily trade some of those items for what they needed.

Ty looked at her the way one might look at a confused
child. "We don't want to alert them to the fact that
we have a witch with us, or tip them off to what we're
doing by revealing the ingredients we need. So," Ty said,
invading her personal space, and looking down at her.
Gaia, he was still so tall. Ena hated the way that, despite
everything, her stomach still flipped at his nearness,
just as it had all those years ago. "If you so much as

breathe a word about who we are, or who *you* are, people will get hurt. Do you understand?"

Ena ground her teeth together, and stared into his green eyes with all the venom she could muster. Truthfully, she was appalled that these men would choose to steal from these villagers, but she wasn't really that shocked—they were daemons after all. Still, a mounting feeling of guilt built inside her, knowing it was her supplies, and her spell, that was the cause of this. But she would cooperate, and let them think she was obedient, if only to lure them into a false sense of security. The more they underestimated her, the easier it would be to get the information she needed and escape.

Shoving down her indignation, she took a deep breath and plastered on a saccharine smile. "Yes, Master," she said.

Something flared in Ty's eyes at that, something more than the satisfaction she'd caught last time, something that looked almost...hungry, but before she could fully parse it out, he turned away from her and began to lead his horse directly into the village, forcing her and the others to follow.

As they entered the clearing of the village, Ena was now certain that it was not one of the villages along the Chasm Road, and that therefore they had indeed traveled west, because she didn't recognize it at all. The village was small—tiny, really. Maybe ten worn-down stone houses sat clustered around a crumbling well. Their thatched roofs were clearly old and needed replacing, as significant patches of rot were visible on some of them. Towards the edge of the settlement was a large stable, and it was probably the best-kept building in the village. It was big enough to house probably twenty horses—far more than this village could need. Across from it was an extremely run-down guesthouse. Ena could tell it was a guesthouse because it was bigger than the other single-story stone houses, and had a dilapidated second story that Ena desperately hoped did not collapse while they were inside. Past the houses, deeper into the forest, she also glimpsed a second clearing in the trees and what looked to be an agricultural field. She couldn't say for sure, but from this distance, she guessed it to be a field of recently threshed hay and a small orchard of what looked like apples and other tree fruits.

Since the villages this side of the Chasm Mountains thrived due to prolific trade routes, most were accustomed to visitors and travelers, providing hospitality for them as a way to create mutually beneficial trade relationships. The more relationships and ties a village had to others, the more security they had. That way, if one village was impacted by bad weather or misfortune affecting their crops or trade goods, they could rely on their trade relationships, and oftentimes the goodwill from previous trades, to get them through the hard time. This village, given what Ena could see, likely raised orchard fruit and horses, and used those resources to trade for other things they needed, just as her Coven traded their potions and spells.

Ty strode confidently through the village and up to the stables just as a young stable boy emerged. He jovially greeted the boy, handing him the reins to his horse, before confidently explaining that they were metalworks traders scouting for new trade relationships.

The boy's eyes widened in excitement. While many villages had their own blacksmiths and could make some metal goods, the most significant deposits of metal ore were located near the Chasm Mountains, and thus metal goods were harder to come by the further west the village was. The high-quality metal goods these daemons carried were likely highly coveted by most of the mortal villages, and for that fact alone, they were probably welcomed with open arms at most places they went. Ena had to admit, it was an ingenious cover for their true purposes.

After handing their horses off to the stable boy to be fed and watered, they made their way over to the dilapidated guesthouse. The off-kilter door creaked as they walked inside to find a cozy, albeit slightly crooked, room, almost as if the foundation had sunk on one side, causing the whole room to tilt. Five or six small tables with mismatched chairs and one very old-looking couch were scattered around, and at the far end was a decent-sized hearth with a roaring fire that was putting off more than enough heat to make the room comfortable. To their immediate left was a short bar with two stools, where a burly, middle-aged man was wiping down mugs with a stained cloth.

Only a handful of patrons filled the space, but Ena couldn't tell if they were visitors, like her, or if they lived here. Three older men were playing cards in the corner, each with a cup of what looked like brown ale, and a couple, a man and a woman aged somewhere in their forties, were huddled together at a table eating bowls of something soup-like.

Placing his hand on the small of her back, Ty guided her towards a table near the back of the room. The sudden intimacy and gentleness of the gesture made Ena flinch, and Ty, clearly having noticed, rescinded his hand as if she'd burned him. But Ena took the hint and followed him and Turner over to an unoccupied table, while Steig went to the bar. She sat down in the old wooden chair that Ty pointedly pulled out for her next to where Turner sat, then watched as Ty went to converse casually with the bartender.

She couldn't help but shift uncomfortably in her seat. She'd never been undercover before and didn't quite know what to do with herself. Was she pretending to be with one of them? Was that why Ty had touched her like that? Should she make small talk with Turner? Luckily, Ty returned a few minutes later carrying two mugs of ale for her and Turner, giving her something to do other than fidget nervously.

Looking suspiciously at the thick brown beer, Ena cautiously took a sip. Looks were certainly deceiving because it was delicious. After not consuming anything but apples, a hunk of cheese, hard jerky, and water for the last two days, the beer filled her stomach wonderfully. She chugged half of it before consciously making herself slow down. She needed to keep her wits.

While Steig remained sitting lonesome at the bar, Ty sat down with her and Turner, his own mug of ale untouched in front of him. Before Ena could fret over having to awkwardly make fake conversation with these daemons, the bartender approached them. He was balding on his head, most of his hair having migrated to his face, where his thick beard and mustache nearly covered his mouth.

He rubbed his hands together in front of his large, rounded stomach as he greeted them. "Welcome, welcome to Tritam, travelers," he said jovially. "How is the ale treating you?"

"It's wonderful, thank you," Ty said, smiling widely and turning on the charm.

"We also have some soup if you'd be interested? I think it's vegetable barley."

"Thank you kindly, good sir, we would love some," Ty replied.

"Of course, of course," the man muttered, bumbling off through a doorway which must have led towards the kitchen. Ena watched Steig eye him as he left, clearly tracking the location of the kitchen.

Within a few minutes, the friendly bartender returned, carrying three small bowls of soup and a basket of bread in his large hands. This village clearly didn't have much, but social conventions dictated that visitors be offered food, drink, and shelter for a reasonable length of time, without requiring a trade of equal value. This, of course, was predicated on the assumption that visitors were there to foster beneficial relationships which could be drawn upon for trade in the future, which they weren't.

Ena gave the man a watery smile as she took the bowl of soup, her guilt eating at her yet again.

After placing the basket of bread in the center of the table, the bartender turned to Ty. "I hear you're metalworks traders. We don't get many of those around here. I'm sure Tomas, the head horseman, would be delighted to meet with you to discuss what we might offer you in exchange." The man gestured at the table in the corner, where the three men were playing cards. "He's the bald one in the hat just over there."

"Excellent. Thank you kindly, good sir. I think I will go introduce myself."

Ena nearly rolled her eyes at Ty's over-the-top good manners. He rose to standing and patted the bartender on the shoulder in thanks before he strode off to talk with Tomas.

Turning her attention away from Ty, she focused on her soup—her hot, delicious-smelling soup. Eagerly raising her spoon to her mouth, she blew on it before taking a bite. Unlike the ale, the soup was...not good, to say the least. It was overly salted, with way too much barley and not enough vegetables. Next to her, Turner took a cautious bite and visibly gagged. Ena had to stifle a laugh at the pained expression on his face. He pushed his bowl away from him and reached for a piece of bread instead.

Ena continued to take a few more bites until Turner quietly asked her, "How can you stand to eat that stuff?"

Turning to look at him, she finally registered his face up close. He was definitely younger than Ty and Steig, but older than she'd originally thought. He was probably around her own age, but he had an inno- cent-looking face with soft features that made him appear younger. His blue eyes were large and prominent on his face, but up close now, she saw that there was an edge to them—a hardness which wasn't all that surprising, given the way he'd callously burned down Heran's house. His dirty-blond hair was slightly too long, too, and mussed in much the same way that Ty's used to be when they first met, which also contributed to his child-like appearance. The recollection sent a pang of hurt through her, so she looked away and focused back on her soup.

"It's rude to reject an offer of food as a visitor. Even if it tastes like shit, you should eat the entire bowl and wipe it clean with your bread or you'll offend them," she said.

Turner sighed and glared at his bowl, but he brought the spoon to his mouth again and continued eating. Maybe he just wanted to maintain their cover and not ruffle any feathers, but Ena was surprised he chose to do so, given he seemed unfazed that they were here to steal from these people.

Theoretically, she realized, she could simplify this whole operation—and bypass whatever plan Ty was enacting—if she were to use her Gift. All it would take was compelling the bartender to give them what they wanted, and to keep quiet about it. Of course, she'd never used her Gift before, but if what Heran had said about it was true...then maybe she could. But Heran had also told her to never use it unless given explicit permission, and even though she *was* serving Gaia by trying to figure out what they were up to, she hadn't been given that permission. Besides, there was already far too much of Iblis's will at work here, and she did not want to lose control and unwittingly add to it, so she turned back to her food in resignation.

When she and Turner had eaten their bowls of soup and finished off the entire basket of bread, she turned back to her ale and nursed it slowly, taking in the room. Ty had joined in the card game with Tomas and the others and was busy making small talk with them. In between rounds, she saw him pull out the bejeweled dagger he'd brought in with him, likely lying through his teeth about all the metal objects he wanted to trade. By the time most of her ale was gone, Ty had the men laughing in stitches at a joke he'd told, and Ena couldn't hold in the scoff that came out of her.

"It's annoying, isn't it?"

She whipped her head to Turner as he spoke, seeing that his own ale was drained now too. "What is?"

"How good he is at lying."

Ena raised her eyebrow at him. Did he know how intimately aware of that fact she was? She didn't think so, but either way, she was surprised that he would talk about his friend this way.

"Don't get me wrong," he continued. "It's a necessary skill in our line of work. But man, what I wouldn't give to be that smooth with it."

"You're not smooth with it?" Ena asked curiously.

Turner scoffed. "Please, with this face?" He gestured with one finger at his big, innocent-eyed face. "I can't hide a damn thing."

Ena smiled despite herself. "Why'd he let you come then, if you're such a liability? A lying liability, I mean."

The ale had definitely gotten to her a bit as she giggled at her own joke.

Turner side-eyed her companionably. "He's my cousin, and he's always looked out for me. There's no way I would've let him do this alone."

Turner spoke with such admiration and...love in his voice that Ena didn't know what to say. She was silent as memories from long ago resurfaced. She remembered that night by the beach...remembered Ty telling her all about his cousins, and especially his younger cousin who followed him around like he was a god among men. It clicked for Ena that Turner was probably that cousin. Clearly, Ty hadn't lied about that, and she didn't quite know what to do with that information. She'd been so caught up, rightfully, in her anger at Ty and his companions, wanting to see them only as the evil creatures they were, that it caught her off guard how human Turner seemed in this moment, and how...normal his familial relationship with Ty seemed.

Ena was shaken from her thoughts as she suddenly heard raised voices coming from the men playing cards. They had all been playing companionably with one another, but now one of the older men, who was lean with gray hair, seemed highly upset at the other. His weather-worn face was screwed up in anger as he pointed a bony finger and yelled at the one the bartender said was named Tomas, accusing him of cheating.

Out of the corner of her eye, Ena saw Turner surreptitiously make eye contact with Steig.

Something was happening.

Ena glanced back over at Ty, who was leaning back serenely in his chair, holding his cards. At first glance, it appeared he was bored and uninterested in the argument, but looking closer at him, she saw that he was, in fact, concentrating heavily on the man pointing his finger. His gaze was unblinking and slightly sinister. What was he doing?

The argument between the two men escalated, as the one yelling at Tomas stood up, walked around the table, and grabbed Tomas by the shirt collar. Ty's gaze flicked to Tomas as Tomas abruptly stood up and shoved the other man back. There was more yelling and shoving until Tomas reared back and punched the other man in the face, sending blood flying across the table.

Oh, shit. This must be the distraction.

The fight between the two men escalated as Tomas was thrown down onto the table, his face bloodied by the repeated punches raining down on him. The bartender approached, attempting to get between them. The third man who'd been playing cards, who, up until now, had been watching the argument like a deer caught in a hunter's sightline, finally stood up and tried to help the bartender pull the men apart, only to get caught in the fray himself when Tomas kicked him in the gut.

All the commotion was now drawing the attention of the other couple in the guesthouse, who were quickly gathering their belongings and fleeing the area, lest they get in the way of the brawl.

As if this was what he'd been waiting for, Ty glanced briefly at Steig, who quickly went around the bar and through the doorway to the kitchen. Ty retreated from the altercation surreptitiously and walked over to Ena and Turner. "Time to go," he said, with menacing calm.

Ena was still trying to figure out exactly what had just happened when Ty grabbed her arm and led her outside. Walking quickly to the stables, Ty yelled loudly for the stable boy, demanding he fetch all three of their horses as quickly as possible. Feigning outrage, he ranted indignantly that they wouldn't be doing business in a place such as this, that treated visitors with such disgrace. The stable boy clearly didn't yet know what he was referring to, but he muttered his hurried apologies and went to the stalls to retrieve their horses.

Turner, Ty, and Ena quickly led the horses back through the village and into the woods. She tried hard to keep her eyes straight ahead and not look behind her at the guesthouse, although she could still hear the sound of crashing furniture and raised voices coming from inside. She was tempted to glance around for a sign of Steig, too, but she kept her eyes straight ahead.

She was still frantically trying to understand what had just happened when they arrived at the agreed-upon meeting spot in the woods. Once she looked around to make certain they were well out of ear and eye shot of the village, she whirled on Ty.

"You did that. Didn't you?" she asked, not bothering to hide the accusation in her voice.

"Did what?" he said, not looking at her and instead tightening the girth on his saddle.

"Started that fight somehow."

"Yes," he said flatly, still not looking at Ena.

"How did you do it? Some kind of...mind control?" Ena asked, hoping they didn't notice the way her voice wavered on those last two words. This was the first time Ena had met a daemon with a Power similar to her *visanis*. She'd heard that daemons often had Powers of the mind, and Heran had told her that her Gift was likely shared by daemons, but to see it in practice was something else.

"Do you really want to know?" Ty asked, finally looking at her.

"Yes," Ena replied sincerely.

"Fine. I guess there's no harm in telling you now you've seen it. Yes, I started the fight. I have the power to...incite rage, anger. I feed on what little is there and escalate it until—well, you saw. We call it *furor.*"

Ena stared at him. It was not the same as her *visanis*, or what little she knew of it, but it was still the most similar Power to hers that she'd heard of. Somehow knowing that made her feel slightly less afraid of her Gift, and infinitely more...curious.

"How does it work?"

Ty stared at her, looking thoroughly surprised at the question. "What do you mean?"

"I mean..." Ena paused, trying to figure out how to put her curiosity into words. "How does it feel when you use it?"

Ty narrowed his eyes at her, assessing her intentions, but it wasn't a trick. She was curious to know how a mind Power like her own worked, what it felt like, how she could...control it so it wouldn't overwhelm her like it had been about to do during her Summoning.

Clearly realizing it wasn't a trick, he answered her. "It feels like...a tiny spark inside someone, that I can sense. And if I focus on them, I can form a thread between us. A channel. I use that channel to feed them my own rage and anger, stoking their spark into a flame, and then a wildfire, until they can't think straight. All they can do is lash out like a wild animal."

"So..." Ena hesitated, seeking to understand. "It was your own anger that started that fight. Your own rage that you fed to those men."

"Yes." Ty took a step closer to her, clearly mistaking her hesitation for fear. He peered down at her menacingly with that intense gaze of his. "Does that scare you, little viper?"

Ena paused. *Was* she scared? Knowing a bit more about how her Gift might work was comforting, but hearing about all the rage Ty must have inside to be able to do what he did...she answered his question truthfully.

"No," Ena said, meeting his gaze unerringly. "I just feel sorry for you. Being that angry all the time must be a hard way to live."

Ty stared at her as his brow furrowed, like he didn't even know what to say to that, when they heard a rustling through the woods, and Steig emerged. He was red-cheeked and out of breath, and he was carrying a sack full of goods.

"How'd it go? Did you get everything?" Ty asked quickly, turning away from Ena and all that had transpired between them.

"Yes," Steig replied, as he started digging around in the sack for something. "The fight was calming down by the time I was finished, so I had to go out the back and loop around the outside of the village. Here," he said, tossing something to Ena. It was a dark-blue women's cloak.

Ena was surprised. He'd taken this for her? "Thanks," she said, staring at the cloak. It was slightly worse for the wear, but the quality wasn't bad.

"Don't thank me. I only did it because he insisted you'd freeze to death without one," Steig replied harshly, gesturing at Ty.

Ena looked over at him in shock.

"I just don't want you dying before we can get what we came for," Ty said dismissively. "Now let's go," he ordered before Ena could respond. "We gotta get back and check those traps before it gets dark."

Not knowing how to even begin to process this new information, Ena quickly tossed the cloak around her shoulders and secured it tightly before pulling up the hood. Ensconced in her new warm cocoon, she followed the daemons' lead as they all mounted up and headed back the way they'd come.

CHAPTER ELEVEN

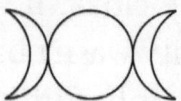

IT WAS PAST DARK by the time they made it back to where they'd camped the previous night. How they navigated to the area in the dark, and without a witch's Knowing, Ena had no idea, but the remnants of their campfire and the imprints they'd left on the ground plants and leaves proved it was without a doubt the same spot. After dismounting and tethering the horses nearby, Steig went off to check the rabbit traps while Ty and Turner gathered dry branches and leaves to start a fire. Turner, of course, was able to light it quickly using his Power.

Ena wrapped herself in her new *borrowed* cloak—she insisted to herself that she would return it when all this was over—and tried not to read too much into why Ty had had Steig take it for her. The gesture was thoughtful, yes, but it was also in his best interest. She shouldn't feel *grateful* to him for doing the absolute bare minimum to keep her, their captive, comfortable.

She pushed her extremely confusing feelings towards Ty aside and instead contemplated what was coming next. It had been several years since she'd completed a locator spell. The last time she'd done one had been when one of their best sows had run off, and they'd used the spell to find her. It had been tricky because the animal was on the move, so Ena had only been able to see where the sow was at that precise moment, and then they had to track her from there. They, of course, found her safe and sound, farrowing under a hollowed-out tree stump, but the litter of pigs she'd given birth to there had grown to some of the biggest her Coven had ever had, so it was a memorable event.

Ena remembered the ritual well. She knew the ingredients, the process, the spellword. But she knew it would require great concentration and calm to do it right, so she began now by staring into the fire and reaching down into her Knowing. All spells and potions required connecting with one's Knowing and moving through the ritual of the spell or potionmaking with intention and purpose. It was only through this intense concentration and connection with Gaia that her magic could be reached and harnessed.

Her preparations were temporarily disturbed when Steig came tromping back through the woods, holding two dead rabbits in one hand. He wordlessly tossed them at Ena's feet, then went to sit around the fire with Ty and Turner, who were huddled together talking quietly. All three of them now sat around the fire, staring at her expectantly.

She looked down at the two grayish-brown rabbits. Their fur looked so soft, and she Knew when she reached down to pick them up, they would feel like silk in her hands. Their black eyes were open and still, and their necks were elongated in an unnatural way where they had been broken. Ena used her Knowing as much as she could to sense what their lives had been like, but dead things did not have nearly as many signs as the living.

After a few moments, she finally raised her head to look at the daemons as they watched her. "I will need absolute silence while I prepare these rabbits and complete the spell. The ritual begins as I gather the ingredients, and any distraction that breaks my concentration could cause it to fail. Is that understood?"

They looked seriously at her with bated breath, and one by one, nodded in understanding.

"Okay, good." Then she spoke to Ty directly. "I'll need a knife."

They looked at each other in unspoken communication. Giving her a weapon, she knew, was a risk for them. Her Gift may not work on them, but a knife to the gut would sure as shit do some damage. Would he take the risk? Whatever this amulet could do, whatever they needed it for, seemed important enough for him to have taken several risks already.

Ty stood up, slowly removing the large dagger from the sheath at his waist and flipped it in his hand, passing it to her handle first. He watched her like a hawk as she grabbed it.

But she wasn't an idiot. One knife would not be enough to take down three large daemons on her own. Still, she loved the glimmer of fear she saw in Ty's eyes as her hand wrapped around the hilt, and she contemplated for a second what it might feel like to shove it into his cold, unfeeling heart.

Taking the dagger, the rabbits, and the sack filled with the other ingredients Steig had stolen, she set to work preparing the spell.

She began by slitting the throats of the rabbits and dribbling the blood that emerged in a wide circle around her. She heard the blood drip, drip, drip into the dirt on the forest floor, just as it had dripped down her face during the Summoning. She felt Gaia in the presence of death. The death was her sacrifice and it showed Gaia that she respected the balance.

Laying one of the rabbits on the ground in front of her, she used the dagger to cut off each of its feet, and then its head. Then she cut a small slit in the loose fur on its back, and ripped hard with both hands, peeling its skin off its body in one fell swoop. The wet, ripping sound of the hide parting from the muscle underneath was as familiar to her as breathing, and she lamented that she likely wouldn't be able to save the hide for future use in these conditions. Wasting it felt like an affront to Gaia and disrespectful to the rabbit, but none of this was in her control, so she pushed those feelings aside and did what she had to do.

She flipped the rabbit onto its back and sliced it down the center. The headless, footless, skinless carcass hardly resembled a rabbit anymore, and she unfeelingly cracked its breastbone and removed its heart. Then, starting with the lungs, she scooped her hand through the cavity and removed the entrails. She tossed those parts outside of her circle in a tidy pile, Knowing that the coyote whose scat she'd seen in the area would find them tomorrow and feast.

Now came the tough part. The rabbit was prepared for cooking, but she still needed to remove the leg bones. The bones had to remain fresh and uncooked for the spell to work, so she cracked each joint, separating the rear legs from the pelvis, then used the dagger to cut them clean off. She delicately slit the dagger into the muscle surrounding each of its rear leg bones. It was slippery, so she had to be careful lest she cut herself. The muscles there were dense and tough. She Knew that the rabbit had lived a relatively long life of running from predators. Using her hands, she poked the end of bone through the muscle and sinew, and clawed it the rest of the way out.

It was messy and not graceful. Her hands were slippery with blood by the time she was done, and the leg muscles were mangled beyond usefulness. She gently placed the rest of the rabbit carcass outside of her circle, hoping she'd get to enjoy the fresh meat cooked over the fire after this was done.

Picking up each hard-earned leg bone sequentially, she snapped them in half, then scattered each piece inside her circle of blood in the four directions. Aquilo. Auster. Occidens. Oriens. Gaia existed in all four directions. Knowing this would help her locate the amulet, and the legs of the rabbit would help her travel there in her mind.

She reached into the cloth sack at her feet and intentionally picked up the apple that was inside. She laid it in front of her in the bloody, dirty mess where the rabbit had been and sliced the apple in half. In the pale flesh, she could see tiny holes where caterpillars had gotten in and nibbled on the sweet meat all the way to its core. She read its signs and Knew that the tree it had grown on was old and healthy. It had flourished in the past year, which had been particularly cool and wet, leading to the creation of this fruit, whose only goal was to be eaten and decay, leaving its seeds in the soil to propagate anew.

Slicing again, Ena now cut the apple into quarters. She placed them carefully between each piece of bone in her circle of blood. Apples represented knowledge. Placing the apple around her circle signaled to Gaia that she wished to Know.

Finally, she removed the bunches of dried herbs that Steig had stolen, then tossed the empty sack outside of her circle. Bay leaves, belladonna, sage, and worm-wood—herbs which enhanced wisdom and were used in divination. One by one, she took a sprig of each in her hands and crumpled them delicately in the circle around her. They were brittle and aromatic; likely a year or two had passed since they'd been cut from the living plants they'd once been a part of. The herbs crumbled easily between her fingers, leaving a residue behind once she was finished. Once combined, Ena breathed in deeply and lowered to her knees in the center of her circle. She could feel Gaia's presence in her every heartbeat.

Now for the most critical part. She didn't know much about this amulet. She'd never seen it in person. But she concentrated her thoughts on the description Ty had given her. A deep-purple, uncut amethyst stone in a circular setting of silver, hung on a chain of braided silver strands. She thought about the way the light would reflect through the amethyst, and the way the cold silver would feel in her hands. She closed her eyes and spoke her spellword.

{*Locus*}

***

Images flashed quickly through her mind's eye. She saw the amulet; it was beautiful. The stone was multicolored, fading from a vibrant deep purple at its center to a pale white-purple at the edges. The circular setting was large. She thought if she were to hold it in her hand, it would cover her entire palm, but the symbols etched into the silver confused Ena. She recognized the triquetra, often used as a symbol of the three Covens, the Goddess, which was Gaia's symbol, and the horned God, often used to represent Iblis, but she didn't recognize the final one. She'd never seen it before in her life, despite her rigorous studies, and she couldn't fathom what all these symbols together might do.

The image changed and she saw the amulet sitting in a simple wooden box. The box had a lock on it, and it was closed shut.

The image changed again and she saw a large leather-bound trunk in a dark room filled with trunks and bookshelves. It looked similar to Heran's altar room.

The image flashed one more time to reveal a large wind-beaten wooden house with new wooden shingles. She breathed in deeply and, though she knew her physical body was still in the woods, the air smelled salty and fresh, but also slightly fishy. The house was two stories and had large circular windows. An over-grown fenced-in garden surrounded it, reminding her so much of home that her heart ached to see it. In the distance behind the house, she caught a glimpse of sand dunes, and just as she heard the crash of large waves pounding into the shore, her eyes snapped open.

***

She was out of breath as she looked frantically around her, trying to regain her bearings. The woods around her were dark, the only light coming from the fire in front of her.

Ty, Turner, and Steig were all standing, clearly on edge, and staring at her intently. She had no idea what she'd looked like as she was receiving the vision, but Turner and Steig had their hands on their weapons sheathed on their belts and their brows were furrowed. Ty, who had given his weapon to Ena, was closest to her and looked like he was two seconds away from jumping into the circle and yanking her out of it.

She placed her hand over her chest and took sever-al deep breaths, willing her heart to calm down. The visions were disorienting to say the least, but she was familiar with the aftereffects. After several moments, she felt calm enough to look up and address them.

They were still all standing in silence, clearly unsure of whether it was alright to speak again, so she spoke first.

"I found it," she said.

Picking herself up, she stepped outside of her circle and rejoined the men around the campfire. Their body language calmed instantly as she approached them.

"Where is it?" Ty asked hurriedly.

This was the tricky part. She needed to give the men enough information that they wouldn't suspect her of lying or leaving anything out, but she didn't want to give them all the information. She needed to retain the upper hand for when they let her go if she had any hope of thwarting their plans.

"It's on the coast of the Endless Ocean. I had a vision of its location, and during it, I smelled... well, I can't say for sure since I've never been, but I think it was the ocean, and I heard the crash of waves."

"Where is it on the coast? Did you see anything else?" Ty asked.

"I saw a house, a big one with large round windows and a fenced-in garden around it. That's all I saw," Ena said, keeping the additional details of its location to herself. "I think," she added, "I think it's with the Occidens Coven."

"Good, that's good," Ty said, nodding and looking at Steig and Turner. "That's a lot to go on. We'll head there first thing in the morning. It should take us several days, but if we keep our stops minimal, we should make it in less than a week."

"Wait," Ena said, something about the way he spoke setting her off. "*We*? *Us*? Are you including *me* in this? I thought you said you'd let me go if I helped you with the spell!"

"We *will* let you go," Ty said reasonably. "But only after we get the amulet. You're the only one who will recognize the house for sure, so we'll need you to point it out so we can be in and out of there as quickly as possible. Plus," he added, glaring at Ena like a kid caught stealing all the sweets, "there's no way we're letting you go now so you can run right to your Coven and warn them about what we're doing. You're coming with us."

Ena's heart plummeted. They weren't letting her go. On some level, she wasn't surprised. She'd seen this coming. She knew they were unlikely to let her go that easily. But suddenly, shame filled her. What if she really had just helped them find the amulet? She'd kept some details to herself, hoping she'd be able to thwart them once she was free, but now she had no idea when that would be, because now they were going to—

"Whoa, whoa, whoa. Wait a second." Another thought occurred to Ena, one almost as upsetting as being kept by these daemons. "You don't understand," she explained. "I *can't* go to the Occidens Coven. It's forbidden. They are our rivals and we have a very strict treaty with them not to infringe on their territory. If I'm caught there, my life could be forfeit."

The smile that graced Ty's face was downright malicious. "I know," he said. "Now you'll have just as much motivation to keep quiet as we will."

Ena didn't know what to say to that. He was right. If she went with them to the Occidens Coven to steal the amulet, she'd be better off keeping quiet and sticking with them than revealing herself to the rival Coven. Ena was not exactly sure what had caused the rivalry, but she knew to willingly break it would be to her detriment. There had apparently been some disagreement hundreds of years ago that had since been long forgotten, only the bitterness and mistrust remaining. To Ena and the rest of the witches, it seemed like it had always been this way. It was simply fact that the other two Covens, Aquilo and Auster, did not get along with Occidens, so there was a treaty between them that specified that Auster and Aquilo witches were not to trespass on Occidens territory, and vice versa. The territory line was somewhere just past the Sacred Pool she'd visited with Heran, and the punishment for breaking the treaty was up to the discretion of the Coven who was wronged, but it could include death. She'd heard stories about witches losing their tongues or hands as punishment for attempting to trade with villages over the treaty line. One witch had been burned alive just for walking along the beach near the Occidens Coven's village.

No, one thing was terrifyingly clear—if she continued on with them into Occidens territory, she'd have no choice but to help them find the amulet as quickly and quietly as possible in the hopes that they'd let her go afterward. But, of course, maybe they'd just kill her once they had it. Or take her back to the Underworld as their prisoner.

Turning away from the fire and telling them she had to relieve her bladder behind a nearby tree, her thoughts whirled furiously.

There was no way around it, no putting it off any-more. She couldn't stay with them. Staying left her with no good options.

It was time for her to escape. Tonight.

CHAPTER TWELVE

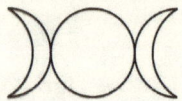

ENA PRETENDED TO SLEEP on her side, facing away from the fire. Unfortunately, Turner stayed awake to take watch. She shouldn't have been surprised; it was the smart thing to do. There was always the chance that her Coven would catch up to them, or that those bandits she'd heard about might cross their path, but she'd passed out so quickly and thoroughly the previous night that she wasn't sure if any of them *had* actually stayed awake to take a watch. Now she knew, and it made things infinitely more difficult for her.

Her thoughts whirled furiously, flicking from plan to plan, trying to determine her best method of escape. She contemplated trying to start a very small, hopefully manageable forest fire as a distraction, or maybe she'd wait for Turner to take a pee break and then sneak away as fast as she could. Her mind went through plan after plan, discarding them as too unrealistic or dangerous. Soon, the sun started to rise and Ena lay frustrated and exhausted, no closer to freedom than she'd been the night before.

The next day passed in much the same way. After a heartier breakfast consisting of the roasted remains of the rabbit carcasses, Ena mounted up in front of Ty and the four of them again headed west. Ena was keenly aware that every step they took was one further from her home, and closer to the dangers of the Occidens territory. Not only that, but she was getting sick and tired of trying to ignore the stone wall of a body behind her. Every step of the horse rocked Ena's body back into contact with Ty's. She felt his thighs flex every time he spurred the horse on, and his arms grazed her waist every time he lifted the reins to direct the mare. It was a constant reminder of things she needed to forget, of things she never should have done, and the extremely masochistic feelings that haunted her still.

While she yawned and scowled in the saddle, the daemons seemed to be in better spirits than ever before. Up until now, the three of them had been fairly stoic, only exchanging a few words to each other out of necessity. But clearly, now that they had a new destination and renewed hope for finding the amulet, they had loosened up a bit, and proceeded to laugh and joke with one another incessantly on the journey.

Apparently, Ena learned, Steig had a wife and several unruly kids back home, and Turner was explaining to Ty how the youngest of them had taken to causing absolute chaos during meals by dumping her food on the floor and then climbing on the table to stomp on everyone else's food the second Steig or his wife moved to clean up. This had happened again and again over several nights, with the other children encouraging her and laughing it up, until Steig's wife, Lara, stormed out of the room declaring she was never cooking again and that they could all eat cold, uncooked vegetables for all she cared. Steig didn't participate in the telling of the story, but Ena saw the warm smile that graced his face at the mention of his family.

"Sounds like she takes after you, Steig," Ty declared, chuckling at Turner's story.

"Pfft, what are you talking about? I was the well-behaved one. It was you who was the troublemaker," Steig retorted.

Ty barked a laugh. "That I won't deny, but who was right there with me half the time?"

Steig rolled his eyes but couldn't hide his smile. "Only because you convinced me, and I didn't want to see you get killed."

"Right, sure... I distinctly remember it being your idea to go, and I quote, 'deeper than we've ever gone before' into the under caves."

"Yeah, only after you convinced me you had an infallible sense of smell and would be able to follow our scent trail back out. The irony of that has never escaped me."

The two friends laughed together at that, although Ena wasn't sure what was so ironic about that. But it struck her again how normal their lives seemed to be. She had never given much thought to the lifestyle of daemons in the Underworld, but from their description, it was maybe not actually the place of nightmares that she'd been told it was.

Not only that, but she'd never forgotten the story Ty had told her about getting lost in the caves with his best friend, who she jarringly realized must be Steig. She remembered how she and Ty had laughed together that night about it, how they'd scooted closer to one another afterward, sending a jolt of butterflies to her stomach as their arms brushed, and how connected she'd felt to him. And now...

The pang to her heart overwhelmed her for a second, and she had to look down at her hands where they rested on the pommel to hide the tears that filled her eyes. She had to get away, not just for her physical safety and to disrupt the daemons' plans, but for her own sake. She couldn't be around Ty anymore. She couldn't look at his face, her mind and heart filling with memories, and be reminded at every turn how little she meant to him. How he'd used and discarded her like trash. She just couldn't take it anymore. She had to be done with him, once and for all.

That night passed much the same as the one before, except that when dawn neared, Ena had so exhausted her mind and body that she actually fell asleep for a few hours. When she woke up, she cursed herself thoroughly. Since she hadn't been able to come up with a foolproof pre-planned escape, she figured she would play it by ear and seize an opportunity when it presented itself. She trusted that Gaia would do this for her. But what if she had missed her opportunity to escape the second she fell asleep and another one never presented itself? She grumbled all through the ride the next day. Luckily, the men didn't address her much, except to offer her food and give her instructions about where and where not to pee when they stopped for breaks.

As she sat atop the horse, steadfastly ignoring the men around her, she found her mind turning to her visions of the amulet. The combination of the symbols that surrounded it was so unique, and she wracked her brain, trying to recall anything she could about them. There was the triquetra, the Goddess, and the horned God, which she knew of. But the Goddess and the horned God, representing Gaia and Iblis respectively, were never used together. That went against everything she had been taught about maintaining the balance. And the triquetra was only used when drawing on the magic of the three Covens, something which hadn't happened in centuries because of the rivalry. And then there was the last one...it had looked like four inter-locking petals surrounded by a circle, but she didn't recognize it at all. She was certain Heran would know of it, and could give her some answers when they were reunited. Not for the first time in her life, she was so grateful for the matriarch's guidance. She missed her and Greya painfully. Perse and Thyla too. What were they doing now? Were they worried about her? Looking for her? She was certain Jon, an older male witch in their Coven whose Gift of *arsa* made him especially skilled at building houses and other structures, was probably well underway rebuilding Heran's house. Her heart ached at the thought of them all.

She laid down by the campfire that night, dirty, tired, and sad, but she forced herself to stay awake, more motivated than ever to get home to her family.

Hours passed yet again while she pretended to be asleep, using her Knowing to listen and feel for any sign that now was her chance. It wasn't until the others—besides Turner, who was awake yet again keeping watch—were fast asleep that she heard a wolf howl in the distance. The sound echoed through her bones, chilling her to her core, and she Knew—

Gaia had granted her.

It took her all of one minute to figure out her plan. She had to act fast, before the wolf wandered too far away.

She focused her gaze on where the three horses were tethered to a tree, huddled together for warmth. She reached down into her Knowing. She could sense the charges of energy in the air, the way they bumped up against each other. The same way she could sense the water present there, and draw it out using her spellword, she Knew how to arrange them to create the spark she wanted.

Using a particularly loud pop from the fire as cover, she quietly spoke her spellword.

{*Ignis*}

Halfway down the tether connecting one of the horses to the tree, a small spot of light and heat erupted, causing the tether to break and flop to the ground. The horse, spooked by the appearance of the flame on its tether, reared back and fled into the darkness of the woods, its hoofbeats clomping through the downed leaves. The others, sensing that something was off, thrashed uselessly on their tethers, unable to flee.

"Damn," Turner said, noticing the commotion. He quickly walked over to Steig's sleeping form and nudged him awake. "Take over the watch, Steig. One of the horses spooked and broke its tether. I gotta go get it."

Steig grumbled something in affirmation as he sat up, looking bleary-eyed. He moved to add a few more logs to the fire, which had burned down to a hot bed of coals, as Turner jogged off into the woods after the horse.

Using another particularly loud pop of the fire, Ena whispered to the air next.

{*Aeris*}

The wind began to blow—not too harshly, not enough to attract attention, but enough that it pushed the scent of the horse that had fled directly toward where Ena had heard the wolf howl. The breeze was cold, whirling and swirling around their campfire, stoking the flames higher. The trees that stood around them began swaying and dancing in the wind Ena had made, and she saw Steig wrap his coat tighter around his body.

Not so far in the distance, the wolf howled again. Its call was eerie and lonesome; the sound of it made the hair stand up on the back of Ena's neck. But then, another joined its chorus, and then another. There wasn't just one wolf; there were three.

Steig's attention whipped to the sound. He clearly realized that the howls were coming from the same direction Turner and the horse had gone. Listening intently and staring into the darkness of the woods, Steig waited.

Out of the darkness, Ena heard the horse whinny in terror. She no longer feigned sleep as she sat up to listen to the commotion.

Snarls echoed through the darkness, and then came Turner's yell.

"*Steig!*"

Sounds of a struggle erupted through the quiet woods. It was somewhat deafened by the sound of wind whipping around their campsite, but it was clearly not very far away. Ty was awake now, too, and he made eye contact with Steig as they both stood.

"I'll go," Steig said, answering his unspoken question, then darted into the woods towards the cry for help.

Shouts and rustling leaves, snarls, and frantic hoof-beats made it clear there was a desperate struggle in the dark. Ena stood up now, too, as the horse whinnied again, only this time, it sounded pained.

She started to feel afraid. Maybe she hadn't thought this plan through. The wolves were close—closer than she'd intended them to be. She'd just wanted the escaped horse and the sounds of wolves to be a distraction. Even though she didn't like these daemons, didn't trust them, she didn't necessarily want them or the horses to be eaten alive by wolves.

Her heart started pounding in her chest, but she was committed now. This was her chance, and whatever happened, she had to deal with it.

Ty stood next to her, his body vibrating with unspent energy. He was staring daggers into the woods, towards the commotion, trying to make out what was happening just beyond the sightline of the fire. He looked ready to bolt at any second.

Then Steig's cry of pain echoed through the woods.

Turning to Ena, Ty seemed to suddenly come to a decision. "Stay by the fire," he said, fear flickering across his face. "You'll be safest here."

For a split second, Ena couldn't tell whether his fear was for his friends, or for her, or both. But either way, she responded with as much calm conviction as she could muster.

"I will. I promise."

His brow furrowed ever so slightly at that word, *promise*, as if something about the way she said that concerned him, but then another strained grunt came from the woods, and he reluctantly turned away from her, running off into the dark.

Seizing her chance, Ena used her spellword again to break the tethers of the other two horses. The more distraction and confusion she could create, the more it would benefit her escape. Instantly, they, too, were darting off into the woods, luckily away from the commotion of the struggle.

Then, leaving no trace, Ena disappeared into the woods, trying to ignore the chaos she'd left in her wake.

CHAPTER THIRTEEN

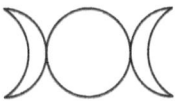

ENA RAN SILENTLY THROUGH the woods, her heart pounding in her ears.

Years of tracking animals using her Knowing had taught her how to move delicately. The key was to understand where the leaves were and what they would signal if she stepped on them. If she stepped on them the right way, it sounded like the wind, and not like a footstep. And if she avoided branches that would snap, she could pass herself off as a deer, or a different creature of the night. She couldn't mask her scent, but daemons, while known for their strength and speed, did not have heightened senses, so she figured that was okay. And, Gaia granted her, because her dress was black and her cloak dark blue, making her nearly invisible in the dark forest.

The sounds of the struggle got quieter and quieter the further she moved away from the campsite. Still, she didn't look back or slow down until she was several miles away.

Eventually, silence settled over the forest. The unnatural wind she'd made had died down, and the natural breeze through the trees was once again the only sound.

Inside, however, her head was loud with thoughts. She had to actively stop herself from thinking about the potential destruction she'd left behind. There'd be time for that guilt later. Now, she had to focus on putting as much distance between her and the daemons as possible.

Another hour went by before she was fairly confident she wasn't being followed. She stopped running and hurriedly assessed the trees around her. Choosing a tall, sturdy pine with a sufficient number of low branches, she scrambled up the rough trunk and climbed higher and higher until she could see the night sky.

Gaia had granted her again.

It was a relatively clear night—only a few wisps of clouds covered the stars—and the moon was nearly full. Far to her left in the distance, she saw the darkened mass that was the Chasm Mountains. She oriented herself using the Southern Star and was pleasantly surprised to see that she had already been heading the direction she needed to go.

Yesterday, she'd been able to catch some glimpses of the sun's position through the canopy of trees. She was able to figure out that they'd been traveling northwest, which meant that the village they'd visited was roughly southeast of here. She briefly considered traveling back to that village and asking for a horse so she could ride home quicker, but she remembered Ty's warning.

People will get hurt.

If she did travel to the village and the daemons caught up with her, she did not want the villagers to be dragged into the middle of it, not after the role she'd already played in the theft against them.

She also considered traveling directly south until she hit the River Wry, and then following that upstream to her Coven's village, but she figured that the daemons would suspect that, and would probably head that way to try to catch up with her. Not to mention, that would mean a week or more of traveling, and with no supplies or horse, that would be incredibly grueling.

No, her plan was hopefully something they would not expect. She would head southeast until she was parallel with the Lost Sister, the jagged twin-peaked mountaintop that Heran had used to orient them when they'd traveled to the Sacred Pool. Ena knew that the Sacred Pool was somewhere parallel to that peak, and given how many days they'd already been traveling west, she was likely only a few days past it.

The Sacred Pool was her best chance to get help. Not only did the water have special qualities that were useful for potions and spells, but it was also a divining pool—its waters could be used to send messages to other witches. She'd never practiced a spell like that herself, but she knew how to do one—theoretically. It was a blood-to-blood spell. Sacrificing her blood in the pool and speaking the proper spellword would allow her image to appear within whatever body of water was closest to the blood relative she sought to speak to. Through that connection, she could speak to Greya, and she prayed to Gaia that she'd catch her when she was doing the laundry or filling a pot of water. If she could get a message to Greya, then she'd tell the Coven about what the daemons were planning. Then Heran could intercept them, and send someone with supplies and a horse to come get her.

It was a good plan, she told herself.

It was her only plan.

Her palms scraped on the rough bark as she scrambled down the tree. She knew when the sun rose that she'd likely find them filled with splinters—her skin had always been so thin and susceptible to them. But she ignored the uncomfortable spots of pain and continued to jog silently through the woods.

She moved this way all night, but as the sun started to lighten the sky, exhaustion finally hit her. The stitches in her sides became unmanageable, and she felt like she was going to collapse, so she allowed herself to slow down to a brisk walk.

The movement of birds and the shuffle of squirrels masked her sounds even more, and she began to think that maybe she'd succeeded in losing them. She still kept an ear out for sounds of hoofbeats or large male feet, but her mind relaxed enough to, unfortunately, start drowning her in guilt.

Why she felt guilt, she couldn't exactly say. The men had come to her village and *kidnapped* her, then forced her to do the locator spell, and had been prepared to drag her to an enemy Coven where her life would be at risk, all for their own nefarious, daemonic purposes.

Not only that, but Ty had lied to her, tricked her, all those years ago. He'd manipulated her into thinking he was mortal—for what purpose, Gaia only knew—and then he'd discarded her. And now that she thought about it, he'd probably done the same thing to dozens of other women by now.

But hearing those screams from the woods, the snarl of the wolves... No. She wouldn't dwell on that. Besides, daemons were fast and strong, and she'd only heard three wolves. Three full-grown daemons could likely fight off three wolves, right?

She just hoped the wolves hadn't severely injured any of the horses. The sound of that pained whinny replayed in her mind, and her guilt sparked anew. But, she told herself, if one of them had been killed, that was perhaps a necessary part of Gaia's balance. The horse's body would feed the wolf pack and any number of critters in the woods for weeks.

She forced herself to think of other, more urgent things. Like how she was going to find something to eat today. She did, Gaia be blessed, come across a small stream around midday. It bubbled cheerfully over colorful, polished rocks, and the sight of it lifted her spirits immensely.

She spent longer than she should have drinking her fill on its banks and collecting bittercress, an edible plant which grew in copious amounts on the water's edge. It didn't exactly fill her belly, but it at least took the edge off her hunger, which had only worsened as the day went on.

She also patted herself on the back for having had the foresight to bring the waterskin that the daemons had given her. She filled it and looked longingly at the stream. Part of her wanted to follow it. She knew it would run into the River Wry eventually, and being

close to a water source made things so, so much easier. She could, of course, use her magic to pull water
from the air in emergencies, but she could only get
small amounts at a time, and doing so regularly would
exhaust her energies. But alas, streams could meander
widely, and following it might add several extra days to
her journey. Sighing, she parted from the stream when
it began to flow west, and continued on her way south.

By the late afternoon, her feet were aching in her
boots and her muscles were terribly tight from running all night and walking all day. The adrenaline, lack
of sleep, and inadequate food had begun to wear on
her immensely. Her stomach grumbled painfully. She
longed to stop and rest, but before she could, she knew
she should try to find something else to eat.

She focused her Knowing on the signs around her.
The forest was stuffed full of pine and oak trees, with
the occasional birch and ash sprinkled in. Abundant
plant life covered the ground, not much of it edible.
Maybe she'd get lucky and find some mushrooms. It
was the prime season for many species.

The squirrels were busy collecting acorns, so she
could do that, too, but they were very cumbersome to
process and cook—she didn't have time for that; she
needed to keep moving. She looked up into the canopy
to see what the birds were doing. The birds were—

There!

Gathered in a plop of white and purple on a dangling
oak leaf were some bird droppings with pieces of blackberries in it. Ena looked up at the trees surrounding her
and spotted a noisy wide-winged purabeak. She read its

signs and Knew it was not migrating yet, and that it had been hopping around gorging itself on the fall bounty in this area for some time.

She watched it flit back and forth between the trees, flashing the bright-purple feathers under its wings, as she followed it, and after a while, it led her to the blackberry bush itself. Most of the berries were past their prime, the season of plenty nearing its end, but the coolness of the forest had kept some overripe and slightly withered berries on the vines. Ena ate as much as she could before the sun fully went down. Then, deciding that this spot was as good as any to rest, she gathered downed leaves and moss to create a crude nest and finally laid down to rest.

The temperature in the forest dropped quickly, and Ena desperately wanted to start a fire, but she didn't dare risk it. There was a chance that one or more of the daemons was still on her trail, and she didn't want to attract their attention. She curled up tighter under her cloak and drifted off to sleep immediately.

***

She awoke shivering just before dawn as light drops of water began to pitter-patter on her cloak. Emerging from her cocoon, she looked up to see that the clouds had rolled in while she'd been sleeping, and it was starting to rain. She groaned in miserable frustration.

Her muscles were tight from the cold and overuse, and she was really, really starting to hate this dress.

What she wouldn't give for a full meal, a hot bath, and a fucking change of clothes that fully covered her chest.

She was able to find a few more uneaten blackberries on the bush which served as her breakfast, then took a swig of her waterskin before she once again climbed the tallest tree she could find to check her positioning. The sun was invisible behind the dense layer of rainclouds, but she could still make out the Chasm Mountains. She'd made less progress yesterday than she'd hoped. Her search for food in the afternoon had taken up more time than she would have liked. By her estimation, she still had a day or two of travel before she was anywhere close to the Sacred Pool. She scrambled down the tree and continued walking.

For the first time since she'd escaped, she started to feel apprehensive. Would she be able to find the Sacred Pool? Would the spell to send a message work? Maybe she should have come up with a different plan of escape. Maybe she should have gone to the village and gotten a horse. Maybe she should have stuck with the daemons until they got to a different village. Maybe, maybe, maybe.

All her doubts and misgivings hit her like a load of bricks and dread filled her. She was alone out here. Yes, she had water, for now, but food was going to be a constant struggle until she made it home. She'd camped in the backwoods many times in her life, but she'd always had a horse, ample supplies, and the company of other witches. Not to mention most of her travel had been done in the summertime, not in the late fall. Her solitude was already starting to wear on her, and she desperately hoped this had not been a poor decision.

Just then, the clouds burst open and it started to rain in earnest. Heavy droplets thudded on her shoulders and the hood of her cloak. Within minutes, her cloak was drenched through and she knew it was only a matter of time before her dress was too. She looked around, but there was no type of shelter in sight—no caves, no overhangs, no hollowed-out stumps big enough for her. This part of the landscape was distressingly flat. She had no choice but to keep moving to keep warm, and hope that she happened upon a spot to hunker down for a while.

She trudged on and on, focusing only on the squishing of her boots into the muddy forest floor. One step. Another step. Another step. Another. Soon enough, the rain soaked through all her clothes, her socks, her boots. She started to shiver, and her fingers and toes started to hurt. She knew she'd need to risk a fire tonight.

Later in the day, she happened upon some myelle mushrooms clustered around the base of an ash tree. She picked as many as she could and gathered her dress in front of her to form a makeshift container for them. She'd have to cook them later over the fire lest she risk a stomachache, but that would be doable. The thought of that fire was the only thing that kept her going.

Her waterskin was empty now, but she wasn't thirsty. The rain ran down her face, in her eyes, and dripped into her mouth. She'd never been this wet, and her worries only increased as the sun began to set and the temperature dropped yet again. Try as she might, she couldn't bring any warmth back into her hands. Moving them was getting tough, especially since she needed one to hold on to the mushrooms cradled in the fabric of her dress.

Gaia be blessed, just as the sun went down, she came upon an unused hollow beneath the base of a fallen tree. She nearly ran to it and kissed it she was so relieved, but she didn't have the energy.

The tree that formed it had been huge, its gigantic roots splayed in all directions where they had been ripped from the earth. Shivering and stumbling, she climbed down into the massive hole that remained and dug it out a bit more, but the angle of the tree and its roots only offered so much coverage from the rain, so she gathered some large, downed branches that she found and laid them across the hollow to form a crude lean-to. Then she layered the branches with moss to shield her from the elements even more.

It was hardly waterproof, but better than nothing.

Once she had most of the branches in place, she slipped inside the crude shelter, placing the last branch to cover the gap she'd used to get in.

Her hands moved incredibly slowly as she gathered up the soggy sticks and leaves she'd tossed inside to make her fire. Her body shook like a leaf, but she ignored it as she reached into her Knowing and used her spellword to light the soggy pile on fire. She had to restart it several times, because everything was so wet, the small flame she created kept blinking out.

After several tries, the materials dried out enough that she was able to get a decent fire going. The warmth and light buoyed her spirits immensely, and her makeshift shelter warmed enough that she slowly regained the movement in her hands. She took off her cloak and laid it on the ground underneath her to dry. Since there was no room to hang it up, it was the best she could do, and she also removed her boots in an effort to dry her socks by sticking her feet near the fire. She was cramped and dirty in her little hovel, but she was starting to feel slightly more hopeful.

One by one, she cooked her mushrooms using a forked branch to hold them over the fire. A few of them got badly singed, but she was pretty sure they were the most delicious things she'd ever eaten regardless.

Once she'd eaten them all, she stared into the fire for a while. The rain still pounded into her shelter and several leaks had formed, causing drips of water to drop into the fire and sizzle. She was afraid if she went to sleep, her fire would burn out, and then she'd have to start it all over again. But she was so, so tired. The stress of her escape, the elements, her loneliness, all weighed on her. She didn't want to admit it, but at least when she had been with the daemons, she hadn't felt so...alone. Yes, she had been there against her will, and yes, they'd forced her to help them find the amulet, which was bad. But by the end, she had at least felt physically safe with them. They hadn't hurt her. They'd given her food. In her quiet moments of fear since escaping, she sometimes wondered if staying with them would have been better than this.

But she was close. So close. With a blessing from Gaia and a quick pace, she could make it to the Sacred Pool tomorrow. She was more confident than ever that she really had gotten away from the daemons. There was no way they'd be able to track her in these conditions. She was filled with conviction once more as she laid down and wrapped herself in her cloak. She fell asleep almost instantly.

***

Sometime in the night, she was jerked awake when a pile of frozen moss and tree branches fell on her, bruising her cheek with an ice-cold slap. Startled out of her deep sleep, she frantically looked around her.

Her makeshift lean-to had collapsed.

Reaching to move the branches and moss off of herself and the coals of her fire, she felt that they were covered in a slick layer of ice. Outside of her hollow, she could hear the sound of ice tinkling through the trees and onto the ground. The drippy, sadness-inducing rain had turned into the ice-cold menace known as freezing rain.

Fucking perfect.

As the freezing rain broke through her collapsed shelter, it drenched Ena's fire in seconds, putting it all the way out. She knew it would be futile to try to start it again, as all the sticks and branches in the area would be encrusted with ice. She'd experienced freezing rain before in her village and knew how destructive it could be. It always led to significant damage to roofs when tree branches inevitably broke under the weight of the ice and fell, and often led to broken bones, too, when people slipped and fell trying to walk around on the slick ground. She had no choice but to huddle as close as she could to the tree's roots and wait it out until dawn. The rain would hopefully let up at some point, or at the very least, when the sun rose, the temperature would rise above freezing and it would switch back to regular rain.

But she soon found that waiting it out might not be possible. Her head and torso were protected from the worst of it by the tree's base and roots, but her boots stuck out into the rain despite her best efforts and soon they were covered in a thick layer of ice. Her toes began to go numb inside her socks, and without the fire, she could feel her still-wet clothing starting to freeze too. She tucked her hands close to her body, but they too were beginning to hurt again. *Fuck.*

Fear started to grip her. Frostbite and hypothermia were a real concern here.

Crack!

She was pulled from her spiraling thoughts by the deafening sound of a breaking branch. She peeked her head out of her pitiful shelter, looking up at the canopy of trees overhead, only to hear the cracking sound again.

Her Knowing screamed at her to move. She scrambled out of her hollow on all fours just as a huge tree limb, covered in a thick layer of heavy ice, came crashing down into the hollow where she'd just been.

She knelt on the ground just next to the branch as she stared at it in horror. The branch covered the hollow entirely, and there was no way she'd be able to remove it by herself. The only shelter she'd found was now gone.

She had no fire. She had no shelter. And the freezing rain continued to fall, crusting her cloak in minutes.

Ena was alone, afraid, and she knew in that instant that she had made a very, very poor decision.

Chapter Fourteen

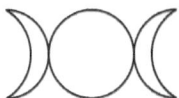

Ena decided she had no choice but to continue walking, both to try to keep warm, and in the hopes that she might reach the Sacred Pool before she lost any appendages to frostbite. There was a cave there that she, Heran, and Greya had spent the night in when they'd visited. Reaching that shelter was her only guaranteed way of surviving.

She was shivering uncontrollably when the sun finally rose, and the temperature mercifully crested above freezing.

The rain didn't stop, but at least now it was normal rain, and not freezing rain.

Her muscles ached and she felt like shit. Her teeth chattered in her skull and she'd lost all feeling in her fingers and toes. Her nose was next.

Around midday, she knew she needed to climb another tree to check her position, but she was worried about the branches not holding, especially after last night. She picked the youngest, sturdiest pine she could find, and battered her frozen fingers climbing its branches until she rose above the tree line.

The clouds had lifted a bit and she could see the Chasm Mountains to the east, and the sun, blurred by the clouds, already dipping west. After walking most of the night and morning, she was finally, mercifully, right in line with the Lost Sister. She should be close—very close—to the Sacred Pool.

The branches held as she climbed down from the tree, although her feet slipped a few times on the slick ice that still covered them, causing her heart to pound nearly out of her chest. But at least that had the benefit of bringing a bit more blood flow through her body.

Now, instead of moving south, she started to wander around, moving slightly east, then zigzagging slightly west, trying to find signs of the Sacred Pool. She continued that way for several hours, looking and listening for any signs of the cave, the pool, or the stream that fed from it, but everything looked the fucking same—the same forest she'd been traveling through, the same flat landscape. She could barely see more than twenty feet through the forest because it was so dense.

Terror started to fill Ena as the sun began to get low in the late afternoon and she found herself going in circles. Where the fuck was it? There was so much ground to cover here, and she had no idea where exactly it might be. What if she was wrong and the Sacred Pool was further east? Or further west? All she could see in every direction were fucking trees. She knew she might not make it with all her fingers and toes intact if she had to spend another night exposed to the elements.

Just when she was starting to panic, she heard it.

Underneath the high-pitched sound of the falling rain, was the low bubbling of water. She moved toward the sound like a moth to a flame, and it led her to a delicate, crystal-clear stream running through a bed of fine, light-brown sand.

The water was so clear, she could see straight through to the bottom, where pebbles of white and brown and green dotted the streambed. The banks on either side were covered in a bed of moss and ferns that looked comfortable enough to sleep on. It looked so beautiful, so dreamlike. She hoped to Gaia it wasn't a hypothermia-induced hallucination.

She frantically walked upstream, knowing that if this was the stream she remembered, she would find the Sacred Pool at its source. The elevation began to change as the landscape sloped gently upwards. As she walked, every so often, she saw small eddies and pools where the natural cold springs added to the stream's flow. She knew that if she stepped into one, her foot would sink down, down, down into the liquid sand on the stream bottom. How deep down the freezing-cold quicksand went, she didn't know. She and Greya had spent a significant amount of time testing the limits of the springs by sticking longer and longer branches down into them, but they never found the bottom.

It was this memory that gave her hope as she dragged her shivering, aching body one step at a time, following the stream for over an hour until she came to its source.

Ena nearly broke down sobbing at the sight. The pool was just as she remembered—a deep, oval-shaped pond about twice her body length in one direction, and three times it in the other. The water was a light, murky blue from the minerals that filled it and, occasionally, a bubble of air rose to the top and popped. The pool itself was a natural cold spring. It created the stream that she'd been following, which eventually flowed into a creek, likely the one she'd drunk from two days ago, which in turn fed the River Wry.

Beyond the pool, formed into the rock wall behind it, was the cave she remembered. Well, she called it a cave, but it was more of an overhang formed into the small rock outcrop that had been carved out by the moving water of the spring over time.

Taking a moment to breathe deeply in relief, and thank Gaia for her blessing, she began to gather what she needed for the spell. Time was of the essence. She desperately wanted to hunker down in the cave and start a gigantic fire, but the sun was setting and she wanted to get the message for help sent now. Who knew what else would befall her, or what the daemons were up to in her absence. She'd do the spell, and then she'd focus on getting warm.

Since her blood was required, she'd need something to cut herself with. She wandered around the surrounding area until she found a sufficiently sharp stone, then she squatted on the banks of the pool, and peered into its murky depths.

She hoped to Gaia that this worked. This was her only shot at getting help and not having to face the rest of the journey home alone, in the freezing rain, without supplies, and recovering from frostbite.

She reached down into her Knowing as she attempted to push her pain and fear from her mind. She concentrated on the light-blue color of the water, the constant sound of rain falling into the pool, and the solid stone in her hand.

She pictured Greya in her mind's eye, the way her pale-blonde hair reflected the light, and her brown eyes warmed with a smile. She concentrated on the way Greya made her feel safe and loved when she was in her presence. She focused on her desperate urge to speak to her sister, to see her. She lifted the jagged stone to her palm and then—

"I can't let you do that."

Ena spun to look for the source of the voice and lost her balance at the edge of the pool. She felt her body tip and she pinwheeled her arms to no avail. The last thing she heard before she tumbled into the murky blue water was the voice shout her name in fear.

"Ena!"

The next thing she knew, her head was underwater and she was falling, falling towards the bottom of the deep pool. Her arms and legs thrashed wildly, her cloak getting tangled around her. She could hardly see in the dark water, and it was cold—freezing cold. Her fingers and toes already lacked feeling, but the water was a shock to her lungs, making them seize in her chest.

She heard a loud splash next to her, or maybe that was just her own thrashing, and then a large arm encircled her waist and pulled her back against an equally large chest. She saw and felt the person's other arm and legs push and kick them both towards the surface.

As soon as her face broke from the water, she gasped for air. Her rescuer, holding on to her under her arms, swam her backwards towards the edge of the pool. Ena swiped frantically at her eyes, clearing them of water, and continued to gulp air into her shocked lungs. The person holding her spun her around and lifted her towards the bank, which she grabbed greedily as she pulled herself up. She coughed and sputtered on all fours until she was confident her feet would hold her. Then she rose to her feet, turned around, and came face to face with Ty.

"You," she said breathlessly, her heart plummeting in an instant.

"Me," Ty replied, standing before her soaking wet, and looking incredibly pissed off.

"H-how did you find me?" Ena asked in disbelief, her teeth chattering. She almost had to shout to be heard above the sound of the rainfall.

"I tracked you. You're welcome, by the way," Ty said as he moved to pick up the saddlebag he'd discarded on the bank of the pool.

"What?" she barked. She was about to absolutely lose it. This could *not* be happening. Not after everything.

"There's n-no way. I'm a w-witch. I left no trail. You c-couldn't have been tracking me this w-whole time, not unless you have heightened senses, and the only people who have that are witches with the G-gift of—"

"*Venator.*"

"You k-know about the Gift of *venator*?"

"I have the Gift of *venator*."

"W-what? No, no, no. Your Power is *furor*. You t-told me." Ena was feeling slightly hysterical now, her entire plan having blown up in her face. She was shaking and shivering, feeling more delirious on her feet by the minute.

"I have both."

"Both?! How is that p-possible?"

"Do we have to discuss this now? You're fucking freezing and so am I. We need to get under that shelter."

"Yes! Answer the d-damn question."

"Fine!" he yelled, looking completely exasperated. "I'm half witch. On my mother's side. Happy?"

"What?!" Ena had to sit down. She was actually feeling lightheaded. This was way too much information to absorb when only minutes ago, she'd been about to contact Greya and had finally been on her way to getting out of this nightmare.

She swayed and stumbled backwards to a tree, but Ty caught her arm, steadying her.

"As much as I'd love to stand here in the freezing rain while you descend into hysterics, I'm cold as shit, so let's get under that overhang before you completely lose it, okay?" Ty said pedantically.

Ena jerkily nodded her head, and followed him around the pool to the overhang.

She felt instant relief as she stepped under it, the rain finally ceasing its incessant pounding onto her hood and shoulders. She swayed again slightly as she made her way to the rock wall, and proceeded to slide down it until her ass hit the ground. She cradled her face in her hands and tried to hold back the sorrow that threatened to overwhelm her.

"While you do... whatever it is you're doing, I'm going to start a fire so we can dry off a bit," she heard Ty say. But she didn't look up. She didn't even move.

Ena vaguely heard him puttering around, gathering sticks and breaking them, as she shivered in her corner. Her mind had ceased working for the most part, too overwhelmed by the cold and the new information to function properly. By the time she dragged her head out of her hands, she saw that he'd arranged a nice pile of small and medium-sized sticks with some dry leaves from just inside the cave. He proceeded to strike his knife on a piece of flint he pulled from his pocket, and the sight of it got Ena's brain slowly functioning again.

"S-stop with that. Let me," she said, her teeth still chattering incessantly. She still didn't quite know what the fuck was going on, but she knew she needed to get warm.

She approached Ty's pile of sticks and leaves and spoke her spellword.

{*Ignis*}

The leaves caught fire instantly, but it took longer for the soaked-through branches to catch. Ena had to start the fire again with more dry leaves from the cave entrance before they held any sort of flame, and then Ty fed the fire slowly, grabbing progressively larger pieces of wood until a nice, consistent blaze burned before them.

Ena was enraptured with it and didn't move a muscle as she held her hands as close as she could possibly get to it without burning them. The numbness slowly left them, but was quickly replaced with a painful, stinging sensation.

She finally looked up at the sound of movement to see Ty taking off his shirt and coat. She couldn't help but notice that his arms and shoulders were covered in more tattoos, like the ones that were on his head, and they rippled as he proceeded to wring as much water out of his clothes as possible before laying them down on the ground next to the fire. Next, he moved to take off his pants.

Ena averted her eyes. On top of everything else that was making her hyperventilate, the last thing she needed was a glimpse of his perfectly chiseled ass.

By the time she looked up again, he'd put on a spare shirt from his leather saddlebag. The shirt was long and ended at his mid-thigh, making him semi-decent again.

He walked over to her, holding out another spare shirt. "You can have this if you want to get out of your wet clothes."

She looked up at him. His face was hard and businesslike, with no hint of kindness or concern. Although she hated the idea of taking favors from him, she took the shirt anyway, knowing it was best for her.

He turned his back to her as she removed her shoes and cloak, putting them as close as she dared to the fire. Then she removed her soaked socks and, thank Gaia, her sodden black party dress. Lastly, she pulled her shift over her head and, before the chill could take her, she shrugged into the spare shirt. It was big and soft, albeit slightly damp from being in Ty's soaked leather saddlebag, but significantly drier than the clothes she'd been wearing. Her shorter limbs swam in the excess fabric, so she rolled up the sleeves. But it smelled like Ty, and she didn't like that.

As the fire warmed the small indent of their cave, she wrung out her hair and began to feel slightly more human. She could feel and move her fingers and toes again, but they stung and throbbed painfully. She knew from her experiences healing others that frostbite like this would pass in time, and as long as blisters didn't develop on her fingers or toes, she likely wouldn't lose any.

Questions began whirling in her mind once more, and she knew she needed to breach the silence with Ty to get some answers, but the first one that came out surprised her.

"Where are Turner and Steig?"

Ty looked at her from where he sat across the fire. He seemed surprised too. "They went ahead to the coast. We lost one of the horses to the wolves, so they took the remaining two while I tracked you on foot. We'll rendezvous with them in Attax before continuing to the Occidens Coven."

Ena felt a smidge of guilt that her actions had, indeed, cost one of the horses its life, but it was instantly swamped by a flood of helplessness.

Attax was the closest major village to the Occidens Coven. She was instantly reminded of everything they had planned for her, everything she would be forced to take part in.

"So that's it then," Ena said, her voice filled with resignation. "I'm stuck with you again." Tears began to fill Ena's eyes and she looked away from him. She felt so angry she could scream—angry at Ty and the daemons, yes, but also angry at herself. She had failed in her escape, and now, everything she'd gone through was for naught.

Ty watched her for a beat, and when he spoke, his voice was gentler than it had been. "I told you. We need your help to see this through. I promise I'll let you go once we have the amulet."

Hearing him use that word *"promise,"* the last word he'd said to her all those years ago, brought up another wave of bitter emotions. She was trying to shove those back down, but then she remembered something.

"Wait a second—you said my name."

"What?" Ty replied, in a tone that implied that she was slightly unhinged and vaguely exhausting.

"When I fell into the water, you shouted my name."

"So?"

"So, I never told it to you. Not to mention, how did you know I couldn't swim and would need help when I fell in?"

Ty looked away from her and stared pointedly at the fire, poking it with a stick, his face carefully blank.

"You do remember me," Ena said quietly, realization dawning on her. There'd been a lot of new information thrown at her in the last two hours, but this realization shocked her the most.

At first, she felt elated at having figured it out, and relieved that he did remember her—he must. But then she realized what it meant, and her blood started to boil with anger.

"What the fuck, Ty? Why did you let me believe I was a stranger to you? That you didn't remember me?" Her voice was louder now; she could hear it getting shrill as it echoed around the quiet forest.

Ty still did not respond or even look up from the fire, and Ena lost it.

"Look at me, Ty!" she yelled.

For a second, the only sound was the rain falling outside the cave, and the pop of the fire.

Then Ty raised his eyes to hers, and the look in them could've killed. "Of course I remember you."

Ena stared at him for several seconds. Rage filled his eyes, and if she had a mirror, she was certain she'd see the same emotion reflected in hers too.

"Why?" she asked, struggling to control the waver in her voice. "Why didn't you say anything? Why did you let me believe you'd forgotten me?"

Ty took a deep breath and sighed, finally breaking eye contact with her to look back at the fire. "Because I'm not the person you remember. And I wish I could forget any of that ever happened."

His words were like a knife to her heart, and all of a sudden, it was hard to breathe. She didn't know why she was reacting this way. That summer had haunted her, too, and she'd tried her hardest to not think about it anymore. Even before learning who he really was, and all the reasons they should never have been together, she'd told herself that she needed to get over it, that everything that had happened wasn't a big deal, that she'd moved on. But now, as she watched the harsh planes of his face in the firelight, even knowing what he was, she knew that wasn't true. That she'd been lying to herself.

She hadn't moved on. Not really. Not in the ways that mattered, not in her heart. And when she'd thought he'd forgotten her, that had hurt, but it had allowed her to hate him for it, and she'd latched on to that hate like a lifeline.

Now, somehow, this was worse. Knowing that he remembered everything, just as she did, and regretted it—regretted the moments that she'd replayed over and over for years before she'd forced herself to stop, it tore at something deep inside her she thought she'd shed long ago.

Dashing her hand across her cheek before he could notice the tears starting to fall, Ena fell silent. There was nothing more to be said.

They sat in silence, staring at the fire as the sun set. And even when she'd been shivering in the freezing rain, she'd never felt more alone.

CHAPTER FIFTEEN

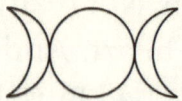

ENA AWOKE TO THE sounds of an ax chopping wood. She looked blearily around, not remembering where she was for a minute. Then she glanced over her shoulder and saw Ty using said ax to split a downed log into firewood and it all came crashing back. An instant wave of grief swept over her entire body, like a heavy blanket weighing her down.

Her escape had failed. Ty had tracked her. She was once again at the whim of a daemon, being used for Iblis only knew what purpose. And on top of all that, she was stuck with the man who'd carelessly taken her virginity and broken her heart. She would have to look at his stupidly handsome face all day, knowing he regretted what had been some of the most romantic and perfect days of her life. Knowing she was just a mistake to him.

But she'd be damned if she'd let him know how much this all hurt, so she shoved it all down, down, down, and focused on what was right in front of her. She had no choice but to continue on with Ty and his plans. She couldn't use her magic against him, and she couldn't escape—not with his heightened senses. Her only choice now was to see this through and hope to Gaia that he spoke the truth and would let her go afterwards.

So she was back to her original plan. Whatever they wanted with the amulet, she still needed to learn. If she could figure that out, at least she'd have something to bring back to her Coven. Something to show for the absolute shittiest couple of weeks of her entire Goddess-damned life. Doing this, and foiling their plan, would be her revenge.

Ena stood up slowly and stretched her muscles. The rain had stopped sometime in the night, and the Sacred Pool seemed to glow in the early-morning light. It was undeniably beautiful, the way the trees framed the pool, leaning over it as if reaching to touch it. Tendrils of light-green moss dangled from the branches like curtains, adding a feeling of mysterious enchantment to the pool. She had been so cold and shocked yesterday, in more ways than one, that she hadn't truly taken notice. Now she did, and she took strength from the sacredness of this place. It was a source of Wiccan power, meant to serve her kind. She drew on that knowledge and used it to fill the broken places in her heart before readying herself to face what was ahead of her.

Feeling around for her wet clothes, she was pleased to see that her shift and socks had dried fully overnight. Her dress and cloak were still slightly damp, but that was to be expected, since the wool took forever to dry. Having little choice, she turned her back on Ty and stripped down as she dressed in her own clothes. He could watch if he wanted; she was done caring about what he did.

Once she was fully dressed, she went to relieve herself behind a tree in the forest. When she returned, Ty had taken out some provisions from the pack he'd brought.

"Here," he said, handing her a piece of the jerky that she had been coming to loathe, but now felt like a delicious treat after the last several foodless days.

She took it wordlessly, along with a hunk of cheese and an apple he offered her, and inhaled them, barely tasting them as they went down.

Seeing that she was done, Ty slung the saddlebag he'd converted into a pack onto his back and kicked out their fire. "Come on," he said. "We're heading north."

Then he took off into the woods, not bothering to check if she followed.

The bastard had the nerve to seem upset with her, as if she had been the one to take him from his home, force him to serve an evil god, and feign ignorance about his identity. Well, she *had* technically done that last thing, but she had only been following his lead.

Ena walked behind him in silence. Trekking with him on foot was much different than on horseback. His strides were so long that she had to occasionally jog to keep up. Every step she took felt like a huge loss. She was once again heading in the opposite direction of her home, losing all the progress she'd made on her escape. She knew they would be heading northwest again to meet back up with Steig and Turner in Attax. That would mean almost a week of traveling.

Alone. With Ty.

Gaia, help her.

They stopped at the same delicate stream she had followed the day before and filled up their waterskins. Ena found some more bittercress as a snack, but she didn't share any with Ty.

All the silence gave Ena ample time to think about everything that had happened, and everything she still needed to do. The past seemed to weigh heavily between them now, since there was no more pretending. It was like a physical entity that hung in the air. Everything they'd once shared seemed to contrast sharply with everything they now were to one another, but neither of them acknowledged it. They'd clearly come to an unspoken agreement after last night to leave the past in the past. It was better that way.

One thing she'd learned stuck with her, though, and there was only one way to get the answers she needed, so she was the first one to break their silence.

"You said your mother was a witch."

It wasn't the smoothest transition into a delicate conversation, but she didn't have any patience for small talk right now.

Ty, who had clearly been lost in his own thoughts, seemed startled to hear her speak. He looked back at her skeptically. "I did," he replied, in a tone that said he was wary of where this conversation was headed.

"How is that possible?"

"Are you asking me how babies are made?" He grinned mockingly at her. "You're a little old to still be wondering about that."

Ena scowled at him. The fucking nerve of this man.

Biting back a growl, she replied over-sweetly, "No, I mean, how is it possible that your mother was a witch and your father was a daemon? We're opposites, foils, enemies. Intercouplings don't happen."

"It happened with us," he replied matter-of-factly.

Even the brief mention of their time together had Ena clenching her jaw in shame, remembering what he'd said to her last night. And the way he said that…"happened," as if he didn't purposefully and willfully lie to her and manipulate her into thinking he was mortal.

Fuck, what had happened to their unspoken agreement to leave the past in the past? Maybe this was her own fault for poking at old wounds.

The silence between them was deafening.

Forcing her jaw to unclench, something else occurred to her then that hadn't before—she *had* slept with a daemon. Blessedly, no child had come of that misbegotten union. But what would that look like? Her curiosity grew, and she had to know more.

"Were they together? Did she live in the Underworld with you?"

Ty sighed in frustration, and for a second, Ena thought he wouldn't respond, but then he did. "No. I never met her. My father took me after she gave birth to me, and I never saw her again. I don't know much, but I know their union wasn't forced, if that's what you're implying."

"No," Ena said hurriedly, horror rushing through her at the thought. "No, I wasn't implying that." Then after a beat, she asked, "So what happened to her?"

Ty was quiet for a second, seemingly focused on dodging some particularly protuberant tree roots. Ena was aware that she was prying into private matters, but when someone kidnapped you, lied to you, and casually threw the loss of your virginity in your face, you had a right to be somewhat tactless, right?

"Her Coven banished her and she wasn't welcome in the Underworld, so she left. I don't know where she went."

Ena was quiet after that. She hated Ty, for everything he'd put her through since she'd met him, but she'd be lying if she said she didn't feel a little sympathy for him. She'd lost her parents at a young age, too, but to know that your mother had likely suffered because of your birth was a lot to deal with. She felt the urge to change the subject quickly, so as not to force either of them to dwell on the past.

"How does your Gift work then?"

"The *venator*?"

"Yeah. I mean, I've heard of it, but I've never met another witch who had it before."

Ty looked over at her in surprise. Did she say something wrong? Before she could dwell on it, the moment was gone, and he answered her question.

"Well, I can see really far, farther than most humans, even in the dark. I can see a wider spectrum of colors, too, than I used to, before I got my Gift. And I have an unparalleled sense of direction. It's virtually impossible for me to get lost. And I also have a heightened sense of hearing and smell, like a hellhound." Ty smiled to himself at that. Ena had heard of the mystical beasts that kept the daemons company in the Underworld. She'd thought they were a myth, just like so many other things having to do with daemons. Ty spoke about them with something like...affection on his face, which bewildered her to no end.

"That's what allowed me to find you, even in the rain," he continued. "You were surprisingly fast, I'll give you that. And you were right—you didn't leave much of a trail, but I could still smell you."

Ena scrunched her nose up at that. That was...weird. She wondered what she smelled like to him. "How did you get your Gift without a Summoning? Do daemons have a Summoning?" she asked, changing the subject away from her smell.

"Sort of. We have a version of it where we receive our Powers from Iblis. It's...intense."

Ena was quiet for a second, wondering if she should pry further. She didn't know how much he'd be willing to share, but surprisingly, Ty continued on his own.

"Daemons believe that in order to prove ourselves worthy of Iblis, we must face our own suffering and chaos. The Trial, as we call it, is where we do that. All daemons go through it at age twenty-seven, and if we survive, we are granted a Power from Iblis and are bound to serve him forevermore."

"Face your own suffering and chaos? What does that mean?"

"Essentially...we are left alone in the deepest part of the Underworld for days on end. No light, no food, no water. It...does things to you. To be alone, in the dark, that long." Ty's face took on a haunted look, like he had been dragged into the memories of his own Trial. "After a time, if Iblis shows himself to you, you receive your Power. Only then are you allowed to emerge."

Ena paused at that. That sounded...horrific. The worst she'd had to do was drink the burning psilovenom. Granted, it had made her hallucinate and then feel like shit the next day, but to essentially be left to go mad in a dark cave for days on end was unimaginably cruel and terrifying. Ena couldn't believe Ty had gone through that. Turner and Steig too.

"So when..." Ena hesitated, not wanting to dredge up painful memories. "When you went through that, you emerged with a Power *and* a Gift?"

"Yes."

"But how is that possible? Did Gaia come to you too?"

"I don't know," Ty replied. "I don't think she did, but I've never... I don't know much about her, really."

This whole conversation was starting to make Ena's head hurt. How Ty, a half-witch, could have received his Gift from Gaia without her directly Gifting it to him made no sense. Ena went silent as she contemplated this new information. Once again, she was struck by how similar daemons and witches were. Both received their magic when they were twenty-seven. Both had to undergo a special ceremony of sorts to receive it. She guessed it made sense, given what Heran had told her about all magic coming from the same source. She wondered what else they might share in common.

They continued on the rest of the afternoon in relative silence, stopping to rest once or twice more when they came across a water source. Ena was pleased that her fingers and toes seemed to have returned to normal today, and her muscles were clearly adjusting to the long days of walking, because they didn't hurt quite so much anymore.

Still, Ena was grateful when the sun began to get low in the sky, and Ty declared that they should stop and make camp.

Ena built the fire herself this time while Ty went off to set a trap for small game—if Gaia granted them, they could have something other than dried jerky to eat in the morning—but Ena didn't try to escape while he was gone. She knew it was futile after hearing about his Gift.

By the time he returned, Ena had cleared the area of sticks and pokey plants, then made a small nest of leaves on a bed of moss and was getting as comfortable as possible. Everything was a bit muddy still from the heavy rain, but it was better than nothing. Gaia, she was getting incredibly tired of sleeping on the ground, and she thought that she might just spend an entire week in bed when she got home. The plus side of falling into the Sacred Pool, however, was that her dress and cloak were slightly cleaner than before. She'd take what she could get right now.

Turning her back on Ty and the fire, she started to lay down.

"Uh-uh, little viper. You're sleeping with me tonight."

She jerked back up to find Ty beckoning her over to where he was sitting on the other side of the fire.

"What?" she asked incredulously. He had to be joking.

"You're. Sleeping. With. Me," he said slowly, over-enunciating every word like she was hard of hearing.

"There's no chance in the Underworld I'm sleeping next to you." She realized the irony of invoking the Underworld, given that this man was a daemon, but still, it got her point across.

"Look, I spent all last night keeping watch so that you, little miss flight risk, would not take off again. I need to sleep tonight. And the only way I'm doing that is if you're right next to me. I sleep lightly, so I'll know if you move even an inch. And if you need more motivation, you should know I still have those ropes, so we can do this the easy way or the hard way."

Ena swallowed. This man was her enemy, and not to mention they had an incredibly complicated and fraught history, so she absolutely did *not* want to sleep next to him.

Still, she couldn't help the way her body reacted to the thought. Her heart beat a little faster and butterflies filled her stomach. *Fuck.*

She thought about telling him that she wasn't going to try to escape again. Maybe she could convince him it was the truth. But what reason would he have to believe her? No, she knew Ty well enough at this point to know that there would be no dissuading him from this.

"Fine," Ena said, rolling her eyes to disguise her body's brief lapse into what had to be insanity. "But if you're forcing me to sleep next to you, the least you could do is come over here. I made a makeshift bed of moss and leaves. It'll be much more comfortable."

"Alright," Ty said, seeming way too pleased with himself. He stood up and walked around the fire to where she'd made her nest, then he paused for a second as he stood over her. His eyes seemed to glow in the light of the fire as he stared down at her with that intense gaze of his. Always so intense.

From where she sat on the ground, he loomed above her, his body tall and menacing, his bearded face half-shadowed in the light. Looking up at him, an energy passed between them as she met his gaze. One that she hadn't felt in a long time. Nine years to be exact.

Ena quickly looked away, clearing her throat. The spell they'd been under mercifully broke, and she curled up on her side facing away from him. She felt Ty lower himself and lay down behind her on his back.

She thought he'd stay that way, keeping as much distance between them as possible, but then she felt him turn towards her, so their bodies were only separated by a few inches of empty air. She could feel his warm breath on the top of her head, feel the heat of his body coming off him in waves. She knew that if she were to shift her body just the tiniest bit, she could nestle back into him like a spoon. But the time for that closeness between them was long past, and even then, it had been a mistake, as Ty had so thoroughly reminded her last night.

So she stayed exactly where she was and closed her eyes. But just as the exhaustion overtook her and she drifted off to sleep, she heard him whisper.

"Good night, Ena."

CHAPTER SIXTEEN

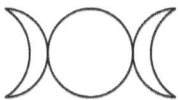

ENA AWOKE WITH A deep feeling of warmth and contentment. Her face was pressed against something impossibly hard, and her nose was filled with the scent of
stone, woodsmoke, and honey. She nuzzled deeper into
the hard thing and the smell, sensing in her half-asleep
state that closer meant warm, and to pull away would
be cold. She felt the hard thing surround her, wrapping
tighter around her, and as she shifted her leg, she found
it was sandwiched underneath something heavy, and
her hip was pressed up against... Oh, Gaia.

Ena cautiously opened her eyes. Her face was nuzzled
into Ty's hard chest, his arms were wrapped around
her, her leg was in between his, and yes, that was indeed
his extremely erect cock pressing into her hip. Ty's
breaths were still even and slow, so he was clearly still
asleep. She went to extract her leg from between his and
tried to turn out of his grasp, but his embrace was like
iron. There was no way this wouldn't be awkward.

"Ty," she whispered gently. "Ty, wake up."

He stirred slightly and rolled his hips, pressing his
cock more firmly against her. Heat shot straight to her
core, followed by an intense wave of embarrassment.

She began to struggle slightly against him, and the act of her shuffling caused him to wake up fully.

All at once, his arms loosened and he lifted his legs apart, allowing her to escape.

She rolled away from him and stood up quickly. "I have to pee," she announced awkwardly, and practically ran behind a nearby tree.

She heard him stand up, cough in an extremely masculine way, and then heard the stream of his own morning urination nearby.

How he managed it with his cock in the state it had been, she did not want to know.

Ena took her time, only to buy herself some additional space to clear her head. She heard Ty wander off after a minute, presumably to check the traps he'd set last night, so she came out from behind the tree and set to work building up the fire.

By the time he returned, she had decided that the best thing to do was to not reference the state they'd awoken in at all and continue on with the day. She did not have the mental energy to dissect what had happened. It was all far too confusing.

Blessedly, Gaia had granted them breakfast. Ty came out of the woods holding a decently large squirrel by its furry tail. He sat down wordlessly and proceeded to skin and gut the animal deftly, then speared it on an appropriately large stick before starting to roast it over the fire Ena had built.

The smell of the roasting meat made Ena's stomach grumble, and while she waited patiently for it to cook, she re-braided her hair and obsessively picked small pieces of moss and sticks from her woolen cloak and dress.

Once the squirrel was cooked through, Ty pulled off some of the biggest pieces of meat tenderly with his large fingers and handed them to her. The freshly cooked meat scalded her fingers, but she popped the pieces into her mouth one by one, not caring if they burned her tongue. They were absolutely orgasmic.

After Ty had picked over the rest of the squirrel carcass until all that remained was bones, they put out their fire and continued on their way. Ena was surprised that Ty did not seem to have to stop and get his bearings the way she had. He seemed to intuitively know what direction they were heading without orienting himself to the mountains or the sun's path. That was clearly because of his *venator*. He'd said he had an unparalleled sense of direction, but damn, seeing it in action...Ena was reluctantly impressed.

They had been walking at a brisk pace and making good time, so Ena assumed they were only a couple days of travel away from the Western Road. She doubted they'd travel directly on it to get to Attax—two people on foot would draw too much attention—but they'd likely walk parallel to it and make their own path. At least that's what Ena would do, but who was to say what Ty would do. He was constantly, annoyingly, surprising her.

Around mid-morning, they came to a stream that bisected their path. They stopped at it to rest for a while and refill their waterskins. Ena had taken up residence against a fallen tree while she snacked on a pawpy fruit that Gaia had granted her. The season for pawpy fruits was still in full swing since the oval-shaped yellow fruits didn't fully ripen until around Samhain. The trees were rare, though, and only grew sparsely on the banks of creeks and streams, so she was blessed to have found one, because their fruit were absolutely delicious. The creamy-textured pulp inside was sweet and floral with an ever-so-slightly rancid undertone. They were definitely an acquired taste, but they were highly nutritious. Not to mention, their branches were extremely pliant and were excellent for making animal traps. She wondered idly if she would be able to convince Ty to cut some with his axe and bring them to use at their campsite tonight.

Ena had been so lost in the deliciousness of her foraged fruit that she had barely taken note of what Ty was doing. Standing up to rinse her sticky hands and face in the water, she noticed that he was staring at the stream in a calculating fashion. He walked up and down the bank a few times in either direction, like he was looking for something. Eventually, he came back, a look of decision on his face.

"We're going to ford the stream up here," he announced, pointing just around the bend where she couldn't see. "Crossing it is the quickest way to get where we're going. There's some stepping stones and downed logs that should make a fairly easy way across."

Ena stared at the stream in horror. It wasn't as big as the River Wry, but it was certainly no babbling brook. It looked quite deep in places and was flowing pretty fast. Did he not remember that she couldn't swim? What if she fell in? For fuck's sake, she'd had more than enough of almost drowning, not to mention being sopping wet and cold.

Ty seemed to understand her train of thought. "You'll be fine, I pro—" He cut himself off suddenly, realizing what he'd been about to say. "I mean, you'll make it. It's not that bad," he ended gruffly. At least he had the presence of mind to not use the "P" word with her anymore. She'd be out of her mind to trust any promise he made ever again.

Ena followed him huffily to the spot he had selected. There were, indeed, a few well-placed stones scattered throughout this section of the stream that would allow them to get halfway across, leading to a downed log that they could use to cross the rest of it.

Ena stared at it cautiously before turning to Ty. "You first," she said, with a saccharine smile.

Ty gave her a bland look before using his long strides to gracefully step from one stone to another, then, making a small leap, he landed on the downed log before balancing across it to the bank on the other side. He made it look way too easy.

Ty stared at her haughtily from across the stream, his arms crossed, and an impatient look on his face. She recognized this for what it was—another challenge, just like when he'd pushed her to climb the cliff. *Are you as brave as me?* he seemed to say. *Are you going to let me win?* He knew she really fucking hated to lose, and she'd never back down from his challenge.

Steeling her courage, she began to cautiously walk on the stones, following the path Ty had taken. They were slipperier than they looked, and she had to use all her concentration to focus on keeping her balance as she stepped from one to the next. She was beginning to feel fairly proud of herself, until she came to the leap that was required to get her onto the downed log. She was significantly shorter than Ty, and therefore the distance would be that much harder for her. She paused on the last stepping stone, the water rushing around her. She looked cautiously up at Ty, who stared back at her, seemingly unconcerned. Fuck it. There was no going back now, she thought.

She launched herself off the stone, stretching her leg as far out in front of her as possible, reaching, reaching for the log. Her foot made it! But just barely, and the log was slippery too. As her full weight landed on the log, she began to lose her balance. She felt her foot lose purchase on the wet bark and her body started to careen towards the water.

Then, something gripped her arm, stopping her fall. Looking up, she saw Ty balancing on the log in front of her, his hand wrapped tightly around her upper arm. Ena reached towards him to steady herself, gripping his shoulder before getting both feet once again on the log and regaining her balance. She stared up at him in surprise. She knew daemons were fast, but Gaia, he had gotten to her in seconds. They both breathed a little heavily as they stared at one another for a second too long.

"Thanks," Ena breathed. He was entirely too close for comfort. Her body hummed in his presence.

Ty released her arms, but didn't move away. "Don't mention it, little viper," he said, continuing to stare down at her. "Besides, I didn't want to have to stop and make a fire to dry out your soggy ass again."

Ena scoffed at him as he finally turned away from her to walk back across the log to the other side. "Don't call me that," she said, scowling as she, too, balanced her way across the rest of the log until her feet blessedly landed on the bank.

"What? 'Little viper,' you mean?" he asked innocently.

"Yes," she snapped.

"Why not? It suits you." The bastard was clearly enjoying this. His wide smile took over his face, in stark contrast to the mean, impassive look he'd been wearing the last week.

Gaia, this man was confusing. One minute, he hated her and treated her like the bird shit on his shoe, and the next, he was cuddling her in his sleep, saving her from a watery fate, and teasing her. Ena did not know what to make of it all, and it annoyed the fuck out of her.

"Because it's extremely condescending. I'm not 'little.' I'm a grown-ass woman."

Ty made a show of glancing down appreciatively at her rear end. "Okay, fair point," he replied.

Ena stared at him incredulously, her mouth hanging open. She could not *believe* he'd just done that.

Seeing her face, Ty burst out laughing.

It was the first time she'd heard him laugh like that since...well, since the last time they'd been together. The sound of it transported her right back to when she was seventeen. Ty had one of those extremely infectious laughs, and the sound of it, coupled with the light it brought to his eyes, and the way his face transformed from attractive to devastatingly handsome when he smiled, tugged at her heart for a second.

She hurriedly looked away, as if blinded by the sun, and had to remind herself where she was. Who he was. She was not seventeen anymore. And maybe she could admit that he was still very good-looking, but she wanted nothing to do with him. Not anymore. Not after everything.

"My apologies," Ty said, his laughter dying down. "You set me up so perfectly for that joke I couldn't help myself." After a beat, he added, more seriously now, "And I don't think calling you 'little viper' is condescending. Vipers are extremely dangerous, even the little ones," he said, winking at her.

Ena just rolled her eyes at him and kept walking.

***

The mood between them was significantly lighter after that. By the late afternoon, they began to head due west, and found themselves walking directly into an amazingly beautiful sunset. The forest was bathed in an otherworldly golden glow. Ena tried not to notice, but the light did beautiful things to Ty's face. The red in his beard shone with a warmth she hadn't noticed before, and his eyes, as always, seemed to reflect the extra light around him, making them even more piercing. The altered light played across the side of his shaved head, making his tattoos appear darker against his skin.

They were so intricate; she'd never seen them this well before. Whirls and dots of ink formed swirling, circular patterns that bled into one another, running across the sides of his skull before wrapping around the back and dipping down onto his neck. They seemed to progress from one to another, as if telling a story, and she remembered the way they'd continued down his shoulders and arms when she saw him with his shirt off.

Ty turned to her, catching her staring. Ena would've been embarrassed, but instead, she realized the turn in his attitude could be a good opportunity to get some more information out of him. Though his beauty was...distracting, she couldn't forget where they were headed, and why. Not for one second.

"What are your tattoos?" she asked.

He eyed her skeptically. "You really want to know?"

"Yes," she replied. "They're...unique."

Ty looked at her again, as if assessing whether or not she was telling the truth, before he spoke. "We call them *onata*. They're given to us each time we complete a mission from Iblis."

Ena almost stopped in her tracks. For some reason, she hadn't been expecting that, and she was suddenly appalled that she'd been admiring them so much. She figured they had something to do with daemonic culture, but not this.

His tattoos were a visible reminder that he was a servant of Iblis. They were a written record of all the chaos, discontent, and discord he had spread, of every time he had disrupted the balance that witches worked so hard to maintain. Ena began to wonder how many of the horrible events she'd heard of in recent years had been caused by Ty's own hand—the famines, wildfires, earthquakes, population collapses, violent incidents. Given his Power of *furor*, he would've been able to provoke mortals or animals into conflicts that could lead to all sorts of terrible outcomes. She knew, theoretically, that he had done those sorts of things. But now, seeing the evidence of it, it all seemed so...real.

"Oh," Ena replied lamely. And then something else horrific occurred to her. "And is that what this is? A mission from Iblis to find the amulet?"

Ty was silent for a second, as if debating whether or not to answer. "No," he said. "I guess you could say it's...extracurricular."

Ena didn't know what to make of that. She had so many questions. What could they possibly want with the amulet that didn't have to do with Iblis's mission? Ena opened her mouth to ask more questions, but Ty shut her down before she could.

"Don't even try it, viper. That's all I'm going to tell you. For your sake, and mine."

Well, that was cryptic as shit.

Forbidden from asking what she wanted to know, Ena turned silent again until the sun had fully set and they stopped to make camp.

That night, as she laid down beside him, sleep took a long time to come to her. She replayed what he'd said over and over again in her mind. She'd always thought that they'd been planning to do something nefarious with the amulet, something utterly destructive and chaotic. And that had always worried her. For Gaia's sake, the evidence of all they had done was written right there on Ty's body. It was highly likely they'd use it to do more of those things. But she couldn't shake the feeling after what he'd said that there was so much more going on than she knew.

So tonight, for the first time, she was both deeply afraid and completely unsure of what he intended to do with the amulet.

CHAPTER SEVENTEEN

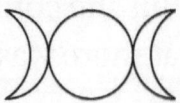

THE NEXT FEW DAYS passed similarly. They walked as far as they could each day, trapping and eating what they could along the way. They continued to sleep side by side every night, and every morning, they awoke entwined in some new, embarrassing way that they both refused to acknowledge. Ena blamed the cold weather and the natural morning tendencies of the male physique for the bulk of the awkwardness.

She was fairly certain that they were now traveling parallel to the Western Road and were only a few days away from their destination, but she didn't exactly know how to feel about the prospect of joining back up with Steig and Turner. She and Ty had developed a truce of sorts. He'd been kinder to her, more friendly, and less guarded. She worried that joining back up with the others would ruin their newfound...well, friendship wasn't the exact word she would use, but it was certainly a new understanding.

But she also knew this feeling of...comfort with him was dangerous. It reminded her too much of the way things had once been between them. Ty saw their time together as a mistake, and for that reason alone, she needed to protect herself from dredging up old feelings, not to mention the whole mortal enmity thing. So maybe reuniting with Steig and Turner would be for the best.

Either way, she'd come to accept that escaping wasn't in the cards for her, and she was committed to seeing her plan through, but she dreaded leaving the safe anonymity of the forest and venturing into unfriendly Occidens territory. She hoped to Gaia that she was able to keep her head down and get through whatever plan they had to steal the amulet without much trouble. But in truth, that was likely a fool's hope.

One night, when they were only a day or two out from Attax, Ena slept nestled into Ty like a spoon. They'd pushed themselves to their limit the day before, walking even past sunset, so she didn't have the energy to resist when Ty placed his arm over her waist and tucked her into him. She gave herself over to the warmth and fell asleep instantly.

There were still several hours until dawn when her Knowing woke her. She couldn't exactly say what was wrong, only that there was a sudden sense that something was not right.

Her eyes flew open, but she didn't move. She looked across the coals of their fire into the dark woods, but couldn't make anything out besides the endless vague shapes of trees. She reached down into her Knowing, focusing intently on any and all signs around her. She heard a stick snap in the darkness, and then she Knew.

There was something nearby with a dangerous intention.

Ty's arm was slung across her middle, and she squeezed it firmly, digging her nails ever so slightly into his flesh. She felt him stir awake just as the sound of a shuffled footfall echoed through the forest.

She felt Ty's body go taut behind her as he, too, instantly realized that something was off. His muscles coiled around her, pulling her ever so slightly tighter to him. Then she felt his breath over her ear. "Don't move until I say," he whispered so quietly she almost couldn't hear him.

Ena lay still, pretending to be asleep, even though her heart was pounding in her ears and her legs ached with the urge to jump up and run, run, run. She couldn't shut her eyes though. No—those she kept wide open, watching from the dark cave of her cloak's hood, waiting in fear for what might emerge.

Slowly, out of the woods appeared several human figures. It was nearly pitch black in the forest, the only light the glow of embers from their nearly burnt-out fire and the glimmer of the moon through the trees. She couldn't tell much about the figures, but by their size and gait, they appeared to be male.

And there were a lot of them. Seven at least. They moved quietly, slowly surrounding Ena and Ty's campsite. Were they witches? Mortals? Her Knowing was screaming at her now to move, move, move. These men wanted to take, to hurt, to kill.

One of them was close enough now that she saw he held a knife in his hand. Its sharp edge glinted in the low light of the fire.

He approached Ena and Ty, clearly believing them to still be sleeping. With her hood up, Ena was certain she appeared that way, and Ty's face was hidden, buried in the back of her neck.

Ena saw the man turn slightly to one of the others, gesturing toward the large saddlebag that lay next to Ty. It was filled not just with food and supplies, but some of the metal goods they pretended to trade in. And next to it lay his axe. Ena had admired it several times; it was elegantly designed and expertly made.

Was that what they were after? Were they thieves? All at once, Ena remembered what Perse had said in the days leading up to Samhain, about the group of bandits that had formed, and how they were terrorizing the region north of their village. Had they made their way south now?

The man drew closer to them and mimed dragging the knife across his throat to one of the other men. She saw the white of the other's teeth flash as he smiled in reply.

Ena started to panic. Why wasn't Ty doing anything? Shouldn't they be running? He'd told her not to move, but maybe she should call on the wind and knock them back? Or start a fire to distract them? Ena was keenly aware that she was not a trained fighter, and she'd never used her magic against a mortal before. She'd never had to.

Then the man holding the knife began to lean over her, and everything happened fast.

Ty's arm shot up and grabbed the man's wrist, pushing the knife up and away from her. Simultaneously, Ty sat up and must've pulled his own dagger out, because he shoved it under the man's rib cage, pushing up towards his heart.

The other man closest to them saw this. "Son of a bitch!" he shouted. Then he threw himself at Ty.

Ena scrambled away on all fours as Ty stood up and slashed out at him with his dagger faster than Ena could register. He must've picked up his axe, too, because all of a sudden, it was in his hand and there was a loud thunk as he spun and embedded it into the skull of someone approaching them from behind.

He kicked the man back, pulling his axe from his head, and Ena stared dumbfounded at the rush of blood and gore that came pouring down the man's slack face. She was only broken from her stupor when she heard another attacker come at her from behind. Ty threw his dagger, embedding it in the man's eye just as he was about to grab her.

Ty whirled to face her and pulled Ena to her feet. "There's too many of them," he said quickly. "You have to run."

Ena tried, but her feet didn't move.

Sensing her hesitation, Ty gripped the sides of her face. "Don't worry, I'll find you. Go!"

Ena did as he commanded and stumbled blindly into the dark. Behind her, she heard Ty immediately engage with another attacker, the sound of his axe slicing into flesh followed by a scream of pain.

Ena ran, stumbling over roots, too terrified to move silently. Her Knowing screamed at her again and she sensed the man right before he came at her from behind a tree. Ena didn't even have to think about it; her body thrummed with adrenaline and all of her magic was right there. She spoke her spellword.

{*Aeris*}

A huge gust of wind shoved the man back into a tree so hard it nearly split. He was knocked unconscious instantly and slumped to the forest floor.

She didn't pause to contemplate what she'd just done; Ena continued to run. She heard shouts coming from her left and saw through the darkness that there were three more men running, heading for the conflict.

How many more men were out there?

She needed to hide.

She looked around and saw a dense thicket of thorny blackberry bushes and ran behind it, crouching down so she couldn't be seen.

She tried to force aside the panic that was flooding her. Her heart pounded and her mind was frantic. She tried to get a hold of a logical thought, but they kept slipping from her. She took one breath. Then two.

The rest of the men hadn't followed her; they were clearly too focused on Ty.

Ty, who had told her to run and now was fighting against Gaia-knew-how-many men. Could he take them all alone?

No, she finally realized with a bone-deep fear. No, he couldn't take them all. Ty would be killed.

Ena was shaking and she was so, so afraid. But the thought of Ty being killed terrified her even more.

Before she could think about why that was, she forced her body to move and ran at a full sprint back the way she'd come.

Back at the campsite, Ena saw five men already dead or unconscious scattered on the ground, while Ty engaged two more. He dodged the point of a deadly sharp sickle wielded by one of the men. The man's face was screwed up in rage, and he lashed out blindly with his weapon, clearly overexerting himself. Ty dodged him easily, then ducked as another one of them swung a fist at his face. Ty struck out again with his dagger, which he'd somehow retrieved, hitting the man in the gut, then spinning around to slit the throat of the other. Ena realized then that he must have been using his Power on them, making them careless with rage to gain an advantage.

But he didn't see the three men who had arrived from the woods approaching him too. They were just running past the dying embers of their campfire when Ena spoke again.

{*Ignis*}

The campfire blazed to life, the flames instantly reaching the height of a fully grown man and exploding out in all directions. The three men who had been approaching Ty screamed as their clothes caught fire in the blaze. They dropped to the ground, rolling around frantically and patting themselves to put the flames out. Their screams echoed around the woods, and Ena smelled the burning of their clothes, the burning of their flesh.

But she knew it wasn't enough. They'd get up in a few minutes, burned but alive. And they'd try to hurt her again. They'd try to hurt Ty.

Something came over Ena then—a feral feeling she had never had before. She didn't think she'd ever drawn on her magic this much, and it filled her from the crown of her head down to the tips of her toes. Her Gift was there, too, thrumming under her skin, waiting to be used, but she ignored it for now and, instead, she crouched down and placed her hands on the earth.

She gripped the soil in her hands, feeling it push under her fingernails, and she spoke again.

{*Terra*}

Her magic rumbled through the earth, splitting it in two. Radiating out from her hands, a deep fissure cracked open through the ground. The men she'd burned with her fire fell into it where it opened beneath them, and she barely heard their cries for help as it closed around them. Soil and debris rained down on them, filling the crevice like a shallow grave. Their cries became slowly muffled by the earth as it swallowed them, until she couldn't hear them at all anymore, and she Knew they were dead.

She stood up and looked around, her heart pounding and her muscles twitching with adrenaline. She turned just in time to see Ty, still locked in battle with the only two men who remained alive. The blaze of the fire she'd started lit up the forest as she watched. One of them had a large butcher's knife that he swung at Ty's head. Ty kicked him away so hard that the man flew into a tree a horse's length away and went slack. But doing so exposed Ty's side to the last man, who shoved his knife deep into Ty's abdomen. Ena felt the blow like it was to her own body, and fear flooded her anew.

"Ty!" she screamed.

Ty made a pained grunting noise before taking two steps back and yanking the dagger out. She watched him swing his axe into the chest of the man who'd stabbed him, then turned towards her, his face grave with pain and concern.

Some movement out of the corner of Ena's eye caught her attention. Another figure was running out of the woods, his knife raised at Ty while his back was turned.

Ena was too far away to reach them and Ty didn't see him; he was too busy looking at her. She felt her Gift growing inside her again, begging to be used, and she didn't know what else to do, so she reached for it.

It grew through her like a vine, a torrent of power exploding through her like a blazing wildfire, and she gave herself over completely to the unknown of it. It didn't matter if she lost control now; everything was already out of control.

All at once, she felt a channel open between her and the attacker and she felt the man's intentions like never before; she felt his mind, his thoughts, his being *just there* for the taking. The instinct came to her naturally, like she was finally learning to walk, when all she'd done before was crawl. She latched on to it and spoke through the channel.

{*Stop.*}

Ena's voice sounded strange, even to her own ears. The tone wasn't quite right. She sounded calm, even though she didn't feel it, and even though it was only her speaking, there was a simultaneous echo, as if two of her were speaking at once.

The man running at Ty froze instantly, his knife poised to strike Ty in the back. Ty whirled to look at the would-be attacker, his eyes going from the point of the knife, now placed right above his heart, to the man's face, etched into a permanent snarl. Then he turned to look at Ena. Horror and confusion played across his face, but he didn't say a word.

The man was frozen like a statue; Ena wasn't even sure if he was breathing. But she didn't care. She knew what to do next.

{*Draw the knife across your throat.*}

The man obeyed as if in a trance. He lifted the knife and drew it slowly, deeply across his own throat. Blood spurted out frantically as it sliced across his flesh, leaving a bloody gash visible in the firelight. Ena watched his mouth fill and gurgle with blood until his legs collapsed underneath him and he fell to the ground. She watched as the light went out from his eyes, until he stared vacantly at the sky, and Ena Knew he was dead.

CHAPTER EIGHTEEN

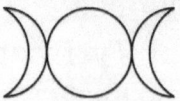

EVERYTHING WAS QUIET FOR a minute. Maybe two. Ena had no idea how long it was quiet, actually. All she could hear was her breathing. All she could feel was her fear. Every nerve in her body felt alight and ready to fight. Her Knowing was alert, waiting for more threats, but her eyes remained focused on the man she'd just killed with her Gift.

"Ena?" Ty spoke gently, like he was speaking to a spooked horse.

Her mind barely registered the strain in his voice as she dragged her gaze from the dead man to look at him. He was kneeling on the ground, surrounded by bodies. He was clutching his side with both hands, and his face was a mixture of pain and concern. "Are you okay?" he asked.

Was she okay? She didn't know.

"I think they're gone. We're safe now."

Safe. Was she safe? She didn't feel safe. She didn't think she'd ever feel safe again.

Ty tried to stand and let out a pained groan with the effort. The pitiful sound somehow snapped Ena out of whatever trance she was in and she rushed over to him.

He was breathing hard and Ena placed her hands on his wound. Standing closer now, she could see it was gushing blood. Had the attacker gotten him in a vital organ of some kind?

But Ty wasn't looking down at his wound. He was looking up at her. "What in the Underworld was that you just did?"

"I-I don't know," Ena said. Her voice was shaking and sounded weak. So different now from the one she'd just used to kill that man.

She felt the fog of her fear lifting slowly and her brain began to put thoughts together.

"It was my *visanis*. I've never used it before. I...didn't know what else to do. It just came out."

"Your Gift is *visanis*?" Ty asked, his eyes wide with shock.

"Yes, but now is not the time, Ty. You're hurt." She had a million questions, too, as she knew Ty did, but his blood gushed over her hands where she placed them at his side, and she could tell his body was going into shock as he started shaking. "We've got to cauterize this wound to stop the bleeding, I don't think stitching it will be enough."

"I know." Ty groaned as she made him sit back against a nearby tree. "But we should leave. I don't know if there's any more nearby, and we're in Occidens territory now. If anyone was attracted by the commotion...we can't be found here."

Ena nodded in understanding. What they'd done would attract attention eventually. It was best they were far away before anyone found the evidence.

She ran over to one of the dead men that lay on the ground and removed his shirt. The man was heavy and it took longer than Ena wanted to lift the dead weight of his limbs. She ran back over to Ty and had him press the shirt over his wound, then grabbed his discarded dagger. Rushing over to the remains of the fire, she shoved it deep into the burning hot coals. Every second seemed to last an eternity as she waited for it to heat. She could tell every breath was causing Ty pain as he bled into the flimsy shirt in his hands.

Deciding she could wait no longer, she pulled the dagger out of the coals and brought it over to Ty. She lifted the stolen shirt away as well as his own, revealing the wound as it seeped blood. It wasn't too wide, only about the width of the blade itself, but she could tell it went through several layers of skin and muscle. She would need to cauterize inside it as much as possible.

"This is gonna hurt, I'm so sorry," Ena said, her voice shaking.

"Just do it," Ty said, gritting his teeth.

Ena shoved the hot dagger into his wound as deep as she dared. She heard his blood and flesh sizzle around the hot knife as it burned his skin, sealing the open wound inside his body. Ty's eyes were clenched shut tight as he breathed and whimpered through gritted teeth.

By the time she was done, he was drenched in sweat, his body shaking from the trauma. Ena took the blood-soaked shirt and tore it into strips before wrapping them around the freshly cauterized wound.

Ty groaned as his head drooped back against the tree. Was he about to pass out?

"Fuck," Ena said. "Can you stand? Can you walk? We need to get to a safer place and then I can clean and stitch it." She knew Ty had a needle and thread in his pack—she'd seen him use it to repair a button on his coat a few days ago—so she grabbed his pack and put it on her back before coming back to Ty.

"Yeah, yes, I can walk," Ty said, but his voice was shaky.

As she grabbed Ty's forearm and lifted him to standing, he put his arm around her shoulders to support some of his weight on his injured side, and they hobbled slowly into the woods.

They walked like that for about a half hour before Ena had to stop. Ty was very heavy, and the weight of him had her thighs shaking and her back aching after only a few minutes. She didn't know how much farther she could go supporting his weight. She guided him gently down to the forest floor, where he sat and leaned against a tree.

"It's okay," he said. "I can walk on my own for a bit. I just need to rest for a minute."

"No, you can't," Ena said harshly, looking at him. He was still clutching his side and his face was pale, but he looked at her and gave her a pained smile.

"If I didn't know any better, I'd say you were worried about me."

Ena didn't respond. She just sat for a minute before lifting Ty up again and continuing on. They kept walking for another hour until they reached a decent-sized stream.

Hoping that they'd made it far enough, Ena suggested that they rest here so she could assess his wound better. They were deeper in the forest now, miles away from the Western Road. She hoped it was enough and that no one had tried to follow them.

Ty collapsed on the bank of the stream and closed his eyes, leaning against a large stump. Ena set to work building a fire next to him— small enough to avoid attracting too much attention, but big enough that it would provide enough light to see his wound better. Now that they were in the clearing of the stream, Ena could blessedly see the moon. It was waning, but only a few days past full, so it, too, provided some light to see by.

Starting the fire was harder than she thought. Her body and her magic were so exhausted. She'd never felt this drained before. It took her several tries to get the spark she needed, but once the fire was alight, Ena perched down next to Ty.

"Here, have some water," she said, offering him the waterskin from his pack.

He took the waterskin and drank deeply. Even the act of lifting the waterskin to his lips seemed to tire him, though, and he collapsed back against the stump.

Ena went to lift his shirt. "Are you ready?" she asked gently.

He closed his eyes and nodded in response.

After untying the crude wrapping she'd done, she lifted his shirt to reveal the deep stab wound. It was crusted with burned skin now, but it looked like the bleeding had slowed.

"I'll need to stitch it," Ena said, trying to keep her voice steady. "And then hope that it didn't do any significant damage internally." Ena knew that it very likely could have, and if the cauterization hadn't done its job, stitching up the wound on the outside wouldn't do much to help him, but she would do all she could.

"Just stitch it. I'll be fine," Ty said. When Ena stared at him skeptically, he continued. "Really. It's not my first stab wound. I heal fast," he said, trying to smile but grimacing instead.

Ena went into his pack and pulled out a small leather folding case that contained a bone needle and two wooden thread winders with simple black silk thread. She also took out one of his spare shirts and tore it into strips. She desperately wanted something to disinfect the wound with, but there were no pots with which to boil water. She didn't dare pour river water over it. That would be asking for infection.

As if sensing her train of thought, Ty gestured at his pack again. "Grab the flask in there."

Flask? Ena had never realized he had a flask. She dug around in the bag until she pulled out a small metal flask with a cork stopper that was attached to the bottleneck by a sturdy string. The craftsmanship was beautiful. It was decorated intricately with whirls and dots, not dissimilar from Ty's *onata*. Ena figured daemons could likely get whatever they wanted in return for trading these in the mortal villages. She'd never seen anything like it.

She cautiously removed the cork. Wine would certainly be better than river water for disinfecting, but why would he carry such a small amount of wine around?

As soon as the cork popped off, she knew it wasn't wine. A spicy, smoky aroma drifted out of the flask, and she brought it to her nose to take a bigger sniff. The scent instantly burned her nostrils, and she had to cough and snort to clear it from her sinuses.

"What in Gaia's name *is* this stuff?"

Ty, despite his weakened state, seemed highly amused by her reaction. He even tried to chuckle, but it quickly turned into a cough, and then a pained whimper. Once he'd made it through all that, he explained. "We call it woodwater. It's alcohol, stronger than wine or ale."

"Okay..." Ena said cautiously. If she hadn't been fervently trying to stop Ty's wound from bleeding, she would have asked how it was made. She'd have to save that for another time.

She made Ty lean forward slightly so she could remove his shirt all the way. She tried not to, but she couldn't help appreciating the way the muscles of his chest and shoulders were cut. The *onata* tattoos that trailed down his shoulders and arms highlighted their size, and even covered in blood, his abdominals were a sight to behold. A rich layer of soft, dark hair covered his wide chest and lower stomach, trailing below his pants. She noted absently that this had not been there before, all those years ago. One more marker of the time that had passed, and the ways they'd both changed.

After heating the needle in the fire to clean it and threading a long section of silk thread through the eye, she prepared to pour the woodwater over his wound. She knew it was pointless to warn him again, because it would hurt like a bitch either way, so she didn't hesitate as she dumped half the flask over the open wound.

Ty clenched his teeth and grimaced in pain, barely holding in the cry that must've been on the tip of his tongue. She gave him a second to recover from the stinging pain, before she set to work carefully stitching the wound closed.

Ena had stitched several wounds before, but never in the dead of night, and never with such rudimentary supplies. She had often assisted Heran with healing, both for witches in her Coven when accidents inevitably happened, or mortals who traveled to be healed by the matriarch. Heran was the best healer among all the Aquilo and Auster witches, both because of her vast knowledge of healing potions, and because of her Gift of *tempus*. It allowed her to manipulate time in small amounts and was an exceedingly rare Gift among the witches. Slowing down time often bought Heran critical seconds when treating a hemorrhaging wound or a quickly advancing illness. Ena was all of a sudden overcome with an intense wave of longing for the matriarch's calm, sturdy presence.

Ty closed his eyes tightly while she stitched the wound closed, but he didn't make a sound. When she finished, she wrapped the wound with another torn strip of shirt and was relieved to see that, while a little blood appeared, it no longer soaked through the makeshift bandage.

Ena wished she could do more. If he was mortal or another witch, she would gladly forage for the necessary herbs to make a disinfecting and healing poultice for the wound and imbue it with her magic to speed his healing and stave off infection. But she knew it was likely futile. Not even her Knowing worked on him, so her healing potions probably would not either.

Having done all she could, Ena helped Ty put his shirt back on. He leaned back against the tree, his eyes closed again.

Ena didn't know what to say. She didn't know what to think. So she mostly sat in silence, trying not to relive everything that had happened.

Ty was silent for so long, she thought maybe he'd fallen asleep. But then he spoke. "I didn't know you could fight like that," he said, his voice quiet and tired.

Ena turned to look at him. He was breathing shallowly, as if still in pain, but his face wasn't quite so pale anymore. She thanked Gaia for that.

"What do you mean?" she asked.

"The fire. The earth. Your *visanis*. It was...impressive. You truly are a force of nature." He spoke the last few words reverently, in a way that communicated so much more than his words said, and it was all too much for Ena to comprehend right now.

Did he remember when he'd called her that before? Did he mean it? Did she deserve to be complimented on her actions? She'd never done...anything like that before. Using her magic against mortals. Using it to kill. The use of magic in self-defense was theoretically allowed among witches, but it didn't happen very often. Witches were critical to the maintenance of the balance, so their lives were sacred and to be protected. But killing, except for the purpose of sustenance, was almost never Gaia's will. For witches to use their magic to kill was a slippery slope, one that could lead to chaos and discord between witches and mortals.

But Ena couldn't stop thinking about how easily it had come to her. How easily her *visanis*, which Heran had forbidden her to use, had come out of her. It had felt almost like...another side to herself that she'd never known was there before. She had been terrified, ready to fight for her life, and her mind had been so chaotic, it had almost felt like...

"Thank you," Ty said, interrupting her spiraling thoughts. "For helping me."

She looked up to find him staring at her. Their gazes connected, and the sincerity and vulnerability in his eyes made Ena's heart skip a beat. She hadn't seen him like that in so long. The light of the fire danced across his face, making his eyes glow in the dim light.

"You're welcome," Ena replied, giving him a tight, haunted smile in return. But she meant it. She didn't quite know where they stood, or how to feel about everything she'd done to those men, but she knew saving his life, helping him, was the right thing. Even if he was a daemon, even if it wasn't Gaia's will, it was hers.

"You should get some rest," she said.

He nodded solemnly at her, but didn't close his eyes right away. He just stared at her, watching her, as if reluctant to have her leave his sight. But exhaustion clearly won out, because after several minutes, he leaned his head back, and she heard his breathing slow and even out.

And then Ena was alone, staring at the fire as it burned down to ashes.

Chapter Nineteen

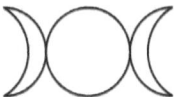

AT SOME POINT BEFORE dawn, Ena must've drifted off to sleep. When she opened her eyes, it was midmorning. Even though it felt like no time had passed, she had to have fallen asleep for several hours. She looked over at Ty, who was still leaning against the tree, passed out cold.

She set to work building up the fire again and took stock of their surroundings. The stream bubbled gently, its constant, steady flow a balm to Ena's nerves. The bent and leaning pine trees that lined its banks were friendly-looking, and Ena was pleased to see that the world was much the same as it had been before...everything.

She foraged around the banks for some bittercress and found some edible mushrooms. She knew that Ty's stash of jerky and apples was almost gone, so she decided to go deeper into the woods to set a trap for small game. She used her Knowing to locate a rabbit burrow, then, using the knife and twine she'd taken from Ty's pack, she whittled the sticks she needed into points and drove them into the ground, arranging them with the twine to create her trap just outside the entrance.

Once the trap was set, she started to walk back to where she'd left Ty. She really hoped her trap was successful, but if not, she wondered how she might use Ty's shirt as a net to catch one of the fish she'd seen jumping teasingly out of the river. She had just come to the conclusion that this was likely more trouble than it was worth, when she returned and saw Ty was awake.

He hadn't moved, but his eyes were open. He was staring blankly at the stream. When he heard her approaching, he whipped his head towards her, seeming startled by her appearance.

He stared at her like she was a mirage. Some raw emotion crossed his face that Ena didn't know what to make of. Relief? Joy? Desperation?

"What?" she asked, feeling suddenly concerned that something had happened.

"I thought you'd gone," he said, his voice tight.

"Oh," Ena replied, understanding dawning on her. He thought she'd run off and left him like this? "No, I was just setting a trap."

Ty nodded and quickly looked away from her. He was acting strangely.

"How do you feel? Do you need help?" Ena asked, reacting to the uncomfortable look on his face.

"Well," he said, dragging his hands down his face and clearly trying get whatever emotions he was feeling under control. "I feel like I've been run over by an elk, but mostly, I just desperately need a piss."

"Oh," Ena said again, laughing slightly in relief. She walked over and took as much of his weight as she could, helping him as he stood up stiffly. They stared at each other awkwardly for a second.

"Do you want me to...?" Ena asked, gesturing vaguely down at his crotch.

"No, no," he reassured her hurriedly, smiling. "I think I can manage on my own."

Then he shuffled off behind the nearest tree to relieve himself. He seemed to have a bit more strength this morning. Though he walked slowly, he didn't seem quite as weak and pained as he had last night. Maybe he really did heal as quickly as he'd said.

When he returned, Ena handed him his waterskin, the last of the jerky, and some bittercress. Once he'd eaten a little, he wordlessly laid down on his back and fell asleep again.

Ena spent the day fervently trying not to think about what had happened, and what in the Underworld she was doing. Ty had clearly thought she'd tried to escape again. Why hadn't she done that? The thought hadn't even crossed her mind.

Flashes of the night before kept coming back to her. Ty pulling the knife out of his side, then turning to look at her. The blaze of the fire as it engulfed those men. The sound of the man's head smacking into the tree when she used the air to shove him back into it. The way her *visanis* had felt flowing through her as she reached through the channel into the other man's mind.

She knew her life had been under threat, and so had Ty's, and she'd acted the only way she knew how at the time. She felt guilty for having to kill those men, and using her Gift when she was forbidden to. But the worst part? Part of her had loved it. She'd been completely out of control and yet completely *in* control for the first time in her life. It had been terrifying and empowering, and what that said about her, she wasn't sure. And that part scared her most of all.

Later in the day, she went back out to check her trap to find that Gaia had granted her a fat rabbit. When she got back to their camp, she saw that Ty was awake again. He sat up against the tree stump, drinking some water. He seemed less startled when he saw her emerge from the woods this time.

"I got us some dinner," she said, holding up the rabbit triumphantly.

"Great," Ty replied cautiously. Something in his tone was off. Like he was trying too hard to be nice. Something had changed between them, and she wasn't sure yet what it was or how to deal with it.

She brought the rabbit near the stream and proceeded to skin and gut it, letting the innards float away in the water. Then she speared the carcass on a large stick that she'd sharpened and set to work roasting it over the fire.

Ty was watching her pensively. A few times, he opened his mouth as if to speak to her, and then closed it again like he'd changed his mind. She could tell that now he was awake again, there were things to discuss. But she wasn't sure where to start, or if she was even ready to discuss anything, so she kept silent and focused on her task.

Once the rabbit was cooked, Ena and Ty passed the carcass back and forth, picking it clean and washing down the greasy meat with their waterskins. Ena was tempted to take a swig of the woodwater to steel herself for what she knew was coming, but she figured the smart thing to do would be to save it, in case of potential future injuries.

They finished eating in silence. The sun was just starting to get low in the sky when Ty finally spoke.

"Ena," Ty said quietly. That one word was heavy with unspoken sentiment.

She turned to look at him. The same vulnerability that had been in his eyes last night was there, the same emotions she did not know how to acknowledge.

"Why are you still here?" he asked simply. "You could have left hours ago and had half a day's head start on me. Iblis," he sighed, shaking his head. "I don't even know if I'd be able to track you successfully in this state. I think you know that too. Not to mention, you could have kept running when I told you to last night and left me to my fate, but you didn't. You came back to fight with me." He paused, pinning her with that intense gaze. "Why?"

Ena took a deep breath. She'd been asking herself the same question all day, and if she were being honest with herself, there were a lot of reasons. But one of them was because there were some things she needed to know.

"I'll answer that, if you answer something for me too," she said, meeting his gaze. There was no more beating around the bush. It was time to address hard truths. And Ty clearly agreed.

"Okay," Ty said, conviction in his voice. "I'll tell you whatever I can."

"Well," she said, wondering where to start. "First of all, I'm not a cold-hearted bitch. I couldn't just leave you to be murdered in cold blood while I fled into the woods. And I couldn't leave you to bleed to death with no help either. And then, well..." She fell silent for a second. This was maybe more than she'd been prepared to share with this man who'd betrayed her trust, but she felt it needed to be said. "I've never used my magic like that—to harm others. And I've never used my Gift before. I was forbidden to use it, unless expressly for Gaia's will. And... I used it to kill a man." She paused, letting her words sink in. This was the first time she'd admitted it out loud, and the truth of it hit her like a ton of bricks. "I don't quite know how I feel about that," she continued. "And so, I'm not sure I'm ready to go home right now. I'm not sure I could face them," she finished quietly, shame coloring her voice.

She hadn't admitted that out loud either, but it was true. She didn't know how she'd face Heran and Greya and the rest of her Coven after what she'd done. What would they think of her now? Witches were meant to maintain Gaia's balance and help mortals. They allowed death, didn't fight it when it was necessary, but they didn't actively encourage it, and they never purposefully caused it. But she had, and she'd felt so alive doing it. And now, deep down, she wasn't sure she was worthy of serving Gaia anymore.

Ty seemed to hear everything she didn't say. He was quiet for a minute, listening to her. Then he spoke softly, but confidently. "Ena, you acted in self-defense. I can't believe your Goddess, or your family, would fault you for that. Yes, the man was attacking me, your sworn enemy," the corner of his mouth curved up slightly at that description, "but had he killed me, he would have come for you next. And honestly...I didn't recognize those men, but there's a good chance their lawless state was a direct result of daemonic intervention. That guilt should be on me, not on you."

Ena was surprised. This was the first time she'd ever heard him express any sort of regret for serving Iblis. She didn't know what to make of that. She tried to take his words to heart, though, and they did soothe her guilt ever so slightly.

She nodded at him, but there was something else that weighed on her—something she'd barely been able to admit to herself. And Ty, being what he was, was the safest person she could think to say this to.

"I think," she started quietly, "when I used my magic like that, when I gave myself over to my Gift...I think I was channeling Iblis's will, not Gaia's."

Ty stared at her, his brow furrowed in concern. "What makes you say that?"

"Well, Heran told me that some Gifts could be shared between daemons and witches because our magic comes from the same source. We were created jointly by Iblis and Gaia." Ena waited to see a strong reaction at this information, but when Ty didn't give one, she continued. "I know that my Gift is one that daemons usually have, so maybe, when I use it, I'm naturally more inclined to channel Iblis, rather than Gaia. I mean, I felt so scared and chaotic during the fight, I didn't know what to do, so I let something...else inside me take over.

Something that felt disordered and disruptive, and not at all like Gaia. But," Ena added, looking away as tears of shame flooded her eyes, "I didn't dislike it. I felt powerful and...I know in the moment, that saved me, but it was wrong."

Ty reached out with his hand, as if to comfort her, then brought it back as if thinking twice. He was quiet for a minute as her words sunk in. "Look at me, Ena," he said. When she didn't, couldn't, lift her gaze to him, he reached out gently with his hand and tilted her chin towards him. Their eyes met, and his were solemn and filled with understanding. "Violence...it requires that. It requires you to give in to the absolute chaos of life and death. Even if you didn't want to, you did what you had to do, and it sounds like you know that. Who's to say whether it was Gaia's will or not? I won't judge you, and no one else has to ever know."

He gently released her chin but she didn't look away. His words warmed her heart more than they should. For a minute, she felt like she was speaking once more to Ty the young mortal, not Ty the grown daemon. The way he seemed to understand her, and she him. How had they gotten so far from this? How were they back here once again?

"Can I ask you something then?" Ena asked, her tone serious.

"Alright," he said. The sunset illuminated his face in golden purples and blues, and he met her stare with his eternally intense gaze.

"Why didn't you come back? All those years ago." Ena's voice shook, even though she tried to steel it. "You promised you would. And...I know you regret it. I understand that it should never have happened, because of what we are." Saying those words, though she'd tried to convince herself a thousand times over that they were true, still felt like a knife to her heart. "But I need to know. Was it all a lie?"

Ty looked away from her to stare at the fire. For a second, she wasn't sure if he would answer, that maybe she was wrong to bring this up and they should have left the past in the past, but then he looked up at her again, and that intense vulnerability was back in his eyes. There was sadness there, and regret, and longing, but underneath it, Ena could feel his simmering rage.

"I wanted to come back, Ena. So badly," he said quietly, intensely. "I tried, the next year. I tried to convince my uncles to let me go back, but they wouldn't. That summer..." He sighed, shaking his head slightly. "You probably guessed this already, but we weren't on that trip to establish trade relationships for our metal goods. We were there on a mission from Iblis to spread disease. It was my first mission, actually. My first time mingling with mortals and witches. One of my uncles has the power to amplify the spread of infectious diseases through touch, and so he mingled with travelers during your Litha celebration to spread a plague that they would carry back to their home villages. I was there to assist him and add to the cover."

Ena stared at him in horror, memories from the fall and winter after they met clicking into place. "I remember the outbreak that year. We worked constantly that fall and winter to keep people from dying in villages all up and down the Chasm Road. That was you?"

"My uncle, but yes," Ty confirmed, a defensiveness in his voice. "It was us. That's what daemons do, Ena...whether we like it or not." His eyes turned hard as he stared at her.

"And you don't like it?" Ena asked. She'd never thought of daemons as being reluctant servants of Iblis. She thought they all did it gladly and willingly.

"No, I don't," he replied, looking back at the fire. "Not always. But it doesn't change what I have to do. And that's why I couldn't come back. That next summer, after we met, I tried to convince them to bring me on another mission with them, thinking I could sneak off and go see you. But they wouldn't allow it. I think they knew," he said ruefully. "I was supposed to mingle with the witches and the mortals that summer, to maintain our cover, but I think they saw that I got a little too...invested in you."

Ty paused, as if waiting to see if she would say anything, but Ena was speechless. This was more than she knew what to do with.

"The summer after that," he continued, "I went on my own. I wanted to see you that badly." He smiled sadly at this confession, shaking his head at his own foolishness. "I made it halfway there before they caught up with me and dragged me back. They beat me within an inch of my life and said they'd do the same to you if I tried it again. And that's when I realized that I was a fool." Ty's voice turned hard again, the rage he felt creeping into it like a spreading wildfire. "I was so incredibly stupid for ever thinking something could be possible between us."

He looked at Ena then, and his eyes were filled with a desperate, cold certainty. "You didn't know I was a daemon, but I knew you were a witch. And I knew what happened to my mother. So, after they finally beat some sense into me, I decided to forget you. In fact," he scoffed, seeming to get angrier now at these recollections, "I spent years sleeping with anyone and everyone who would have me, trying to get you out of my head, but it didn't help. I never forgot you, Ena. Never. In fact, I'm so obsessed with you, I think you've ruined me for anyone else for the rest of my life. And part of me hates you for it, because I know I can never have you."

His green eyes were glowing in the fire as darkness fell around them. His face was hard, and there was pain behind his eyes, mixed with the rage that she knew was always there, just under the surface. Whether it was for her, or his uncles, or the whole Goddess-damned world, she wasn't sure. But hearing his words, hearing his confession, she felt it too. And it was too much; it was all too much.

"You hate *me*?" Ena asked incredulously. She couldn't believe the hypocrisy of that statement, and everything she'd worked so hard to push down, down, down, came exploding out of her. "I waited for you that next summer, and the next, and the next. I asked every traveler I saw if they knew how to get a letter to Yalta, but no one had even heard of it. I was pathetic," Ena spat. "By the fourth year, I knew you weren't coming back and I felt like such an idiot."

Ena quieted then, shaking her head. She spoke her next words carefully. "I know you're not the same person you were back then—you've made that abundantly clear. I mean, Gaia, I thought you were mortal. But I'm not the same girl you met either. Something died in me when you didn't come back. Something broke. And I'll never get it back."

Tears filled her eyes at the truth of those words. She'd felt so broken, so lost, since that summer. She'd never been able to get back the feeling of being alive like she was when she was with him. It was as if she'd put all her hopes and dreams for her life into one person, who had abandoned her, leaving her empty. And Gaia, she knew how pathetic that sounded, how fucked up that was, and it made her even angrier.

"I've pushed away every single guy who's tried to get close to me since then. For fuck's sake, I haven't even—" Ena paused, shaking her head. Some wounds were too deep to reveal, even now. "I told myself I just didn't want a relationship, that I hadn't met the right person, but I think a part of me has always been waiting for you to come back. And now, here you are, you came back. And you've absolutely ruined me. So you know what? I think I hate you too."

She went quiet, letting her confession echo through the woods. All she could hear was her heart beating, and all she could do was fight back her own tears.

Ty watched her in silence, the energy crackling between them. Eventually, he looked away, staring back at the fire. "Well, at least we have that in common," he said sadly.

Together, they watched the fire dwindle, and when Ena had finally calmed down enough, she curled up on her side under her cloak to fall asleep. Ty did the same, laying down on the opposite side of the fire on his uninjured side.

Ena was cold, but she'd never admit she secretly longed to sleep next to him again. That the feeling of his body heat and his steady breathing would be a comfort after all the emotional and physical distress she'd been through.

As she drifted off to sleep, Ena wondered vaguely whether it was normal to yearn so deeply for comfort from someone you hated.

CHAPTER TWENTY

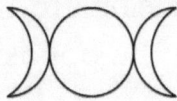

ENA WOKE UP BEFORE Ty and was glad for it. She loved the peace of the early morning. The simplicity and the quiet. And now more than ever, she needed some space to clear her head.

As she walked through the woods to check her traps, her mind replayed all that had been said last night, each word stabbing deeper and deeper into her heart.

Ty hadn't been pretending. He had actually cared for her. He had tried to get back to her. Those thoughts warmed her in ways she felt scared of. While they made her feel slightly less like an idiot for clinging to the memory of that summer for so long, they'd also rekindled a hope in her that she knew was unhealthy and unwarranted.

But hearing about the things he'd done, the things his uncles had done... He was bound to serve Iblis, no matter whether he wanted to or not. Like he'd said, that's what daemons did. And she was a witch. She could never condone the things he was forced to do. So it was all the more clear why they could never be together. Why it would never work. Part of her mourned that loss, even now. Even this many years later, and after everything that had happened.

But maybe it was a good thing that she finally knew the whole truth. Maybe now, she could finally move on.

She knew she was still stuck with him until he decided to let her go. He was healed enough now that he'd come after her if she tried to leave. But, like she'd shared last night, she wasn't sure she was ready to face her Coven. Not now. Not after everything. Maybe if she saw this through and was able to find out why they wanted the amulet—or, better yet, if she was able to take the amulet for herself—she could face them again. Then she'd have a way to atone for the ways she'd disrupted Gaia's balance.

A plan started to take shape in her mind. She'd told Ty and the others only where the house was and what it had looked like. They didn't know about the trunk, or the box inside it. If she could somehow get to it first, and hide it, then she could try to escape again. Or hopefully they'd let her go when they didn't find it. She'd admit, it wasn't the most well-thought-out plan. There were a lot of variables to contend with. But it was the best she had for now.

She was so lost in her thoughts that it took her a second to sense that something was wrong. Ty had been there when she got back to camp, but he hadn't moved. It was midmorning now, and he hadn't even gotten up to drink water or pee. She approached him to check on him, and noticed he was shivering. She'd built up the fire, so it wasn't that cold where he was. She moved to touch his shoulder, to try and wake him up, and the heat of his body almost scalded her. He was burning up.

Moving around to face him, she shook his shoulder gently. "Ty? Ty, wake up," she called gently. When he didn't stir, she shook harder. "Ty!"

He slowly, groggily, opened his eyes. They were hooded with fever, his body sluggish as he raised his head.

"Ty, you have a bad fever. I need to check your wound," Ena said. She tried hard to keep herself calm, but she knew fevers like this were very dangerous. Despite what he'd said about his healing capabilities, without access to clean conditions and healing potions, the risk of infection from his wound would be serious.

She helped him sit up and lean back against the tree stump again. She gave him some water to drink, and that seemed to revive him slightly.

"It's okay," he said, sounding tired. "The fever is normal for us."

But Ena wasn't convinced. She lifted up his shirt to reveal the bandage on his wound. She unwound it gently, and checked the stitches. The wound was red and swollen, but that was to be expected. There wasn't any pus, nor were there any red lines coming from it, so it couldn't be that badly infected. Still, his skin was like a million degrees, raging like an inferno. She couldn't believe that was normal.

"Come on," she said. "I want to get you in the river. The cold water will bring your fever down, and it'll help clean all the dirt and blood from around your wound."

"Ena, really, you don't have to fuss. I'll be fine."

She maybe would've believed this if his teeth weren't chattering in his skull like he was naked in the dead of winter.

"Indulge me. Please," Ena said. She stared right into his eyes, giving him her most wide-eyed, pleading look. She was trying to keep her tone light, but inside, her stomach was knotted in worry.

"Fine," he grumbled, "but don't blame me when you're freezing your tits off the rest of the day."

Ena smiled lightly at his joke. He couldn't be feeling that bad if he was cracking jokes, right? She clung to that hope.

She helped him out of his dirty coat and shirt while he was sitting, then she helped him stand and lean against a tree while he undid his pants and slid them down his body.

Maybe she hadn't thought this through. His back was facing her and she saw...a lot. Her eyes roamed his broad, muscular back and shoulders, and lower... Oh, Gaia. The muscles of his ass were rock hard and perfectly sculpted. Fuck, was he made of stone? Maybe that was why he always smelled like stone...She was openly staring now and caught in some sort of trance, almost forgetting why she was making him do this in the first place. Even all those years ago when they swam, and when they were... together, she'd never seen this much of him. It made her regret the way they'd done it frantically and half-clothed like the hormone-crazed teenagers they had been.

She must've made some sound because Ty turned around and caught her staring. Their eyes locked for a second before an extremely mischievous grin came across his face, despite his feverish state. "You know, some people think staring is rude," he said.

Broken from her reverie, and her face heating in embarrassment, she rolled her eyes at him. "Oh, hush," she said. "Just wait right there for a minute and try not to collapse while I take off my dress, and then I'll help you into the water."

He did as he was told while Ena shimmied out of her worn black dress, boots, and cloak. She kept her shift on. It wasn't ideal, since she'd have to take it off and hang it to dry afterward, but there was no reason they should both be naked for this. Things were bound to be awkward enough.

She walked over to Ty and grabbed his arm, keeping her eyes firmly on his face and torso, before leading him to the water's edge. Together, they stepped into the bitter-cold water. The stream wasn't very deep. They navigated carefully over the rocks, which were slippery and tore slightly at Ena's feet, while she took Ty's weight on her shoulders to help him balance.

Ena shivered as the water reached her thighs, then her hips, and eventually her waist, but Ty's arm was so burning hot around her that it was manageable.

They stopped in the middle of the stream where the water came to Ty's hips. Blessedly, it covered his manhood now, so Ena safely turned to him with her arm looped around his waist to support him.

The river swirled around them as it rushed to the ocean. For a second, Ena was transported to a much warmer night, in a much warmer river, many years ago.

Ty had held her then, coaching her through her fear. She looked up at him and saw the same ghost of a memory in his eyes, both of them feeling the ways the past was still present.

Ena dipped her free hand in the cold water and lifted it to the back of Ty's neck. He closed his eyes as the water cupped in her hand ran down his back, then she did the same over his chest. She gently wiped the water over his arms and torso, washing away dirt and blood from the attack, while taking care not to get any in his wound. She brushed her wet hand over his cheeks, across his brow, and through his hair, feeling the rough stubble growing on the shaved sides of it, until soon she became lost in the majesty of his beauty, of his strength. The way the muscles of his arms sloped under her hands, the way his chest rose and fell with each deep breath, and the way his heart beat steadily underneath. She wanted to run her fingers through the hair on his chest, and brush her thumb over his lip. She wanted to trail a finger down his neck and place a kiss on his eyelids. He was so painfully perfect, she wanted to do so, so much more than she should.

"How does that feel?" she asked, her voice coming out quiet after their long silence.

He opened his eyes to look at her, and the same feeling of longing that throbbed in her chest was reflected in his eyes. "Better," he said, his voice low and rough. "Much better."

She saw his eyes flick down to her lips, and the way he was looking at her was too much. Everything she felt was too much. She knew what this could easily lead to, and that it would only bring more pain and heartbreak for them both, so she looked away and removed her hands from him.

They stood there in the water for another minute or two, until slowly, slowly, she felt his body temperature come back down, and she guided Ty out of the water.

After they'd both gotten dressed again, Ena built up the fire as big as she dared to try and warm herself up. Ty resumed his spot by the fire, laying on his side. He was asleep again in minutes. Everything was quiet as Ena watched him sleep. She didn't need to—she knew he was likely fine, just as he'd insisted—but she couldn't help herself from reaching over to him and touching his shoulder lightly. His temperature was still warm, but better now, and she felt thoroughly relieved.

She finally dragged her gaze away from him, wondering how they both might feel about this tomorrow, and the next day. She knew that they were walking a very dangerous line now, but she couldn't bring herself to regret it.

CHAPTER TWENTY-ONE

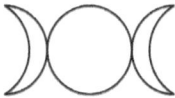

"I'M FEELING WELL ENOUGH to continue on today," Ty announced the next morning.

"Okay," she replied, side-eying him with skepticism. There was no denying that he did look significantly better today. His fever was gone, his color was normal, and she'd taken another look at his wound to find it already half-healed.

"I told you, the fever yesterday was normal. Daemons heal substantially faster than mortals and witches. It burned whatever infection was there out of me, and now I'm fine," he said patiently, as if explaining something rudimentary to a child.

"Alright, if you say so," Ena said, as she lovingly ate the mushrooms she'd cooked over the fire this morning.

"I still need you to come with me," he said cautiously, as if it wasn't obvious. As if something had changed between them.

"I know," she said. She'd already decided to see this through, knowing it was the only way to redeem herself to her Coven, and to Gaia. Now was not the time to get stubborn about it.

"But I meant what I said. I promise I'll do my best to keep you safe, and once you help us find the amulet, I'll let you go."

Ena paused as she ate, wiping her fingers off on her cloak. "You have a history of making promises you can't keep, you know," she said, not unkindly.

Ty looked at her with sincerity. "I know. And for what it's worth...I'm sorry. For not coming back when I said I would."

His face was serious, no hint of the joking Ty, or the angry mask Ty liked to wear. She knew he meant it, but it didn't make the fact that he hadn't come back any easier. It didn't erase the past. But still, it meant something to hear him say it.

"I know," Ena said again, quietly.

After packing up the rest of their stuff, which wasn't much, and putting out their fire, she let Ty's impeccable sense of direction lead them as they continued heading west.

"How far do you think we are from Attax? I know we lost some time after the...attack." She said the last word cautiously. She didn't like talking about it. She didn't like remembering it. Every time she did, her heart started beating faster and her palms got sweaty. She wondered when that would stop.

"I'd say we're about a day out. We should be there by tomorrow afternoon. We'll meet Steig and Turner at the guesthouse there and then continue on together to the Occidens Coven."

Ty watched her to gauge her reaction to that, but she just nodded and continued walking.

They moved in amicable silence most of the day. The air between them did seem to be clearer after their confessions and whatever they had shared in the river yesterday.

But Ena knew, despite the feelings they'd had in the past, that wasn't where they both were at now, or at least, it shouldn't be. They might have been friendly with one another, but if anything, they were adversaries. He was using her. She was attempting to thwart him. It was a strictly platonic, adversarial relationship.

I'm so obsessed with you. I think you've ruined me for anyone else for the rest of my life.

His words from the other night came back to her, and they brought a strange twisting feeling to her chest. Despite his insistence that a part of him hated her, and that he had been foolish for thinking they could be together, she remembered the way he had looked at her in the river yesterday. And when she'd returned from the woods after he thought she'd left him. And now the apology... She didn't quite know what to make of it all, so she did what she did best and shoved all her confusing feelings and thoughts aside so she could focus on the task at hand.

They made good time, even though Ena insisted on stopping and resting more frequently out of concern for Ty's injury. They camped once more in the back-woods that night. Ty was back to insisting that she sleep next to him lest she escape. Admittedly, she thought his reasoning was pretty flimsy at this point; they both knew she was unlikely to try to escape again. But she didn't complain. The weather was starting to turn colder, and she wanted his body heat.

They awoke with the dawn to continue on their way, and by midafternoon, they finally, blessedly, came to a large, busy dirt road. The road was significant—just as established as the Chasm Road. It was about twenty feet wide with rutted tracks from all the carts that went up and down it. Every few minutes, a group of travelers passed by, mostly on horseback, although there were a few people on foot pushing handcarts. Ena knew from studying old maps that this part of the road was highly populated with villages, so it made sense that some people would travel on foot between them.

They kept to themselves and tried to keep a low profile as they traveled along it for a few miles before they came to a bustling village— Attax. Their timing was blessed by Gaia, because as they approached, rain clouds tumbled overhead, threatening to pummel them with rain any second.

Attax itself was fairly large, about as large as Northumbra, the closest mortal village to her Coven. It had all manner of stone and wooden houses and buildings, including a stable, a wood mill, a small blacksmith, and even, it looked like, a book binder's shop. In the distance, she saw plowed agricultural fields and large animal pens with cows and pigs. It appeared as if it was a substantial trade hub, catering to travelers coming to and from the coast on a regular basis.

They wandered down the main dirt road through the village until they came to the guesthouse. It was a large, two-story stone building with wooden shingles, several chimneys, and likely enough space for ten or more guest rooms. It even had a wide porch that wrapped around the entire structure, where Ena saw patrons relaxing in chairs drinking mugs of ale.

She was distracted, taking in all the sights and sounds, when suddenly, the clouds broke and it started to rain. Ena was shocked as Ty grabbed her hand and rushed her under the cover of the porch.

"Thanks," she said, looking up at him breathlessly.

"I think we've both been wet enough lately, don't you agree?" he asked, flashing her a charming smile before pushing open the door into the guesthouse.

It was a cozy place, with a large, warm fireplace at the back, and a half-dozen sturdy-looking wooden tables dotted across the room with an abundance of chairs scattered around them. Several different groups of travelers were clustered around the room, some standing by the fire, others sitting and eating. And everyone was drinking and talking.

Ena hadn't realized how isolated they had been in the backwoods for so long. It felt so *nice* to be around people again—to hear their vibrant chatter, smell the scents of freshly baked bread. Not to mention, just being in a warm, sheltered environment felt like absolute heaven.

Looking around the room, Ena saw that there was no bar like at most guesthouses. Instead, there was a large desk near the front door where a brown-haired man in his mid-forties sat writing in a record book. Ena and Ty approached him as he looked up at them with a genial smile, removing his glasses from where they'd been perched on his nose.

"Great timing, eh?" he said, gesturing to the down-pour occurring outside.

"Indeed, my good sir," Ty replied, smiling charmingly and putting on the same overly polite air he'd donned at Tritam. Ena resisted rolling her eyes at the act. How did people keep falling for this?

The man looked them both over with a slightly judg-mental air, clearly noting their bedraggled appearance. "Been traveling a long time, have you?" he asked.

"Yes, my good sir, we come from over the Chasm Mountains, from a village known as Yalta. We have a great forge there where we make all sorts of metallic goods we were hoping to trade. Alas, my wife and I were set upon by bandits on the road, and most of our goods, including our horses and our cart, were stolen from us."

Ena whipped her head at him. She didn't know what shocked her more: his use of the word "wife," or him bringing up the bandits as a cover story. He didn't even flinch or look at her. Clearly, this was a cover story he'd prepared ahead of time, and she guessed it made sense and would make them look less suspicious. But a little head's up would've been nice, if only to save her from the shock.

"Oh dear!" the man replied. "I do hope you are alright. We've heard rumors of a group of outlaws roaming the woods near the Western Road as of late. Most of them hail from Ternan, a small village just northeast of here that was destroyed by a wildfire not six months ago. Many of the residents were absorbed by other near-by villages, but there's often only so much room, you know, and what with winter setting in soon... Oh dear." The man tsked and shook his head in sympathy.

Little did he know, that group of outlaws wouldn't be a problem anymore. Ena wondered how long it would be before word spread of the massacre in the woods. Clearly, no one had found the bodies yet.

"Yes, I'm sure the circumstances were tragic," Ty replied, placing his hand over his heart in a sympathetic gesture. "We survived unharmed, thank Gaia, but alas, we only have so many objects left to trade. However, we were hoping to spend the night and secure a horse so we can journey home." Then Ty looked over Ena appraisingly for a second before adding, "And get a new dress for my wife here."

Ty gestured at her with this last word, and while she should've been mad that he was calling her out on her disheveled appearance, she was so happy to be getting a clean dress that she had to stop herself from verbally thanking him. She hadn't mentioned anything to him about her slow, building hatred for this dress, but clearly, her appearance was so rough that he'd figured it out on his own.

"Yes, yes, that should be able to be arranged. Let's see what you've got." The man gestured to Ty's pack.

"Sweetheart, why don't you go settle in at a table while I negotiate with this good man here." Ty looked at her expectantly, clearly wanting her to play along.

She gave him a quick death glare, before smiling sweetly and wandering off to an empty table.

She watched from afar as Ty took out the few remaining weapons and metal goods he'd brought and haggled with the recordkeeper. After several minutes, they seemed to reach an agreement as the man recorded their transaction in his book and Ty came over to sit with her.

"They said someone will be out soon with some food and ale for us. They'll bring a dress your size to our room, and I had to trade one of my good daggers, but I was able to secure us one of their best horses."

"Well done, sweetheart." Ena smiled with faux sweetness at him, and he chuckled lightly in return.

"I knew you'd hate that," he said, smiling widely. "But it just makes sense for our cover, you know, so be a good girl and play along."

Ena narrowed her eyes at that, but something about the way he said it made her stomach flutter.

He was right, though. She didn't want to be found out any more than he did at this point, not this close to the Occidens Coven. She'd pretend to be his wife, she'd pretend to be a trader from the other side of the Chasm Mountains, as long as it kept her identity as an Auster witch hidden.

"Yes, Master," she replied.

Ty whipped his head to her, his eyes flaring with desire. So she hadn't been mistaken the last time she'd called him that—Ty *did* clearly like it. How interesting... The corner of her mouth tipped up mischievously at him just as a woman in her mid-forties approached their table.

The woman, possibly the wife of the recordkeeper, brought them two large mugs of ale, some cheese, beef stew, and freshly baked bread. Ena was so overwhelmed by the prospect of eating food other than jerky and bittercress that she almost teared up. But, deciding there wasn't time for all that, she simply dug in without another word.

Ena and Ty ate companionably in silence, clearly both exclusively focused on the delicious food they'd been given. When she'd finished everything and was wiping her bowl clean with a piece of bread, she felt like she finally was able to think rationally again. The first thing she realized was that, ostensibly, their daemonic companions should be joining them soon, but she hadn't seen any sign of them.

"Where are Turner and Steig?" she asked, looking around the room as if they might pop out from behind one of the tables.

"I inquired about them with the recordkeeper. They've been staying here on and off, posing as bards, but they're out right now. They should be back soon."

Ena almost spat her ale out. "*Bards*?!" she asked, as she wiped some of the beer from her chin.

Ty laughed at her reaction, wiping some ale she'd sprayed at him off his sleeve. "Yes, bards," he said. "Steig has quite a good singing voice, actually."

Ena was still trying to wrap her mind around that when the woman returned and offered to show them to their room. Suddenly aching for an actual bed, Ena eagerly followed her as she led the way up a wide, angular staircase to the second floor. The building was actually three floors; it looked like there was a third attic level without windows that contained rooms, as well, but their room was on the second. She led them down a dark hallway into a nice-sized room tucked at the back of the house.

"If you'll be needing a wash, there's a communal bath-house just downstairs past the kitchens. I can have one of the girls prepare it with hot water if you'd like," she said, as she held the door open for them to enter.

"Yes," Ty and Ena spoke simultaneously, their tones indicating their eagerness at the idea.

The woman smiled and nodded at them before leaving them to settle in.

Ena took in the room with awe. It was clean and simple, with a bed large enough for two and a small dining table complete with two cushioned chairs. In the corner was a washstand with a pitcher of fresh water and a basin for washing. The room was fairly dark, but there were several candles lit around the room, and a small window that faced the woods behind the guesthouse. There was also a small fireplace stocked with cut wood and dry kindling.

All in all, it was nothing special, but after weeks of sleeping on the ground and foraging for her own firewood, it felt so wonderful to have all these amenities right at her fingertips. She almost started to tear up again.

Ty barely seemed to notice her overly intense reaction. He simply put his pack on the ground and got to work building a fire in the hearth.

Ena walked over to the bed to find that a clean dress and shift had been left for her. The dress was long-sleeved and plain, made out of a simple handspun wool dyed the color of mud. It had a built-in bodice that laced in the front with sturdy cotton laces—much more practical than the decorative ribbon on her current disaster of a dress. And, Gaia be blessed, the neckline was significantly more modest. She was eternally grateful that her chest would be warmer and her breasts at significantly lower risk of spilling out going forward.

After starting the fire to warm the room, Ena and Ty walked back downstairs, through the dining room where they'd eaten, and past the kitchens to the small communal bathhouse that was adjacent to it. It was a tiny room with a large copper bathtub that took up half the space, a stool, and a vanity with a mirror, basin, and pitcher. Someone had kindly filled the bath with steaming hot water and set out a fresh bar of soap and two worn towels on the stool.

Ena stared at the bath like it was a vision of Gaia herself. Assuming she'd take the first bath, which was only kind enough, considering she was here by force, she walked into the bathhouse elated, and so, so ready to get in the warm tub, but as she went to close the door behind her, Ty stopped it with his foot.

"Uh-uh, viper. I'm coming in too," he said with a cocky grin on his face.

"Excuse me?" Ena hissed, trying to keep her voice quiet so as not to attract attention.

"There's a window in here." He gestured to the small, foggy-glass window behind her. "I'm not leaving you alone in here so you can run off again."

Ena looked at the window, then she looked at Ty. There was no possible way she could even fit through that fucking window and he knew it.

"Ty," she said, mustering all her patience. "I just want a bath. Desperately. I'm not going to run anywhere. Besides, that window is tiny. I don't even know if I'd fit, and I know you'll just come chasing after me anyway."

Ty made a show of considering this for a second, then said, "Nope, sorry, I can't take that chance."

Ena glared at him. She knew what he was playing at. This wasn't about stopping her from escaping. He was toying with her. Pushing her buttons on purpose. This was just another one of his challenges to see if she'd back down. She knew if she fought him on it, he'd likely love that even more and still come in anyway.

She let out an extremely put-upon sigh, then asked, "Is this payback for me staring at you before we got in the stream?"

"Sure, let's call it that," he replied, grinning wolfishly.

She rolled her eyes and opened the door wider so he could follow her in.

"Don't worry. I'll let you go first," he said, gesturing to the fresh water.

She eyed him before turning around to start unlacing her dress. She heard him settle on the stool behind her, and looked over her shoulder to see that he had his back to her and was facing the door. His attempt at protecting her modesty was laughable considering she knew expressly why he'd insisted on coming in with her. The dirty pervert.

She turned back and shrugged quickly out of her dress. She wondered absently if they'd be able to launder it for her so she could keep it with her as a spare, then she stepped delicately into the bath.

The water was so hot it hurt a little bit at first, but Gaia, it felt amazing. She let out an indecent moan as she lowered herself into the water and tilted her head back to dip her hair in too. Out of the corner of her eye, she saw Ty inconspicuously adjust himself under his pants while he stared studiously at the wall. Ena smiled privately to herself, pleased that she was at least inflicting some revenge on him. That's what he got for insisting on coming in. If he thought to get a rise out of her and throw her off, well, she would not make it easy on him.

Ena took her time scrubbing herself down with the lavender-scented soap. The almost two weeks' worth of dirt and grime took a long time to come off. Then she took her time washing her hair—twice—and finally, after all that was done, she sat low in the tub, soaking her bones and absently picking out the dirt from under her fingernails.

"Are you done yet?" Ty groaned. "Iblis, you're taking fucking forever. You've gotta be a prune by now."

Ena rolled her eyes, even though he couldn't see her. "Fine," she sighed loudly. "Hand me that towel then."

Ty went to grab the towel from where he'd placed it on the vanity, and, as he turned to hand it to her, she stood up in the bath.

The water dripped down her body, sliding over her chest, her stomach, her hips and thighs. Her long, wet hair just barely covered her breasts, and she knew exactly what she was doing.

She innocently reached out to take the towel, as if it was no big deal, but Ty's eyes were frozen on her chest. Then they went lower. She saw his throat bob as he swallowed, then he lifted his eyes to meet hers. His gaze was predatory, as if he was watching her every movement, taking in every facial expression.

"You're playing a dangerous game, viper," he said, his voice deep and rough with desire.

"Game? Who's playing a game?" Ena asked innocently, raising an eyebrow. "I'm just all wet and cold," she said, crossing her arms over her breasts as if to warm them and giving them a gentle squeeze that served no purpose but to squish them together. "Please can I have that towel...Master?"

The word "Master" seemed to break him, and he growled. He threw the towel at her and turned quickly around.

She let out a sultry laugh as she wrapped herself with it, thoroughly pleased with herself at having ruined his power move.

She stepped out of the bath, lamenting her exit, and turned her back as Ty removed his clothes and got into the significantly dirtier water.

She put on the new, clean shift that she'd brought with her, then she spent an absurdly long time combing her fingers through her hair, trying to get the tangles out before she re-braided it. She heard Ty splashing around in the bath, presumably cleaning himself, but, feeling that she'd already had her revenge, she gave him his privacy.

By the time she was done with her hair, Ty had gotten out and dried off with his own towel. She kept her back turned while he got dressed, and then when he indicated he was ready, they walked back to their room.

The sun was setting now, and with her belly full for the first time in weeks, her body finally clean of all the dirt, grime, and persistent campfire smoke smell, she suddenly felt exhausted. The room was warm now, the fire having warmed it thoroughly while they were gone, so Ena crawled into the bed without another word to Ty. She knew they'd be sharing the bed—there was no question about that—but it didn't concern her since they'd already been sleeping next to each other for the last week.

Ty didn't follow her right away, though. He watched as she tucked herself in, then he took a seat at the table. She saw him take his whetstone out of his pack and slowly, methodically, begin to sharpen his knife.

Ena fell asleep in seconds to the soothing sounds of the whetstone dragging across his blade.

CHAPTER TWENTY-TWO

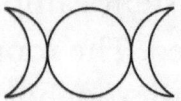

ENA WAS RUNNING THROUGH the dark woods, her heart pounding, but she didn't know where she was going. She turned around when she heard a man laughing—an evil, menacing sound that echoed through the woods.

Behind her, there were five men holding Ty down on the forest floor. He was struggling in a blind rage, spitting and thrashing like an animal. She watched as one of them raised a sharp dagger and thrust it deeply into Ty's chest again and again, stabbing him repeatedly. His blood spurted everywhere until he was drenched in it and it pooled around him like milk spilled on the floor.

She opened her mouth and screamed, her fear and rage and helplessness flooding out of her. She felt her Gift growing, growing, growing inside her. Her head was full of terror and chaos and she wanted them to *die*.

She knew it was wrong, and that Gaia would abandon her for it, but she reached for it. She let it grow through her, making her powerful, giving her control. She cracked open her mouth to speak when a blinding white light appeared.

Raising her arm to shield her eyes from the light, Ena was reminded of the bone-deep terror she'd experienced during her Summoning, and all at once, she Knew. Gaia had come to punish her—to take away her magic. She cried out to beg for mercy and then—

"Ena," a voice gently called to her. "Ena! Wake up."

Ena's eyes snapped open and she sat up, looking around frantically. She was in a dark room and it was stiflingly hot. She turned to her right to see Ty, shirtless and sitting up on the bed next to her, reaching out as if he was about to touch her, but was unsure of himself.

"Ena, are you okay? You were having a dream," he said.

A dream. It was a dream.

Ena rested her head in her hands as she remembered where she was. The guesthouse in Attax. She was in a room with Ty. She'd fallen asleep, and slept deeper than she had in weeks. The room was warm because the fire had just died down after burning hotly for hours, and Ty was sleeping next to her, putting off his own heat like an inferno.

She took a deep breath, calming her pounding heart. "I'm fine," she replied quietly. "Sorry, I-I was having a nightmare."

"It's okay," Ty said gently. He continued to watch her, clearly unsure of what to do. Ena just sat there, making no move to lay down again.

"Did you want to talk about it?" he asked cautiously.

Ena didn't know what she wanted. She'd been trying hard not to think about it all, and since they'd arrived in Attax, there'd been plenty of distractions helping her keep her mind off it. But the dream had made her viscerally remember the fear she'd felt during the attack. She remembered running through the dark, fearing for Ty's life, and using her magic in ways she never thought she could. Using her *visanis* to make that man slit his own throat. She remembered wanting them to suffer—to die—and part of her thriving in the knowledge that she was capable of doing it.

She remembered those dark feelings, and her guilt and shame over them mixed with her fear as tears came to her eyes. Then she looked over at Ty in the dim light, and she remembered other feelings that were equally as dangerous. And all at once, everything came crashing down in such painful clarity.

She was in bed with a daemon. The same daemon she'd foolishly, willingly fell for years ago, and had never moved on from. A daemon who, if she were being honest, she wasn't even trying to get away from anymore. A daemon who was drawing her in, making her care about him again, making her *want* him.

Gaia, what in the Underworld was she doing? She was losing her grip on herself. She'd always been one of the best witches in her Coven. Always helping people, perfecting her potions and spellwords, serving Gaia, and maintaining the balance. That was her path.

What path was she on now?

All at once, she felt so out of control and scared and...unworthy. The tears started to spill over and she turned her face away from Ty so he wouldn't see.

"Hey, hey," Ty said, sensing her distress. "It's alright, Ena. You're safe here, you're safe. I won't let anyone hurt you. You know that, right?"

She nodded as he wrapped his arms around her gently. But he didn't know that it wasn't others she was afraid of. It was herself.

She started to sob, but she couldn't bring herself to say it out loud. Ty had never judged her over what happened. He'd understood she'd done what was necessary, and she wanted nothing more but to allow him to comfort her, to hold her, and reassure her that she was still good. And that Gaia still loved her. She knew, if given the chance, he would tell her that, all of that, and he would make her feel seen and worthy again. And she was so, so grateful for that. For him.

So she let him hold her, and slowly stroke her hair, as she sobbed quietly into his chest.

When her crying gradually stopped, Ty laid her down gently on her side and curled up behind her. She felt her body calm down as he slowly stroked her hair, her arm, the side of her thigh. His touch felt so right, and despite her fear and her guilt over her feelings for him, she felt drawn to him. The same way she'd been all those years ago.

She didn't want to think about the man she'd killed anymore. She didn't want to think about what Heran or her sister would say about it, about any of this. She just wanted to stop thinking. And his hands felt good. Gaia, they felt so good.

How could something so wrong feel so good?

So she decided to let go. She decided to lean in to what felt good and right and safe, in a world where everything increasingly felt bad and wrong and unsafe.

She arched back into him in silent invitation, pressing her ass softly into his crotch. She felt his cock through his pants, already half-hard, and she knew it was a bad idea, she knew it would only add to her guilt and all her confusing feelings, but she was so, so tired of fighting what felt good, what felt right, what called to her.

"Please, Ty," she whispered quietly.

She felt his body freeze behind her, finally understanding her meaning. For a second, she wasn't sure if he would continue. Maybe he would be the rational one, and put a stop to this right now, before any more lines were crossed.

Then he took a deep breath, his head nestled into the crux of her neck, breathing in the scent of her skin and hair, and he groaned. "Fuck, Ena," he said. "This is a bad idea."

"I know," she said, "but I don't care."

He paused for just a second, as if holding himself back, before sliding her hair off her shoulder and kissing her neck gently, tenderly. The single kiss sent shivers down Ena's body. She couldn't even comprehend how many times she'd dreamed of having his lips on her again.

"Fuck it. Me neither," he said.

Then he unleashed himself.

He kissed her neck again, open-mouthed this time, licking her, tasting her. She loved it. Gaia, she loved it so fucking much, and she wanted more. She arched deeper into him, feeling his rock-hard cock behind her, and she ground into it. She brought her hand up to tangle in his hair, holding his mouth to her as he continued to kiss up and down her neck, nibbling at that sweet spot just under her ear.

She squirmed and writhed in front of him, and sensing she wanted more, he slowly lowered the hand he'd been stroking her arm with to pull up her shift, bunching it around her waist. Her bottom half was fully exposed now, and his hand felt so big and warm as it slowly traveled up over her stomach, tracing circles with his fingers, until it came up to cup her breast.

He squeezed gently, kneading it softly as she arched back into him with a moan. He began to swirl his thumb over her nipple, making it peak and driving her mad until he eventually pinched it. The sharp shock of pain drove her crazy, making her gasp and sending a throb right down to her core.

Ena tilted her head back and moaned. "Fuck, Ty."

"More?" he asked, his voice breathless from kissing her neck.

"Yes, fuck yes."

He lowered his hand back down her stomach and paused above her mound. She could feel the dripping wetness gathering in between her thighs, and Ena wanted nothing more but to have him inside her. Any part of him. Right the fuck now.

But instead, he teased her as he took one long finger and gently stroked her right down her center. He did it again, and again, and again, until she thought she might explode right then and there. She whimpered and squirmed against him, begging him wordlessly for more.

He chuckled darkly at her unabashed desire. "Ena," he whispered into her ear, "I want you to hear me."

She turned her face towards him so she could see him. His gaze locked on to hers. His eyes were dark with desire and his pupils blown wide, as if they were trying to take in everything they could, absorbing every part of her body as she lay half undressed and writhing before him.

"I've thought of you every single day for nine years." He sunk one long finger into her. "I've pictured your face when I took others to bed." He brushed his thumb over her clit, swirling in tight circles. "I think of you every time I fuck my own hand." He started to move his finger in and out, slowly at first, then faster and faster. When he sunk a second finger in, the heel of his hand now perfectly hit her clit as he moved his fingers in and out in the perfect rhythm. Ena's eyes started to close, her pleasure building, her orgasm getting closer and closer as she rocked into him.

"Look at me," he commanded.

Ena did as she was told and opened her eyes again to look at him, and the intensity she saw on his face made her not want to look away again. She knew he wanted to see.

"I've dreamt of you for nine years. You're mine. Do you hear me? You're *mine*." His words pushed her over the edge, and she kept her eyes on him as her climax shattered through her.

She clenched tightly around his fingers as she shouted, "Yes! Fuck...yes, Ty." *I'm yours, I'm yours, I'm yours,* she thought to herself, all of her walls and hesitation having been shattered by his words and her orgasm.

He continued to move his fingers slowly in and out, wringing every last drop from her pleasure. When he finally pulled his hand away, Ena was breathing heavily, but she could still feel his rock-hard cock pressed against her back, and the tightness in his body. She turned around in his arms so she was facing him and slowly lowered her hands to stroke it gently over his pants. He groaned and bucked into her as they locked eyes again.

Ena could tell they weren't done. Not even close. Nine years was a long time to wait for more of this.

"Get on your knees," Ty told her, his gaze filled his raging desire.

"Yes, Master," she replied, her lips quirking slightly.

Ty growled, then moved with her as she sat up and went to the edge of the bed.

There was a loud knock on the door.

They both froze, their heads swiveling to the door as if they couldn't possibly have heard correctly. Then they heard a voice—

"Ty! You in there?"

It was Steig.

CHAPTER TWENTY-THREE

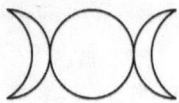

ENA AND TY LOOKED at each other, then frantically moved to fix their clothes and stand up.

"Coming!" Ty replied angrily. He clearly had tried to keep his voice steady, but even she could tell it sounded annoyed and tight with unspent desire.

Ena glanced at the window and could just barely see the early-dawn light peeking out from behind the curtains. It was morning already? She smoothed her shift and went to sit down casually on the chair as Ty threw on a shirt and strode to the door, pulling it open.

Steig stood in the doorway with a concerned, suspicious look on his face. He glanced over at Ena, then back at Ty, who was standing in front of him.

"Can I speak to you in the hallway for a minute?" he asked, his voice clipped.

Ty glanced at Ena, his eyes flicking briefly to the window behind her. She knew he didn't like leaving her alone and was considering whether there was a chance she'd run again, but he clearly decided it wasn't likely, so he closed the door behind him and stepped out into the hallway.

The door wasn't very soundproof. Their voices were muffled slightly, but Ena could hear Steig clearly when he spoke in a hushed voice.

"What the fuck did I just interrupt?"

"It was nothing. We were sleeping," Ty replied defensively.

"Don't give me that shit. I could sense the lust leaking from that room a mile away. What the fuck are you doing? Do you just have a thing for witches or something? Please don't tell me this is some mommy-abandonment shit..."

"What? No! I don't...I don't have a *thing* for witches. It's..." She heard Ty release a big sigh. "Okay, look, I'm sorry I didn't tell you this earlier, but it's *her*. She's the same witch."

Steig went eerily silent on the other side of the door. Ena couldn't see his face, but the silence was heavy with anger. When Steig spoke again, his tone was low and menacing.

"Are you fucking serious, Ty? This whole time, you didn't say anything? I left Lara and the kids home alone for this. I followed you on this fool's errand because *you* convinced me things could be different—*better*. Tell me the truth. Was that all an excuse so you could find this girl again?"

"No!" Ty answered loudly before quieting down again. "*No.* I promise, it wasn't. I didn't go looking for her on purpose. It was pure chance that she found us, and then I *did* have a good reason for taking her. I promise, we are still doing this, finding the amulet—it's still my main goal."

"Really? Because last I checked, we kidnapped her and burned her house down. She has every reason to hate us. Yes, we need the information she has, but you can't trust her, Ty. What if she's manipulating you?"

"What? No, she's not. And besides, I haven't told her anything."

There was a weighted silence from Steig on the other side of the door.

"Look, I hear you," Ty continued. "It was a mistake, and it won't happen again. She's going to help us get the amulet, she knows it's not worth her effort to try and escape, and then we'll let her go and we'll be long gone before she tells her Coven about us. That's still the plan."

"It better be, Ty. Because I'm not gonna watch you get all torn up again over this girl. Need I remind you, you almost died the last time you refused to let her go? This won't end well. For either of you."

She heard Ty sigh again on the other side of the door. "I know," he said. He sounded resigned and exhausted.

"Good," Steig said, sounding annoyed but convinced, then she heard him mutter something about going to get Turner, but Ena wasn't listening anymore.

She stood up hurriedly and started putting on the clean dress she'd been given. Now that the desire had drained from her body, she was flooded with shame.

What the fuck had she been thinking? Her sad, lust-addled brain had led her so far astray it wasn't even funny. This was bad. It was worse than bad—it was fucking delusional. She and Ty couldn't do this. They could not be together. She needed to get her shit together and focus on why she was here, why she had chosen to stay. She needed to find a way to get the amulet before them and take it back home to her Coven. That was her path.

Ty opened the door and came back into the room. She could tell in an instant that things had changed between them again. This was no longer Ty, the man who'd comforted her; this was Ty the daemon, who would complete his mission at all costs.

He looked her over once, taking in the fact that she was dressed, then said sternly, "Come on. Let's head downstairs. We'll meet with Steig and Turner over breakfast."

He turned, and Ena followed him wordlessly out the door and down the stairs. The tension between them was palpable. Clearly, they were both having second, third, *and* fourth thoughts about what they'd just done. They'd gotten way too carried away, too lost in their own world, and now that Steig and Turner were back, all the reasons why they couldn't and shouldn't go down that path came screaming back at her.

You're mine.

The words he'd whispered to her as he made her come ran through her head. Had he meant them? Fuck, did it even matter if he had?

They walked into the dining room to find Steig and Turner sitting at a secluded table near the fireplace. Ena and Ty sat down, and the same woman they'd met yesterday brought them some ale and a delicious-looking breakfast of eggs, sausages, and bread with apple preserves. Ena ate greedily as she listened to the three men catch up, and tried desperately not to think about the fact that she could still feel the ghost of Ty's fingers inside her.

"We've been scouting out the Occidens Coven's village and we think we found the house the witch described," Steig explained, gesturing harshly at Ena.

They were back to this? It all seemed ridiculous at this point, and Ena was tired of it.

"My name's Ena," she said. "No use pretending everyone doesn't know it anymore."

Steig turned slowly to look at her. "Okay, fine," he replied, giving her an untrusting look. She wondered mildly why he seemed to hate her so much. Was it just because she was a witch?

Turner, sensing the tension, interrupted with a practical question for Ty. "The issue is, we need to find a way to get into the house and look around for a while without being disturbed. We saw several witches coming and going from the house, but there's no major gatherings coming up that will ensure everyone is occupied."

"It might help if we had more specifics to go on," Steig said bitterly. "Did you see anything else in your vision? Anything specific about where the amulet might be in the house?" he asked Ena.

"I already told you everything I saw," she replied curtly. It was a lie, of course. She had a very specific idea of where the amulet was, but since it was the only advantage she had at the moment, she was keeping it.

"I could start a fire as a distraction," Turner offered. "We could sneak in while everyone's busy putting it out."

"I don't think we should alert them to our presence unless absolutely necessary. There will be too many variables to control," Ty explained, his tone taking on the assuredness of a commander. Ena again wondered vaguely what his position was among the daemons that enabled him to command such respect, but before this debate could go on any further, an idea occurred to Ena. It was risky, but maybe for the best.

"I could help with that," Ena said.

All three heads swiveled towards her.

"What do you mean?" Ty asked sternly.

"My Gift is *visanis*. I could use it to...temporarily incapacitate the witches that live in the house. Make it easier for you to search for the amulet without attracting attention."

"Your Gift is *visanis*?" Steig asked in shock. "Did you know about this?" he asked Ty.

"Yes, but I only found out recently. It's a long story," he said dismissively. "But I figured there was no way she'd use it to help us." He pinned her with his gaze. "Why would you help us?" Ty asked her, clearly suspicious of this offer. He knew about her restrictions around using her Gift, but this was different. She knew this was the safest and best way to get out of this whole mess—a mess, she'd acknowledge, that was partially her fault at this point. She had done the spell that had led them here. And she'd do what she needed to do to get out of it while causing the least amount of harm possible.

"I figure this way, if I use my *visanis*, I can ensure that no witches get hurt. I can put them to sleep or something. Clearly, you all are going to go search for the amulet no matter what I do, and I'd rather it not descend into a bloody battle or a forest fire," Ena explained, looking pointedly at Turner. "So I'll help, but I want something in return."

There it was. Ty leaned back in his chair, his arms crossed defensively. "Okay..." he responded. "And what's that?"

"If I help you break into the house using my *visanis*, I want your word that you'll let me go whether you find the amulet there or not."

The three of them looked at each other, clearly calculating whether or not that was a good idea.

"And why *wouldn't* it be there?" Steig asked skeptically.

"Any number of reasons. You only gave me a vague description of it, so the spell might not have worked properly. Or they could have moved it since then. Take your pick. I did my part, but I can only control so much, so if I do this, that's it. You let me go afterwards."

Ena needed this guarantee. She knew Ty planned to let her go when they found it, she didn't doubt that, but if everything went according to her plan, they *wouldn't* find it, and she didn't want them dragging her all over creation indefinitely searching for it. She needed this to be over.

"Fine," Ty replied. "I think you've proven to be about as useful as you're going to be, anyway."

Ena's chest tightened at his words. She would be lying if she said that didn't hurt, especially with the ghost of his kisses on her neck. Clearly, he was trying to tell her something with his cold tone and harsh attitude. He was trying to push her away again—and he would succeed. Yes, she'd certainly outlived her *usefulness* with these daemons.

"Okay, that's settled then," Turner said cautiously, looking between Ena and Ty as they stared daggers at each other.

"We'll leave as soon as the rain lets up," Ty declared.

***

Unfortunately, the rain continued all day and well into the evening. Ena hung around the dining room most of the day, listening to Ty, Turner, and Steig strategize now that they knew about Ena's *visanis*. When they took breaks to gather supplies or tend to their horses, she spent the time observing the other patrons at the guesthouse.

There was a family with several children who spent a significant amount of time playing a rowdy game with marbles that Ena had never experienced before. She couldn't help but smile at their communal joy, but it made her miss Greya fiercely.

Then there was the duo of glassblowers who had traveled to deliver some commissioned items to a few people in the village. She overheard some gossip that indicated that Dirk the butcher had been way over-charged for the glass pitcher he'd ordered, but that was no business of hers.

The everyday human moments kept her company and soothed her while it rained and she tried fervently not to think about everything that had happened with

Ty. The kind woman who'd served them their food kept her well-provided with ale after ale, and by the time dinner rolled around, she was pleasantly inebriated.

It had been a long time since she'd been drunk, probably since the Litha gathering this past summer, but Ena was thoroughly enjoying the feeling.

It wasn't until she'd finished eating her dinner of chicken, roasted potatoes, and mashed carrots, that she realized there was a commotion in the corner of the room.

The dining room was packed with patrons, both guests and village residents, but Turner and Ty had cleared out quickly after dinner. Ena had been given express instructions to "stay here where Steig can see you," and honestly, with the pleasant feeling of the ale buzzing through her brain, she had no desire to be anywhere else at the moment.

Looking over at the corner in question, Ena saw Steig sitting in a place of honor with patrons gathering around him.

Oh, Gaia. Was he about to sing? Ena hadn't truly believed it when Ty had said he was posing as a bard. He *so* did not strike her as the musical type. He was gruff and harsh, not touchy-feely at all. But as the room settled down, and he opened his mouth, she realized how wrong she'd been.

Steig sang a slow, long ballad, his deep, smooth voice reverberating throughout the room. And it wasn't just any song—it was a love song. His voice seemed to drench the room, enrapturing even the noisy children. His pitch-perfect notes cascaded fluidly as he sang of a hunter who fell in love with a seamstress. They loved each other madly and couldn't keep their hands off each other, so every time he left for a hunting trip, they'd make love frantically in farewell, and every time, he'd return to find her pregnant. The couple had fifteen children, who grew up to found a new village, and their prosperity benefited everyone.

It was an interesting story, Ena granted him. Highly unique. And she didn't miss the effect it had on the patrons of the guesthouse. Slowly, one by one, couples peeled off together into dark corners of the room, kissing and canoodling. A few even left before he was done to run up to their rooms. Ena liked the song, sure, but she didn't seem quite as impacted by it as everyone else.

Eventually, way slower than she would have if she hadn't been drunk, she realized what was happening—it was *cupido*. She'd heard of it, of course—the Power that some daemons had to enhance lust, greed, and ambition. She'd always wondered what Steig's Power was, and now it clicked. His Power came from his singing. His *lustful* singing.

Gaia, Ena had never been more grateful that daemonic Powers did not work on witches. She'd dealt with more than enough consequences of her ill-conceived lust for one day.

When Steig finally finished singing, only two other patrons remained in the room to applaud him, but he didn't seem concerned. He bowed slightly to the two who'd clapped and left his chair of honor to drink a mug of ale at another table.

Maybe it was her drunken state, or maybe she just needed him to know that she knew what he was up to, but she found herself approaching his table.

"I guess it makes sense now," she said to him as she sat down.

"What does?" he asked her, barely making eye contact.

"Why you have so many kids," Ena said.

He looked at her with his eyebrows raised, realizing that she'd put two and two together about his Power. "You got me," he said, before looking back down at his mug.

Gaia, you would've thought she'd killed this man's family with the cold shoulder he was giving her. She was just trying to waste the time with some mindless conversation so she didn't have to think about Ty and what in the Underworld she would do if she had to sleep next to him again tonight, but this guy just wouldn't give an inch. What the fuck did she ever do to him anyway?

"What the fuck is your problem with me?" she asked, the alcohol completely obliterating her brain-to-mouth barrier. "Do you just hate all witches? Is that it?"

Steig looked around frantically. "Keep your voice down," he hissed. "Do you want them to know what you are?"

She rolled her eyes. There was no one here anymore anyway. They were all back in their rooms fucking like rabbits.

"Fine, don't tell me. Don't suppose it matters anyway," Ena said. She'd never admit it to him, but it did matter.

Turner seemed fine enough with her, kind even, but Steig had always had a stick up his ass about her, even before he knew who she was to Ty. And in Ena's mind, he had no right to treat her this way when she'd done nothing to him. He was the one who'd kidnapped her, forced her into this. The least he could do was not be a constant asshole.

Steig looked over at her, clearly noting her drunken state, and she thought she saw a flash of pity in his eyes. "I don't hate all witches. I mistrust them. There's a difference."

"Okay...and why do you mistrust us?" Ena asked.

Steig rolled his eyes, as if that was the dumbest question he'd ever heard. Ena was about to get up and leave this pointless conversation, when he spoke again.

"I was there, you know," he said, pausing to make sure she was listening. "After Ty tried to get back to you. After they beat him nearly to death. I was there."

Ena froze where she sat. She'd known they were friends, best friends, but she never thought about that, never guessed that he'd been there for Ty, all those years ago.

"The beating hurt his body badly. He couldn't walk for almost a month after that. But his heart... that was worse. The loneliness and the regret that haunted him in the years that followed. He was never the same." Steig shook his head as he took another gulp of ale. "You fucked him up good, witch."

Ena bristled at his tone. As if that was her fault. As if she wasn't hurting and fucked up herself after that summer.

"Yeah, well, the feeling was mutual," she said, her hands finding her own mug for another sip.

"I can see that," he said, looking at her appraisingly. "I don't know how I didn't figure it out earlier, actually. Who you were. I should've known."

"And you blame *me* for that? For him being hurt and all that came after?"

"No, I don't blame you. But I know what it is to love someone fiercely. So fiercely, that you're willing to ignore all the bad that comes with the good. And seeing you two together...seeing the soft spot he's had for you since the minute we took you...I'm worried about my friend."

Ena was silent as she took in his words. She could understand his concern for his friend. But love? That wasn't what she and Ty had. They were drawn to each other, yes, but it wasn't love. How could she love someone who'd hurt her so badly? Besides, she didn't know how to tell Steig that he didn't need to be worried. Things between her and Ty were over, and they both knew it.

Those words were on the tip of her tongue, but for some reason, she couldn't bring them out.

Steig looked over at her again before draining his cup. "Just take some advice and keep your distance from him. For both your sakes." He stood up, leaving her alone at the table before going upstairs to his room.

Ena watched the fire burn down alone until she'd finished her mug. She swayed slightly as she walked up the stairs to her room. Walking in, she saw that the bed was empty, but Turner was passed out in a nest of blankets with a pillow on the floor in front of the fire. They clearly didn't want her to be unsupervised all night, but she silently thanked Gaia that Turner was here and not Ty. It was easier that way.

Because she wanted to take Steig's advice. She wanted to keep her distance. She knew it was the only path forward. For both of them.

CHAPTER TWENTY-FOUR

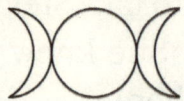

IN THE MORNING, THE rain finally stopped. It felt strange waking up alone after so many nights next to Ty, but at least Turner, who was already awake, was there to instantly distract her from the small ache that grew in her chest.

"Sleep well?" he asked as he built up the hearth with logs.

"Shouldn't I be asking you that? You're the one who slept on the floor after all," Ena replied groggily.

Turner smiled at that. "I didn't mind it. It was warm by the fire," he said.

Ena watched as he used his Power to light the fire. His hand seemed to glow and burn as if it were the hottest coal in the hearth. For a second, she was captivated watching it. It was similar to what a witch could do with a spellword, but also different, and she couldn't stop her curiosity.

"How does that work? Your Power, I mean... I thought daemons mostly had Powers of the mind," she asked.

Turner looked at her in surprise, but answered kindly.

"We call it *incendia*," he said. "And yes, that's true. Powers of the mind are more common, but some of us have corporeal Powers too. They're an extension of our other corporeal abilities, like speed, strength, and healing. I'm able to generate additional heat in my body, and concentrate it into my hand."

"Oh," Ena said, feeling fascinated despite herself. "So you don't have to draw on the environment around you like I do when I use my spellword?"

Turner shook his head.

"Fascinating," Ena mused.

Turner smiled at her. "Ty always said you were smart. I'm surprised you didn't know that already."

Ena's stomach jolted at the mention of Ty. He'd talked to Turner about her? He'd said she was smart? Fuck, the mushy feelings that brought up in her were the last thing she needed right now.

"We weren't taught much of anything about your kind," Ena said shortly, the statement a harsh reminder of the separation between their peoples.

Turner left to give her privacy to dress, and after a hearty breakfast eaten in relative silence, she and Turner met Steig and Ty by the stable to ready their horses.

Ty was busy tightening the saddle on a beautiful mare with a glossy black coat and a long mane, and he didn't acknowledge her approach. She hadn't seen him since yesterday afternoon, and he'd clearly been busy securing supplies for the rest of their trip, because the horse's saddlebags were packed full. The sight of him, as always, caused her heart to jump, but she didn't show it. He was keeping his distance, and so would she.

Ena focused on the new horse as she approached it. She read its signs and Knew it was calm and good-natured. It loved to gallop and could do so for miles without tiring, but it would respond quickly if redirected to slow down. The horse also really wanted an apple. Ena stroked its neck gently and turned to Ty.

"Did they tell you her name?" she asked, breaking their silence. There was no way they'd be able to get through this without at least exchanging a few words.

"Apparently, it's Mahnin," he said, not making eye contact.

"Hello there, Mahnin," Ena crooned to the beautiful horse as she offered her hand for it to sniff.

"Ah, I see," Steig said as he approached. "This one you're friendly with. Does that mean you won't lure it into the woods to get eaten by a wolf?"

Turner laughed behind her, and Ena shot him a dirty look, but she didn't have much of a retort. She still carried guilt for what her actions during her escape had caused.

Ty gestured to her that the horse was ready, so she mounted up on her own. She was expecting him to mount up behind her, but instead, Turner did, as Ty took Turner's usual brindled horse.

A sharp bolt of rejection and disappointment shot through her, but she quickly pushed it aside. It was for the best, for both of them. Like Steig had said.

Once they'd all mounted, they rode out of the village and back onto the Western Road. Ena was terribly sad to see Attax go. She didn't know when she'd be able to stay in such nice accommodations again. Maybe not until after she made it back home. She had their word now that they'd let her go once they searched the house from her vision, so she'd be home in no time, she told herself. Soon, this would all be a bad memory.

They rode along the Western Road for most of the morning. It was fairly busy with travelers going to and from the coast, but their little group, with no cart and only a few riders, didn't seem to attract much attention. Steig and Turner had told them that the Occidens Coven's village was only about half a day's ride away, so Ena was not surprised that by the afternoon, they branched off from the road to travel the rest of the way through the backwoods. Ena understood that this was for the best; they couldn't be seen riding into the Occidens Coven. They'd have to find a way to enter the village undetected, and to do that, they'd need to keep their distance from the main roads.

Turner was pleasant enough to ride with. He kept her busy with idle chitchat—stories about learning to ride horses in his youth, and his deep love for spice buns, which were apparently a daemonic delicacy. Ena could tell he had a kind heart, and honestly, that confused her. Steig and Ty, while they each had their moments, were both harsher, harder, and more what she expected daemons to be like. But with Turner, well, she'd never expected a daemon to be so...nice.

But despite his attempts to keep her engaged in conversation, Ena's eyes kept drifting unbidden to Ty—his broad back and the way his muscles rippled on his forearms as he gripped the horse's reins. Her mind conjured up images of the two of them in bed together the night before last. The way he'd comforted her, pleasured her. For that brief time, she'd felt so safe, and, if she were being honest, it had felt *right*. Like coming home.

She found she missed his sturdy presence behind her on the horse. She missed being surrounded by his scent. She missed the new understanding they had come to, their pseudo-friendship. A lot had changed between them, especially after the attack. And somehow, he had come to be the only person who understood all the conflicting feelings she wrestled with about her Gift. And now that she thought about it, maybe he was the only person to ever really understand her at all.

She knew this new separation was for the best. But still, it hurt to look at him. The way he'd avoided her last night, and again this morning. The way he was treating her, once again, as if she were nothing. It brought back those old feelings of rejection, reopened those nine-year-old wounds that had never fully healed.

The other night, they'd been so close to going so far... Ena wasn't sure when she would've stopped herself if they hadn't been interrupted. And the things that he'd said to her... That he'd dreamt of her. Yearned for her. Had he meant it all or had he just been caught up in the passion of the moment? How could she trust anything that he had said when he could just go back to ignoring her so easily? Maybe he was just doing the right thing and keeping his distance, or maybe that night was just another thing about her that he regretted.

But no matter how hard she tried, she couldn't bring herself to regret it. Any of it. She never could. Maybe once she was away from him, she would. Maybe then, she could finally, finally, move on.

All roads led to the same place: she needed to get the amulet and end this.

***

They stopped once along the way to relieve themselves and eat some of the provisions they'd brought for lunch. As the sun got lower in the sky, Ena thought the air started to smell...different. It was fresher somehow, and salty. A more significant breeze was blowing through the trees now, whipping her hood back so she had to pull it up constantly.

Then she heard it before she saw it: the smooth crash of waves in the distance. At first, it sounded like the wind, but as they got closer, she could distinctly hear the persistent ebb and flow of water on sand, louder and more constant than anything she'd heard from the River Wry.

One step, the forest looked normal, and the next, as the trees gradually began to thin, she suddenly saw nothing but blue beyond them.

As if this world abruptly ended, and a new one began.

Ena sat forward in the saddle, excitement gripping her. She'd never seen the ocean before, never seen where the land ended. A loud, large white bird that she'd never seen before flew overhead, squawking. She felt the breeze whipping against her cloak as they reached the end of the forest.

And that's exactly what it was—the end. The trees simply stopped, and the land dropped down into a sandy cliff. Below, Ena could see rolling dunes of light-brown sand, decorated with tufts of grass and scraggly, beach-dwelling plants.

And beyond that was endless blue.

The ocean was huge, bigger than she could possibly have imagined. Staring at it, she couldn't see where it ended, or discern if it ever did.

She stared at it in awe. She'd seen it at a distance, of course, from the top of the gorge near her village, but its presence in person surrounded her. Overwhelmed her. The waves crashed into her very being, her Knowing inundated with new signs and intentions. There was so much *life* here. Staring at it gave her the same feeling she had looking out at the mountains that dwarfed her: like she was a part of it, and it was a part of her.

She looked over to find Ty studying her from atop his horse, his face unreadable as always. But was that, possibly, a hint of tenderness she saw?

He turned away before she could figure it out, snapping instantaneously back into his role as commander.

"We'll leave the horses here," he said to the others.

Ena dismounted, as did the others, and then they loosely tethered the horses to separate trees so they could graze while they were gone. One by one, Ena and the daemons slid and scrambled down the sandy cliff onto the beach.

By the time she reached the bottom, Ena's boots were already filled with sand. She wanted to stop and dump them out, but Ty barely waited for her to stand up before leading them on down the beach, and she struggled to keep up. She didn't realize how difficult walking through the deep sand would be; it was as if a heavy child clung to each of her legs, dragging her down with each step. But she'd never let Ty and the others know it, so she trudged on in silence, breathing heavily.

The group kept to the forest line, navigating between the dunes of sand to keep them hidden. Between dunes, Ena caught glimpses of the water. She longed to take off her sandy boots and walk into it, to feel the water and the sand squish on her toes as the ocean rushed back and forth, back and forth. But she wouldn't go too far, because the violence of the crashing waves was intense in its consistency, pounding water onto the shore in a never-ending rhythm. The Endless Ocean was a vast and beautiful unknown, and just like so many others, it both terrified and enthralled her.

It wasn't until they got closer to the Occidens village that Ena's fascination with the ocean turned into intense anxiety about what was to come.

She knew the plan; they'd discussed and debated it at length the day prior. They'd leave their horses hidden at the edge of the forest, and walk along the coastline hidden in the dunes. Once they got closer to the village and the house from Ena's vision, Ty would use his *venator* to see who was in the house and where. Steig and Turner had scoped out the house briefly when they posed as traders visiting the village to obtain a potion to cure warts, and they'd seen three women regularly coming and going from it.

There was much debate as to whether they should wait for the three witches to be asleep before going in, but Steig insisted it was less suspicious if they were to be seen walking around the village in the early evening, rather than the dead of night. Besides, Ena had never used her Gift on a sleeping person before, and apparently, according to Ty, Powers of the mind often worked differently on people who were asleep because they were unable to see or hear in a normal way. Her *visanis* might only be able to impact their dreams, and not their real actions.

Only once Ty discerned where the witches were in the house would they move in, and Ena would incapacitate them one by one, allowing the four of them to search the house for the amulet.

Yes, Ena knew the plan well, but it hadn't felt real until this very moment.

As the sun was setting, they came to the edge of the village. Crouching low behind a dune, they watched it from afar. It was large—larger even than her own village. The land flattened here, with a less drastic cliff between the edge of the forest and the sandy beach. The houses were wooden, not stone, and looked far more wind-beaten than the ones back home. Their windows were rounded instead of square, with far less moss growing on the wooden shingles that made their roofs. Ena could see various fenced-in gardens tucked behind them, partially inside the safety of the forest. But some of the houses, those closer to the water, were gardenless and raised up on stilts.

Not for the first time, she wondered what had caused the rift between the Covens, and why they had required a treaty to keep them divided in the first place, because aside from some aesthetic differences, nothing about this village indicated that these witches were significantly different from those in her own Coven, and the thought deepened Ena's dread.

"We believe the house from Ena's vision is just down there," Steig spoke quietly, pointing to the largest house Ena could see from their vantage point. It was tucked closer to the forest and wasn't raised up, and she could see from here that it was well-maintained compared to some of the other houses. It had a second story, and what looked to be a brand-new roof. It had large, rounded windows and a stone chimney with smoke curling out.

There was no doubt; it was indeed the house from her vision.

All of a sudden, Ena felt like she might throw up.

This was really happening. She was going to have to break into that peaceful house with these daemons and find the amulet.

The Occidens Coven were their rivals. But, while she knew all this in theory, she didn't have anything against these witches personally, and now she was about to steal from them.

Taking two or three deep breaths, she tried to calm herself.

These daemons were going in no matter what, and she needed to get that amulet before they did—both for the sake of these witches, and herself, because if the daemons got it first, Gaia only knew what they planned to do with it. Ena had tried to ferret that out, but the three of them had been extremely close-lipped about it. The best indication she'd gotten was what she'd overheard between Steig and Ty—that somehow, they thought this amulet could make things better for dae-mons. And what Ty had said about finding it not being a mission from Iblis. That could mean any number of things, and likely did not bode well for mortals or witches.

She didn't like it—in fact, she was close to panicking at the thought—but this was the only course of action she could take.

"Is that the house from your vision, Ena?" Ty asked her seriously. The other two waited with bated breath for her confirmation.

"Yes," Ena said, trying to hide the shaking in her voice. "That's it."

Ty nodded and looked back at the house, studying it intensely from afar. "It looks like all three of them are on the first floor. I see two in front of the hearth in a sitting room knitting and mending clothes, and the third is in the kitchen. If we go in through the cellar door, Ena and I can take care of the one in the kitchen first while you two subdue the ones in the sitting room until we get there."

Steig and Turner nodded silently in understanding. Despite her internal pep talk, Ena was quickly crossing the line from nervous into panic. Her breath was com-ing in short gasps and she couldn't feel her fingertips. She knew she'd agreed to this, but Gaia, it felt like there was no turning back from this. What if it all went wrong and they were captured? What if she accidentally hurt someone with her Gift? What if she couldn't get to the amulet first and the daemons got it anyway?

Ty grabbed her hand and hooked his finger under her chin, raising her face until she looked at him. "Ena, breathe," he said calmly, those green eyes boring into hers. "You can do this."

She met his gaze, finding solace in those eyes—finding strength. She forced her body to mirror the calm, steady breaths rising in his chest. She felt his grip on her hand, the rough calluses on his palm familiar and grounding.

He didn't know what she planned, that she intended to betray him, but she took his strength anyway, and she felt her body calm slightly as she nodded at him.

Then he released her chin, and they started moving.

CHAPTER TWENTY-FIVE

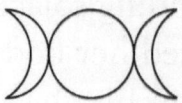

THEY WALKED AS QUICKLY and quietly as possible, keeping to the sides of houses and avoiding open spaces, trying not to attract attention as they entered the village.

They saw a few other folks outside, closing up their garden gates or wrangling children inside, but no one seemed to pay them any mind, likely thinking they were travelers returning to their camps for the night.

As they approached the large house from her vision, Ena started to reach down into her Knowing in earnest, listening and watching for any signs that might give them away. She felt her Gift there, too, waiting inside her, but she didn't reach for it yet.

They'd debated at length whether the Occidens witches' Knowing would alert them to Ena's presence. But, deciding there was no way around that, the daemons hoped that being with them would mask Ena's intentions somewhat. This thought occurred to her again as they entered the back gate of the garden surrounding the house. What if they sensed her coming and were prepared? What if they attacked her?

Turner walked up to the wide cellar door at the base of the house and opened it, revealing a steep staircase leading down into darkness.

He slipped inside, and Ena, Ty, and Steig followed him wordlessly, Steig closing the door silently behind them.

Once they reached the bottom, Ena found herself in a dark, cold storage room filled with potatoes, onions, baskets of freshly cut herbs, and other foodstuffs. It smelled like earth and rosemary, and the familiarity of it all calmed her a bit.

Then, coming from up the short set of stairs that connected the cellar to the rest of the house, she heard the muffled sounds of talking and laughter. That was where they needed to go.

Holding Ena's hand protectively, Ty led her quietly up the stairs and through the door at the top. It opened into a dark hallway, but there was a doorway to the left through which she could see light and heard the sounds of chopping. Ty clearly heard that, too, indicating silently with his head that they should follow that sound into the kitchen. Steig and Turner would be on their own finding their way to the sitting room.

Ena's heart was pounding and she had to swallow the saliva that pooled in her mouth several times, keeping herself in check. She felt her Gift on the tip of her tongue, begging for her to reach for it, all the way, to unleash it, but *not yet*.

They pushed through the doorway into the kitchen to find the space was sparsely lit with a few candles, illuminating a large cooking hearth, a dining table with chairs, and extensive wooden counters cluttered with dishes and jars. Ena's eyes scanned over these elements only briefly before they went to the middle-aged woman with dark-blonde hair piled high on her head. Her back was to them as she stood at the counter chopping garlic, but upon their entry into the room, her head turned to them. Just as her eyes widened slightly in alarm, Ena reached for her Gift, letting it flow through her, and like slipping instantly into a long-neglected instinct, she spoke.

{*Do not move.*}

She heard her voice emerge in the same eerie way it had in the woods when the bandits had attacked. It sounded like her and not like her at the same time.

{*Put down the knife and lay on the floor.*}

The woman did as she was told, putting the knife down on the counter, and laying on her back right there on the dirty floor of the kitchen.

{*Sleep until the sun rises.*}

Ty looked over at her. His eyes were filled with some mixture of admiration and horror, but Ena couldn't focus on that right now. Her *visanis* was surging through her and she felt powerful—completely lost and utterly in control at the same time. Her nerves had been replaced with clarity as she gave herself over to the magic, and with every beat of her heart, she felt the warmth of her Gift tingling through her. She wasn't done.

Barely glancing behind her, she abandoned the woman she'd forced into sleep on the floor and strode calmly back into the hallway, looking around for the sitting room. Ty was forced to follow her now, and he did so without a word.

The voices she'd heard from the cellar had stopped talking, replaced with the minor noises of a struggle—feet shuffling and a small squeak of fear. She walked down the hallway, following the sounds and the dim light of the fireplace, to find Steig and Turner holding the two other witches in the sitting room. Their eyes were wide with fear as they struggled against their captors, the daemons' hands covering their mouths and preventing them from using any spellwords.

Ena vaguely registered how young they were—both were in their early or mid-teens, and clearly didn't have their Gifts yet. They were most likely sisters, given the way they resembled one another. She saw the panic in their eyes, but it barely impacted her; she was too caught up in the flow of her magic. She focused on them and spoke.

{*Stop moving.*}

The women went limp in Steig and Turner's arms and they proceeded to lay them down with care on the floor. She noticed that focusing on both at once with her *visanis* felt difficult, and her magic seemed strained. So instead, one by one, she gave them the same command as she had to the woman in the kitchen. She watched as the witches' eyes slowly closed and their breathing evened out. Within seconds, they appeared to be in the deepest kind of sleep, their bodies calm and their faces peaceful.

She knew in the back of her mind that her job was done, but she didn't know how to loosen her grip on her Gift. It burned through her still, and she loved the feeling of power it gave her. She felt drunk on it, and a part of her never wanted to let it go, wanted to live in the ordered chaos of it forever.

He must've recognized her struggle, because Ty stepped into her line of vision. Gently, he grasped her by the shoulders and looked into her eyes. "You can let go now, Ena," he said. "It's over."

Seeing those familiar green eyes and the calm they held somehow broke her hold on her *visanis*. She felt her magic start to fade slowly from her body, retreating to where it dwelled deep inside her. Her breathing slowed and her mind cleared. She dimly started to become aware of the horror of what she'd just been able to do to the three witches. So quickly. So *easily*.

Before she could feel anything more, Ty grabbed her hand, gently stroking his thumb over the back. "Nicely done," he said, giving her a small, cautious smile. "Turner and Steig, you start searching upstairs." He gestured for them to return to the hallway. "Ena, you stay close to me and we'll search down here."

Steig and Turner exchanged a look, seeming to notice how Ty had gravitated back towards her the moment they'd entered the danger of the enemy village. Neither of them called him out on it, though, they simply nodded and left to go find the stairwell.

Ena followed Ty out of the sitting room and down the dark hallway towards the front door of the house. Holding a candle in one hand that he'd grabbed along the way, Ty opened and closed a few the doors that lined the hallway, clearly looking for one room in particular.

Eventually, he opened a door that led into a large altar room. He obviously believed this was the most important room to search first, and he wasn't wrong. This was the most likely place for a witch to keep ceremonial objects.

Ena stood hesitantly in the doorway as Ty entered the room and immediately started looking over the bookshelves. In the low light, she could see that there were several of them all around the room, adorned not only with books, but various trinkets used for potions and ceremonies—ceremonial chalices, animal skulls, ornately carved wooden boxes, and various glass bowls sat packed three rows deep on the shelves. There were several low tables covered in decorative cloths, as well, the remnants of potion ingredients laid out in bowls and mortars, and spellbooks opened to the last pages referenced. Several large trunks lay around the room, too, and Ty began throwing them open at random, digging around inside cursorily before moving on to the next.

Then she saw it.

There, tucked into an obscure corner of the room, lay the large leather-bound trunk Ena had seen in her vision. Glancing over at Ty, she found him distracted, digging through a trunk on the other side of the room, opening and dumping out every possible receptacle that could hold an amulet.

This was her chance.

Ena walked cautiously to the trunk, hoping he'd think she was simply helping him in his search. The lid was unlocked, so she lifted it. Inside, it was filled with folded lace tablecloths—high-quality ones—and the same style of handfasting ropes her Coven used. There was also a trove of candles of every shape and size. None of the contents seemed particularly special or unique. She wondered why they would keep the amulet here, of all places.

Rifling through the contents, Ena felt around for the large wooden box she'd seen in her vision, but she found nothing of the sort. Was she mistaken? None of the other trunks in the room looked at all similar to the one she'd seen. It had to be this one.

Stepping back to assess it again, she glanced over her shoulder to see that Ty was blessedly focused on pulling out all the drawers in the writing desk at the other end of the room, and that made her think.

Feeling around on the bottom of the trunk again, her finger found a small notch in the wood, just big enough for a finger to slip in. Doing just that, and tugging lightly, she felt the bottom of the trunk move.

It had a false bottom.

She quickly threw the contents of the trunk out onto the floor and removed the bottom altogether. There, underneath, was the wooden box from her vision. She quickly went to open it, but found it was locked. Quietly, feeling for the metal components she Knew were inside, she whispered her spellword.

{*Clavis*}

The box opened in her hands, and there, laid in the center, was the amulet.

The description of it provided to her by Ty did not do it justice, nor what she'd seen of it in her vision. It was beautiful. The uncut amethyst in its center was a deep purple, so dark it was almost black. Looking into the stone, it felt endless. Like she could fall into its void and keep sinking, sinking, sinking forever. The color drained from the stone as it reached the edges, leaving it a pale white-purple where it met the circular silver setting that surrounded it. The setting shone as if it had been recently buffed, and was etched with those four confusing symbols, just as she'd seen in her vision. The braided silver chain it hung on was long and intricately made, and if she were to touch it, she Knew it would feel as delicate as hair.

Ena was so enthralled by its beauty and power, she did not notice that the sounds of Ty frantically searching the room had stopped. As she moved to touch it, his voice jolted her out of her trance.

"Ena," he said quietly behind her. "You found it."

She turned around to face him, still holding the box. She stared at him, and he at her. Some unspoken communication transpired between them, and his brow furrowed. He looked down at the box in her hands and extended his hand towards her.

"Give it to me, Ena," he said, his voice low with warning. Then, after a beat, he added gently, "Please."

Fear and vulnerability shone in his eyes. His beautiful eyes. Ena stared at him for a moment, frozen. Part of her wanted to give him the amulet, despite everything, if only to see him happy. If only to wipe away that deep look of concern and desperation that had settled on his face.

But she knew she couldn't do that. She couldn't stray that far from Gaia, not after everything she'd already done. This was the end of the road for them. She couldn't let him and his people take the amulet. She had to protect her Coven, and everyone else, from them.

So she picked up the amulet, and slipped it around her neck.

She couldn't exactly say why she did it. She figured Ty could overpower her and take it if he really wanted to, but somewhere in the back of her mind, she also knew that amulets were made by witches, for witches, and that they held enormous power. And something about this amulet seemed to recognize her as one of its own. It called her to use it, wear it, own it. Putting it on felt as easy as breathing.

The instant the stone fell upon her chest, Ena's vision went white.

***

Images came to her, quick and disjointed.

She saw faces she didn't recognize. She saw a moonless sky and a darkened forest.

Three women were holding hands, standing in a sacred circle. They chanted spellwords she'd never heard as they surrounded another woman kneeling on the ground.

The kneeling woman was bloodied and weeping. Ena felt her fear and her guilt. She saw the tears track down her face, leaving lines in the dried blood there.

She saw an athame drag across someone's wrist—she couldn't tell whose. Then she saw the blood collecting in a golden chalice. Ena's wrist burned as if her own had been slit. It *hurt*, and her vision was blurred.

She saw the amulet. It somehow seemed to glow in the moonless night as one of the women, one of the witches, held it by the chain and dipped into the chalice until it was covered in blood.

She heard the kneeling woman beg for mercy as the amulet was placed over the head of one of the witches—a brown-haired woman with gray streaks, her blue eyes impassive and cold. She felt the woman's disdain and hatred for the kneeling woman as if it were her own.

Then the kneeling woman screamed as if her heart was being ripped from her body, and Ena screamed too. She watched the woman collapse on the ground as the amulet stopped glowing.

The brown-haired woman smiled as she removed the amulet from around her neck, and Ena felt her satisfaction. She turned to hand it to one of the other women who'd been chanting. She had pale-blonde hair and hazel eyes. Ena felt her wariness and concern.

She saw the three women leave the forest, abandoning the body of the woman who had kneeled. The woman was still alive, she was breathing, but something seemed...different about her. Something seemed *less*.

Finally, she saw the amulet, sitting innocuously in the box she'd found it in, and as the lid snapped closed, Ena's reality returned to her.

***

She lay on the floor, staring up into Ty's face.

"Ena?" he asked frantically, his voice tight with fear. He stroked her hair from her face. "Can you hear me now? Are you okay?"

Clutching her head, she sat up and looked down at her chest to find the amulet gone.

"What the fuck was that? What happened?" Ty asked, still searching her body as if he could find a physical wound.

"I—I don't know," Ena said as she looked around. They were still in the altar room. Everything had been turned over, and she lay on the ground next to the trunk she'd found the amulet in.

"Did you see something? Your eyes they...went white. And you were screaming. You didn't respond to me and then you collapsed on the floor."

"I... Where's the amulet?" she asked, suddenly realizing that it was gone.

"I took it off you," Ty said harshly, as if this was obvious. "It was hurting you."

Ena's mind frantically tried to understand what had happened, what she'd just seen. It must have been a vision, triggered by the power of the amulet. She knew that visions were possible, but extremely rare. They were usually sent by Gaia herself and would occur in sacred spaces or when someone came into contact with a sacred object.

But what had it been a vision of? The past? The future? Because she saw the amulet end in the box she'd just found it in, she had to assume it was the past. What had they been doing? Ena wasn't entirely sure, but whatever it was had felt...wrong. So wrong.

Whatever it was, she Knew it was an abomination of Gaia's power.

Ena looked up at Ty again. "Tell me why you need the amulet, Ty."

Ena had never asked him directly, not since that first night. But after everything she'd just seen, everything she'd just felt, she needed to know. Something horrible had occurred, and Ena had a feeling there was much more to this amulet than she had originally assumed.

He shook his head. "Now is not the time. We have to go. You made a lot of noise when you screamed, and we need to get out of here before we are found."

At that moment, Steig and Turner came bursting into the room, weapons drawn.

"What the fuck is going on? Did you find the amulet? We heard Ena scream." Steig glanced furiously between the two of them, his brow furrowed in confusion.

"Yes, I have it, but we can talk about it later. We need to move now before we're discovered," Ty replied, dragging Ena to standing.

With Ty's arm around her waist, they fled the room. As they ran through the hallway, Ena caught a brief glimpse of the girls in the sitting room, still peacefully asleep on the floor. They flew down the stairs into the cellar, then erupted out of the door and into the night.

Worrying less about keeping to the shadows, they moved as quickly as they could back through the village the way they had come.

Once they hit the sand past the village, they started running. They tore over the dunes they had crossed coming here, their energy renewed with adrenaline. Ena's mind whirled, trying frantically to process everything she'd seen in spite of her fear.

They were all thoroughly out of breath by the time they reached the cliff above which they'd tethered their horses. Ena struggled to scramble up it, sliding down several times, until Ty, already at the top, offered a hand to pull her up. Steig and Turner quickly mounted their horses as Ty turned to Ena, reaching for her to place her on the horse, but she backed away.

"I'm not going any further with you until you tell me what in the Underworld is going on. Tell me why you all want the amulet."

"I'm not leaving you, Ena, but we can't talk about this here. Get on the horse," Ty said, his tone brooking no argument.

"No!" Ena erupted. She was far too confused, too afraid. Her plan had fallen apart, again, and she didn't have the amulet. There was no way she could get it from them now. But she needed to know what they wanted to do with it. Something was horribly wrong here. She needed to know *now*.

"Leave her, Ty. We need to go now!" Steig said, his horse stamping around, sensing his impatience.

"No!" Ty growled at him. "I said I'm not leaving her. She saw something back there when she put on the amulet. We need her." He turned to Ena once more and grabbed her by the shoulders. "Ena, I promise I'll tell you everything, but we need to get to safety first."

Just then, they heard a commotion coming down the beach. Voices. Shouting. Ena saw torchlights coming over one of the dunes in the distance approaching them.

"Fuck!" Ty said. He pulled the amulet from his pocket and handed it to Steig. "Take this and go. Both of you. Now!"

Steig didn't hesitate—he shoved the amulet into his own pocket and spurred his horse instantly into a gallop.

Turner glanced back at them, his face filled with unease, but then he, too, took off after Steig.

Ty moved to lift Ena onto the horse once more. She didn't fight this time, and once she was seated, he climbed up behind her.

The sounds of pursuit were getting closer, but it wasn't just the pursuers on the beach anymore. Ena turned to see several witches emerging from the woods around them. Then she heard a deep male voice speak.

{*Spiritus*}

She felt the air leave her lungs in one fell swoop. She couldn't breathe. She bent forward on the horse, panic setting in. She couldn't *breathe.*

"Ena!" Ty shouted, his voice filled with fear.

{*Aqus*} another voice said, and the horse collapsed underneath them, water sprouting from its nose and mouth as if it were drowning.

Ty leapt from the horse, removing his dagger. "Let her go right fucking now," he said, his voice more menacing and dark than she'd ever heard it as he approached the male witch who had her under his spell.

"What did you do to my family?!" the male witch screamed.

Quicker than she could blink, Ty threw his dagger at the man. It struck him in the shoulder, causing him to fall to his knees and breaking his concentration on her. She felt her lungs fill with blessed air once more.

Ty removed the ax from his back as another female witch threw out her hands. The ground around them began to shake as the roots of the nearby trees grew and stretched like vines, reaching for Ty's feet.

As they touched him, they turned to dust.

"He's a daemon!" one of the other witches shouted.

{*Aeris*} another one spoke, and the leaves began to swirl around them as the wind picked up into a fierce tempest. Ena could barely see in the dark as branches and rocks hit her face, scratching her, bruising her.

"Ty!" she yelled. She couldn't see him anymore, but she could hear the sounds of a fight. Grunting and yelling. Someone screamed in pain.

She ran blindly toward where she'd seen him last, but a gust of wind threw her back. She felt a sharp pain at the back of her head and the cold earth on her cheek before everything went black.

CHAPTER TWENTY-SIX

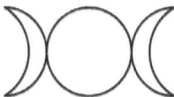

ENA SLOWLY OPENED HER eyes to reveal a strange room. Her head was throbbing and her throat was dry. Looking around, she saw that the room she was in was small, almost the size of a closet. It held a simple table and chair, and the walls were bare. There was no fireplace, so it was cold, and as she raised herself up to sitting, she realized she was laying on a small, hard bed. There were no windows in the room, but light seeped in under the doorframe, and she could tell that it was daytime.

Where was she?

Using her Gift to put those women to sleep. Finding the amulet. Her vision of the past. The attack in the woods. Ty.

It all came back to her in a series of swift realizations. She was with the Occidens Coven. They'd captured her, and where was Ty? The last she'd seen him, he had been fighting off the witches single-handedly. Had he gotten away? Had they killed him?

Ena's heart started to pound as she stood up, fear gripping her once more. She went to open the door, but it was locked.

{*Clavis*}

She spoke her spellword quietly, but nothing happened. She tried it again, jiggling the door handle and pulling with all her might, but still, nothing happened.

She forced herself to calm and investigate her surroundings. There was a candle on the table, and she tried to light it with her spellword, but again, nothing happened.

They must have spelled the room against the use of magic.

She'd heard of it being done before, oftentimes to protect young children who hadn't yet learned to control their magic, but she'd never felt the effects of it herself, and usually it required the person's blood.

Ena reached up to touch the back of her head where she had hit it in the woods, feeling a large, tender lump. She winced at the pain, and saw on her hand the dried remnants of her own blood.

She went over to the door again and knocked gently. "Hello?" she called, her voice sounding small and desperate. "Is anyone there?"

There was no response.

Ena began to feel claustrophobic. It was dark. She was trapped. She started to pace frantically, searching for a way out of the room, feeling the walls and testing the floorboards. She felt so helpless without her magic.

Why were they keeping her here? Where was Ty? Was he okay? Had Steig and Turner gotten away with the amulet?

Suddenly, the door opened and light flooded the room. Ena shielded her eyes as they adjusted to the change.

A figure walked into the room holding a lit candle. She walked over to the table and used it to light the one already sitting there. With the candles now brightening the room, Ena found herself staring into a familiar face.

It was the woman from the kitchen that she'd used her *visanis* on. Seeing her more closely now, she saw that she was probably in her mid-forties. Her face had gentle lines around her eyes, and she was thin. Her dark-blonde hair was tied back into a bun and her hazel eyes watched Ena like a hawk.

"It's good to properly meet you, Ena. My name is Syrelle," she said.

Ena stared at her cautiously, not knowing what to say. How did she know her name?

"Are you feeling alright? You took quite a fall in the woods, I'm told." She paused, waiting for Ena to respond, then continued when she didn't. "Of course, I wasn't there. I found myself incapacitated until the sun rose this morning."

The woman looked at Ena knowingly, clearly trying to gauge her reaction. But Ena gave nothing away.

"Where am I?" Ena asked. She had many questions, but asking this one seemed like a good place to start.

"You're still with the Occidens Coven. I apologize for the sparse accommodations, but we needed to make sure you were secured for now. The room is spelled against magic. But something tells me you already figured that out." The woman gave Ena a tight smile and moved to sit down in the chair. "Please, sit," she said. "I think it's time we had a conversation."

Ena sat on the edge of the bed, her body tense and ready to run or fight. She waited for the familiar surge of her *visanis*, but she couldn't feel it at all.

"We've contacted your Coven," Syrelle said. "When it became clear to us that you were a witch, we sent Aquilo and Auster a message asking if either of them claimed you. Your matriarch, Heran, and your sister, I believe, are on their way here as we speak to negotiate for your release."

Heran and Greya were on their way here? Ena was immediately filled with an intense feeling of relief, followed by guilt, shame, and trepidation. How in the world was she going to face them after everything?

But another concern crowded that one out.

"Where's Ty?" Ena asked, her tone deathly serious.

"The daemon you were with? Interesting that you would ask about him," she said, tilting her head to the side and examining Ena like she was a curiosity. "Your matriarch explained that you were taken from your home a few weeks ago and haven't been heard from since. Daemonic activity was suspected. But..." She peered studiously at Ena. "I was told about the way he defended you when my people found you in the woods... Maybe all is not as it seems."

Ena did not want to antagonize this woman. She could not be seen as having been in league with daemons. Her position was already precarious, but if she could convince them that she was forced to go along with the daemons' plan, maybe they would let her go. That was the truth, after all. They just couldn't know that there was...more between her and Ty.

"I was taken by them," Ena explained. "They forced me to come here with them and told me they would not release me until I helped them...steal something."

"Ah, yes. The amulet. It seems they succeeded in that. While your...friend—Ty, was it?—was captured, the other two got away. Do you know why they were after it?"

"No," Ena answered truthfully. She still did not know what they hoped to accomplish. But her vision had left her with so many questions, and she knew she needed to be cautious with what she revealed to this woman.

"You know, we were lucky you were with them, actually. Without your involvement, the seer in our Coven would not have been able to foresee the attack. Of course, they were not able to warn us about everything, but they saw enough that when my husband arrived home from his travels to find us lying on the floor, they knew where to find you in the woods."

Hearing that description of events, Ena was struck with a deep pang of guilt. She didn't trust these witches, but she still had not wanted to do what she did. Even if she could still recall the pleasurable feeling of power that had enthralled her, it had come with consequences.

She cleared her throat lightly and tried to let the sincerity of her next words come through. "Syrelle, I deeply regret what I did to you and your family. I was hoping that the use of my Gift would remove the necessity for bloodshed and violence while the daemons searched for the amulet. I only agreed to it because...because they said they'd let me go. But I know it must have been terrifying for you and those girls. For that, I am truly sorry."

"I believe you," Syrelle said gently. "My Knowing tells me that you are being sincere."

Ena flinched slightly. Of course she was using her Knowing on her. They were from enemy Covens, and she'd come here with nefarious purposes. But it still grated on Ena's sense of propriety to know another witch was violating her privacy that way. She hoped she couldn't discern her feelings for Ty—that would only complicate matters—but she feared that that was exactly what was happening here.

"Now," Syrelle said, standing up as if to leave before Ena could say anything else. "I'll have someone bring you some water and food. There's a chamber pot beneath the bed if you need to relieve yourself. I'm sorry to say you'll have to remain in here until the members of your Coven arrive, for security's sake, but I'll leave the candles."

Ena nodded in resignation. Syrelle moved to the door, and Ena knew it wasn't smart, that asking likely revealed too much, but she needed to know. "And...the daemon? Does he still live?" she said quietly.

Syrelle gave her a pitying look. "For now," she said. "But he took something powerful from us and wounded several of our people in the process. The Coven is debating what to do with him. I don't think he'll live long."

Relief filled her to hear he was still alive, but was quickly snuffed out at the prospect that, soon, he might not be. What could she say to sway her that Ty should live? Would anything she said matter?

"He's half witch, you know," Ena blurted out. She hoped he would forgive her for telling them this. He might have had his own plans to escape and needed his Gift to remain a secret, but maybe if she could show them that he wasn't all bad, if she could communicate that somehow, they would be more lenient.

Syrelle looked at her knowingly. "Oh, we know. It's one of the only reasons he still lives," she said.

They already knew? Had Ty told them? Why would he have done that?

"If I may be so bold," Syrelle added, a cautioning look on her face. "There have been witches before you, some from this very Coven, who have been led down a dark path by daemonic intervention. It can be natural to...pity them, but it never ends well. You'd do well to let go of whatever sympathy you may have for him, before it festers and grows."

With that, Syrelle closed her in once more. Ena leaned back on the bed, her mind whirling.

He was alive. For now, at least. And Heran and Greya were coming for her. They'd be able to sort it out. Syrelle had seemed like she believed Ena, and hopefully didn't blame her for everything that had happened. They might be able to get her out of this.

But Ty...how would he get out of this? Did Syrelle and the other members of the Occidens Coven know about the amulet and what it was for? Did they know why he'd taken it? And what was that about other witches from their Coven being led down a dark path? She'd never heard another witch express pity for daemons before. Did Syrelle know something she did not?

Ena couldn't shake the feeling that there was way more going on than she knew. The witches she'd seen in her vision had done something extraordinary with the amulet, something that had felt wrong. And Ty had mentioned that getting the amulet was not Iblis's will. Then Steig had said that whatever they wanted to do with it would help daemons... That could mean anything, of course, and was not necessarily good for mortals or witches.

But everything she'd seen and learned since the daemons had taken her made her realize that maybe not everything she had been told about them was true. And maybe, just maybe, Ty didn't deserve to die for this.

Or maybe she just didn't want to let him go.

She knew it was wrong on so many levels to feel this way, but even after everything, she still cared for him. And she knew it was foolish, and naïve, and something she'd thought had died in her long ago, but a small, desperate part of her wanted to trust him.

She needed to talk to Heran and get more information about the amulet. Maybe then she'd be able to help Ty. Maybe if she could prove that taking the amulet had not been in service of Iblis, they'd let him live. He'd clearly already told them he was half witch, and that revelation had swayed some to his side. But why would he have done that? It didn't seem like him to reveal that information willingly.

Unless...maybe he hadn't told them. Was it possible they knew his mother? Was that what Syrelle meant by witches from Occidens walking a dark path? Ty had never said what Coven she was from. Did he even know?

If that was true, if his mother was an Occidens witch and they somehow recognized him, then clearly some members of the Coven were hesitant to put him to death because of that. And maybe, if Ena could figure out what he wanted with the amulet, it would be enough for them to let him go.

In her heart of hearts, she knew that was a fool's hope. Half-Occidens witch or not, he was still a daemon; there was very little chance the Coven would allow him to live, especially not after what he'd done. But it was the only hope she had right now. She was not ready to face the possibility of losing him. So she would cling to this hope like it was the only buoyant thing in the Endless Ocean, and pray to Gaia it kept them both afloat.

CHAPTER TWENTY-SEVEN

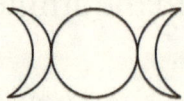

DAYS WENT BY AND she was going out of her mind. With nothing to occupy her in the small, dark room, she had little to do but sleep.

So she slept, and dreamt of Ty. She dreamt of the two of them together, writhing together in pleasure and in pain. She dreamt of the vision she'd had, and the violence of it intertwined with her memories of the bandits in the woods.

She woke and ate the food they brought her, and she paced around the room. She thought about everything that had occurred over and over and over until she drove herself half mad trying to figure out all that she didn't know.

Then, on her third day after waking up, a knock came on the door.

"Come in," she called. The Occidens witches had never knocked before; they just came in when they brought her food and emptied her chamber pot.

She almost couldn't believe her eyes when Greya walked into the room. "Ena!" she cried, rushing towards her and scooping her in her arms.

Ena froze there for a minute, too shocked to move or speak. When she finally realized that this was, indeed, reality, and not one of her wild dreams, she wrapped her arms around Greya and felt tears instantly start to fall.

Greya's scent surrounded her. The familiarity and the warmth of her sister seeped into her bones, buoying her when she'd been drowning. The sisters held each other for several minutes, rocking and weeping and drinking in each other's presence.

Eventually, Greya pulled away. "Are you alright?" she asked, wiping tears from her eyes. "I've been so worried, Ena. So, so worried."

"I'm fine," Ena replied, sniffling. "I promise, I'm unharmed." They moved to sit together on the bed as Ena asked, "Where's Heran?"

"She's meeting with the matriarch of their Coven. Syrelle, I think her name is. They're discussing whether any reparations need to be made because of the breach of the treaty, but Heran is confident that they'll let you go. They seem to understand that this was not your doing or your choice."

Ena nodded silently, relief flooding through her.

Greya studied her in the way only a big sister could. "Ena, what happened?" she asked, as if she'd been holding this question inside for weeks. "They said you arrived with three daemons and helped them steal an amulet? There's been a lot of consternation about that. They said...they said you used your Gift on them." Greya spoke that last part cautiously, as if not wanting to offend Ena.

Ena took a deep breath, steadying herself. She needed to tell the truth, and pray that Greya would understand her choices. If she had any hope of redeeming herself with her Coven and her Goddess, she needed to come clean and accept the consequences.

"It's true," Ena replied. "They took me on the night of Samhain. They were looking for the amulet in Heran's house, and when I found them, they forced me to come with them and do a locator spell. It led them here, and they told me if I helped them, they'd let me go. I tried to escape but..." Ena trailed off, tears filling her eyes again as she thought of how close she'd come to getting a message to her sister.

"Shh, shh, it's okay, Ena. You don't have to explain yourself. You did what you needed to do to survive." Greya stroked her hair soothingly. But a pit of guilt hit Ena's stomach.

"No, no, you don't understand. I did use my Gift on them...and others. I know it wasn't Gaia's will, but I thought it would save them from violence...I thought it would save *me*." Ena buried her face in her hands as tears began to fall. She cried for all the fear she'd felt, all the guilt. All her sadness and her confusion spilled out with her tears as they turned to sobs, and through it all, her sister held her in understanding, making soothing sounds and mumbling calming words.

Eventually, Ena began to calm down. Her tears dried up, and her breathing slowed once more. But still, she could barely bring herself to meet her sister's gaze, because there was something else she had to admit.

"There's...there's something else you don't know," Ena said, taking her head off Greya's shoulder, her eyes puffy and swollen. "One of the daemons who took me...was Ty."

"Ty?" Greya asked, her brow furrowed in confusion. "The mortal from all those years ago? Are you sure?"

"Yes. He's not a mortal. That was a cover. He's a dae-mon."

Greya paused, a look of utter shock on her face. "Oh, Ena," she said, her voice filled with anguish for her sister. Greya had been there when Ena had waited, year after year, for Ty's return. She knew the heartbreak Ena had felt in his wake, and she knew, Goddess damn her, that a part of her had never healed, that a part of her had always been waiting for him to come back.

Greya brought her closer as if to hug her again, as if to comfort her, but Ena shook her off. She'd had enough of crying, and mentioning Ty reminded her of what she still needed to do. She needed answers.

"Did they tell you anything about the amulet?" Ena asked, pulling back to look at Greya.

"No," she said. "Why? Do you know why the daemons wanted it?"

"No, but Greya, there are some things that don't add up. When I put it on, I had a vision. I saw three witches, and they were doing a ceremony with the amulet. They were hurting someone. I don't know who it was, but it felt...wrong. So wrong. I don't know what Ty wants with the amulet, but I'm not sure it's bad."

"Ena," Greya started, her brow coming together in confusion and disbelief, "you can't be serious. This man just kidnapped you, burned Heran's house, attacked this Coven. He can't be trusted. He's manipulating you. Who's to say exactly what you saw?"

"I know what I saw," Ena said through gritted teeth, her anger rising. "Look, Greya," she said, trying to calm herself and speak clearly. "I can't explain it, but somehow... I think I trust him."

"Trust him?! Ena, are you drinking fucking psilovenom?" Now it was Greya's turn to feel anger. "I know this is hard for you. I know you've been hung up on this guy for years, but you're letting your feelings cloud your judgment. He *cannot* be trusted."

"That's not what this is about, I—"

Ena's words were cut off as the door opened again and the sisters went silent.

Heran walked into the room, her gray eyes darting between the two of them. "Am I interrupting something?"

"No, my apologies," Greya said as she stood up, smoothing her dress and fixing her composure. Ena hoped they hadn't been overheard arguing with one another; that would not be good for the Coven's image.

Heran turned to face Ena, her arms outstretched. Her face was wrinkled and her eyes kind. Her brown- and gray-streaked hair was tied tightly back in a bun. "Ena, my child. Are you alright? We've been so worried."

Ena smiled warily at Heran, her heart and mind still thrown from the argument with Greya, and moved closer to embrace her. "Yes, Heran."

The smell of lavender surrounded Ena as Heran held her. Heran's body was small, but sturdy. The feel of it comforted her, and she felt her own body calm slightly. It felt good to be safe again, with people she trusted.

Pulling back, Heran held Ena by her shoulders and studied her intensely. "We have much to discuss. The Occidens witches have agreed to let you return home with us. They do not consider this a willing breach of the treaty, so you will see no punishment."

Ena breathed a sigh of relief at that, but tensed at Heran's next words.

"Greya, would you please step outside for a minute? I would like to speak to Ena alone."

Greya looked warily between her and Heran, but nodded dutifully and stepped out of the room, closing the door behind her.

"Sit, my child," Heran said, gesturing to the bed. She herself sat on the lone chair in the room and reached out to grab Ena's hands. "I know you have been through much and must have a lot of questions, but I need to know: the amulet that was stolen, did they tell you why they wanted it?"

"No, Heran. They didn't tell me anything. But..." Ena paused. She was cautious to share what she knew, especially after the way Greya had reacted. "I was the one to find the amulet first. I intended to take it and hide it from them, and hoped to bring it home with me when they let me go." She looked at Heran for assurance. She wanted her to know her intentions had been good. She had tried so hard to serve Gaia and to disrupt the daemons' plans. "But when I touched it...I saw something." Ena paused again, gauging Heran's reaction.

"You had a vision?" Heran asked calmly.

"Yes. And what I saw...well, it was unsettling." Ena described her vision in as much detail as she could to Heran. Heran remained silent as she spoke, slowly stroking her thumbs over the back of Ena's hands in comfort. When she was finished speaking, she released them with a gentle pat.

"Thank you for sharing that with me, child." Heran's reaction was not what Ena had expected. She did not seem surprised or confused, only calm and contemplative. She rose to stand and turned away from Ena. She paced the room a few times, before seeming to come to a decision as she sat back down.

"I believe Gaia has seen fit to reveal this vision to you, so I will tell you what I know." Taking a deep breath as if to steel herself, Heran continued. "Hundreds of years ago, when witches and daemons came to the split, it was true that many daemons willingly chose to serve Iblis. But it is also true that some did not. You must understand, it was a dark time. There was significant discord and disillusionment between witches and daemons. It was decided that, although some daemons wanted to remain connected to Gaia and continue serving both their Master and our Goddess as they saw fit, they could not be trusted. Daemonic gifts were too insidious, too disruptive to be allowed access to Gaia. They were simply not suited to serve her. So, one witch from each Coven came together to bind all daemons into servitude with Iblis, removing their ability to access Gaia's power and interpret her will. It was a necessary sacrifice, one which has allowed witches and mortals to thrive, relatively free of daemonic influence. The daemons have since been confined to the Underworld, and though they occasionally emerge to create chaos and disrupt the balance, witches have been able to, for the most part, maintain control."

Ena was silent for a minute as she tried to process this information. "So, the vision I had when I touched the amulet. That was the binding ritual?"

"Yes, I believe that is what you saw. The amulet is a crucial conduit which allowed the witches to terminate the daemons' connection to Gaia. I am not certain of the details, those have been lost to time, but I believe the daemons who took you intend to use the amulet to break the bond to Iblis."

Ena's mind spun. Was this true? Was this what Ty and the others intended to use the amulet for? To regain access to Gaia and her power? What would that mean for them, for witches, for mortals? Ena didn't know how to feel about this.

Heran, misinterpreting her confusion for distress, reached for her hands once more. "Do not fret, my child. The daemons may have the amulet, but Syrelle and I are confident that they will not be able to break the bond to Iblis on their own. It was done with witch magic, and daemons alone cannot break it, even with the amulet."

"Oh...okay," Ena replied flatly. That was the least of her concerns right now.

"But Ena, I'm not certain why Gaia has seen fit to reveal this to you. Only time will tell, but this information is strictly guarded. Only Coven matriarchs have been entrusted with it, and it must remain that way. You cannot tell anyone, not even Greya. Do you understand?"

No, Ena didn't understand. She didn't understand at all. Why was this being kept secret? Why were they so sure that cutting off daemons from Gaia's power was a good thing? She wanted to ask these questions, and so many more, but that was not her place. She had never argued with Heran, so instead, she lied.

"Yes, I understand, Heran."

Heran nodded and cupped her cheek gently. "Good. Now come," she said, rising to stand once more and bringing Ena with her. "We were given nicer accommodations for the night, and you've been given permission to come stay with us. We'll leave for home first thing in the morning."

Ena sighed deeply. She was more than relieved to be leaving this tiny, dark room, but as Heran moved to open the door, Ena's heart sank.

Heran had said only Coven matriarchs knew about the amulet, which meant Syrelle already knew. There was no new information Ena could tell her that might sway her to let Ty live. She had no more cards left to play.

Her mind spun in frantic disbelief. Maybe they'd decided to let him go anyway. Maybe his heritage had been enough. Heran had been talking with the Occidens matriarch, so she must have new information.

"Wait," she said, her voice shaking as she stopping Heran. "The daemon I was found with. Did they tell you if they came to a decision about what to do with him?"

"Don't worry, my child. He is to be drowned in the Endless Ocean at dawn. He won't be able to haunt you anymore."

CHAPTER TWENTY-EIGHT

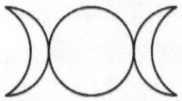

IT WAS THE EARLY evening when Ena found herself in the bath. Heran had led her through the house she'd been held in and down the street to a larger home where they had been given a nicer room. Ena's legs moved automatically, but she didn't see or feel a thing.

Ty was to be put to death. He was to be drowned.

She was given food, which she ate out of habit, barely tasting a thing. Then she was shown to the bathhouse, where she was provided with a warm bath and a clean dress, one of her own that had survived the fire. Greya had brought it with her from home.

She sat in the bath and stared at the water, and all she could think was that soon, the water would drown him. The water would fill his lungs and he'd stop breathing. His beautiful eyes would close forever. He'd never laugh at her again. Never touch her again. Never look at her with those eyes that saw everything—even the words she couldn't say.

Ena silently began to cry, her tears falling into the water.

Why did she care? He was a daemon and she should hate him. He had abandoned her and lied to her and she should hate him. They could never be together. She owed him nothing. She should let him go and move on.

But it wasn't that simple. Yes, he was a daemon, and yes, she had plenty of reasons to hate him, and yet she didn't. The way he made her feel...like she was powerful, and beautiful, and brave. The way his laughter drew out her own. The way he had fought to get back to her, despite everything. The way he was reckless and pushed her to do more than she ever thought she could. The way he understood her, and always, inexplicably, made her feel safe. There was a magnetic force that pulled her to him, even after all this time, and she'd be a fool to deny it.

No, she couldn't let him die. She wouldn't.

Everything Heran had told her ran through her mind, and she started to plan. If daemons succeeded in breaking the bond to Iblis, if they were able to access Gaia's power, who knew what they would do. She'd always been told that they couldn't be trusted and that they would inevitably bring destruction and devastation to her world.

But what if it wasn't that simple?

She couldn't shake the feelings she'd experienced in her vision. The wrongness of it all. She didn't believe that cutting off the daemons from one half of their natural magic had been Gaia's will. And for some reason, she remembered all those years ago, when she'd first met Ty, and how fascinated he'd been when he saw that Canus Elk in the woods. He was half witch. Was it right that he remained cut off from Gaia's power just because of his daemon blood? What about Turner? And Steig, with his family? What might they be free to do with access to Gaia?

All at once, she was filled with certainty. She had to speak to Ty. Tonight. She needed to understand and hear it from his own mouth.

And if it was true, then she needed to say goodbye.

***

Later that night, she feigned sleep in her bed. When she was certain that Greya and Heran were asleep in the beds next to her, she slipped on her boots and her borrowed cloak and grabbed the saddlebag filled with food and clothes that Greya had prepared for her for their journey home tomorrow.

As quietly as possible, she slipped out the door. Gaia be blessed, now that they'd agreed to her release and were assured that she wasn't a threat, they weren't watching her so closely anymore, because the door was unlocked and there was no one outside her room.

She walked quickly down the hallway. Her Knowing assured her that the witches whose home it was were blessedly asleep upstairs on the second floor, and the kitchen was quiet and dark, but a fire burned in the sitting room and she Knew someone was awake there. She'd intended to make her exit out the front door, but there was no way the witch wouldn't sense her as she crept past the sitting room.

What were the chances there was someone at the back door too? Fuck. She changed course and timed her steps to the loud pops of the hearth fire and instead moved to the washroom to regroup. She'd been worried that they might still be guarding the entrances to the house. Even though they'd been assured that Ena was no threat, she, Heran, and Greya were still from an enemy Coven—they still could not be trusted. She opened the door of the small chamber that contained a pitcher, ewer, basin, and tub, and tried to steady her breathing as her heart pounded.

She could use her Gift on them, of course. She knew she should feel guilty about being so willing to do that, but she was too deep into this to care now. All that mattered was getting to Ty and getting him out. But she also knew there'd be similar circumstances wherever they were holding Ty, and the more she used her magic, the more it would drain her, so she wanted to save it as a last resort. She wracked her brain, thinking of a way to escape the house without having to use her Gift.

Then her eyes landed on the window.

It was small, but maybe just big enough for her. She tried not to think about the irony of sneaking out of the bathroom window when Ty had given her such shit about potentially doing it in Attax. Instead, she stepped into the dry bathtub at the base of the window and lifted the well-oiled latch. Gaia be blessed, it was naturally windy this close to the ocean, and just as a particularly large gust rattled the house, she swung the window open, letting in the cold night air.

The drop from the window onto the ground of the garden below looked manageable, so Ena tossed the saddlebag she carried through the window, hearing it land with a gentle thud on the soft soil. Cautiously, she lifted one leg through the window, using the edge of the tub below to awkwardly straddle the sill. Then, crouching low, she ducked her head through the window and slid down until one leg landed ungracefully on the ground, the other still caught on the edge of the sill. She lost her balance and fell as she pulled her other leg down to meet her, her hands slamming into the sandy, rocky dirt as her body smashed the woody sage plant below. But she didn't stop to worry about the damage as she stood and closed the window behind her. She fled silently through the house's garden and out the small gate that led into the forest. Once in the dark of the woods, she followed a light path through the trees until it wound between two of the houses next door, leading her back to the main road that ran down the center of the village.

She wasn't entirely sure where Ty was being held, but she followed her instinct as she crept down the road to the small house that she'd been held in. She'd figured out through observation that no one currently lived there, and that was why it had been chosen as the easiest place to house her as the Coven's unexpected prisoner.

She'd bet everything that Ty was being held there too.

She slowly opened the front door, which unfortunately gave a loud creak. Ena winced as she slipped into the house, then closed it quickly behind her and froze, listening. There was no way someone hadn't heard that. They'd be ready for her now.

Her heart pounded in her ears as she walked down the hallway. The door to the first room on the right was open, and she saw light coming from within. She Knew someone was there. She had no idea which room Ty was being held in, and there was no way to get to the rest of the house without passing by the witch in that room. So as she walked towards the light, she reached down into her Knowing, feeling for her Gift. Guilt over using her forbidden Gift didn't even touch her as a plan formed in her mind.

Besides, if she played her cards right, no one would ever know.

A man in his fifties with short black hair speckled with gray sat in a large, upholstered chair in front of the fireplace, a discarded book in his lap. Ena wasn't even scared as his eyes landed on her, confusion filling his face. She reached for her Gift and it flooded through her, swamping her like a wave, and before he could speak, Ena did.

{*Don't move.*}

The eerie voice of her *visanis* echoed around the room as the man's movements froze.

{*Tell me where the daemon is.*}

The man stared at her, confusion locked on his face and his body frozen in his last position. Only his mouth moved as he answered her question.

"Upstairs, the third room on the right," he replied, his voice afraid.

{*Tell me where everyone else is in the house.*}

"Ben is at the back door and Elyse is outside his door." The man's voice shook, but not a muscle in his body moved.

{Ignore any sounds you hear until morning. Forget that you saw and spoke to me.}

After finishing her instructions, Ena gasped for breath. That was the most commands she'd given using her Gift, and she felt the strain on her magic already, but she kept going.

The man instantly turned back to his book as if nothing had happened, and Ena walked quietly towards the back of the house. She saw Ben there, sitting in a chair that had been dragged next to the door, whittling something out of wood. She recognized him as one of the witches who'd been bringing her food the last few days, and he stood up at her approach, realization dawning on his face.

He moved to speak, but Ena was faster.

{Forget you saw me. Sit down and sleep until someone wakes you.}

He sat down in a trance and closed his eyes instantly.

Turning her back on him, Ena returned to find the stairs. She hoped her movements hadn't already alerted the final witch's Knowing, but that hope was dashed as she crested the top and heard Elyse speak.

{Aeris}

A gust of air threw her off balance and she fell halfway back down the stairs, landing awkwardly on the saddlebag she carried as it partially cushioned her fall. She scrambled to right herself, ignoring the throbbing on the side of her head where she'd whacked it on the banister, and looked up to see Elyse glaring down at her. Ena felt her Gift surge through her anew, her anger rising. Before Elyse could do anything else, Ena spoke.

{Lay down, close your eyes, don't move.}

The woman froze, her face screwed up in anger, before laying down and closing her eyes. Ena righted herself the rest of the way and walked up the stairs to stand in front of her. She breathed heavily as she drew on her exhausted magic to finish the commands. She was dizzy from her fall, but she hoped this effort would cover her tracks.

{I was never here. When someone finds you, tell them a daemon came and forced you to unlock the door. Then he knocked you unconscious and left with the prisoner.}

The woman didn't move or show any acknowledgement that she'd heard Ena, but she wasn't asleep, so Ena hoped the compulsion would work as intended. She released her grip on her Gift in sudden exhaustion, then stumbled to the door of Ty's room.

Her magic was nearly exhausted, even her Knowing seemed dimmed, but she dredged up what she could to feel for the metal in the lock on the door and spoke her spellword.

{Clavis}

Thankfully, she heard the lock click. She turned the handle slowly, and stepped into a dark room.

CHAPTER TWENTY-NINE

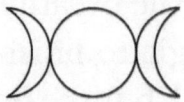

A SINGLE CANDLE BURNED low on a table. Ena squinted in the dark, trying to make out where the furniture was, and where Ty might be, when an arm reached out and looped around her waist from behind. She opened her mouth to speak just as a hand reached out and covered it.

She squirmed and mumbled incoherently into the hand, but he didn't let go, so she bit him.

"Damn! Easy, viper," Ty said from behind her. He released her mouth, shaking out his injured hand, but kept his arm still looped around her waist. "What are you doing here, Ena?" he asked in surprise.

"I need to talk to you," Ena replied angrily. His arm finally loosened around her waist, so she spun to look at him. She could just make out his face in the dimly lit room, and it still took her breath away.

Somehow, in the days they'd been apart, she'd forgotten just how beautiful he was. Thick lashes framed his light-green eyes as they bored into her. His perfect, kissable lips were parted slightly as his dark brows lowered in confusion. The candlelight danced in his beard, making the mix of lighter blond hairs glow against the darker browns and reds.

"Are you okay? Did they hurt you?" he asked, concern etched on his face.

"Asks the man who just grabbed me when I came in the room," she said, still feeling a bit irked at his welcome.

"I wasn't sure who you were at first. My *venator* doesn't work in here and I heard a commotion outside the door. Are you sure you're okay? I've been asking about you, but they wouldn't tell me anything."

Her temper softened at his distressed tone. "I'm fine. They're letting me go," she said, giving him a small smile.

He nodded in relief before flicking his eyes to the door behind her. "What happened to the witches standing guard?" he asked, watching it like someone was going to burst in any second.

"I took care of them," Ena said with conviction.

Ty looked at her then, a hint of suspicion creeping in. "What did they tell you?" he asked cautiously.

"That you're to be put to death tomorrow," Ena said, swallowing her fear at the thought. "Drowned."

He nodded, a look of solemn understanding settling on his face. But there was no surprise. He expected this. "Come to say your goodbyes to a doomed man then?" he asked, giving her a sad smile.

"Doomed?" she asked. She didn't like hearing him talk this way. "You're giving in so easily?"

Ty shrugged. "I won't go down without a fight. And if I do, Steig and Turner already got away. I know they'll keep going without me. And you...you'll be okay too," he said, as if trying to convince himself.

"I never pegged you for a martyr," Ena said, feeling annoyed that he was so accepting of his death. Why wasn't he fighting? Insisting they flee right now? Part of her was screaming to, but she needed answers first.

Ty just rolled his eyes, as if this conversation about his death was pointless. "What did you want to talk about, viper?" he asked, sitting back on the table.

Ena took a deep breath, studying him for a few seconds, but she allowed the change of subject. "You told me you'd tell me everything. I want to know why you want the amulet."

"Why?" he asked suspiciously. "So you can run and tell the rest of your Coven? They've been asking me that same question for days, along with a surprising number of questions about my mother," he said ruefully.

Did he suspect the same thing Ena did? That the only reason they'd kept him alive so long was because of his mother? Ena didn't know, but now was not the time to open *that* jar.

"No," Ena said, trying to control her annoyance. She'd come here to help him, and he was just clinging to this bullshit. She took a deep breath. "Look, I...when I put on the amulet, I had a vision. I saw a ritual being done, and it seemed...well, it *felt* wrong. And when I spoke to Heran about it, she told me something, something I didn't know before. She told me that witches were the ones who bound daemons to serve Iblis. That it wasn't their choice. She told me that's why you want the amulet. To break that bond. Is that true?"

Ty hesitated for a second, watching her, gauging her reactions. He'd clearly kept this information to himself for so long, she knew it went against his nature to admit to it. Finally, he sighed, as if coming to the same realization she had: that it was time for them to be on the same page. "Yes, it's true," he said.

"Why?"

"Why what?"

"Why do you want to break the bond?" Ena asked, feeling exasperated again.

"Isn't it obvious?"

"Not to me," she said flippantly.

Ty sighed again, as if he were dealing with a difficult child, and rubbed the back of his neck. "How much do you know of our kind and the Underworld?"

"Not much. Only what I've been told, and clearly not all of that was the truth," she said, not even trying to keep the frustration from her voice.

Ty nodded. He understood her frustration, he understood her anger, and he looked at her with that understanding as he told her the truth.

"It's true that your kind bound us to Iblis hundreds of years ago," he said. "But even before then, witches and daemons were constantly struggling for dominance over one another, fighting for power over the land, the resources, and alliances with the mortals. Your kind was suspicious of us, because our Powers were often of the mind, more subtle and insidious than the earth magic of witches. Disagreements occurred, mistrust grew, and witches, to maintain their control, well, let's just say they decided to control the narrative. They blamed all chaos and disruption on daemons, causing mortals to mistrust us as well. Eventually, we became so, for lack of a better word, demonized, that we were no longer welcome in mortal villages, so we settled in the Underworld."

Ena had never heard any of this before. She'd always been told that daemons chose to live in the Under-world, not that they had been forced there through a power play.

"Soon after that," Ty continued, "the three Covens used the amulet to bind us to Iblis, cutting us off from being able to interpret Gaia's will or access her magic. And the rest is history," he said, as if it were that simple. "But, of course, there were consequences for what the witches did. Their magic could no longer be used against us, and vice versa. No one is quite sure why that happened, but powerful spells can often have unexpected ripple effects."

Ena stared at him, rapt with attention as he continued, his tone filling with anger now.

"Of course, while your kind and mortals thrived above ground, daemons suffered below. Forced to interpret and carry out Iblis's will in exchange for our Powers, for our way of life, we survived only on what we could steal, or the little we could make and catch for ourselves around the entrance to the Underworld. We traded a little with mortals, using the natural metal deposits in the Underworld and our skills in metallurgy to create a cover for our missions. But, of course, we couldn't make ourselves too well known, for fear of being found out. So, for a long time, daemons lived this way and came to accept our fate. Eventually, the amulet and everything the witches had done became myth, and we started to internalize the lies that had been spread about us. That we were evil. That we were only good for spreading chaos, discontent, and discord. But I know that's not true. And that my people deserve better. They deserve a chance."

The room was silent with Ty's declaration. She'd never heard him speak this way before—so passionately, so full of righteousness. Part of her wanted to argue that her kind would never be so cruel, could never be so power-hungry and malicious with their magic, but the more she thought about it, the more she knew it to be true. Just because witches served Gaia did not mean they were immune to greed or apathy. She'd seen the ways the Covens played politics with one another, vying for influence and power over the mortal villages. And while it was true that they helped mortals, their help always came at a cost, a trade to better the Coven. And sometimes, even though help was requested, it was denied because of Gaia's will. But now, after all the lies, Ena was starting to wonder, how much of it was truly Gaia's will, and how much of it was witches'?

"How did you learn all this?" she asked. "How did you find out about the amulet?"

Ty looked at her, as if deciding how much to reveal. He'd clearly never shared this all before. Ena wasn't even sure if all daemons knew. He made it seem like they probably did not.

"A few months ago," he began, "I was on a mission from Iblis in a village to the west of the Aquilo Coven.

The people there were flourishing too much, or so we were told. Their alliance was strengthening the Aquilo Coven, and Iblis feared the power of the witches was growing too strong, so I was sent to disrupt it."

"By using your *furor*?" Ena asked.

"Yes. Unchecked rage can really throw a wrench in alliances," Ty replied with a rueful smile. "I was there for a while, undercover of course, and I made...a friend." Ty looked away again, guilt briefly washing over his face. "He was a mortal, a book binder in the village. And he was a collector and purveyor of rare books and manuscripts. He shared with me the myth of the amulet. Of course, he didn't know who, or what, I was. Not until it was too late." Ty went quiet again, and when he looked up, Ena could see the pain in his face. "After that, I started looking for more information about the amulet on my own, until I found a vague reference that led me to believe it might be in the matriarch's house at your Coven. Obviously, that was incorrect."

Ty went quiet again, but Ena sensed that there was more to the story.

"What happened to him? Your friend?" Ena asked quietly.

Ty met her gaze with purpose, as if what he was about to say next would be extremely consequential. "He was killed when one of the targets of my rage started a house fire that spread quickly throughout the village," he said.

Ena had to hold in her gasp, putting two and two together. "When was this?" she asked, trepidation in her voice.

"About six months ago." He looked at her with guilt in his eyes. He knew what she was realizing.

He *was* the cause of the fire that had wiped out the village of Ternan, precipitating the loss of homes and livelihoods that had led to the bandits resorting to thieving and killing. That had led to them attacking her and Ty in the woods.

Ena was silent for a moment. She didn't know what to say. The fact that Ty had ultimately been the cause of such destruction, and that it had come with such horrible consequences, shocked her.

"Do you regret coming here now? After hearing what I've done? I told you, Ena, this is what daemons do. This is what *I* do. At least until I can break the bond." He didn't speak with acceptance, but instead with resignation, as if willing her to see him and judge him. As if he *wanted* to be punished for it.

But she saw the sorrow in his eyes, the regret. This was not something that he'd chosen. Forced by Iblis and the daemonic hierarchy, she knew this was not something he relished. No, she might have been upset by this information, but she didn't blame him for it, even if he blamed himself.

"No, I don't regret it. I know you didn't choose this, Ty, any more than I chose what happened when the bandits attacked us."

He looked away from her then, hiding his guilt as if her acceptance of him overwhelmed him.

"But there is one more thing I need to know," she asked, forcing him to look up at her again. "What *will* happen if you break the bond? What will daemons do?"

Earnestness shone in his eyes, like he willed her to see what he saw, what he knew. "My hope is that those of us who wish to serve Gaia will be free to do so. We won't be forced to do Iblis's bidding in exchange for our Powers. We'll be able to interpret Gaia's will, in the same way we do Iblis's, and we'll have a choice. With time, and goodwill, we may be able to reintegrate with mortals," he paused, looking at Ena before he said, "and witches."

Ena stared at him. She didn't pretend that she knew this man well. Once, maybe, she'd thought she did. But nine years was a long time. Somehow, though, she knew he was being sincere. The vulnerability in his eyes was one she had not often glimpsed since their reunion. The passionate way he spoke about his people, and his hopes for the future—it wasn't faked.

Ena smiled lightly. "It could be a fool's errand. None of what you hope for could come to pass."

Ty smiled back at her, like a wolf. "Maybe so...but at least I'll fuck some shit up on the way."

Ena would never admit it, but the way he said that sent a thrill through her. Something, somewhere deep inside her, urged her to join him in his chaotic endeavor. To forge this new path with him, and the thought both terrified and enlivened her.

Stooping, she picked up the bag of supplies she'd brought with her and tossed it at his feet. "Go," she said. "The witches guarding the house have been compelled to ignore and cover your escape. No one will stop you. You can go to the stables and take a horse. You'll be long gone by morning."

He looked down at the bag, but he didn't pick it up. Instead, he smirked at Ena, a knowing, joking look on his face. "I thought you just came here to talk, and yet you had this bag of supplies for me the whole time?"

"I had a feeling about what I might hear."

Ty chuckled, but then grew quiet. He looked at her seriously and said, "What about you?"

"What about me?"

"You should come with me."

Ena stared at him in shock and confusion at his offer. "Come with you? Come with you where?"

"To the Underworld."

Ena scoffed at him, her mouth agape. He had to be joking. But his face was set, and he looked dead serious.

"I've been gone too long. I need to return for a while. But I have resources there. You could help me figure out how to break the bond, now that we have the amulet. Besides, I'm not leaving you here to take the fall for my escape. And if you come with me, there are...ways to protect you, to keep you safe."

She paused. The sincerity of his offer touched her in a way she couldn't describe. Clearly, he didn't want to let her go, either.

"I covered my tracks coming here. They won't blame me," Ena said. "And either way...I can't do that," she said quietly. "My place is with my Coven, with my sister."

Ty shrugged, as if he'd expected this. "If you say so."

He played it off, but she could tell this answer disappointed him. They stared at each other, the tension crackling between them. All that was left was to say goodbye. It was the reason Ena had come, and yet she couldn't make her mouth form the words.

Ty moved to pick up the saddlebag at his feet, and then he took a few steps towards Ena, stopping when he was close enough to touch. Ena craned her neck to look up at him.

"I guess this is goodbye, then," he said gently.

"I guess so," she replied.

"Try not to pine for me for the next nine years, okay?" he said, that cocky smile reappearing on his face.

Ena scoffed, not breaking eye contact. The absolute nerve. "Oh please. You and I both know the second you get to safety, you'll be thinking about me while you fuck your hand."

The corner of Ty's mouth lifted slightly as he took a step closer so their bodies were touching. "I won't deny it."

"Good," Ena said, feeling slightly breathless now.

"Great," he replied, squishing even closer into her.

"Bye, then." Ena glanced down at his lips.

"Stop talking," Ty said, and then his mouth was on hers.

CHAPTER THIRTY

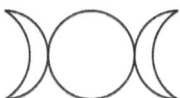

HIS KISS WAS RAW and demanding, his tongue instantly parting her lips and driving into her mouth. His hand came to the back of her head, grabbing her hair and holding her in place. She kissed him back with the same ferocity, her arms looping around his neck and pulling him closer to her.

Ty nipped at her lips and sucked on her tongue, so frantic, as if he wanted to do everything all at once. Ena could barely keep up as he lowered his hands to her backside, squeezing it through her dress and lifting her up. She looped her legs around his waist, pulling at his hair and arching further into him. Her breasts pushed against his chest as she sucked on his lower lip, making him groan loudly.

She was dimly aware that he was supposed to be leaving, but fuck it all. If this was goodbye, if this was all they would ever have, then she wanted everything.

She grabbed at him like her life depended on it as he took two long strides to the side of the room, forcing her back against the door. Her hands came to his shirt, lifting it up so she could feel his skin. She stroked her fingers down his chest, the sensation of hard muscles and soft hairs driving her absolutely wild.

Leaning her weight back against the door, she looked down and started to undo his pants. She could feel his cock already hard underneath, begging to be released. She couldn't get his pants all the way down in this position, but she stroked him through the fabric, swirling her thumb around the tip that was exposed.

"Fucking Iblis, Ena," Ty gasped. Then, still holding on to her rear, he walked them over to the small bed and threw her down on it.

As she stared up at him, he looked like some sort of dark, vengeful god. His shirt disheveled and his pants halfway undone, his hair unkempt from her hands working into it—she took it all in and relished the view, committing it to memory. He stared down at her with an intensity that made her heart skip.

"Get that dress off," he commanded.

Ena did as he asked and undid the laces on her bodice. She quickly kicked off her boots and shimmied out of her dress and shift until she was kneeling naked on the bed before him.

His eyes roamed over her breasts, her stomach, and down between her legs. "I can't tell you how often I regretted not getting you fully naked before me all those years ago. You are fucking stunning, Ena."

If Ena wasn't quite so mad with lust, she would have blushed, but as it were, she just shook her head and said, "No time for that," as she reached for him and yanked his shirt over his head before she moved to pull his pants down too.

As he stepped out of them, his hands came up to cup her breasts. He groaned as he squeezed them gently, his thumbs stroking lightly over her nipples. He lowered to his knees before her so his head was at their level, and he took one nipple into his mouth, swirling his tongue over it before biting it gently between his teeth.

Ena instantly felt her core fill with wetness. Her clit began to ache, begging to be touched as he fondled her breasts more and more.

Her hands came to his shoulders, his neck, his hair, then lowered down his chest to stroke his cock. It was silky smooth and yet absolutely rock hard. She felt him shudder as she touched it, and she knew it felt as good for him as it did for her. She stroked him several times, up and down, pumping him with her hand as she kissed him. Imagining what it would feel like in her mouth, in her pussy. Then she couldn't wait anymore.

"Ty, fuck. Please fuck me," she begged, squeezing him tightly in her hand.

He straightened up to look at her, his eyes mirroring the frantic desire she felt in her body. "Lay down," he said, his voice rough.

She did as she was told and lay back on the bed. She expected him to come on top of her, but instead, he tugged her legs to the edge of the bed. As she lifted her head to ask what he was doing, she felt his hand part the lips of her sex as his tongue lightly licked up her center.

She threw her head back instantly in ecstasy. No coherent words came from her mouth as he continued to tease her clit with his tongue, lightly at first, then harder and harder. Then she felt one of his long fingers enter her, pumping in and out slowly, tortuously. She squirmed under him, running her hands along the shaved sides of his head as she felt her body tighten, her pleasure ramping higher and higher until he slid a second finger inside her and she exploded. Her orgasm tore through her body instantly, making her cry out. She felt her muscles clench around his fingers as he worked them in and out, still licking and sucking at her clit. When the shocks left her body, she was shaking and limp. Only then did he stop and climb on top of her.

They locked eyes as he cupped her cheek gently. The look in them stilled her heart for a second. So reverent, so filled with tenderness.

"Are you ready for me, Ena?" he asked gently.

"Yes," she replied, her voice still shaky from her orgasm.

Slowly, he reached between them to grasp himself and line his cock to her entrance. As he did, she suddenly got nervous, and he must have sensed her tension, because he stopped and looked at her once again.

"What's wrong?" he asked.

"Nothing. It's just...I just haven't been with anyone...like that...in a while." In over nine years, to be exact.

"Do you want me to stop?" he asked.

"No, no. It's just..." she spoke quietly, as if hesitant to admit this. But she needed him to know. She needed him to know what this meant to her. "There's only been you, Ty. I haven't been with anyone since the night we were together."

Ty was silent for a second as his eyes filled with emotion. "Oh, Ena," he said gently. Relief filled his voice as he cupped her cheek again, stroking it with his thumb before lowering his brow to hers. "You really are mine, aren't you?" he whispered.

Not able to speak for fear that he'd hear how true that statement was, she simply nodded in return.

He sighed into her, and then kissed her, tenderly, lovingly. When he pulled away, she had to ask. She had to know.

"And you?" she asked quietly. "Are you mine?"

He pulled back to look into her eyes, and the look of adoration in them brought a twisting feeling to her chest. "I've always been yours, since the moment we met, and I always will be."

Bringing up her hand, she traced his cheek with her finger. She gently skimmed it down his face, along his bearded jaw, and over his lower lip. She traced his face as if to memorize it—memorize the way he was looking at her, and the way he felt on top of her.

"I'm ready, Ty," she said.

He took himself in his hand again and slowly pushed inside her. Her eyes went wide as she felt her body stretch around his. There was some pain, but somehow, it felt right. Just like the first time, it felt like she was home.

Once he was fully seated inside her, he stopped moving, giving her body a chance to adjust to the size of him. Ty brought his head down and kissed her again, sweetly this time, as if he wanted to savor every part of her.

Feeling the burning start to lessen, Ena began to rock her hips cautiously up against him. He moved with her, slowly, deeply at first, then faster and faster. Their breathing turned ragged as sweat began to cover their bodies.

With every push of his pelvis, she felt her muscles get tighter and tighter as he pounded against her clit. She clutched at his back, dragging her nails down so hard she had to have left marks. She felt a feral wildness come over her. Driven by some instinct she couldn't name, she urged him to go faster, harder. She wanted her body to remember this tomorrow. She wanted to feel him inside her even after he'd left. She wanted him to mark her. She thrust up into him as he reached down with one hand, grabbing her hip hard enough to bruise as he lost control entirely, driving into her with wild abandon. She felt her orgasm rip through her body as he spilled inside her. The waves that rippled through her were duller this second time, but all the more satisfying with him inside her.

Ty bent over top of her, keeping his weight on his forearms. For a while, the only sounds were their ragged breaths, and the incessant beating of their hearts.

Slowly, slowly, the world came back. Ty rolled off her to lay beside her, squished close together on the small bed.

All at once, Ena felt her heart break. This man beside her, he was...everything. Everything she'd ever wanted. Everything she'd been waiting for. She *was* his, even though she'd denied it for years. And now, after all this time, he was hers too. How could she say goodbye? She had barely been able to do it the first time, all those years ago, and yet here they were in the same situation again.

She got up and dressed silently and automatically as she felt tears roll down her cheeks. Ty dressed himself beside her, then picked up the saddlebag she'd brought. Wordlessly, he extended his hand to Ena, and she took it.

They walked out of the door, passing the witch lying on the floor of the landing, and down the stairs. Through the hallway, Ena saw the witch in the sitting room obediently reading his book, none the wiser to their presence. All had gone according to her plan, so they slipped out the front door, and into the cool night air.

Ena guided Ty towards the stables that she'd scoped out earlier that day. They kept to the shadows of the houses, but they didn't see anyone else out. The stalls were dark and warm, filled with the sounds of resting horses. They approached one of the larger horses, better for a man of Ty's size, and Ena watched him as he located a saddle and put it expertly on the horse.

She knew she should go. He had this in hand now. He didn't need her anymore to get away. If anything, having both of them here would draw more attention. She should go back to her room, where Greya and Heran slept. She should be with her family, with her Coven, where she belonged.

He had his job to do. He needed a chance to break the bond and make things better for his people. And she'd done her part by letting him go, and giving him that chance. Now it was time to return to her path.

Ty looked back at her as he led the saddled horse out into the night. She kept telling herself she should turn back now. He was far enough away, he was safe. They walked into the dark woods behind the village, and started heading deeper into it. Soon, she could barely make out the houses in the dark. She could still hear the ocean, but it was getting fainter. And yet she walked, and she walked.

She couldn't stop. She couldn't say goodbye. And Ty, sensing this, didn't mount his horse. He simply walked beside her, just as afraid to let her go. And in that moment, Ena realized what that draw to him was, the one she'd always felt, because she realized how much they'd always *fit*. Like when she looked at the vastness of the mountains, or the endlessness of the oceans, and knew she was a tiny piece of a bigger whole. Just like those, it was as if she and Ty were a part of each other, ebbing and flowing together like one being, one whole.

Realizing this, she stopped in her tracks, and Ty stopped too.

Turning to look at her, his eyes were filled with sorrow. "So this is it then?" he asked. Steeling himself, he looked at her and said, "Ena, I—"

"You'll need a witch."

"What?" he said, his brow furrowing in confusion.

"You'll need a witch. Likely more than one, to break the bond."

"Ena, what are you saying?" His face lightened with hope.

Ena took a deep breath, and dredged up her courage. She looked into the face of the man who'd always made her feel powerful and alive. A man who felt like home, and who was, and always would be, *hers*. And although she knew she should return to her path, standing beside him in the dark of the woods, she was suddenly filled with a sense of clarity.

She didn't want to return to that path. She didn't know if she fit there anymore, not like this, not after everything she'd done and learned. Maybe she'd never really fit there. And she *wanted* to help him break the bond. Wanted to right this wrong. Maybe that was why Gaia had given her the vision.

So she would follow a different path. An unknown one.

"You'll need me to help break the bond," she said. "So I'm coming with you. To the Underworld."

END OF BOOK ONE

Wondering what was going through Ty's mind after he found Ena at the Sacred Pool? Don't miss out on a special bonus version of Chapter 15 from Ty's POV!

You can find the bonus chapter on my website at https://melissamparks.com under Bonus Content.

***

Ena and Ty will return in book 2 of the Omnis series, *The Unknown Daemon*, coming Winter 2025!

Follow M.M. Parks on social media or join her newsletter for book 2 updates.

ACKNOWLEDGEMENTS

First of all, I would like to thank you, the reader, for giving this little indie book a chance. To all of you who have been incredibly supportive and enthusiastic about this book on social media from the start— you encourage me every day and give me faith that I can actually do this indie author thing!

Eight months ago, I started writing this book on a whim, just to try it. I'd been feeling incredibly unfulfilled in my life and at my job—a career I'd been working towards for the past seven years. I quickly found that, not only was writing fiction incredibly fulfilling and fun for me, but it felt like it *fit*. My entire life, I've been obsessed with love and love stories, especially fantasy ones. I inhaled every romantic movie, book, and TV show growing up (my favorite was and still is *Titanic*). I watched and re-watched *Lord of the Rings*, *Star Wars*, *Vampire Diaries*, *Twilight*, *Harry Potter*. I lived and died by the stories I consumed. But while this was always a hobby, I never saw myself as a writer. I was an academic, a social scientist. I wrote non-fiction and essays—I wasn't creative enough for fiction, I told myself.

But when I started writing Ena and Ty's journey, I knew that wasn't true. I fell in love with writing, and I never looked back. I decided to follow an unknown path and quit said unfulfilling job to pursue my passion. I found the strength to do this as Ena found the strength to follow her unknown path, too, and I haven't looked back.

To my beta readers, thank you all for engaging with this story from the beginning. Your kind words and feedback were incredibly valuable.

To my sister— thank you for believing in me from the get go and understanding implicitly that this fit for me. I could not have done this without your unwavering support. Thank you for talking through plot points with me, letting me spoil you on the entire series, and listening to my anxiety spirals weekly. We are and always will be the Power of Two.

To my parents—thank you for your support and for me believing in me as I pursued an unconventional career path. Your marketing and small business advice means everything.

To Louve -ch, my newfound friend and critique partner— you've inspired me to become a better writer. I rely on your feedback and advice daily, and couldn't imagine writing book 2 without you. Thank you for being my world-building guru, pushing me to go darker, and letting me temporarily get mad at you when I don't like your comments.

To my kids—thanks for sharing mommy with her computer during downtime, and for your own wonderful and endless imaginations which inspire me daily.

To my husband— thanks for being the inspiration for this book. Thanks for listening to me rant about my characters and obsess over the plot, even when you didn't want to. Thanks for your ideas and your input, even when I ignored them. Thanks for being supportive when I decided to quit my job. Thanks for being the dreamy male main character in our own second chance romance, and for keeping our lives interesting by being both my enemy and my lover. I love you always and forever.

ABOUT THE AUTHOR

M. M. Parks is a fantasy romance author living in Oregon, USA. Her work is inspired by her love for nature, romance, and culturally diverse fantasy worlds that explore other ways of knowing and being in the world. She has a PhD in Anthropology and loves growing paw paw trees on the hobby farm where she lives with her husband and two children.

www.ingramcontent.com/pod-product-compliance
Lightning Source LLC
Chambersburg PA
CBHW030227120726
47903CB00005B/1392